PRETTY MAIDS ALL IN A ROW

1. ~~Jill Fairbunn~~ ****
2. Marjorie Evanmore ***
3. Hilda Linder *
4. ~~Jeannie Bonni~~ **
5. ~~Mary Holden~~ *
6. Peggy Linski ***
7. Rochelle Hudson ***
8. Anne Williams **
9. Marie Amis ***
10. Sally Swink **
11. Kathy Burns **
12. ~~Yvonne Mellish~~ **
13. Sandra Seymour **
14. Alice Patmore *
15. Sonya (Sonny) Swingle **
16. Mona Drake ***
17. Barbara Brook **
18. Betty Smith ****
19. Hetty Nectar ***
20. 'Looby Loo **
21. Mrs. Mortlake (?)

Other books by Francis Pollini

Francis Pollini

Pretty Maids
all in a Row

CORGI BOOKS
TRANSWORLD PUBLISHERS LTD
A National General Company

PRETTY MAIDS ALL IN A ROW

A CORGI BOOK 552 08491 3

Originally published in Great Britain by
Neville Spearman Ltd.

PRINTING HISTORY
Neville Spearman edition published 1969
Corgi edition published 1970

This book is set in 9/10 pt. Plantin.

Corgi Books are published by Transworld Publishers Ltd.,
Cavendish House, 57–59 Uxbridge Road,
Ealing, London, W.5.
Made and printed in Great Britain by
Hunt Barnard Printing Ltd., Aylesbury, Bucks.

. . . and pretty maids
all in a row

FRAGMENT: AN OLD NURSERY RHYME

I

Ponce de Leon found the body. It happened this way: he had excused himself, politely, from Miss Smith's Eng. Lit. class to go to the lavatory and masturbate. Or, more precisely, find a suitable and relatively private receptacle for the torrent of stuff that screamed to leap out of him. For Miss Smith drove him wild. With those gorgeous, soft curves under those gorgeous outfits she wore – the sweaters! – and that gorgeous smell, *that fragrance* of hers, which you could always tell a few corridors off and could *only* be her, Ponce just about went off his rock. He sat as long as he could in her class. Then, panting practically, he just had to excuse himself from the class, almost always, and no fighting it. He was in love with Miss Smith – often referred to by the kooky elements in the school as *Miss Snowy-Paws* and by certain other plain crude elements as, and Ponce hated the thought, *Miss Purry-Twat*. These latter elements were an extremely tiny minority, needless to say. But they bothered Ponce, nevertheless. For he never, never could have that kind of thought. He was in love with her, and had always been, since the day he had first set eyes on her. She filled his dreams. He was her Lancelot. *That gorgeous hair !* His heart thumped, he flushed, he blushed, he was extremely warm and bothered whenever he saw her. And when she talked to him! He lost *all* contact. He was in space, far, far out, orbiting Venus. *He was mad about her*. He had just entered the lavatory. He was just about to plunge into a cubicle, with his heart throb, unzip himself, and haul out the red hot, when he spied the body. Not that at that precise moment he realized it was a body. He stopped in his tracks, puzzled, then, astounded. And he had a conflict. For the matter was hot, and urgent. There was the cubicle. He wanted to go into that cubicle, no doubt about it, body or no body, the pressure was not trifling. But – he didn't. He stood there, gazing at that sight, and things gradually eased inside, and matters started taking a descending course, leaving him freer and freer to stand and ponder, at the sight. Which was: the rump of a female form jutting out of a cubicle, her head stuffed down the head as far as a head can get, no less. Ponce stared, taking in more details. Her feet were more or less flat on the floor, her knees against the toilet bowl, she was propped up that way, she might have been trying to touch her toes. Ponce stared and stared, he was in a minor panic by now, for he was well aware that here, before his innocent eyes was a catastrophic happening, not to mention tragedy, of gross proportions. But he was extremely curious, also. He was that kind of boy. It was the school Guidance Counselor himself, Mr McDrew, *Tiger*, of course, who always said he was a lad whose mind, and eyes, had to *know*. At the moment, his eye was on that rump, sticking curiously up in the air, exposed to any and all eyes that might care to stare. Ponce stared. Her dress, he noted, was pulled up over her waist. Her panties were a very pleasant pastel shade, not unlike a rose that had caught his eye only this morning, on his way to school. But something more. There was something pinned to the flimsies – a sheet of paper, Ponce noted, finally, after his eye had traveled up and down the exposed posterior, the shanks, the flanks, the thighs, the ankles, at least half a dozen times, or more. What's more, Ponce noted, something was written on the paper – in capital letters, three words at least, and if he wanted to see them he would have to move closer, no doubt of it – No easy thing to do, transfixed as he was, rooted there where he stood. But – he moved, after a terrific effort of will, he moved, however hesitantly, for he was no lad, as everyone knew, to be pinned down by that arch tyrant, that ancient enemy of man, though at times friend too, well he knew: Fear. He moved, or rather stumbled, his way toward that rump, nicely rounded, and the paper. *Who was the girl?* The question, at this point, began to arise in him. It had a certain academic as well as human interest to him. *Who could it be?* Certainly, from this angle, in that position, he could not really see. He couldn't tell by the panties. He was closer to the paper. It was just an ordinary sheet of school paper, plain, unlined, State-supplied. Eight by ten inches, at least. And written on it – now he could see –

SO LONG, HONEY

He stared, pondering the message. Never in all his life had Ponce encountered such a reality. *Who was Honey?* Should he go even closer, take a look *down there* – and see? Her legs were lovely. He saw the paper. He inched his way closer, heart pounding, until he was less than a foot away from the undeniably well-formed behind on her. He stopped. His heart was bounding,

8

pounding, he was aware that at any moment anyone, someone, could burst upon the scene, through that lavatory door, for the lavatory in his school was a place that was religiously frequented, almost. His highly developed sense of discretion, not to mention propriety, was now a high-pitched whine within him – a siren almost. It was no use though. He couldn't help it. An opportunity like this presented itself – how many times in a lifetime? Up to now, Ponce hadn't met it. It just was something which in his wildest moments he couldn't have dreamed of. Was it something God in his wisdom in collusion with Lucifer had arranged specifically for him, to supremely test him? Was it his very own *special trial*? Ponce, in those few moments oscillating between wildness and lucidity, tried to think of it, some sort of answer to it. His mind flicked back a few weeks to Sunday School. It was a rather shadowy memory, mixed up as it was with a dance at the high school the night before, but somehow it seemed apropos. Not that Ponce was fanatically religious. In fact, at this point in his life curve, he was experiencing a not insignificant amount of soul-searching on the entire issue. What was the score? Was there any meaning or significance at all to it? But, the memory had jogged up in him. The voice of the Sunday School teacher jogged and jogged in him, bizarrely. And he saw a hand, near him. *God's way*, *His way*, *Testing us*. Ponce saw the hand, moving. While his head bounded, and rebounded, and spun, and pounded, he definitely saw the hand, his hand, *nobody else's*, slowly, irresistibly, moving. He understood it. Moving. It reached the panties. Trembling, the fingers touched them. Just lightly, brushing them. Ponce's heart hammered. His fingers never wavered. They moved across, and upward. The flesh still radiated a certain warmth through the panties, the flesh was white and soft and lovely, he knew, this was a true fact of life, indisputably – *astonishingly*. Upward. Skirting the weird piece of paper. The very top of the silkies. His fingers reached the elastic edge and tremulously, mysteriously, slipped under it, coming into direct contact with flesh, without a doubt still warm. Lovely, warm flesh, *Whoever*. And now his heart, his whole being thundered, his rock was a rock again, hot, crying out for expression, life, action. His hand moved under. *Wonder*. His hand, wandering, sliding under. He felt the marvel of it. *He wasn't dreaming*. The smooth, soft, indescribably beautiful feminine rump under it. He trembled. His hand glided. A violent trembling. The reverberations in his body blinded him, *for the first time in the whole of his life he had his hand on one.* A hot, brilliant, white light was enveloping him, as his hand, magnificently, unhindered, *gloriously*, glided, slowly. *The smoothness of it.* The utter wonder of it. More than he had fantasied it would be. Hundreds, thousands, of fantasies, at least. *Miss Smith's is like this. It must be like this.* He was totally enveloped in the white light, he was aware only of his hand, wandering. *How it wandered.* He thought he would come apart with a violent explosion there. The lavatory, the whole school would be blown to bits by it, the force, the heat of it. Seismographs would register it. He shook like a paint mixer. He was about to do something. His other hand was definitely trying to reach out, take hold of the silky frillies, pull them away from the lovely hump, *down, down*, over the lovely shanks, the flanks, *down, down*, if he could, *if he could only control the shaking.* His hand reached out. He heard a strange sound. In the white light, his hand was gaining ground. Definitely, this strange sound – and his hand lost ground. The sound registered. *Someone was approaching the lavatory.* The hot light receded. *There was the outer door of the lavatory, just opening.* The ever-alert, ever in contact part of himself had heard it. And, with that astonishing presence of mind so characteristic of him, he panicked. His hand flew out from under the panties. He was sweating now, as well as trembling. The force of the swift withdrawal was just enough to upset the uniquely precarious postural balance of the unknown but greatly admired young feminine. She tumbled sideways, grotesquely, as Ponce, horrified, frozen, and intensely curious, stared. Her head popped out of the toilet, she fell like nothing he had ever known. For now she was known. Ponce, in that split second, full of terror, staring at the blond hair and familiar features, had crossed the unknown. It was *Jill Fairbunn,* Ponce tried to hang on, *Sawyersville High's Head Cheerleader,* Ponce fought like a lion, hanging on, and he turned, knowing he had to turn, in the next bit of that second, for there was the door, opening, and Ponce knew what to do, suddenly: He rushed for it. He rushed with all the power and strength at his command for it, bowling over a figure he fleetingly recognized as Mr Mummer, among other things Mathematics teacher, Programmed Instruction champion. . . . He rushed howling, in a wild charge, and Mummer never stood a chance. He trampled over him and shot out like a bullet, or Sawyersville's ace halfback at least, which he wasn't. He hit the hallway, skidded, pivoted, got his balance, and tore down the long, long hallway, screaming, all the way. It was one long echoing howl, terrifying to one and all, as he raced down that hall, for one destination: The Principal's office – Mr Proffer . . .

2

Mike McDrew – *Tiger* – sat in his office. At this moment, when the entire school was about to be plunged into historically unprecedented chaos, he was administering a Bernkrokkler Personality Inventory to one of the most interesting personalities of Sawyersville High School, Marjorie (*Madge*) Evanmore. The way he was administering it was even more interesting, for she was sitting on his lap, cuddling him. She was an attractive, healthy, well-formed miss, and no doubt of it.

'Mr McDrew –' she said, '*Tiger* –' she said, 'Are you *sure* the door is locked? I mean – ' she trailed off, turning her face toward him, her eyes closed, her lips inviting him.

'Listen,' Tiger said, 'Sure it is.'

'Well, I'm glad it is,' she murmured.

'Ha ha ha –' he laughed softly.

'*Honey* – '

'Ah ha – '

'*Bunny* – '

'Ha Ha – '

'*My bunny-honey* – '

'What are you wearing?'

'You tell me – '

'How can I tell you?'

'Tell me – '

'Aren't you nice and warm – '

'*Tell me, tell me* – '

'Hear how they're wearing them in England?'

'Do you like my legs?'

'They're gorgeous legs.'

'*Put your hand on my legs* – '

'Just gorgeous legs – '

'*Tiger – higher* – '

'Shall I go higher?'

'Higher, *higher* – '

'How high shall I go?'

His hand was up to her knee, pushing her skirt upward, slowly. His hand glided past her knees and reached the delightful thigh region. He lingered, at that region.

'*Tiger – honey –* '

Marjorie was in a warm and trembling state, he felt her pressing against him, her heart pounding. He smelled the fresh, young smell of her – the *heat* of her as her lips, wet, open, sought his, hungrily. He liked her. Her breath, sweet, warm, caressed his face.

Ponce's first screams, at this point, tore through the school. They didn't make all that much impact, however, on the Guidance/Counseling office. Though Tiger's hand, in that moment, did pause in its journey. And he said, casually, 'What was that?'

'What?' she replied, huskily.

Tiger dropped it. The screams went on, but farther off now. Ponce had sprinted by Tiger's door at a terrific pace. At this rate, he wouldn't be long reaching his goal. On they went.

'Nothing,' he murmured, resuming his languid journey.

'*Tiger Honey –*' she murmured, barely.

She had her arms about him in a terrific clinch, and she was kissing him. Tiger was thinking just then that never so far as he could immediately recall had he felt such a pounding hot body against him, almost part of him, on his lap, or elsewhere for that matter. *Never.* And he kissed her. A marvelous, special kiss for her. He kissed and kissed her, totally unaware of anything but the supreme bliss of their kiss there, meanwhile making excellent progress along that exquisitely delightful freeway, Inner Thigh Dreamway.

'*Tiger –*' she gasped, breaking off the stupendous kiss, for a moment at least, and tossing her blond hair – unbleached.

'You little honey –' Tiger murmured, chuckling, softly, giving her little nips, her nose, her eyes, her cute ears.

'*I'm not so little –* ' she said.

'I know, don't I know it – Honey – ' he said.

'Please – *not too slow* – you're really *awfully slow* today – Honey – I'm going to *just scream* – *Tiger Honey –* '

And again he chuckled, in his soft way, reaching into her blouse with his free hand now and touching her soft, young, fabulous breasts, cupping them, one at a time, gently fondling them, the treasures, lingering at the exquisite tips, playing there, maddening the girl, ever more.

'You're a good bunny,' Tiger murmured, 'What a good bunny,

taking it off before getting here – makes things a lot smoother –
doesn't it –'

'*Smoother*, Honey –'

'Doesn't it –'

'*Honey* –'

'Let's see what they look like –'

'*Look at them* –'

She slipped out of her blouse, deftly, revealing them. They
were full, lovely, *perfect*. If they hadn't been there, right before
him, he wouldn't have believed it. He stared at them, loving
them. Almost mesmerized by them.

'*Like them?*' she whispered.

'I'll always like them,' he murmured.

'*Take them* –'

And Tiger took them, burying his face in them, soft and lovely
things, white, marvelous orbs, interrupting his journey between
her thighs to bring both hands into play, holding the glorious
things, caressing them, licking and kissing them –

'*OH! Honey!*' The maid cried out. She was beside herself.
He thought she would melt. He suckled her tips, lovingly.

'*Tiger Honey!*'

How could she control herself? Her need was wild, for him –
McDrew murmured, 'Steady honey –'

'I can't – *Oh I can't – Honey!*'

'You know how it is –' he murmured, 'How nice it is – all in
time – there's plenty of time – take your time – Honey Bunny –'

'I'm going to die – *Just Die! Honey!* Oh kiss me please kiss me
at least kiss me *let me kiss you Tiger Kiss Me!*' She was soaring.

'Sure, honey,' Tiger murmured, raising his head now from the
wet treasures, meeting her sweet open mouth with his now, feeling the luscious mouth on his, and the hot fire of her tongue
entering his mouth, wandering all about. She was moaning. His
hand, parted from the treasures, resumed its work below, on the
thighway, and upward, ever upward, gliding, smoothly, along
that silken way –

'*Now Tiger!*' Her voice was a hot, raw whisper now, as she
broke off the kiss, on fire.

'*Must Be Now, Tiger* –' She was a sheet of flame. He noted
that.

'You been taking your pills? Honey? *You little honey.*' Tiger,
caressing her, down below, murmured lovingly.

'Yes Honey!'

'Nice and regular? Honey?'

'Yes! *Oh Yes! Honey!*'

'Let's go then,' he murmured, lifting her. He stood up, the golden girl still cuddling in his arms. He stripped her, what remained on her. She helped him, somehow, to strip himself. She gasped, as soon as she found his organ. She kissed it, she fell to her knees, kissing it, she caressed it, and glided with it, as it entered her mouth. She played, eternally, with it. Her tongue slid over it, enfolding it – She moaned –

'Let's go, honey – ' Tiger said, gently, murmuring to her, reaching down for her, his hands over both her orbs, and urging her up. She rose, trembling, and fell back, in his arms, back, slowly, under him –

'*You honey bun,*' Tiger murmured, viewing her for a moment as she lay on her back, ready, dying for him, her knees up, her feet flat on the floor, her legs perfect, '*Honey* – ' he murmured, slipping magnificently, masterfully, into her, 'You're a hot river,' he told her, '*What a river,*' he murmured, the full weight of his masculine frame on her massing now behind the thrusts of his formidable organ, into her, as outside, somewhere, a storm of noise, of feet running, of voices excited and babbling, rose and swelled, trying, but making little inroad, in fact hardly any, into the office of Guidance/Counseling, '*You luscious lovely – ever luscious lovely – succulent honey – bun bunny –* ' McDrew murmured, penetrating deeper, and deeper, the farthest reaches, thrusting, plunging, panting in rhythm with her, as she moaned, and moved, as she shook, and rocked, with him, taking his fabulous lunges, '*Don't stop no – Oh Don't Stop Now – Oh Will You – Oh Tiger – Honey!*' She managed, barely, as they rocked on, *and on,* marvelously –

'*Honey!*' Tiger, jolting massively, finally, cried out, '*Honey HONEY!*' The young maid almost simultaneously screamed out, feeling the massive spurt and surge within her, spreading, thrilling her, and '*OH HONEY!*' Adoring the huge, engulfed, jolting organ, the whole of her now in spasm, a long series of ecstatic spasms, with him, for him. . . .

Outside, the stampede of feet and babble of voices rose and rose further, unabated, seeking out a crescendo. . . .

Tiger and the young maid, still linked, clasped in each other's arms, mouth to mouth, rolled over, slowly, and over, so slowly, now murmuring, moaning. . . .

Ponce, at the end of his wild, careening flight, twice during the course of which he nearly overturned himself, burst upon the Principal's office like a madman, or, more precisely, madboy. He hadn't penetrated immediately of course the inner sanctum of Mr Proffer's domain, his private office. Though he would soon do so. What he ran into first of all was the Principal's Secretary's office, that is to say, the Outer Office, and the Principal's Secretary herself, Miss Craymire. This thirty-five-year-old spinster through no apparent fault of her own (certainly, she was not unattractive) was just putting the finishing touches to a project which bored her intensely, to wit, typing up the minutes of the most recent Weekly Teachers Meeting, presided over, of course, by her boss Mr Proffer, the man Ponce was about to present his bit of news to. He was a genial man, and Miss Craymire admired and respected him, among other things. She was, the truth be known, hopelessly in love with him, and had always been. It was a sad, hopeless love indeed, she had spent all these years hiding it from him. She looked up, rather startled, at the entrance of the boy-projectile. Of course, she had heard rather strange noises out in the hallway, but they hadn't registered. Now, Ponce registered. She was, actually, somewhat more than startled. She thought he had 'exploded out' into the 'typical adolescent psychosis,' a phrase she remembered quite well from the times Mr McDrew, among other things School Guidance Counselor, had used it – most recently in a paper he had submitted to the State Educational Journal – though it was a phrase that appeared a number of times in the minutes of Teachers Meetings – and other places. She was, to be blunt, petrified in her chair at the sight of the lad. She was certain he had gone mad. She awaited her doom, utterly rooted there. She was a fatalist and had been from the moment she had been born, the greatest continual wonder in her mind always being, I'm still alive, today. So this was the end. She knew it. She would die at the hand of this lunatic. Bizarrely enough, though, she heard her voice cry out in a squawk, *'What is it, Ponce?'* As if she had to be told. The lad answered, in a voice out of this world, *'Mr Proffer!'* And she answered, though she never knew it, 'He's in there.' So that's who he had come to murder! She resigned herself, naturally.

'*Got To See Him!*'

She heard the lad's words, and just managed to see him lunge across the room and plunge into the inner sanctum, without knocking even.

How would he do it?

He left her wondering about it.

Mr Proffer swiveled around in his chair at the unceremonious intrusion, dropped the mike of the machine into which he had been dictating a preliminary draft of a speech he was scheduled to deliver at the next Rotary Club dinner, and faced the intruder.

'Mr Proffer!' Ponce shouted, less than a yard from him.

'What is it, boy?' The genial Principal inquired, in a voice designed to calm the obviously distraught adolescent.

'She's in the lavatory!' the lad fired at him.

'Who, my boy?' He tried to humor him.

'*Jill Fairbunn! Mr Proffer! She's up there!*'

'What is she doing there?'

'She's Up There!'

'Is she?'

'*She's Dead Up There!*'

'Dead, my boy?'

'*Dead* I said!'

'Where, my boy?'

'In the lavatory – *our lavatory* – I was just up there – I ran all the way down from there – '

'Whose class were you in?'

'WHAT'S THE DIFFERENCE?'

'Now, now, there now, Ponce, take it easy – '

'*Don't you believe me?*'

'Why shouldn't I believe you?'

'*Mr Proffer! Boy! I'll show you!* C'mon with me – *Holy Cow! Wait'll You See! WOW! Right Now!*'

And the genial Principal did begin to conceive that something fairly unusual might just be up. This boy, he knew, was no crazy young pup. On everybody's list, Tiger's especially, he was right up. Furthermore, he had become aware of a certain unusual amount of noise and activity out there, somewhere, all over the school, it seemed. Almost like a herd. Stampeding. Herd. Come to think of it, just before the fiery entrance of the boy he had heard something, yes, far off, it seemed, which might even have been a – *scream*. He got up.

'*HOLY COW!*'

Ponce flew through the door, which was open, fortunately, yelling that out, and Mr Proffer followed, hot on his heels. They flashed by the still petrified Miss Craymire, who looked on, utterly unable to move from her chair. . . . She merely noted, mentally, incredulous as ever, that her beloved Boss was still alive, *somehow.* . . . She was thankful . . . exceedingly . . . though paralyzed – totally.

4

Sawyersville's Chief of Police, John Poldaski, urgently summoned from his normal duty post (for this time of day) (in fact, most of the day) at the corner of Twelfth Street and Whitmaker Avenue– the hub of Sawyersville, where he kept his eye on traffic, strang, ers, friends, relations, acquaintances, the weather, the Roll of Honor, the Pool Room, and this and that, arrived at the high school with a ferocious squealing of tires, and brakes, also. He catapulted himself out of the brand new Borough of Sawyersville Police Car (fully equipped with the latest crime-combating apparatus, including a twelve-gauge Remington, which, from time to time, he used for hunting), sprinted across the well-kept lawn and grounds, and burst into the high school, pistol drawn, though fortunately, and unbeknown to him, with the safety on.

He pushed his way past a cluster of students, and local citi-zenry, among whom were numbered a smattering of Selmo's Bar stalwarts, located next door to the high school, rushed up the short stairway just beyond the entrance, got as far as the landing, paused, turned, as if remembering something, and said to the cluster, '*Where is she?*' in his barking baritone.

A fusillade of voices hit him, from which he learned nothing.

'Goddamnit! Shut Up! SHUT UP WILL YA!' He roared out, 'You – somebody – Hey, *Grotto* – TELL ME!' He added.

The so-named, as it happened, one of Selmo's stalwarts, fired at him, 'Stop wavin' that fuckin' thing! Is it *Loaded?*'

'*Don't piss around!*' the Chief roared.

'Who's pissin'? You wanta kill somebody?' He had thrown at him.

A barrage of voices erupted again. slugging it out before him.

'FUCK!' roared the Chief, turning his back on them. and sprinting off, somewhere. past the landing, past another set of doors, and into a hallway.

'Chief! Oh, thank God you've come!'

Poldaski whirled to his left, gun still drawn, and faced Miss Nectar. School Librarian.

'Where is she?' he demanded.

'Follow me, just *follow me*, Chief Poldaski,' she offered.

'Close all the doors! The outside doors! Lock them! Close the windows! I don't want one window open! Lock them! He's in here! Must still be in here!' the Chief boomed out.

'Certainly, Chief!' Miss Nectar responded.

'*No !* – have somebody else take care of it – *I'm following you* –'

'Chief, listen – just go up those stairs and turn left, it's *down the hallway* – you can't miss it – *everybody's up there* –'

'O.K. then! Don't forget! All the doors! *All Of Them !*' And with this the Chief sprang up the stairway pointed out by the Librarian, while she fluttered.

He reached the upper hallway in record time having taken the stairs two and three at a time. his heavy boots pounding them. And there before him, filling practically all of the hallway. was the entire school population, practically. It *would* soon be the entire population, plus the local citizenry and Selmo entourage he had turned his back on at the entranceway. At this moment they were pouring up that stairway, after him. The Chief plunged, pushed, prodded, butted his way down that hallway.

'It's the Chief!'

'The Chief's here!'

'Here's the Chief!'

'John!'

'Poldaski!'

He heard all about him.

'Where is she?' he yelled out.

Someone had hold of his arm now.

'Thank God you're here, man!' he heard in his ear.

'Who are you?' Poldaski demanded, facing the little man who had spoken.

'Chief! Don't you know me?'

'Hell No! *Who Are You ?*'

'Listen, you gave me a ticket only last week for going through that Stop sign! Remember me?' the man said.

18

'*Who The Hell Are You?*' The Chief reiterated, grasping him by the arm, firmly.

'Mr Hinkle! *Ralph Hinkle!* I *teach* here – *Chief!*'

'Yeh? Do you?' the Chief snarled.

Another voice hit him and looking up he saw someone being made way for by the mob.

'Chief! *I'm here!*'

It was Proffer. He drew up beside the Chief.

'Know this guy?' Poldaski inquired.

'Oh, that's Mr Hinkle, John. He teaches here.'

'Don't you *remember* me?' the teacher asked again.

The Chief nodded, and released his grip, finally.

'Don't run away,' he told him, following Proffer. 'Anybody touch anything?' Now he asked.

'I don't think so.'

'In *here*?'

They had reached the lavatory door.

'That's right, Chief.'

Poldaski surveyed the mob.

'Put some of your teachers outside the door. Don't want anybody else in there,' he said.

'I'll do that, Chief,' he was informed.

They entered the lavatory.

'Huh.'

The Chief said.

'Huh.'

Poldaski said.

Moving to another position.

'I'll be goddamned.'

He said, standing there.

'Jill Fairbunn ain't it?' he finally said.

'That's it, Chief.' Proffer, very quietly, said.

'Huh.'

The Chief said.

And stood there.

'Who the hell'd wanta do that?' he finally asked.

He got no answer.

He looked around. All around. He turned to Proffer.

'Better call in the Staties,' he told him, quietly.

The Chief was referring to the organization which dealt with serious crimes outside the immediate and/or foreseeable capabilities of local Police Forces: *The State Police*, no less. It was the first time he had ever done so.

'Alright, John,' Proffer murmured, nodding his head, unhappily. He was still, the truth be known, in a state of shock, or semi.

'That's the only thing alright,' the Chief told him, in the lowest of tones, Proffer just catching it, 'Get them on the phone right now. I'll hang around.' He added.

'Yes, Chief,' Mr Proffer managed, treading his way out of the lavatory.

'Wait! Where's the kid that found her?' He heard the Chief shout, just as he was about to step out.

The voice of Ponce came from a corner of that lavatory, 'I'm here, Chief.' And that's all.

Poldaski faced him.

'O.K. Stay here.'

'Right, Chief,' the lad said.

Proffer was out of the place, and opening the outer door.

'Don't let anybody out of the building! Not anybody!' The Chief yelled out to him, as Proffer walked shakily out into the teeming hallway.

'Close that door!' the Chief shouted.

'It closes automatically,' Ponce said, quietly.

The Chief turned to the lad again. There were others in the lavatory – four or five teachers (male) and a number of students (also male). Mr. Mummer was there, battered but recovering. He sat on a toilet seat, dazed, bewildered, while two of his colleagues succored him. The Chief reached for a black notepad which he had tucked away cleverly in one of his many pockets. He was somewhat hampered, however, by the pistol which he still held at the ready in his right hand, pointing more or less in the lad's direction. The Chief in fact was getting absolutely nowhere with his free hand, and so finally he holstered the weapon, after a long look around the lavatory. He found the notepad, after a long search, and a ball-point pen also. He flipped open the notepad briskly, and found written on it, *Don't Forget the Butter !* In large letters unmistakable. He ripped out the page angrily, and jammed it into one of his pockets, muttering to himself about Mary, who was always doing this. He would show her tonight, *goddamn her*. The rest of the pad was blank.

'O.K.,' he said at last, 'What happened?'

Ponce stared at the Chief. He was thinking a million things, and he didn't know how to answer. He even wondered if he should answer. How many times, before all this was over, would he be giving answers? He sat there, pondering matters. He finally started to answer.

'Well, Chief – '

'Wait a minute – ' the Chief said, rubbing the ball-point back and forth across the sheet of notepaper in an effort to get the ink flowing, 'Sonuvabitch,' he muttered, rubbing harder.

'Here, Chief,' said one of the teachers, Mr Crispwell, Commercial Studies, handing him a lead pencil.

The Chief mumbled thanks and took the pencil, meanwhile pocketing his stubborn pen, and silently cursing his wife again, in the process. He said to the lad, 'O.K. – what was that again?'

'I didn't say anything,' Ponce said, feeling so low.

'You didn't?'

'Nothing.'

Poldaski eyed him.

'You're Ponce de Leon, right? Britfield Avenue – right?'

.'That's right.'

'Any brothers?'

Ponce responded, puzzled, beginning already to regret he had decided to answer questions, 'I have one younger brother.'

'How old is he?'

'Six, Chief,' Ponce responded, glumly. He had never thought of John Poldaski as an ace crime-buster, the truth be known.

'What sports do you play?'

Ponce hesitated. This was a sore point and a half alright. It was about the most ridiculous question so far, no doubt, and in any case the Chief should know the answer, for he was probably one of the town's most avid sports fans, among other things.

Ponce tried this answer, 'I'm the football team's Equipment Manager.' Which was true, absolutely.

'Yeh!' Poldaski cried, 'Oh yeh! I seen you out there! You're the waterboy!'

Ponce winced, for that wasn't strictly true. His assistant, Billy King, actually performed that function. But – he let it go. It might lead to complications.

'Right, Chief,' he said.

'I thought I seen you out there!'

'That's me. Always out there.'

'What about next week?'

'We'll take them.'

'Sure about that?'

'Tiger – ' he paused, he really shouldn't be bandying about that name, 'The Coach said we would.'

'That's o.k. then!'

A moment.

'Going?' Ponce couldn't help asking him.

'Sure I'm going!'

'It's away, Chief.'

'What's the difference?'

Ponce said nothing, though he knew very well what the difference was. Unlike the home games which the Chief attended free of charge as part of his duties, he would have to shell out at an away game – usually. Though even there, if he spotted the local Police Chief, whom he knew of course, he breezed by the gates. Ponce pondered, knowing he had stepped on a corn. He didn't want Poldaski mad at him, not at this point.

'What's the hell's the difference?' The Chief demanded. No doubt about it, the tone was mean.

'No difference at all, Chief,' Ponce finally said, hoping for the best, hoping the Chief's sense of irony wasn't at its best.

The Chief was eyeing him. Ponce knew he hadn't pacified him.

'What's your age – De Leon?' It was a sinister tone.

'Sixteen,' Ponce told him, 'Nearly seventeen,' he also told him.

'What happened?' The question hit him.

'He nearly killed me, that's what happened,' came a mumble from one of the cubicles, Mr Mummer of course.

'Who are *you*?' The Chief shot at him. His right hand actually touched his holster.

'Mr Mummer,' Ponce barely heard him.

'Oh, yeh – Mummer – ' Poldaski remembered, moving his hand away from the holster, and back to the notepad. 'What the hell you doin' there, Mr Mummer?' he asked of him.

'I just told you – '

'How old are you – '

'Huh, Chief?'

Mr Golden, one of the teachers attending him, said to the Chief, 'He's still in bad shape, Chief. He had a bad jolt out there.'

'*What happened?*'

'Well, I understand Ponce bumped into him and knocked him over.'

'Oh yeh?' He whirled to face the lad again. 'De Leon – what the hell is this – you never told me that!'

'Chief, I was trying to tell you – I was going to – '

'*Don't skip anything.*'

'I won't, Chief.'

'Start at the beginning.'

'Sure, Chief.'

'Where were you?'

'What, Chief?'

'*Stop screwing around with me!*'

'Listen – Chief – '

Mr Crispwell interjected mildly, 'Chief,' he said, 'Why not just have him tell you the whole story – without asking any questions – know what I mean?'

Poldaski exploded, 'Who the hell are you? Oh. Crispwell! Well keep the hell out of this, Crispwell! Think this is funny? Funny game or somethin'? What's your angle?'

'Chief! Listen!' Ponce pleaded.

'I better take you down to the Station. Hell, what can I get outa you here, all these guys buttin' in – Jesus – '

'*Listen, I'll tell you!*' Ponce, in astute form, shouted at him.

It worked. Poldaski stood there. All he did was stare.

'Don't skip a thing,' he mumbled, finally.

And Ponce told his tale, quietly, step by step, carefully, not skipping a thing, hardly.

Poldaski took it all down, laboriously.

'Damn good cheerleader she was,' he was mumbling, writing, at the end of it all, finally, 'We'll get the bastard, don't worry,' he added, his eyes sweeping the room, taking them all in, the girl, the teachers, the students, all of them.

Outside the school building sirens were approaching, screaming.

It was the State Police, speedy and efficient, as ever.

And an ambulance. . . .

5

Mike McDrew was helping Marjorie back into her dress. He himself, at this moment, wasn't yet completely dressed – his trousers were still off, draped fairly neatly over a chair – but she had requested assistance, and of course, he was only too happy to give it to her.

'Where's the hook, hon?' Tiger inquired, softly, fumbling around with the back of her blouse.

'Oh gosh,' she murmured, with a little laugh, 'Can't you *ever* find it?'

'That's not the most important thing to find, is it, honey?' He too laughed softly.

'No, Honey,' she sighed, '*Gee* didn't I scream though, did I scream loud? Think they heard? Anyone – ?' she added, barely audibly.

'Uh uh. No. You know this little old place is soundproof – ' he chuckled. 'Practically.' He kept on chuckling, 'Now where were we – ?'

'Got it?'

'I got it.'

She turned around, warm, glowing.

'Put your pants on. Tiger, *honey* –' she chided him.

'You didn't give me a chance to.'

'Oh hoo.'

'Hoo hoo hoo.'

And they both laughed, softly.

Now Tiger slipped into his trousers, humming a little tune, tucked his shirt in, hanging on to that tune, and Marjorie walked to the other side of the office where the mirror was, and started fixing herself up. She combed her hair, put on lipstick, powder, before Tiger's mirror there.

'Did you hear a sort of – noise? Trampling sort of far off noise?' She mentioned, casually.

'Just changing classes,' he said to her, just as casually.

Marjorie sighed, before the mirror. Her eye caught Tiger's, in the mirror. She smiled, warmly.

'The zip?' Tiger murmured.

'Oh gosh, yeh, Tiger – honey – '

And she skipped over to him, warm, lovely, and stood before him, looking up at him, wrinkling her nose in the cutest way imaginable, at him.

'Go then.'

'*When*,' she said reaching down and taking hold of the zipper-upper, and tugging just a little bit, and then changing her mind, slipping her shapely hand inside, tenderly.

24

'Wuh uh – ' Tiger said.

'*Tiger honey* – '

'Not that way – '

'*Let me honey* – '

'Not today – '

'Oh *let me play* – '

'Up, honey – '

'Honey honey – '

'You little honey – '

'I'm not little – '

'We have work to do.'

'Don't we – '

'C'mon, honey,' Tiger spoke firmly.

She looked hard at him. She pouted at him. She withdrew her hand, slowly. from the organ.

'You could go again,' she murmured, '*Real easy.*'

'Not today,' he reiterated.

'Oh, Honey!' she pouted at him.

'The zip,' he murmured, 'Honey.'

She zipped him up, slowly.

He was dressed.

He grinned at her.

'There,' he said, touching her face, passing his hand gently along the side of that face, as she continued looking up at him, sulking, but smiling, a little bit too, definitely.

'Now where were we?' He said, turning, surveying his desk, 'Just where were we?' He said again, almost to himself, heading toward his desk.

6

Ponce was unhappy. He was ashamed of that long, screaming run, ashamed of a lot of things. He was that way, he couldn't help it. He only wondered, would he have bolted out of there and screamed that way if it had been anyone but Mr Mummer? Because, no doubt of it, the more he thought of it, that's the way he was beginning to see it. True enough, he had planned it, even while the door was just opening. before he could see who it was there opening it. But would he have done it, say, if Tiger had appeared, or Mr Crispwell – or – *anybody* – instead of Mummer? Ponce pondered, miserable. More and more, he thought that must be it. Because Mummer was something, unquestionably. And had been more or less like a final spur, guaranteeing the dash, without a doubt of it. Ponce remembered, sinking lower. That day last term, in the lavatory, when he had discovered something about Mummer that had jolted him, and appalled him: the man had *propositioned* him, and in such a cunning way Ponce hadn't realized it until almost too late. *Almost*, though. For he had realized, finally, and had promptly walked out of there, undefiled. He thought and thought about that, down in the dumps. He hadn't mentioned it to anybody, for he had never heard anything funny about Mummer before, outside of the bug he had for Teaching Machines and Programmed Learning, he was a real fanatic on that, which Ponce (and Tiger too) were thoroughly against. And he had wondered: *Why me? What was so special about me?* Why had he picked on him? That had worried and worried Ponce, but he had never mentioned it to anybody, not even Tiger, for he was just too ashamed of it, and in time he had more or less forgotten about it, though he steered clear of Mummer by a mile at least, except for that Trig class of course, and in any event hadn't ever bumped into him in the lavatory again – up to now, that is. That character. What a character. He almost wished he *had* killed him, or broken a few bones, his skull for example, at least. Now what should he do about him? Tell the Police about him? Tell *someone* about him? *What if he were the one?* Couldn't a pervert like *that* – be just the one? What a sly one! Ponce pondered thinking hard over it, highly disturbed by it, all of it. Once again he was foxed by the thought: Was it possible *no one*, nobody at all, *not even Tiger*, knew about him? He just hadn't heard anything at all like that about him. Certainly, you could never know it *looking* at him! And he was married, with kids, to boot! *Why me?* Ponce was foxed, alright, and worried again, alright, all over again, but now, here, doubly so. For he felt a pressing duty to *tell* somebody. If only he had once heard something, just a little something, about the man, from *somebody!* He wouldn't hesitate to spill the beans. To Tiger, first of all, preferably. Ponce was up the creek. And here he was now, in Mr Proffer's office, with Captain Surcher, of the State Police, who had led him there from the lavatory, not too long ago in fact. He had respect for Surcher, he was serious, obviously intelligent, a tall, well-constructed policeman. In plain clothes, to boot. Not at all like that buffoon Poldaski. *Jesus!* Though Ponce couldn't help grinning. thinking of him. Ponce was answering Surcher's questions. The Captain spoke in a mild voice to him, in fact, his entire manner was mild, surprisingly enough – more like Tiger's, Ponce suddenly was aware, liking him even more. The questions were many and varied, making him forget, for the moment, the worrying thing on his mind, and what to do with it, finally. No matter the Captain's manner, Ponce was unhappy though. Outside the private office, in Miss Craymire's territory, Chief Poldaski, a number of uniformed Troopers, Mr Proffer, and an assorted collection of others stood around, talked, and otherwise busied themselves, as best they could, under the circumstances. The phone kept ringing. Was Proffer himself doing the answering? Ponce wondered. Miss Craymire herself had disappeared. In fact, at this moment, she was stretched out on the very comfortable bed of the School Dispensary, ministered to by the highly competent School Nurse, that well-rounded personality, Mrs Mortlake. Though Ponce, of course, didn't know it. Captain Surcher was writing in his notebook, and Ponce, having just finished answering his thirty-sixth intelligent question at least, watched him doing so. He wondered how long he would continue doing so. The Captain certainly knew what he was doing, Ponce never doubted that. Shrewd observer and interpreter of human nature that he was, even at this tender age, Ponce knew that. He had at once known that. *Should he tell him?* What if Mummer denied it? What if he *had* been the only one ever propositioned by him? And what if, on top of that, he turned out to have no connection at all with this – wouldn't he be a prize duck! Wouldn't he! Ponce kept quiet, reserving the matter for further pondering and profound thought over, on his own.

'Alright, Ponce,' he heard the Captain say, 'I think that just about answers all the questions I have for you – anyhow, I can't think of any more.' he paused, looking understandingly at the boy, Ponce appreciating it, 'How do you feel?' He was asked. 'I'm sorry I had to take all this time with you, maybe you'll understand someday though. That must have been some shock running into a thing like that, I know – I remember the first time I ever saw something like that – ' He paused. a moment, 'And I was a lot older than you – already a Trooper in fact. And I can tell you – I know how I felt, let me tell you. How are you?'

'Uh – ' replied Ponce, 'Not too bad, Captain.'

Surcher nodded, slightly. 'Well, I think you ought to go home maybe, and take it easy for a while. I guess that's one thing though you're not going to find all that easy to do – everybody's going to have a million questions for you – I know. Get set for that, Ponce.'

'What should I tell them ?' the lad inquired, suddenly aware of that fact. And dreading them.

Surcher shrugged, 'You can't get away from them.'

'It's o.k. if I tell them ?' he suddenly said – regretting it.

'What, Ponce ?' The Captain asked him.

'Everything,' Ponce answered, promptly.

Mildly, the Captain eyed him.

'You'll know what to tell them,' he said, finally.

'But it's o.k. by you ?' Ponce asked again.

'It'll have to be,' Surcher grinned at him.

'She was a peach of a girl,' Ponce informed him, sadly, 'I wish I hadn't been the guy to find her,' he paused, mighty low, 'I can't tell you how I feel – honest. It's like a nightmare.' He paused again, 'You'll find the guy, I know you will, Captain.' He stopped there.

'We'll try to,' said Surcher, rising.

Ponce walked out of that private office with the Captain's arm protectively about his shoulders. All eyes in that outer office were turned on him and the Captain. And there was silence.

Surcher spoke, 'Mr Proffer, I think Ponce ought to be allowed to go home for the rest of the day, I think it would be a good idea if you excused him. Can you do that ?'

'Certainly, Captain,' the Principal agreed, immediately, saying to the lad, 'You just take off, Ponce, God knows what you've been through, son. Take a few days off if you want to, I'll see you are notified of any work you miss, and homework – if you're up to it. that is.'

'O.K., Mr Proffer,' Ponce responded.

'Do you want a ride home ?' asked the Captain.

'Uh – no – that's alright, Captain,' the lad answered.

'Sure, son ?' asked Proffer.

'I'll be o.k., Mr Proffer.'

'Maybe though somebody ought to give you a ride home, Ponce,' Surcher said, gently.

'I'll take him home,' said Poldaski.

Ponce's heart fell.

'I think you better stay around here, Chief, if you don't mind my saying so,' he heard Surcher say, gravely. And he breathed a sigh of relief, silently thanking him, as the Chief mumbled.

'O.K.' And no more.

Ponce said, 'Well, I'll go to my home room and get my stuff, Captain.'

'Right, Ponce,' said the Captain. And he turned to one of the Troopers, 'Andy, you go with him and then see that he gets home o.k. – then come back here.'

The Trooper nodded and left the office with the youngster.

'Now, then. Mr Proffer –' Ponce heard the Captain saying as he walked out of the office . . .

In the hallway, where he had expected to see at least a few hundred fellow students congregating, Ponce found hardly anyone – except State Troopers. They had done a good job of it. All the students (and teachers) were apparently back in their classrooms, hard at it. As Ponce walked along he noticed that a Trooper stood outside each classroom door. They certainly were huge, formidable fellows, Ponce also noted, like ex-Notre Dame players, all of them. Ponce felt a thrill, a sense of safety, seeing them. He had a chill of respect for them, these heavily armed, well-disciplined Troopers. He pitied the crooks who tried mixing it up with them alright. Little goose pimples were rising all over him, as they always did when he felt chillingly proud of something. The Trooper striding along beside him was a powerful six-footer at least also. He towered over Ponce, who was only average size and weight, for his age.

'Everybody must be pretty shook up,' Ponce, climbing stairs now, ventured.

'Yep,' Andy answered.

'Gee – her folks – ' Ponce tried, and dropped it.

'Yeh,' said the Trooper.

They passed Tiger's Counseling and Guidance Office. Ponce saw the *Testing* sign up, so he knew he must be pretty busy. No one ever entered the Office or even tried doing so when that sign was up. So even if the Trooper wasn't walking him home, so to speak, he couldn't see him now anyway, which he badly wanted to do. He would have to wait until tomorrow, probably, since it didn't look like he would be heading back to the school today. Would they put a Trooper on his house, Ponce wondered? That would be something. Yes, Tiger was the one person at this hell of a time he most felt like talking to, and maybe even telling the pressing thing on his mind too. Come to think of it, he would be seeing him after school at football practice – or would they cancel it? *Would they cancel the game in fact?* Ponce suddenly thought of that, choking up at it. He would phone Tiger, later, and find out all about that. He sure hoped they weren't cancelling that game. It was an important one. Carverton was tough, real tough this year. Ponce worried about it, thinking about football practice tonight, if there was any. But even if there was and he saw Tiger there it wasn't the same, because he was The Coach there, all tied up with football and stuff, and not the same guy at all, he knew. There was only one place to talk to him and they had just walked by it. Ponce's heart pounded, because he wanted so much to talk to him. Would it be possible just this once to knock on that door despite the sign that was up? He wanted to, but he was afraid to ask the Trooper if it would be o.k. if they turned around and tried just that. There was something about this Andy Trooper that made it hard for Ponce to imagine asking him that. In any case, it was really too late. Here was the classroom which was his Home Room in fact. Ponce sighed, within. He would just have to phone him and find out about things and maybe even arrange to see him, somehow, later on today, if not at football practice. *So Long, Honey.* The bizarre message came back to him, and he felt funny. He wanted to laugh almost, and that was funny. He didn't though, and immediately felt bad to boot about that impulse, for whoever had pinned that to her was a lunatic and a half of the first and primal order, the lunatic of the year, no doubt of it, and was *that* funny? He only wanted to grin a little bit now, after all. That's all. Painfully. A grin mixed with pain, that was it. Thus it was that whoever might have observed Ponce carefully as he entered that Home Room might have perceived that tiny, barely perceptible, grin on his lips. Just only. Certainly, it wasn't known to him.

'Hey! It's Ponce!' shouted out half the class as he came into view. The male half, at any rate. And suddenly they were milling and crowding about him, in a babble of voices, making remarks, firing questions at him. Ponce heard one female voice somewhere, 'I never heard *anyone* scream like that – ever!' And he was mortified, more than ever. Mr Golden, the Home Room Teacher, was trying to control them, but as always was having little luck at it. He was that kind of guy. Ponce felt sorry for him.

Andy took care of it.

'Stand back! Out of the way! SIT DOWN! EVERYBODY!' he boomed out, impressively. Certainly, Ponce was impressed. It was the very incarnation of irresistible authority, armed, no less. Ponce had a crazy thought, suddenly – maybe Mr Golden – a pistol strapped to him –

'Hey – we just wanta *talk* to him – ' Ronnie Merlin yelled out at the Trooper. And he wasn't the only one.

'Yeh!'

'That's right!'

'Ponce! Some scream that was!'

'Just what did you see? Tell us, Ponce buddy!'

'Buddy!'

'What's up? What's the matter? Can't we talk to him?'

It was a madhouse of voices rebelling against that authority. Ponce felt for Andy. He sure had a job on his hands, unquestionably.

'LOOK, I'M NOT KIDDING!' Andy roared, so that the school shook. Two or three of Ponce's classmates moved back a little. The rest stayed put, and kept firing. It was a massed chorus of cacophony, hitting him.

'Christ! What a *Bastard!*'

Ponce heard from somewhere. He winced at that. He never could swear.

'JUST SIT DOWN IN YOUR GODDAMN SEATS, THAT'S ALL I ASK YOU!' Now Andy roared, above it all, somehow. Ponce stood in awe at the power.

'*I think the sonuvabitch'd shoot us! Know that?*' Somebody yelled, at the top of his lungs.

There was a roar of laughter, and hooting.

'He would, the big Pop! HEY POP POP!' Someone else yelled, Jack Delano, Ponce noted. More laughter, hitting the rafters. Even Mr Golden up there seemed to be heading toward a mild grin. And that was something! Ponce tried to remember, had he ever seen the guy grin? Fascinated, he kept his eye on him. Then, suddenly, for no reason known to Ponce certainly, there was silence and everybody began sitting down, here, and there soon, everywhere. Ponce was amazed. He would never get to the bottom of it, human behavior, that is. And he thought he was actually getting pretty good at it! No less. He stood there, taking it all in. They still had their eyes on him. And he on them. Bizarrely, he thought of Vietnam.

'Get your stuff,' Andy murmured.

Ponce did so.

They left. . . .

7

'Now then, Mr Proffer,' Surcher said to the Principal as Ponce was leaving, 'This is what we have to do – '

'I'm at your service, Captain,' Proffer offered.

'I'm glad to hear that,' Surcher told him, surveying him, 'because I'm going to need your fullest cooperation – '

'You'll get that, Captain, no doubt of it – ' answered the Principal, unhesitatingly.

'I want to find this character without putting your school out of action – ' Surcher informed him.

'That's very decent of you, Captain – '

'Because I know how important Education is, I have a couple of boys, and a girl, of my own – '

'That so? Where do they go?'

'G.A.R. High School – '

'Oh, that's a fine school – '

'I think so. And I think yours is too – '

'Thank you, Captain.'

'If I lived near here, I'd be sending them here, no doubt about that – '

'Where do you live, Captain?'

'Kitston.'

'Oh, well, you're in the right school there – '

'Yes – '

'I guess you know Frank Foley – G.A.R. Principal?'

'Fine fellow. Know him quite well – '

'One of the best, let me tell you. We're great pals. We went through college together – ' Proffer chuckled. 'He's a lot brighter than me though – got his Ph.D., you know – '

'Yes, I know it – '

'My own girls wanted to go to G.A.R.! I have three, Captain. Wouldn't that have been something?'

'Ha Ha. Something.'

The phone was ringing and ringing.

'Do you mind if I answer it?' Proffer said.

'Go right ahead.'

'I'll get rid of them.'

He picked up the phone. At once the voice at the other end

was saying, 'This is Keith Astle, *Times-Record* – can you tell me what happened? I understand something's happened – '

Proffer was rattled.

'Hang on a minute,' he said to the journalist, clamping his palm over the mouthpiece, turning to the Captain, 'I'll be god-damned – *pardon me* – it's the newspapers!'

Surcher was unruffled.

'What's he know?' He asked Proffer.

'I don't know. Not much, I don't think. Doesn't sound like it – '

Surcher nodded, slightly. 'Tell him to go home,' he said quietly.

Proffer stood there. Surcher crossed over and took the phone from him. 'I'll do it,' he murmured. 'What can I do for you?' he said, into the phone. He let the journalist repeat himself. 'No, nothing's happened. Don't worry, if anything happens, we'll call you. Don't we always?' He paused. 'Goodbye,' he added, and hung up.

'I don't want those people around for a while, if I can help it,' he said to Proffer, with the hint of a grin, almost, 'A pain you know where they are,' he added, lighting a cigarette. 'Look, let's sit down and talk in your office, o.k.?'

'Fine, o.k.,' Proffer said.

'Want me in there?' Poldaski said, out of nowhere.

The Captain looked quietly in his direction. He said, finally, 'Would be a good idea, I think, if you went out and took care of that traffic, Chief. Going to build up soon into a jam and a half. Know that?' And that's all.

Poldaski answered, sulkily, no doubt of it, 'Yeh. O.K.' and clumped out of there. Proffer thought he spotted a grin on the Captain's face. He was somewhat hurt by that, for he was fond of John – many years ago he had been one of Sawyersville's great-est fullbacks. He followed Surcher into his private office. He went to his desk and sat down in his own chair, where he felt at home again, finally more in touch with himself and all sorts of things again.

'Sit down, Captain,' he said to the man.

'I like this office,' Surcher said, making himself comfortable, 'Well, what we want to do, Mr Proffer, now is talk to everybody in the school. Teachers, janitor, students – everybody in the school.' He paused as Proffer nodded. What a project! Could he really do it without disrupting everything? How long were those

Troopers going to be stationed outside the classroom doors, for instance ? 'My assistants and I will do this in a way that shouldn't upset your schedule too much. It may take over a week to get through everybody. It looks to me like an inside job, and I imagine it does to you also – am I right, Mr Proffer ?'

'I'd say so,' Proffer said, not knowing what else to.

'We'll work on that theory until proved otherwise, though we keep an open mind all the time, of course,' the Captain went on, 'Because it fits,' he paused again, 'That's how things are in the world of crime. In fact, the world, period. Right, Mr Proffer ?'

Proffer nodded. And kept silent.

'It's all a puzzle, and all you have to do is find the pieces,' he paused, grinning in that slight, almost oblique way of his, 'And that's where all the fun is, if you can call it that, and what drives us around the bend – ' He paused, still grinning, 'I'll bet though you agree with that one hundred percent, Mr Proffer! I'll bet you could write a book or two!'

Proffer gave a mild laugh, and said, 'Brother, could I.'

'So that's what we'll do,' Surcher went on, 'Nice, easy. There's plenty of time, I think, though naturally the sooner we can get the guy the better. And I'm pretty sure it is a *guy* – we'll agree there, won't we ?'

Proffer said, 'It sounds logical – '

'Right. Logical,' the Captain said, putting out his cigarette, 'So that eliminates about fifty percent of the school population already – see how things are beginning to narrow down already ? That's how it works, Mr Proffer –'

'Ha Ha,' offered Proffer, impressed.

The Captain pulled out his notepad and opened it.

'Now this kid Ponce de Leon – he didn't do it – '

'Ponce ?' the Principal exclaimed, shocked, 'My God – he'd *never* do it!'

'Uh uh – don't say *that*, Mr Proffer –' Surcher said, again with that grin, 'You never want to say that about anybody in this entire world, Mr Proffer, including the Pope himself, Mr Proffer, Ha Ha, and that's logical. You're not Catholic, are you ?'

'No I'm not,' Proffer smiled. He appreciated that remark about the Pope.

'I'm not either,' Surcher told him, 'Well, anyhow, my feeling is, until proved otherwise, that boy is in the clear.' Again, Surcher was giving that grin, 'And funny enough, though everything is logical, and part of that puzzle, it's *feeling* that counts most of all in this business, Mr Proffer, and takes you, if you ever do get there, to the culprit –' he paused, looking right at Proffer, 'For instance, my feeling definitely is, without having asked you one question, that *you* didn't do it.'

He let it drop, and Proffer took it like a man, though he had the feeling of being knocked over and tumbled ashore by a wave, mast high, at least.

'And I'm not going to ask you any questions either,' the Captain went on, 'Because it would just be a waste of time and nothing more,' he paused, as Proffer got to his feet on that shore, 'What I'd like to ask you to think about though is this, Mr Proffer: Who in your judgement out of all your students, your teachers, anybody at all you've got around here, *Who* would you say or think or even slightly suspect could be the kind of individual to break out like that and pull such a thing ?' He paused, watching Proffer, 'That's what I ask you to think about. You don't have to give me any answer for a while. Think about it. I want you to have a really good, solid think about it.' He paused and pulled out a cigarette, offering Proffer one, who had to refuse, being a nonsmoker since birth. 'And then you can let me have any names that you come up with. That's all.'

'I'll do that, Captain,' the Principal informed him. And then, suddenly. 'You know what ? I think my deputy Principal can help you a hell of a lot too, Captain!'

'Who's he Mr Proffer ?'

'Mike McDrew – oh. he knows everybody – *thoroughly* – '

'McDrew – ' Surcher thought about it, turning over the thousands of names in his mental filing cabinet with computer speed, almost, 'He's your football coach, isn't he ?'

Proffer nodded. smiling broadly – Who in the whole of the State didn't know that. he wondered – 'That's right, Captain. Heard of him ?' He couldn't help taunting him. The Captain was nodding, with that little grin. 'He teaches Health Education, Civics, Phys. Ed., and direct our plays also, Captain.' He paused, still smiling, 'And – he's our Guidance Counselor,' he added, with a modest flourish, watching the Captain.

Surcher nodded.

'Sounds like quite the fellow.' he said.

'He is, believe me. This school wouldn't be what it is without him!' Proffer proclaimed.

'Does he get paid for all those activities ?' The Captain asked.

'Oh, well, ha ha, it works like this, Captain – Say, you're really getting to learn the ins and outs of the school business, aren't you, Captain ? – ' Proffer paused, chuckling, 'Well, he has a basic salary, you see, and then draws a little extra for his football coaching and Guidance/Counseling activities – '

'I see,' said the Captain.

'We try to take care of him, we do our best,' Proffer said, chuckling still, 'How about if I put a call through to him now ?' He added.

'Where is he ?'

There was a moment of silence. Proffer was aware suddenly of the Captain's formidable figure hovering over him like a Michelangelo sculpture. For a fleeting moment he thought of his visit to Florence one summer, a visit he would never forget as long as he lived, no doubt about it. He thought of Tiger.

'Why – ' he began, trying hard not to seem as if he were choosing his words carefully, 'In his Guidance/Counseling place, I guess this is one of his days for it – he's probably in there now, working away at it – ' he said.

'Call him,' the Captain said.

'Sure, I'll do that,' Proffer said, reaching for his interoffice phone, dialing a number, 'You'll find a friend and a half in Mike McDrew, Captain, believe me. You won't regret it. You ought to hear about some of the situations he's handled – Ah ha – and of course, well, you down there in Kitston – ha ha – and G.A.R. – ah ha ha – know all about him!' He heard the ringing tone. Tiger would be answering soon. 'When'd you last beat us, anyway ?' He threw in.

The Captain, grinning in his way, nodded. He certainly knew the answer to that alright, though not exactly. He remembered the last Sawyersville-G.A.R. game very well – his kids had come home heartbroken. As usual, Sawyersville had triumphed. He himself had not made that game, much as he wanted to – and tried to. He had been called out urgently – as it turned out, for nothing.

He still was bitter about it, whenever he thought of it, for that Sawyersville team was always something to see, no matter how they clobbered old G.A.R. Proffer had something there, alright, to be proud of.

'Hello, Mike ?' He heard Proffer say now, into the mouthpiece, 'Listen, can you come down here ?' He heard him pause, 'About ten minutes ? Good – yeh – hell of a thing – hell of a thing – oh yeh – Well – What ?' Another pause, 'I guess you might as well cancel Practice tonight, eh, Mike?' pause, 'I don't know about the game, we'll have to work on that, o.k.?' Pause, 'Right – right, Mike – oh yeh – Right – oh Christ – ' pause, 'Look, get down here, o.k.? Yeh. Right, see you, boy – Yeh – oh yeh – ' And he hung up.

'He'll be right down.'

Surcher nodded. He was looking around the room, which he certainly liked very much, then at his notepad. He tapped on his notepad. He looked at Proffer.

'It'll be alright if we use your office?' he inquired, 'I mean, when we start interviewing everybody – '

'Sure, perfectly alright, Captain,' Proffer said, though only half-meaning it, for it was like his home, and even more so. 'My god, I'm at your service,' he added though.

'We might need a few more offices. Private.'

Proffer thought about it. He certainly wouldn't touch the Guidance/Counseling office. He mused.

'I think we can scrounge up a few more. We have nooks and corners. Hmmm. I *know* we can,' he finally told him.

'Good. And we'll work out a schedule. You'll see, nothing will be disrupted, or interrupted. All your activities will carry on normally.'

'Great, Captain,' Proffer said, 'That's really what I want to hear. You're one hell of a decent fellow, let me say so.' He chuckled, 'Not at all like the storybook, TV, movie, and radio detectives!'

Silence.

Proffer wasn't sure he had said the right thing, or that the Captain had even heard it. He seemed absorbed in thought. And though there were one or two more things he wanted to take up with him, Proffer kept quiet. He thought he ought.

'Don't you have a few colored students, Mr Proffer?'

The Captain asked him, finally.

'Very few. Hardly any.'

Mr Proffer answered, quietly.

8

Tiger was just beginning to write up his report on Marjorie, who had departed, finally, when the phone rang. It was Proffer. Harry the hatless wonder Proffer. Now what the hell was it this time, Tiger wondered? He was almost chuckling. If he could count the number of times he had hauled that jocko out of it, he'd sure qualify for some prize or other. A computer prize. Or something. Old Mummer, that walking teaching machine, no less, could think of something. Tiger chuckled. Proffer's banal voice still filled his ear as he continued musing over the report. Marjorie was certainly an interesting specimen, no doubt of it. Her place on the Bernkrokkler scale was well formulated, and delineated, and within the corrective coefficient of bilinear and indeed trizonal sigma error, he was sure of it. What the hell did Proffer want this time? He had said yes, of course, in view of everything, and the time of day, free, as he was, in any event. Proffer! Would he ever open up that Radio and TV store and get out of Education as he always, but always, was saying he would? Tiger had to chuckle. He saw the customers walking in and wondering. They'd sure have a lot to wonder about! What the hell was he babbling about – cancel Practice – the game – no less – Tiger shook his head, slowly, wonderingly. What an ace. An Ace he was. He studied the burgeoning report. Already, in his mind, he could see the whole of the report. *Very interesting.* And when he got that store, of course, the School Board would make him Principal. As if he didn't have enough on his hands already. '*Very interesting,*' Tiger murmured, putting his pencil down, just alongside the report, and sitting back in his chair, musing over things, for a couple of minutes at least, before getting up, and heading for the Principal's office. . . .

9

Ponce, on arriving home, wandered about the house awhile, aimlessly, in a state of semicontact. As it happened, there was no one at home, his father, naturally, out working, his mother, no doubt, buying groceries, and Rusty Joe, his little brother, in school up at the Elementary School Building. Only Peppy the cat was moping around snoring, of course, at this time of day, almost. He had seen her crawl behind her favorite studio couch. By this time she would be snoring, without a doubt. He knew. Ponce smiled a little, and sighed, also. If it had been left up to him, to tell the truth, Ponce would have stayed at the school. What was the point of coming home – or rather, being sent home ? Captain Surcher. Andy. Proffer. They all gave him a pain, suddenly. Sure he was shook up, and who wouldn't be ? He felt sorry as anything for poor Jill, that sweetheart of a girl, if ever there was one. But how would his coming home help him ? Or anybody ? The more time passed the more he wondered just how it was supposed to help him. Maybe Surcher just wanted him out of the way ? *What for ?* He wondered about that. He wanted to be in the classroom with all of them, the whole gang of them, and tell them anything – or most anything – they might want to know. He was in the kitchen now, peering out at the back yard and all the leaves starting to fall into it. There was a wind puffing them about and all around, they did a dance out there at the wind's command, a dozen or more times, at least, before settling down. *Jill Fairbunn.* A lump in his throat and a peculiar combination hot and icy feeling crept up his neck and face and hit his eyes finally. She was a girl he had admired for a long time, from a distance of course, in fact, ever since ninth grade, two years ago. The truth was, he had a crush on her, the way he had crushes on girls who were good-looking like that, with blond or red hair especially, and older, and up there. For she was, or had been, a Senior of course, at least a year older, and Captain of the Cheerleaders, of course, *right up there.* He remembered her at the football games, he saw her of course whenever he turned around from his post of duty, or when he was running off the field, after a time out with Billy King, and the water bottles. That terrific cheerleader's uniform. Jesus. She looked the most terrific of them all in it, and no doubt of it. She was the best. That's why she was Captain. What other high school that Ponce knew of put out cheers like Sawyersville? Wasn't that partly why the team had such a fantastic record? Outside of the material and Tiger of course. But those cheers were something. Those cartwheels! Those razzle-dazzle routines all led by Jill! He remembered them. They matched the team no doubt of it. Now she was gone. Gone gone. She'd never be around again. Not ever again. That girl. That peach of a honey dream girl. That sweetheart that angel-girl. Ponce burned with it. He thought any minute he would break down and cry with it. He remembered opening the lavatory door and coming face to face with it. Beautiful! Who had a more beautiful rump? What a hump! For the first the only, the last time he had seen the beautiful behind of that *beautiful* girl. What irony! What could be more ironical than that? In Eng. Lit. class he wished he could bring that up as an example, for what could top that? Nothing could. He knew that. Of course he never would bring it up. not in a million years. It would just have to stay inside, like so many, many other things. That was life. It was, wasn't it? And no doubt of it. He would never see her again. The scream. It came back to him now. as it always would; he could see it for a long time. maybe forever, haunting him. It hit him like a kick. It seemed embedded in his eyes somehow and wanted to flood him, burning hot. What were they all saying about him now? Were they all having one hell of a laugh? What if some wise guy pinned a good name on him? That bothered Ponce a lot, now that he thought of it. For he had two more years to go more or less, at the high school and that kind of a thing could play hell with them, he knew. Ponce winced at the thought. *Screamo!* For example, that. Ponce hoped and prayed, he still felt like crying, and any minute now any second, the flood could burst out of his eyes. But the wince seemed to be doing things for one thing, it held back the crying. The flood was there, massed alright, its pressure enormous – but he wasn't crying. Ponce stood there, staring out of that kitchen window. He wished he had someone to talk to. Should he call Tiger? What was going to happen now? How long was he supposed to stay home, away from school, anyhow? What about Practice? The game? Would they go ahead as scheduled? Who would take over Jill's place? Yvonne Mellish? What did Miss Smith think? What was she doing? What about *Mummer?*

He heard all those questions, and more, inside him, battering at him, and they worried him. There was only one person he could talk all these things over with of course, and that was Tiger. He felt mad at himself for not having had the guts to try his door. What had stopped him? Was he really afraid of that jughead Trooper Andy? Was he out front now, he wondered, sitting in his car, watching the place? Later, he'd take a look. He hadn't mentioned it. He was nothing but a big goon, a dope. Ponce, in his usual astute way, knew it. What about that Captain? That plainclothes State Detective with all the sharp questions? He was no dope. What was he up to? Ponce sure wished he had stopped in to see Tiger, or tried to. Maybe he could phone him. He would talk to him. First of all, find out about Practice. That was important, he had to know! And the game. Everything. He would talk over just *about* everything with him. *That rump though.* Ponce saw that beautiful behind before him, suddenly. He felt his hand moving slowly, beautifully, over it. He saw Miss Smith. *Miss Nectar.* He saw his mother. He saw all these figures before him, moving toward one another and becoming part of each other. He could see them, smell them. His hand moved slowly. Now there was this third-grade teacher of God knows how many years ago, Mrs Hollander, and she too joined them. Then that queen of the Majorettes, the one and only Madge Evanmore. *That honey.* That gorgeous gal with a set on her like – who, anyway? Nobody had a set like that. Nobody. Not even Miss Smith, that dream of dreams, or Jill, poor Jill, any of them. *Any of them.* Ponce was murmuring, *any old one of them, all of them.* Ponce was growing warmer, the figures fusing, his eyes were closing. Now he was murmuring, *and Princess Margaret, that gorgeous little honey, that honey, Oh Honey.* Ponce kept on murmuring. Now the figures were all before him, and he was beginning to feel overwhelmed by them, for the emerging figure, a blend of all of them, was a creature fabulous beyond any of them. *Them,* he murmured, *them, them,* he was murmuring, his eyes closed now, his heart beginning to hammer now, thump thumping now, his body warmer and warmer, his organ hardening, growing. *Her rump, that gorgeous hump, what a hump, that divine hump, the hand gliding over it, his hand, which could have been his organ, gliding, smoothly, over it.* He was dizzy with it. He saw it. *Slipping inside those nifty silkies, those silkies, oh Jesus,* sliding gently, easily, between rump and silkies . . . Ponce was spinning, he was floating off into a world of mysterious colors, sounds, voices, his own world, only, he was floating, driven by the pounding power in him, all of him, *and in the organ*, that sliding gliding thrusting organ, that red-hot organ, *that Jill would have loved she would have loved it*, that any of them all of them *any and all of them* – WHAT AN ORGAN – He heard bells ringing a series of bells ringing, ringing, a persistent drilling annoying ringing. *Smash the ringing*. Ringing. He opened his eyes. He was blinded by the light. *What was that light?* He was on the floor. *What was that ringing?* He saw the organ. In his hands, red hot throbbing. *His organ*. The telephone. He was sure of it. *Formidable organ*. He sat up, listening to the ringing. It *was* the telephone. Should he answer it? Was there any point in getting up reaching out for it, answering it? Who would it be? Who could it? One of Mom's friends? *His organ*. He stared at the hungry, *famished* organ. OH GOD THEY'D LOVE THAT ORGAN! Tiger? Could it be? He got up, slowly. He put it back where it belonged as best he could, gently lovingly.

He picked up the telephone.

'Hello?' He heard his voice somewhere.

'Oh – say – Good morning – pardon me for bothering you – is this the residence of Ponce de Leon, a Junior at Sawyersville High School?'

Ponce wondered. The voice at the other end had a peculiar, irritating nasal quality about it and was a funny pitch too, somewhere between a man's and a lady's voice though neither really. Ponce put his bet on the former. His heart was pounding again, but in a different way.

'Who wants to know?' He asked, finally, most intelligently.

'Who am I speaking to?' said the peculiar voice.

'Who are you?' Ponce asked.

'Is this Sawyersville two-one-one-five-six?' the voice asked, a bit peeved.

'It could be.'

'Is it or isn't it?' The voice was somewhat more peeved.

'Who wants to know?'

'Listen, I got a *right* to know – ' The voice sounded inside a tin can now.

'Yeh?' Ponce replied, brilliantly.

'*Who the hell are you?*' the voice demanded.

'That's what *I'd* like to know,' Ponce responded, honestly slamming down the phone.

He stared at it. He hoped he had made him deaf. But he was scared of it ringing again. No doubt of it. He lifted it off and laid ît on the table. He heard the dial tone. *Now let them try the number.* He grinned at it. What a voice that was!

How would he call Tiger? He wanted more than ever to get in contact with Tiger. There was a public phone down the road in the drugstore. He would use it.

He stared out at the back yard. . . .

10

Over the lunch hour, in the Teachers' Room, McDrew and Proffer spoke to the teachers. Captain Surcher had spent a good deal of what remained of the morning with Tiger – and Proffer. They had decided the best thing to do today was to talk to all the teachers, frankly, openly, and logically, not to mention intelligently. This idea had actually been proposed by Tiger, quickly seconded by Surcher, and agreed to by Proffer.

'We're going to need every responsible person's fullest cooperation, and no doubt about it,' Tiger had said, proposing it, 'And I think we can only expect to get it if we bring them all together and brief them on everything, including all you've told me, Captain, about your tactics, your plans for cornering the culprit. If you keep them in the dark I think I am safe in saying we can't really expect one-hundred-percent, ninety-percent, maybe not even *seventy*-percent cooperation. We're going to need *one hundred* – am I right, Captain?'

That had clinched it, and now here they were.

As to the matter of possible suspects, Tiger had not been able to illuminate that totally obscure area for the Captain – as yet, But he had told him he would certainly give the matter a very, very good think – tonight – tomorrow – every day.

With regard to Saturday's football game. Proffer had suggested it might be best to try to cancel it, in view of the circumstances, especially also as it might even coincide with the funeral of the deceased Head Cheerleader. Of course, Proffer had added, if it proved impossible to cancel, in view of the possible impossibility of arranging another date, and in view, further, of the importance of the game, it might just have to be played – with a few minutes' silence before kickoff of course, and some sort of memorial service to the girl. As for tonight's practice, Proffer left that up entirely to Tiger, who, in fact, decided to cancel, out of respect for the girl.

As Tiger spoke to the teachers, Proffer and Surcher sat by, listening. The teachers gave their most respectful attention to the Assistant Principal, among other things, as he spoke to them, quietly, earnestly. The teachers were hushed and quiet, utterly solemn, many of them obviously in a state of dazed unbelief and bewilderment, in fact.

'I know how you all feel, because I feel pretty much the same way,' Tiger told them, 'This is a horrible situation, no doubt of it, and frightening too, and it's not going to be made any easier either for us when all the parents start bombarding us. I know. We certainly are going to be bombarded. This awful situation is particularly painful to us because of the outstanding caliber of the girl whose life has been snuffed away so brutally right under our very noses.' He paused. There were some sniffles in the room, from some of the female teachers. Tiger spoke even more quietly. 'Not only was she outstanding in the academic area, but also in the personality and extracurricular areas. We all know what a wonderful, warm human being she was.' Again he paused, and the sniffles were more audible. Hetty Nectar, the Librarian, was sobbing quietly, in her handkerchief. Tiger noted. As, indeed, were several others – among them Mrs Mortlake, and Miss Craymire, he also noted. Tiger himself as a matter of fact was having no easy time going on with it, but he knew he had to, no matter what he felt. Proffer was proud of him. He couldn't have carried on. He was thinking just now in fact about the parents and the School Board and the newspapers and other media and the State Authorities, among other things. And he saw them in his mind's eye on a highway, packed on this highway, driving him relentlessly before them, as if *he* were the culprit – and he saw also, suddenly, on the horizon a peaceful, prosperous, well-run, happy little TV and Radio store, proprietor and manager: Harry Proffer. He saw it. *That's it.* In bliss, within, he smiled at it. . . . Tiger went on, 'Well, there's absolutely nothing we can do for that wonderful girl now except pay our respects to her and her family – and pray for her. I'm sure a good many of you know her fine family. *And find her murderer.*' Again, Tiger paused. 'Yes. That's it. Help Captain Surcher here and his outstanding squad of assistants in every way we can – to find that murderer.' And again he paused, visibly shaken, looking them all over. 'I personally ask your fullest cooperation – on behalf of the Principal, the School Board, all of us.' Pause. 'Now specifically, you may ask, for this is the next logical question of course, *How can I help find the murderer?* Well, to tell you more about that I'm going to turn you over to Captain Surcher in just a moment, who will enlighten you on that. But may I just say to all of you, in general terms – cast your minds about, think, as I myself am doing and will be doing, and keep your eyes open, and if you come up with anything, *anything at all* that may be in your opinion of assistance in leading us to this killer – *Please* let us know about it.' He paused again, his voice dropped even lower, 'You probably all suspect, as I myself do, as the Captain does that the murderer is among us, here, in this school. Well, the chances are probably in the vicinity of ten thousand to one that we are right, he *is* in the school, part and parcel, one of us. I myself have no doubt of it. *Among us.* I don't mean right here, in this room of course, one of us. The chances of that are probably *one million* to one.' He paused once more. 'Forget that one.' He paused again. 'And remember, this is very important, you'll have to carry on with your jobs in pretty much of a normal way, you can see what I mean, while you keep your eyes and your minds open.' He paused a long moment. 'Because believe me it looks like we're up against some pretty rough weeks, maybe even months, ahead of us. Well, let's face it and accept it and do the best we can with it. This is a time of testing for us. In one way or another, as you all know, a time like this comes to all of us. Really testing us. For the sake of our children, our school, the community – *all of us* – ' He paused, his voice had dropped so low that only the absolute silence in the room now made it possible for it to be heard, '*Do the best you can.*' He went on, after another pause, in a more normal tone, 'Now, Captain Surcher.' And he sat down, next to Proffer.

The Captain rose. He hadn't been altogether idle during Proffer's and Tiger's remarks. His keen eyes had taken them all in, one by one, unbeknown to them, in a preliminary study of them. They had all passed this preliminary screening, but of course he was reserving judgement. Certainly, it wasn't the end of the study.

He spoke in conversational tones to them, in his mild way.

'I'm sorry to have to make your acquaintance under such circumstances. I've always admired your school – from a distance. My own kids go to G.A.R. – I live in Kitston. I've not only admired your school building, which is very beautiful, and athletic grounds that certainly is a fine football stadium, but also your academic record and standing among the schools in the area. And also, may I say, I've admired that remarkable football team of yours, and from time to time that basketball team also – as a father with kids at G.A.R. you can understand I'm in a unique position to do so!' He paused, that little grin on his face, and from the gathering before him came a subdued but definite murmur of chuckles. Then, silence, quickly. Surcher continued, 'I'm going to get to know all of you a lot better, on an individual basis – and please don't take this the wrong way, because I don't mean I'm going to interrogate you.' He paused again, briefly. 'I only mean that I'd like to talk to each one of you and see just where it takes us in the direction, I hope, of throwing some light, any light, on the identity of the suspect. I'll tell you right now, frankly, we don't have any ideas in that direction. My technical experts have found nothing that could help us. We were hoping to find fingerprints, any kind of a print, on a certain piece of paper, which no doubt you all know about by now. We found nothing. Of course, there is *that piece of paper*. That, in itself, could take us where we hope to go. We'll have to see how things go. It could well be the armored column, let me put it that way, those of you ex-Army men will appreciate that more than others, leading us to our objective. I don't know. I certainly hope so.' He paused. 'And of course, more detailed study of the – body – ' He paused again, having lowered his voice at that word. 'By the Pathologist and the technical experts in the course of the – autopsy – ' Again he paused, 'May reveal a lot more, maybe even everything more. I don't know. Again, I *hope* so. If anything along those lines develops, I'll certainly let you know about it – in confidence, of course. You can understand that.' He paused again, looking them over. 'My own hunch, and probably yours as well, is that the culprit is at this moment somewhere in this building. Where, I don't know. Naturally, we're checking up on all absentees, etc. What I'm trying to say is that he is a member of the school population, I'm pretty sure. If I'm right, the job of finding him will be narrowed down considerably.' He paused again. 'Now, with Mr Proffer's and Mr McDrew's assistance, I've drawn up a plan of operations. Let me familiarize you with it. That's important, because if it has any chance of succeeding I'm going to need your fullest cooperation.' He pulled out some sheets from his coat pocket. 'On these sheets I have the names of all the students in the high school. They're all grouped, further-

46

more, according to home-room teachers. Now, my assistants and I want to talk to the students, each and every one of them. Of course, with the girls it will be merely a formality – and also a way of keeping the killer off balance, making him feel safe and that he couldn't ever be detected by a bunch of chumps, namely me and my assistants, who spent time actually thinking a girl might have done it. It's a way of making him careless and bringing him out in the open. Because another hunch I have is that's what we're going to have to do. I think we're dealing with a pretty peculiar, sinister mind here. I may be wrong, but until proved otherwise – ' He paused. 'So as I say, we want to talk to all the students. We want to find out just where they were when the girl was murdered. We know roughly when that was, and I'll know more precisely later on – late this afternoon – Well, we're going to ask you to confirm their answers. I know this may be something of a problem in some cases, but I would like you to try hard in all cases and to be as accurate as you can. We want to find out all we can about the murdered girl's friends, her close friends, especially her boy friends. And I'm hoping to find some information that may help us when I visit her home today. I don't think this was a random killing by some sex maniac. I think it had a motive. Maybe that surprises you. Well, there may be quite a few surprises in store for you before this is over.' He paused, letting it all sink in. 'Well, that's about all I have to say for now. We're going to try very hard to conduct this investigation with the minimum of disruption to normal school activities, believe me. And a lot will depend on you, how well we do. I hope we can count on everybody here, believe me, we need your cooperation – one hundred percent of it.' He had put the papers back in his pocket. He was about to sit down.

'Are there any questions anybody wants to ask the Captain ?' Tiger inquired of the gathering.

'Yes – ' a female voice called out.

'Miss Nectar – ' Tiger singled her out.

'Yes, Captain – I wanted to ask, when will you start talking to us – I mean, individually ?'

Surcher reflected.

'My assistants will start seeing you this afternoon. I'll probably see some of you late this afternoon. And tomorrow morning. I'm going to the girl's house as soon as I leave here, you see.' He paused, 'Unless you or anyone else has something to tell me that's urgent, in your opinion.'

'No, it wasn't that. Thank you, Captain. I just wanted to know,' replied the Librarian, sweetly.

'Captain –' a male voice, Mr Hinkle, the History teacher, called out, 'I just wanted to ask you – How much of a part will the local Police Chief play in the investigation?'

There was a general silence, but also a few subdued titters, definitely, and many more smiles in spite of everything.

Surcher, with that little grin, answered, promptly, 'None whatever.'

'Thank you' Hinkle told him, obviously relieved, and not attempting to conceal it.

II

Ponce felt lousy. He had walked all the way down Britfield Avenue, across Eighth Street and into Maple Avenue, where the nearest Public Phone was located inside Reynolds' Drug Store, just near the entrance in fact. There were some customers in the place and Ponce was glad of it, because he could just slip into the booth without attracting too much attention, if any at all, that is. Because Ponce, somehow, just didn't feel like attracting any more attention at all – for a long while. He thought of Decoration Day. The parade that passed this way on that day, and on the Fourth of July. Those days. He had always been thrilled to see those parades, the Army Reserve Unit, all local boys, sharp and smart, well drilled, that had especially always thrilled him. The Fire Trucks. American Legion. The State Police. The bands. All the school kids. What parades. . . . All he wanted to do now was talk with Tiger. That's about the only attention he wanted. And just now Ponce felt mighty lousy, because having got through to the high school, finally, that number was busier than anything this morning, he had been told by someone, he didn't even know who it was, that all the teachers and Mr Proffer and Mr McDrew were having a meeting in the Teachers' Room. And when would they be through? Who knew. That's what the answer was. Now Ponce was on his way home, having eased his way out of that Drug Store. He had left a message with whoever it was at the other end (he hadn't inquired) for Tiger to call him. But would he get it? Ponce really felt lousy, hunched over almost, on his way back home now.

'Hello, Ponce!' he heard. Looking up, he saw Ray the mailman.

'Hiya.' he mumbled, trying to walk on.

'No school today?' Ray asked, obviously innocently.

It surprised Ponce. Hadn't the guy heard? He was a walking radio antenna, this guy, with radar thrown in, and he hadn't yet heard? It surprised Ponce, no end. He played it dumb.

'Ah just taking the morning off that's all.'

'Uh ho – not feeling good?'

'Not too good.'

'Seen a doctor? Lots of flu around.'

'Will soon.'

'What's the matter?'

'Pain in the head.'

'Oh oh.'

'See you, Ray.'

'Left a bundle of stuff at your place.'

'O.K., Ray.'

'Saw your mother.'

'Yeh Ray?'

'On Eighth Street. Before. Guess she was out for the groceries –'

'Guess so.'

'All set for the big game?'

'Oh yeh well, things are moving along, Ray –'

'Ha Ha. Bet we clobber them –'

'Hope so. Well – see you, Ray –'

'Ho Kay Ponce. Take it easy, boy See a doctor – don't forget –'

He departed, pushing his mail transporter.

Walking along, Ponce hoped he wouldn't bump into anyone else. Britfield Avenue wasn't exactly bustling at this time of day, so there was a good chance he wouldn't. He was worried about his mother though. If Ray had seen her, she might be home by now. What would she think of that phone off the hook? And had she got the news? Ponce was astounded. actually, that Ray hadn't heard it yet. Reflecting on it, Ponce began to think: Life is full of astounding things, and *no doubt of it*.

All the rest of the way home he mused over that one. In the driveway, alongside the house, there was his mother's car. No sign of any other cars. He felt good seeing that car. But also, scared. He did and didn't want to see her. Slowly, he walked up the three steps, crossed the porch, reached the front door, stopped, turned around, crossed the porch again, walked down the steps and around the side of the house, to the back door. She was in the kitchen, of course. She didn't see him until he opened the door. She dropped a loaf of bread she was just unloading from the bag of groceries, and she called out to him, and Ponce knew she knew, right away –

'Ponce!' she said, 'Oh how awful!' she said, 'I just heard – *I know all about it* –' she said, putting her arms about him, holding him close to her.

He felt like crying. He buried his head in his warm, soft, sweet-smelling mother. He just wanted to cry and cry on her. He realized, suddenly, this is what he had wanted to do, *all morning*, without a doubt of it. He broke down.

'How come I had to find her?' He murmured to her, sobbing profusely on her.

She held him, close to her, she caressed him, tenderly, she spoke softly now, murmuring to him. . . .

12

Marjorie Evanmore, in the school cafeteria now, was just finishing her lunch, sitting at a table with a group of her pals. Two of them, Hilda Linder and Jeannie Bonni, were also Majorettes. Madge, to tell the truth, was very hungry, her appetite was at a high peak at lunchtime, especially on days when she had her favorite class, typing, and most especially on days when she had a session with Mr McDrew, *Tiger*, among other things School Guidance Counselor. She felt a powerful hunger for life on such days, an incredible vigor which defied all assaults on it. She was soaring. Glowing. If the floor of the cafeteria for example had given way, if she found herself plunging downward amid tons of rubble toward the boiler room, or if in fact that battery of boilers had blown up, sending the school with all its occupants to paradise, higher than sky-high, it wouldn't have bothered her. She was on top. Ravishingly hungry. *Happy*. Soaring. *With Tiger*. For she had him within herself, magically, wonderfully, secretly. It was their secret, she was his own, no one would know, oh no. She loved him so. She loved what he did for her so. Who in the whole of the world could so – *so* – She sighed, within, exquisitely alive and warm with him. *She was his.* . . .

Thus it was that although the cafeteria was markedly subdued this day, with hardly any of the near-chaos of any ordinary day, and in fact there hung about it and over it a cloud of depression and fear, as well as a certain bizarre unacknowledged excitement, on less, Marjorie just couldn't get with it. To tell the truth, she couldn't have cared less. She was within herself. It would take a few days at least for her to really get to grips again with the world out there. And by that time she could have been to the Guidance/ Counseling office again. *Unless*, her heart skipped, *unless and if*, how it skipped, the Guidance Counselor, *her Tiger*, sent for her sooner. She closed her eyes a moment, contemplating that happy happening. She even stopped munching a moment, and that was something.

'Gee, I dunno,' a voice drifted in to her, opening her eyes for her. It was Hilda. 'I'm shook – shocked – I feel *all shocked* – numb – you know? I feel *numb*, all over.'

'I feel awful,' Jeannie Bonni informed her.

'Who would *ever* think – who would *think* – ' Hilda put in.

'I mean – ' said Jeannie, 'Who can *dig* it?'

And they were at it again, chattering in that subdued way, about it. About and about it. Marjorie sat silently, munching again only. She gazed at her circle of closest pals with a kind of pity almost. *They were so childish.* Certainly she was sorry about what had happened, and who wouldn't be? Poor Jill was a wonderful girl, and who didn't know it? Who could deny it? Who would dare to deny it? A good kid if ever there was one. All of Sawyersville knew that! She had been a friend, even if not one of her real close friends. Their association with one another actually was mostly connected with their mutual morale-boosting extra- curricular activities. These brought them, or had brought them, closest together, actually. For of course Jill had had her own circle, mainly among the Cheerleaders – which was a clique, a world of its own, as everyone knew. Like the Majorettes, in a certain sense. Marjorie, of course, was *their* leader. So what could she do, Marjorie thought, enjoying her fried chicken and listen- ing to the unceasing talk about it. They acted as if it was some- thing that just couldn't possibly happen in a nice school like this, a terrific place like Sawyersville. Which was crazy, Madge knew, just plain *childish*, she certainly very well knew, *oh how childish*,

51

she would say it like that to *Mr* McDrew, she made a mental note of it, next time she saw him. Life had to be accepted, Marjorie knew, paraphrasing Mr McDrew, *her Tiger Honey*, not that he had to tell her. What use were these childish reactions ? What were they so *shocked* and *numbed* about ? Didn't they know it was the kind of thing that could happen ? Man was a few million years old, things had always happened, as Tiger had told her, and she well knew, in any event. Marjorie took a few forkfuls of broccoli, which she loved, absolutely. The cheese sauce was terrific. *Tiger.* A voice within her murmured sweetly, softly. She took three fast forkfuls, adoring each one.

'They're going to question all of us,' she heard Hilda saying.

'*Us ?*' Mary Holden exclaimed. She was a stunning fifteen-year-old with strawberry-blond hair, long, long. '*All the girls ?*' she said. 'Why *us ?*' she also said, not unreasonably, it seemed.

'Search me!' Jeannie said, giving a cute shrug.

'Did you see that guy ?' Hilda murmured.

'What guy ?' Jeannie countered.

'Well what's his name, the State Policeman – he's in charge of everything – ' Hilda added.

'Oh – *Surcher. Captain* Surcher. Didn't you hear ?'

'Oh, sure I did – '

'Now you know.'

'Well, I *knew* – '

'Is that true ?'

'You're *teasing* me – '

'Well don't say you *knew* – '

'I did know!'

'You're kidding me.'

'Listen, *honey bee* – '

'Oh, stop it!' Marjorie uttered, suddenly, all through with her main course. 'Can't you stop it ?' she said.

Surprisingly enough, they did so. But they stared at their plates, their glasses, all around them, glumly.

'I mean, the poor kid is *dead*,' Marjorie told them, in quiet tones, like a sober mentor, 'What can you do about it ?', she added, buttering another roll, suddenly.

'Well why do they have to question us ?' Peggy Linski asked, in very subdued tones. She was also a fifteen-year-old, but pure blond. And well formed.

'Just think about it,' Marjorie now said, munching the roll,

'Can't you just try giving a *little old think* about it?' She paused. 'Hmmm?' She paused again, 'Let's all do that.'

'I guess,' Hilda said, after a while, 'I guess they're looking for clues,' she told them.

'Clues?' Jeannie burst out, '*Clues?*' She threw out, 'Do they think *we* did it?'

'Listen, no!' Hilda told her, 'Are you a *dodo?*'

'That's probably it,' Mary Holden said accidentally.

'What is?' Jeannie queried, not in her friendliest tone.

'Well I mean,' said Mary, 'See –' Mary said.

'We might give them some *clues!*' Hilda finished for her.

Jeannie stared at her.

Marjorie reached for her dessert, a healthy portion of Boston Cream Pie. She plunged into it. She loved it inside her mouth. She munched slowly. Her eyes, once again, closed for a long moment. *Warm.*

'If you don't understand,' Hilda said to Jeannie, 'Ask the Captain.' And she sipped her Coke.

Jeannie thought about it.

A burst of muffled laughter came from a table near them. They all turned to stare there. It died away . . . presently.

13

Tiger, back in his office of Guidance/Counseling after the very long lunch hour and urgent consultations of one kind and another throughout that hour, sat quietly, staring straight ahead, musing, as often was his custom, at this time of day, in any event. *Now how would the school get over this mess? Out of it?* Was there any way out of it? Would even his great talents for straightening things out be taxed? And how could one view such an event philosophically? The Philosophy of Education was replete with a formidable battery of responses, the most useful, of course, in the circumstances, as always, being the normal curve of probability or distribution, use the term you prefer. Would any of the others do? In the *circumstances?* The architects of the myriad concepts may not have envisaged such a circumstance. Tiger knew that. *Let alone a way out of it.* The thought muffled him.

Tiger, in that moment, sat muffled by it. He struggled until he heard his voice, his train of thought, once again, within himself. He went on with it. As always, on with it. For life, he knew, and so well he knew, would be nothing, nothing at all, without it. He thought of it. *Captain Surcher.* He was impressed with the man. He was certainly very different from what he had expected. He was bright, his IQ certainly would register – at a very rare level, without a single doubt of it, allowing even for the usual bifurcating deviational error to a coefficient say of sigma minus twenty, no less, or more, for that matter. *Allowing for that, even.* Tiger murmured aloud, almost. Not only bright, but formidable. *Very formidable.* How was it he had never met him before? Tiger wondered. He knew practically everybody of any consequence whatever throughout the length and breadth of the entire area, Kitston included, of course, in view of his many and varied activities, at the high school, and elsewhere. How was it their paths had never crossed? Strange. Unfortunate. *Very unfortunate,* Tiger thought. *A man worth knowing.* Well, he was in charge of things and he would certainly see that everything humanly possible would be done to apprehend the culprit to. bring him to Justice, without a doubt of it. *And a lot of good that would do poor Jill Fairbunn!* Tiger, in a deeper mood, couldn't help reflecting. No, it would do nothing at all for that poor, disastrously deceased, ex-Head Cheerleader. He knew. *That little honey.* He mused, merely using a figure of speech, a mode of expression, so to speak, for of course she was a fine size, and he knew it. *That little old honeybunch of a girl,* Tiger further mused now, again figuratively. *That sweetheart,* further yet he mused, almost murmuring aloud. He saw her, *that lovely girl.* That *magnificently formed* girl. Never to be seen, or admired, or spoken to again. *Never.* That girl. Tiger floundered, hit hard by it. He sighed, and shook his head, slowly. *Would Surcher and his crew find the culprit?* If he didn't – what next? Or, rather, and the thought staggered, *Who Next?* Tiger pondered, falling further. Was he, in fact, someone from the school? A student, probably? As Surcher seemed to think? In fact, seemed just about *convinced?* Tiger wondered. *Who could be viewed as someone capable of such flagitious act?* Again, Tiger floundered. It was some problem. He saw Jill Fairbunn as she was during football games, lively, full of energy, *tremendous energy,* leading those lusty cheers which always helped Sawyersville rack up the score, a lust for life, that was it, no doubt of it, Tiger thought, thinking also of his tremendous football team, admired throughout the State, no less, let alone the Conference! He saw her in the hallways, gay, full of life, swinging along so cheerfully, blooming with life, and her love of it, the most popular girl in the entire high school, and no doubt of it, with the possible exception of Marjorie – and – one or two others. He saw her in Civics class, where she was the liveliest mind of all, with the possible exception of course of Rochelle, attentive, yet full of remarks, and questions, stimulating them all to think, and examine things so often just taken for granted. He saw her in Health Education class, where she had one of the healthiest and most open attitudes toward for example sex education than any of them, an area which could certainly create problems for a lot of kids, if the class didn't have at least a sprinkling of girls like Jill, *like she had been.* Tiger reminded himself. He saw her in the plays he directed, for she was quite the thespian, *or had been,* Tiger again had to remind himself, playing her roles with such intense realism and zest, without a doubt of it. *He saw her in the Guidance/Counseling Office.* Stop. Tiger's eyes burned, he almost moaned, his head shook from side to side, he was suffering. *Never, never again.* It seemed incredible. Impossible. *Never.* He was near anguish. *But never.* The full impact of that hit him. It spread through him. For who, now he thought, *Who – of all those who had known her, had come in contact with her, had had anything at all to do with her* – including her parents without a doubt – *Who knew more what that really meant – than he did? How could they? Any of them. He* bore the brunt of it. *Only he* knew the full significance and *agony* of it. *Gone. Forever. Never* again. *Never!* Tiger slumped back in his chair, clobbered. He sagged. A tiny voice in his head though, bizarrely enough, began singing a tune, a faraway, far-off – so far off – sort of – *nursery tune.* He heard the voice, he sat, utterly intrigued by the voice, he paid close attention, now he could actually make out, the words of the tune – *certainly, most of it* – He listened, fascinated . . . *cockle shells and silver bells* . . . It was fading, he concentrated intensely on the tiny voice, he sat utterly still . . . *and pretty maids all in a row.* It disappeared. Tiger listened, but there was nothing more. It was all over, it just wouldn't come anymore. He sighed, finally, and stopped listening for more. He mused over it. Certainly, there was meaning and significance in it. He sat there, musing deeply over it. *And the problem.* Without a doubt an awful problem. The school had never had such a problem. How could the school ever be the same again? Especially – and

Tiger sank at the thought – if the culprit wasn't cornered. *Could Surcher do it?* How best could he help him do it? He searched his mind, parading dozens of names, faces, before it. He was utterly mystified. Certainly he would try. Intensely occupied though he was with all his varied and sundry activities, Tiger vowed he would help him, or try to help him, the very best he could, to the best of his abilities, such as they were. *Jill Fairbunn.* Tiger moved now, though he wondered how. Somehow, he pulled open one of his desk drawers, where he kept his special file. He found it and took it out. He laid it on his desk and opened the folder. Just a plain manila folder. It contained, among other things, all his master plays (and variations on) for the football team. He was constantly studying and scrutinizing these, for they weren't static things. Tiger was a gifted football coach, and had the team to prove it. Everyone knew it. He knew it. And in football, as indeed in life itself, he well knew, things couldn't and shouldn't be static. *Dynamic. Evolving. Ever Changing. Moving.* Those were the key words, and the heart of the secret of his success, well he knew. He had been approached many times by Universities seeking to replace a worn-out or unlucky or just plain mediocre football coach. And not only these. *Others.* A surprising number of others, whose coaches would have been even more surprised had they known of it. Tiger turned them down. All down. For he didn't want to go. He was happy here. He loved Sawyersville. He had a very full, creative, happy, challenging way of life here. It satisfied him.

He merely glanced at the plays now though, for he was interested just at the moment in another part of this special file. He leafed through a dozen or more papers, all concerned with different areas and aspects of his varied activities, and finally found what he was looking for.

It was simply a sheet of paper with some twenty names on it, a list, in short, and he took it in his hands and studied it. His eye ran up and down it. Up, down it. As it were, caressed it. . . .

The list:

1. Jill Fairbunn
2. Marjorie Evanmore
3. Hilda Linder
4. Jeannie Bonni
5. Mary Holden
6. Peggy Linski
7. Rochelle Hudson

8. Anne Williams
9. Marie Amis
10. Sally Swink
11. Kathy Burns
12. Yvonne Mellish
13. Sandra (Sandy) Seymour
14. Alice Patmore
15. Sonya (Sonny) Swingle
16. Mona Drake
17. Barbara Brook
18. Betty Smith
19. Hetty Nectar
20. Looby Loo
21. Mrs Mortlake (?)

His eye finally stuck at the top of the list, at Jill Fairbunn's name, beside which four stars, penciled in red, could be seen. And they had only been put there two weeks ago, no less. Beside no other name did such a number of stars appear. Marjorie, for instance, had only two and a half, though, if anybody, she certainly was due for a move up. Hilda, Jeannie, Mary and Peggy had one apiece. Rochelle, true, had three, but they were in blue and had a very special significance indeed, in a highly unique class of their own, and couldn't be said to represent a challenge in any real sense of the word to Jill's brilliant four. Anne, Sally, Yvonne, had two. Mona, for the moment, none. The rest, with the exception of Hetty, who merited one and three quarters, all had one. Of course, Looby Loo – well – there again, irrefutably, a class (and category) of its own. In fact, he would have to seriously consider: Shouldn't she be on a separate list – on her own? Tiger mused, viewing also now the name of Mrs Mortlake, who wasn't as yet of course on the list at all, officially, that is, at any rate, hence the question mark. That was a problem. No doubt.

Tiger sighed, his eyes almost moist, surveying that first name on the list. That was all he could do, now, of course, that would be all he could ever do, now, from now on, eternally. Gone. *She was gone*. Forever more. *Struck down, in the flower of her life, brutally*. Her stars totaling four. . . .

Tiger sighed again, his throat choking up on him, as hers, indeed – the thought hit him, an awful image filled him – *might have done* – His eyes burned. *Insane brute ! His hands on her. . . .* Tiger now barely contained the hot tears massed behind his eyes. They wanted to rush out, flood everything. . . .

He picked up a pencil, black, indelible, a marking pencil, such as he used to process the Bernkrokkler. He did what had to be done, though most, most reluctantly. He drew a line through her name, with the pencil, slowly, funereally. It was the only way. . . . He reached the end. He was at the stars. He was in agony. He went through them. . . .

The phone rang.

The pencil had just completed its sad journey.

The phone rang again.

His eye strayed slowly now away from the top of the list and moved down the list.

He picked up the phone, murmured a dead hello into it. He held, surveyed, the list.

'Is that you, Tiger?' said a young male voice, in his ear.

'Right,' Tiger replied, barely.

'*Gee* I'm glad to find you!'

Tiger was at number eleven on the list. He lingered there.

'Who is this?' he queried, though he thought he knew.

'Ponce, Tiger! It's me!' said the voice.

He had thought right, alright.

'Ponce! How are you?' he queried.

For he liked the boy. A *most helpful boy*. Sharp as a tack. Industrious too. Wanted to be a *writer*. Tiger grinned. A scribe. Very interested in art, music, that kind of thing. Teaching too. *And football, of course*. For no doubt about it, he was a sort of assistant coach to him, not just equipment manager, as he was supposed to be. College material, and how. The voice was distressed though.

'Well, not too good, Tiger, to tell you the truth,' the lad said. 'In fact, pretty low,' he confessed.

Tiger nodded into the phone, understandingly, 'It's rough, I know, Ponce. A hard one,' he said to the lad.

'*Gee whiz*, Tiger –' The voice said, all choked up.

'Where are you?' Tiger asked, gently.

'They sent me home, Tiger.'

'Did they? Who did, Ponce?' he asked the lad.

'Uh – Mr Proffer – and the Captain –' the answer came.

Tiger reflected.

'Well – maybe it wasn't a bad idea, Ponce – in view of the circumstances –' he finally said.

'But I feel lousy! Lousy!' the lad blurted out. 'Tiger – *can I talk to you?*' he shot out.

Tiger reflected again.

'Sure,' he said, 'Of course you can.' He paused, a moment, 'When would you like to?'

'Anytime,' the lad answered, 'Right now – any time I can – ' he added.

'Well – let's see now,' Tiger told him, his eye absolutely stuck at number fifteen on that list, 'Let's just see now,' he murmured, some life flowing back into him, definitely, his right hand dropping the black pencil now, picking up a red one, straying to no. 15 and carefully inscribing a half-star beside the name, making the total there now one and a half, almost, 'I guess you could walk up here in about fifteen minutes, right, Ponce? You say you're home?' He inquired, putting some finishing touches to his artwork.

'I could make it in ten minutes, Tiger!' the boy answered, obviously pleased.

'Fine. O.K. That's O.K. with me, Ponce,' Tiger said, still holding the pencil. His eye moved downward.

'Thanks a lot, Tiger. I appreciate it. I sure do appreciate it,' the lad said.

'Alright, Ponce,' Tiger told him.

'I'll be there in nothing flat. I sure want to thank you, Tiger,' the lad now said, happily.

'O.K., Ponce.'

'See you!' And the lad hung up.

Tiger held on to the phone, just a moment. Then he replaced it, gently.

His eye, traveling downward, reached Looby Loo.

Without a doubt, she should have a separate list.

He gave her another full star. . . .

He sat back now, reflecting on things, everything. He looked forward to seeing Ponce, who was quite the lad. He could make his day. The only bright spot – well, practically – today. That poor kid. It certainly was a catastrophic discovery he had made. Would he ever be the same? Tiger worried. It would be one hell of a shame if he changed. Not only a shame but a blow, without a doubt, to Sawyersville as a whole – and in particular, the high school. Tiger knew. And what could he do? He hoped for the best. He hoped the lad had resources enough to absorb the profound shock which no doubt it was. Just a few hours ago. All told.

It was a shame. A damn shame. It was life – at its rawest cold. Enough to test someone *twice* as old. It was rough.

The phone rang again.

Tiger picked it up and a warm, low, female voice filled his ear. Tiger loved it, climbing ever more toward the sun.

'What time, Tiger?' the voice said, only.

Rochelle Hudson. How he loved it.

His eye fell on her name on the list.

'Nine-thirty?' He offered her.

'Fine, Tiger,' said the voice, even warmer.

The phone clicked and there was the dial tone, in his ear.

He replaced the receiver.

He sat there a moment.

What a girl.

Picking up the special blue pencil, he penciled in another half-star, beside her name. For good measure.

He awaited his visitor.

14

The story had broken and was receiving wide coverage by the media, locally and throughout the State. Also, having been picked up, it got a certain mention, or at least a glance, here and there, nationwide. But it was the local radio and TV stations that really got Chief John Poldaski down. They left him feeling profoundly frustrated, not to mention bitter, for he never once heard mentioned his name. And no matter how smoothly Surcher had done it, Poldaski was growing more and more aware that he had been elbowed completely out of the case. His role, he slowly realized, was to be that of Chief Traffic Cop, no more, no less. And he resented it. For Poldaski, among other things, had long harbored the knowledge, unbeknown and unacknowledged by others, that he was an extraordinarily gifted crime-buster, of no mean order. He was a clever, formidably astute, cunning culprit duster – and more. He was convinced of it. He had requested Proffer to call in the Staties, true, but for *assistance only*, not to be shoved in a corner. And, definitely, he felt bottled up in a corner, more and more, the more he thought it over. All his years of service to the community of Sawyersville seemed to him suddenly to have acquired a meaning bordering on meaningless, on the face of it, and in view of it. For the truth be known, the Chief had regarded this situation, this case, from the moment he had been urgently summoned into it, as the supreme test of his career, no less. He had been on the verge of tackling it, head on, with certain technical assistance from the State Police, when with a few smooth words from that Statie Captain he had more or less been kicked right out of it. Definitely. And how he resented it.

Just now, in Selmo's Tavern, next door to the high school of course, where he had retired a short while ago for a few quick ones during his first break of the day from his traffic duties, he was fuming. The traffic, as a matter of fact, had increased significantly, the approach to the school, Washington Avenue, being fairly thick with traffic, and where this fine road ran near the school, blocked with it. The Chief had just been relieved by some State Troopers, who had, on top of everything, tried to get him to move his Squad Car out of the way, a request which had led to a fierce exchange on the pros and cons of the matter between the Chief and the Troopers, ending up in the car remaining just where it had been, and would stay, so long as John Poldaski held sway. A shot of whiskey and a beer stood before John on the bar. Quite a few of the boys were putting away generous helpings of Selmo's delicious ravioli and spaghetti, famous far and wide. The sauce was especially alright, in fact a pure gourmet's delight. Responsible for this was Selmo's cute wife.

'Who the fuck those guys think they are I dunno,' he muttered to Selmo behind the bar, and knocking off the shot, his first one, 'Is the goddamn town mine – or theirs?' he added, in an afterglow of free thought and expression, not to mention association.

'I dunno, John,' said Selmo, neutrally.

'I went in right away, Jesus Christ, five minutes after the kid, soon as they called me,' the Chief went on, starting on his beer, 'I talk to the kid, I question him, I get it all down, a half hour almost of stuff, and important stuff, in my notebook – ' He paused, thinking of his notebook.

'That right, Chief?' Selmo said, pouring out another shot for him, and a few more for other clients about him.

'Sure that's right,' Poldaski uttered, sipping half the beer, 'You're goddamn right that's right,' he added, polishing off the beer, signaling to Selmo for another. 'A hell of a lot of important stuff – the kid gave me.' He stopped.

'No shit, John – ' said Abe Muvitz, nearest him, 'Was her head down the toilet?'

'Sure it was,' the Chief informed him, 'Din't I tell ya?'

'And her pants off? Her ass up in the air?' Jake Dalton queried, near the curve of the bar not far from him. He was working on ravioli.

'Her pants wasn't off,' the Chief told him. 'Who told you?' He paused, 'Her ass, yeh right up in the air, oh yeh – '

'When *you* got there?' Ralph Delano, one of Selmo's staunchest regulars, inquired now. He had spaghetti.

'*Nah*,' the Chief answered, somewhat short-tempered, 'The *kid* found her – that's the way *the kid* found her – got it now?' he told them.

'Did he find her?' Delano pressed on.

'*Sure*, he found her. Who you think found her? Selmo? Christ boy!' Poldaski flung out.

'O.K., John.' Delano mollified him.

'And I talked to him one hell of a time. I should have taken him down the Station, that's what. I'd still be talking to him. I'll tell ya – ' the Chief added.

'What for, John?' asked Dutch Belmont, at his post near the middle of the bar, polishing off a long shot.

The Chief glared at him. 'Wise guy?'

'Nuh, Chief. You kiddin'?' Dutch asked.

'Well what you think what for? Huh? Just what the hell for?' Poldaski rapped out at him.

'Yeh but you *talked* to him – ' Dutch put in.

'Not enough I didn't talk to him!' the Chief poured on him. A moment's silence. Selmo filled up some glasses.

'John – ' said someone it was Jack Mizner, 'Hey John – ' he repeated, softly.

'Yeh?' the Chief said, gruffly, obviously deep in thought.

'Hey, listen – ' Mizner told him, in that soft tone. 'Think one of the nigs did it?' he asked, solemnly.

More silence. Poldaski knocked off another shot. Took a sip of beer. Another one.

'Huh?' he said, 'Nigs?' he said, his mind suddenly, and swiftly, working, *the six or seven coons or was it ten that came to the school this year from the all nig school in Caxton the State said they should.* Poldaski's mind worked on. *They didn't even live in Sawyersville!* One of them was on the football squad – *Tiger gave him a break – Jim Green, yeh, that was his name. End. Big kid. Left end. Ran good.* Or was it right? *Left? Right? Which End?* Poldaski grappled with the problem –

62

'Listen, buddy,' Dutch said, 'Maybe you got somethin' there, and how – ' And he looked around the bar, and behind the bar, and up and down the bar.

Abe Muvitz spoke up, 'Ho Buddy!'

'What they let those come here for I'll never know,' Jake Dalton said, 'Black fucks,' he also said, soberly. 'Whudda you think, Selmo ?' Dalton put to the Proprietor in his foghorn voice.

'Ain't thought about it,' Selmo responded, diplomatically.

'Christ, you ain't ?' Jake demanded, ready to ride him.

'Fuckin' Selmo. Sonuvabitch. That Selmo,' Dutch Belmont kidded him. 'I'll tell ya what he thinks about – '

They all chuckled, Selmo joining them. He filled their glasses.

Poldaski was thinking very hard now, his mind working, working double overtime, while they played around, kidding Selmo, a favorite pastime.

'John, boy,' he heard one of them, Jack Mizner, through the chatter, 'You wanta look into that angle. You ask me, that's some angle. Get yourself a medal, buddy!' And he laughed, highly tickled with it. He loved his humor.

Poldaski muttered, 'Yeh – ' Paused a moment, 'Buddy – ' And trailed off, knee-deep in thought, fingering another shot. . . .

15

Surcher was not happy. He had made the sad trip to Jill Fairbunn's home, had met her stricken and bewildered parents, had taken them to the State Police morgue to identify the body (a requirement of law – Surcher didn't like it), had returned with them to their home (with two of his senior assistants), and after dispersing the assorted collection of neighbors, relatives, curious citizens, and others, including journalists, had finally started a systematic search of the house, concentrating especially of course on the late Head Cheerleader's room and belongings. So far, after two hours, he had found very little. She had a very attractive, very feminine room. The colors were soft, gentle, as were the furnishings. He felt like an intruder in it. But he had to be in it. He knew it. There were quite a few letters here and there, in her desk drawers, on her bedside table, and he had made a collection of them to take away, with the parents' permission of course, and study. There was a framed photograph of the girl in her Cheerleading uniform on the dressing table. Surcher stared at it some little while, feeling very low. She certainly was beautiful, blooming with life, without a doubt of it. He tried to reconcile that picture with the spectacle he had seen in the lavatory at the high school and the lifeless form he had just viewed with her parents at the morgue. He couldn't. He just felt very low. He would do all he could to find her killer, but nothing could ever bring about that reconciliation, he knew. That was probably the worst aspect of his work, and the one he always had to struggle with most. He turned away from the photograph, finally, to continue his search. But the letters were all he walked out of there with at the end of it. To cheer him further, a message had arrived in a State Police car for him. It was the Lab and preliminary autopsy reports. The former told him nothing, absolutely. The latter what he already knew: the girl had been strangled – but not sexually assaulted, apparently. And one thing he hadn't exactly known: She had died about nine A.M. that morning. Or thereabouts. It all made Surcher very unhappy. He had been pinning his hopes on the lab crew picking up something. Prints on that scrap of paper, he had prayed for – *anything*. But it was a blank, utterly. Surcher was forlorn. Though a man of solid and steady character, he was definitely forlorn. He knew he had a job and a half on his hands, and he was up against it – already, no doubt of it. He only hoped the letters would shed some little light on things. Anything. He left his two assistants and went downstairs to talk to the parents again, who were in the parlor, sitting very still, near one another, barely there.

Surcher spoke gently to them.

'There wasn't anything. But thanks for letting me look.'

They said nothing.

'Maybe something will turn up in the letters. I'm hoping so.'

Again, nothing. He felt their profound agony.

'Mrs Fairbunn,' he said, very gently, 'Did Jill keep a diary? A record of things? Anything – Something like a diary?'

The stricken woman looked at him. He had to do this. Someday she might understand. Right now, he just hoped she would answer. It was hard enough asking her.

'I don't think so,' she said barely.

'I don't think she did,' her husband came in, adding, 'You didn't find one?'

64

'We didn't.'

'I guess she didn't.'

'Nothing at all resembling one?'

The parents looked at one another.

'Not that we know of,' Mr Fairbunn said.

Silence.

'Mrs Fairbunn,' Surcher murmured, 'Can I just ask you again, did Jill go steady with anyone? Was there anyone very serious about her?'

Now the woman was near tears, as she answered, 'I don't think she went steady with any one.'

'She didn't,' her husband put in.

'Did anyone phone her up a lot?'

'Oh God, she had lots of phone calls,' Jill's father said.

'I can't think of anyone, there just isn't *one single one I can think of*, as I told you, Captain,' the woman said, bursting into tears. Her husband put his arms about her.

Surcher said, very quietly, 'I won't ask any more questions now. I'll just say to you, please contact me if you remember anything, if you think of anything. Can I ask you that?'

'O.K., Captain,' he thought he heard the father say.

Surcher stood there a moment longer, looking at them. Then he went upstairs to see his assistants. Soon, the three of them came downstairs, and departed.

16

'Ponce – I know how you feel,' Tiger said to the boy, immediately seeking to establish rapport.

'I feel lousy, I never have felt so lousy in all my life, that I can recall, Tiger,' Ponce unloaded, looking in fact not too well.

'How do you think I'd have felt if I had walked in there and found her?' Tiger asked, sympathetically, studying the lad.

'I mean, it's the kind of thing you read about, or see movies or TV about, you don't ever expect to run into that kind of thing yourself ever, and that's a fact – ' said the boy.

'That's right,' Tiger agreed.

'There she was – '

'What a crunch – '

'I'll probably see her *the rest of my life*, I'll dream about it – you know how scared I've always more or less been of the dark – Imagine Now! Wow! I'll have to sleep with all the lights on, no kidding. I know I will,' the lad told him.

Tiger said nothing. He merely nodded, slightly and let the boy talk. That was the way. He knew.

'How can I ever go in that lavatory again? *Any* of the lavatories again? Know what I mean?'

Tiger did.

'I do, Ponce,' he said.

'And that Poldaski – and that Surcher – Cripes! You'd think I'd done it! I know that Surcher's going to talk to me again – and again – And what can I tell the guy?'

'Just the truth, Ponce, as you've already told them. What else?' Tiger offered.

'I hope they find the guy!'

'They will, Ponce. A thing like this isn't something just anybody is capable of pulling off. The guy will stick out like a sore thumb, and how. A sore thumb, Ponce, and he'll be spotted alright, sooner or later.' He paused, musing over it, 'Surcher's no dummy. I guess you already saw that. I should say *no Poldaski* – right, Ponce? Ha Ha,' Tiger added.

'Ha Ha Ha!' the lad laughed.

Tiger swiveled around to his right, then to his left, very slightly and gently, in his chair. It was a sort of gentle side-to-side rocking motion. Soon over.

'There's no practice tonight, by the way,' Tiger told the boy.

'What about the game?' Ponce inquired. He was worried.

'We've been working on it. If we can squeeze it in somehow, in the middle of a week, say, probably here instead of away too, we'll postpone it. I've already talked to their Coach and Principal. They're willing to try,' he paused, 'It's not that easy to do though,' he paused again, 'We're trying, though.'

Ponce shook his head from side to side, slowly, 'I don't see the guys doing their best with a thing like this on their heads. Do you, Tiger?'

Tiger surveyed the lad, thoughtfully. He certainly was among the most psychologically astute youngsters he had ever encountered, in all his days. He would be very sorry indeed to see him graduate next year. He thought further about him. He was going to college, of course, and when he was finished? He wanted to be a *writer*, no less, Tiger mused, but that was alright, he could always do that, what did it matter, no matter what the nature of his primary occupation. He'd have material then, Tiger mused, maybe he could write about this, it was pretty unique. And suddenly, out of the blue, Tiger had a vision of what he'd like to see the lad do. *He saw Ponce as a teacher, here, in this school.* And – *Assistant Football Coach.* Tiger got warm about it, though of course took care not to show it. *Assistant Football Coach.* Why not ? The lad certainly had the brains and the drive and the know-how for it, without a doubt, even now he was a hell of a lot more than Chief Water Boy and Equipment Manager, who didn't know it ? He was already practically Assistant, and unpaid for it ! He helped evolve not an insignificant number of Tiger's dazzling and intricate plays, and variations thereon, especially. He was particularly great at improvising something when the team was in trouble, he could do that beautifully, during the hectic, frantic plunge and thrust, and general madhouse atmosphere, of actual games. Tiger, sitting quietly, his thoughtful brown eyes on the boy, was getting excited about it, the more he thought about it. Why hadn't he ever thought of it ? How many games could it be said that this lad, this very lad, probably pulled out of the fire for him ? Would the winning streak be what it was without his help ? Consider the situation at the Franklin game only last week. They had tried everything. But their defense had stonewalled them. And who had noticed the way the defensive safeties hesitated every time Tiger's right end cut to the *left* for a pass ? Who thereupon had improvised that brilliant variation on I-Twenty-four Pass and Run To The Left With Flanker Deployed On Three ? With only five minutes to go in the game! In those five minutes, as a result, three TD's had been scored! Tiger felt warm and glowing about his vision, newborn. Here was a boy who could step in and give him a hand. There was the future of Sawyersville High taken care of, for a long while, at least, a future Tiger was deeply concerned about, for certainly he was well aware he couldn't last forever – even now he was pushing thirty-six, what did it matter if he didn't look it, he was certainly beginning to feel it, and no two ways around it – he knew what the score was, what better than to start thinking ahead, seriously ? In short, Tiger was thinking of a successor. A successful successor. He felt very warm toward Ponce. He was like his own son, almost, in his mind. What was his favorite subject ? Literature ? His thoughts flicked to that extremely gifted teacher of English and American

Literature, among other things, Betty Smith, and he felt even warmer. It was something to have a highly accomplished and evolved young woman like that, of that caliber, teaching Literature, among other things, at Sawyersville High School. Tiger marveled at the good fortune. He appreciated her. He thought of her. She definitely rated another half-star, maybe more. Definitely, Tiger mused, making an indelible mental note of it. *And couldn't Ponce teach Literature? Here?* That would be wonderful. Tiger knew, or pretty well knew, that by the time Ponce had earned his degree, he would be Principal. Proffer was bound to have set up his emporium by then, certainly. Or been kicked out on his ass. Or the two. The combination was possible. The School Board were all crazy about Tiger, after all not only had he brought athletic fame to the community through his outstanding football squads, invincible year after year, but he saved them a not inconsiderable sum by taking on so many extra activities, among other things, for instance, Guidance/Counseling, which alone ordinarily meant the hiring of a full timer costing a pretty penny too, for certainly they didn't come cheap, not these days, at any rate. Tiger liked the vision. He installed it within himself, for growth and nourishment. From now on, it was part and parcel of him. And when the time came – *his successor*. He soared now to the most supreme point of his vision, seeing himself as Principal of the School, *and Guidance/Counselor*, of course, for as long as he could usefully perform that function, *and Ponce as Literature, Civics, Phys. Ed., Health Ed. teacher – his Assistant – and, eventually, Head Football Coach!* He could do it. Certainly, Tiger knew he could do it. He had, among other things, the brains, the IQ for it – on the Stumper he had hit the highest pinnacles, only two or three before, in Tiger's experience, had soared up there. And what a nice kid. One hell of a sweet kid. Everybody liked him. It wouldn't be far out in fact to say they were crazy about him. Tiger knew it. There was something about him – *This lad could do it.*

But that was a vision, for the future, for growth and nourishment. Now, here, at this particular historical, psychological, and sociological juncture, not to mention statistical, Tiger saw little point in mentioning it. The time would come, as it did for all things, fully and properly ripened, and he would mention it. For when it came, when this particular juncture presented itself, Tiger would know it, as he did all things, immediately, intuitively and take action, appropriately.

'You're right, Ponce,' he said to the boy, 'They'll be in no great shape at all, will they?'

'Heck no! Imagine them looking at the stands, and the crowd and the cheerleaders – and no Jill there – *no kidding* – '

'That'll break them up and no kidding, you're right on target there, alright, Ponce – '

'I sure hope it's rescheduled!'

'We'll try our best. I'm going to push it.'

There was silence.

Ponce stared down at his hands.

He shook his head. He spoke softly. Tiger barely heard him –

'Mom was in the kitchen when I got back from the drugstore. She'd already heard all about it. She hugged me, and I cried like a baby, on her. I cried and cried, Tiger.' He trailed off.

Tiger nodded, touching together the tips of his fingers, before him, seeing Ponce's mother, hugging him.

'Then those guys phoning me – ' the lad said.

'What guys, Ponce?' Tiger queried, gently.

'Cripes, Tiger, those newspaper guys – all those guys – '

'Did you talk to them?' Tiger queried, lowering his hands somewhat.

'The first time they phoned, boy what a wise guy, some wise guy, Tiger, I just hung up – and left the phone off the hook – '

Tiger nodded.

'Then they phoned and phoned when Mom came home and put the receiver back – '

'And did you talk to them?' Tiger asked.

'Heck no. I did the same thing. And Mom agreed with me.'

Tiger nodded.

'Then they came to the house' the lad said.

'And what happened then?' Tiger asked.

'Try and get rid of them! Wow, Tiger! I slammed the door in their face and locked it, finally. That's what I did.' Ponce said.

'Good boy, Ponce,' Tiger murmured.

'They went away, finally – most of them – '

'Are some still there?'

'Some are, yeh – in a car, sitting there – I had one heck of a time getting here. They're parked near the house, waiting for me – '

'Um hmm,' Tiger said.

'I went the back way, you know, through the field, across the way there – I told Mom to keep the phone off the hook and the doors locked – all of them – '

'Uh huh,' Tiger said.

'And I got here. And what a jam outside here! You seen it ?'
'I had a look at it.'

'That drip Poldaski out there – directing traffic! How come the Troopers don't shove him ? I mean, the guy's *plain stupid*. You oughta see where his car is! Honest to God, Tiger, right in the middle of it! *That's* what's really jamming everything – '

Tiger was nodding, almost smiling, thinking of John Poldaski, 'He certainly is a menace,' he paused, adding, 'in certain respects.'

'Is he!'

'But nothing to worry about ' Tiger also said. 'Fundamentally,' And he grinned in that friendly way of his.

Silence.

Now Ponce said, with some difficulty, and looking away, 'I sure feel like a prize dope screaming that way – '

Tiger nodded. He had heard about it. That was some sound-proofing, alright.

'Well, Ponce, don't worry about it. Under the circumstances – '

He was a bit surprised though to tell the truth, to have heard about it. It was some reaction. Was there more to it ? He wouldn't ask the lad. If there was, maybe someday he'd hear it. That was the only way. He knew it.

'Yeh but, *gee*, everybody must think – ' the lad halted, looking miserable.

'I'll bet nobody mentions it. I'll just put a bet, Ponce. How about it ?'

Silence.

Tiger waited.

The lad was again looking away from him. . . .

'I sure hope you're right, Tiger. I hope so,' he finally said

Tiger nodded again, and just waited. The boy definitely appeared to be struggling with something. He didn't press him

Ponce said, after a while, once again looking at him. 'I gues Surcher's gonna talk to everybody, right, Tiger ? I heard he went through Jill's house inch by inch – I wonder if he found any clues – '

'I wonder,' Tiger answered.

Another silence.

Tiger still waited.

'What really worries me now though, Tiger, more than any-

thing – ' the lad said, 'is how much they're going to keep after
me. Do you think they'll question and question me? Like I feel,
if they keep after me, I might wind up making a confession or
something – that might happen – it's one of those things that
could happen – right, Tiger? Look at Korea! – All those brain-
washed guys falling over one another to confess things they'd
never done – Heck, you know all you told me about that – '

Tiger thought about it. He thought about Korea his little
sojourn there. His company. His little medal. When and if he
ever wrote his memoirs, he mused, that would certainly take up a
chapter or two. At any rate. He mused quite a few moments over
it. Now there was Vietnam. Uncle Sam certainly could find ways
to keep his troops happy. No doubt of it.

He said at last, 'Well, Ponce, I might be able to help you in that
area, if you're really that worried over it.' He paused, surveying
the boy. 'I'll have a talk with that Captain – also about those
reporters. I'll do that. I think you ought to have some protection.'

The boy brightened up. 'Gee!' he said. 'Hey, that's great of
you, I mean really great of you. Think you can swing it?'

'Sure I do. I'll try my damnedest.'

Ponce knew he would.

'That's really great of you, Tiger,' he murmured, gratefully.

'You deserve it, Ponce. The least I can do for you.'

Silence now. The lad sat quietly. Looking better.

Tiger found himself remembering a dream he had last night.
*There was a garden. There were only trees in that garden. Looby
Loo was standing to the side, where a path ran. She was walking on
it. Not standing. Was she walking on it? Not standing. Was she
walking toward him? She was singing this tune – He was trying to
make out the tune – Now near one of the dozens of trees Ponce
stood – Was it last night?*

'What do you think about the whole thing, Tiger?' he suddenly
heard. 'Any theories? Ideas?' the lad asked. 'Who could have
done it?' He heard him ask.

Tiger looked at the boy squarely, weighing the momentous
question. For certainly it was just that, who could deny it, here,
now, at this juncture. What Sawyersville maid would feel safe
walking the streets, *or the halls of the high school* until that question was answered definitely? Who would sleep peacefully in
Sawyersville until the fiend was apprehended? Tiger pondered
it, weighing his answer. He wished he did have an answer.

'That's the question of the moment, Ponce, and no doubt of it,'

71

he told the lad, 'it's a question that's been occupying the whole of my mind since it happened, let me tell you.' He paused, then added, 'Who knows the answer? I'll tell you, I don't. Not yet, anyway. Does anyone? Well, right now only one person does, on that also I'll put a bet, and you know who that is. Don't you?' He paused again, 'But I'm not despairing. I'm not going to plunge down those stairs to the cellar of despair. As I said before, Ponce, they'll find him, you can count on it. No doubt of it.'

'But *when*?' Ponce asked, astutely.

Again, Tiger pondered. It was just as momentous a one. But wasn't it. That boy was certainly all there, as always. He observed him fondly.

'That's it, isn't it, Ponce?' He paused, a rough analogy coming to his mind, suddenly, 'Just like it's the point about Vietnam, right, Ponce? *When*, *when*. That's the important part. *Will it ever?* That's it, alright, isn't it, Ponce?'

He could see Ponce thinking about it, and seeing it, without a doubt.

And he heard him say, 'Because the guy could do a lot more damage, Tiger –' He said it quietly.

'*Could* be,' Tiger told him.

'I sure hope old Surcher comes up with something at Jill's place!'

'So do I, *do* I,' Tiger said.

'What a lousy mess! Poor Jill! *Jeepers!*'

And silence fell.

Tiger kept on observing the boy.

'What are your ideas on the matter?' He asked, finally, in his quiet way, 'Have you thought about it much, gone over it in your own mind, Ponce, very much? I'd like to hear your theories, if any.'

'You sound like Surcher!'

Tiger grinned, reassuringly, 'I don't mean to – I really would like to know. That's all.'

Ponce shifted around in his chair, looked here and there. Then at Tiger.

'I'm foxed.'

Tiger heard.

'So that makes us even,' he said to the boy.

'You ought to hear though some of the stuff that's going around, I mean, what some are saying, anyhow – I couldn't help hearing, you know –'

The lad paused, as Tiger waited for more.

'Know what they're saying, Tiger. Some of them, around the town?'

Ponce waited.

'What, Ponce?' Tiger queried.

'*One of the colored boys did it,*' Ponce reported, not trying to hide his contempt for it.

Tiger nodded, and sat silently. It wasn't really news to him. Already, he had heard it hinted at, here and there, in the school, by a few teachers – a very, very few – that creep Crispwell, in particular, the lily-whitey, that Hawk, that quasi-John Bircher. It was hard to get rid of a teacher, but Tiger would find a way, he knew, once he got to be Principal. That ultrarespectable would be the first to hit the road. He hadn't heard one student mention it though. The whispers and murmurs had come from that tiny group of teachers, three or four, headed by Crispwell, of course. No, not one student had mentioned it, that Tiger knew of. That was good. Tiger was proud of those kids, they sure showed up that tiny minority of bigots here and there. And their silent followers. For Tiger too had contempt for it. This aspect of the situation had without a doubt worried him, though he had been relieved somewhat on meeting Surcher, the man in charge of the investigation, for he certainly didn't appear to be a racialist. Or a silent follower, either. Not that Tiger could see. He thought of Jim Green, his superb right end, who one day, without a doubt, Tiger knew, would hit All-American. He was a colored boy. Tiger mused now, as he sat there, observing Ponce, over this aspect of the situation. He had been one of the first to welcome the decision to integrate a certain number of colored students from East Caxton into the Sawyersville school system. (There were no Negroes at all in Sawyersville.) It was part of the State drive to break up the 'Negro ghetto schools,' so called, and Tiger had certainly welcomed it. He knew what hellholes they were. There had been a certain amount of hard talk at first and some hot feelings, that was true, but finally the situation was accepted by the school board and, as far as Tiger could tell, the town itself, especially when the insignificant number actually to be integrated became known. Certainly the overwhelming number of teachers felt pretty much like Tiger about it. And so the handful of colored students had arrived, on their special school bus, out of Caxton. There had been no ugly scenes, only a few curious citizens, including of course Selmo's stalwarts, on those first few days, looking on at the unfamiliar sight of black faces penetrating their high school. And these youngsters had done fairly well, most of them, academically. Socially, of course, the story was different – they were more or less ordinary high school kids during school hours and mixed with all the others, but outside school hours, the barriers were as high and as solid as ever. No white girl, so far as Tiger knew, had yet dated a Negro boy, and no white boy also so far as Tiger knew, had taken out one of the not unattractive Negro girls, four in number, to be precise, including of course Mona Drake, Tiger mused on – *that honey*. . . . He smiled, to himself, thinking of her. She certainly was a honey. She was going to be a remarkably beautiful woman, no two ways about that, already she was almost that, and anyone could see that. It was really surprising, he mused, that none of the white boys had dated her – or had she turned them down? He wondered about that. Suddenly, a dream he had just last night came back to him. She was in it. She was walking down the road in front of his house. He was in his study, looking out. She turned and looked up, and their eyes met. And she blew him a kiss. And was gone. Just like that. Tiger mused over that. What was she wearing? He tried to remember that.

'Well,' Tiger said, finally, 'No one knows who did it – ' And he paused. 'Least of all those nincompoops – ' He paused again, 'Do they even know the time of day, Ponce? No kidding.'

Ponce liked that one, and grinned broadly. He felt a little better, Tiger thought. Then he saw the lad go serious again.

'But think of that kind of stuff spreading around though – ' Ponce told him.

Tiger shrugged, 'Who's going to listen to it? Ponce, you know how it is. How many times have we talked about this?'

The boy said, 'Well, I sure hope they find the guy, Tiger – and quick.'

Tiger nodded.

'And so do I,' he said.

'Because if they don't – ' The boy held.

'I know,' Tiger told him, 'In more ways than one, don't worry, and that's why everybody has to keep cool and cooperate fully with Surcher.'

'What do you think of him?' Ponce queried. He knew what Tiger thought of policemen in general, a view he shared fully.

Tiger answered carefully, 'He strikes me, at first observation, anyway, as a fair and competent fellow.'

Ponce nodded, then said, 'Even if he hit a stone wall?'

Tiger pondered, ever more impressed with the boy's astuteness.

'That remains to be seen. What else can I say, Ponce?' he answered, finally.

The lad shook his head, 'Boy, I sure hope it doesn't turn out to be one of them – '

Tiger mused over that one. It would be a bad one.

'It would be pretty bad,' he said, '*Bad*,' he added.

'A kick in the rump' the lad said.

Tiger saw it.

'Would it,' he nodded.

'Not that I think it was,' Ponce said, 'I can't see it, I know them all pretty well by now, and I just can't see it.'

Tiger nodded, 'I'd say the same.'

'I'd put all my money, not that I have any, I'd put *anything at all* against it,' the lad said. And fell silent.

Anything at all against it, thought Tiger, looking at him, surveying him. *What a kid*, thought Tiger, feeling warmer and warmer about his future hopes for the school, and the lad, and everything. What a combination they would make. He could see it. The vision was really growing.

'Can I come back to school tomorrow?' Ponce asked now, quietly.

Tiger answered, 'Sure. Why not?'

Ponce offered, 'I don't see why not.'

Tiger nodded.

Again, silence. The youngster was looking down at the floor. *He's feeling pretty low again*, Tiger thought. *That really was one hell of a jolting shock*, he further thought. He thought of life what a series of jarring shocks that was, from the word go, appalling revelation after revelation piling up, finally burying one. *Unless one finds a way, some way*, Tiger thought. That was it, that was the key, wasn't it? Tiger had fought hard, and worked hard. He thought he had found a way. *At least it's bearable*, Tiger thought. *For a while, anyway*. . . . He had found a way. Each, he knew, in his own way. That was it. Otherwise – resignation, and a longing for release from it, totally, welcoming the burying. . . . Tiger kept his gaze on the boy. What was on his mind now? What was he holding back from him? He felt great compassion for Ponce, fond of him and full of hopes and plans for him as he was. Why did he have to find that body? If he had only got there a few minutes

75

later it would have been Mummer. Tiger shook his head sadly, within himself, thinking of Mummer. There was another one. He would follow Crispwell – quickly, swiftly. Alright. . . . The body. The poor girl, that brutally murdered girl. *that honey*. Tiger grew sadder. Life, he mused now, deeply, growing up was just that though, a series of brutal discoveries – but did Ponce's *first* one have to be *so* brutal? What would it do to him? What had it already done to him? Tiger kept on looking at him, wondering about him, feeling that great compassion for him, while the boy continued looking downward, down in the dumps. In time, Tiger now mused, the shock would wear off, he knew. Time was possibly the greatest and only factor, one might say healer, in such circumstances. Tiger knew it. He thought of his own life. his own jarring confrontations, step by step, all along the way, with brutal realities. He thought of Korea. He thought of Vietnam. He hoped to God Ponce would be spared that. In two years he graduated. Would it be over by then? He thought of all the boys over there now. That Great Earpuller, Old Cornpone, was sure filling the whole place up with them. *In aid of what?* Tiger wondered. He just couldn't help wondering. He never said anything, but he certainly wondered. How many others wondered? He knew Looby Loo wondered. And Betty Smith. And Hetty. Plenty of others. Tiger, now, felt a slightly sick feeling, wondering. What would Kennedy have done? Poor JFK. He certainly made a brutal discovery. . . . Tiger left it, and came back to the present, the here, the now, the boy downcast before him. Another wave of compassion hit him.

'What are you thinking?' he asked him. gently.

'I just feel rotten.' the boy murmured, without moving.

Tiger thought a moment. but it wasn't from any careful thought process that his next words to the boy would emerge. he knew it. They would flow naturally, without his knowing it. That was the way, always. He waited for them.

'She's inside you,' he said, quietly, finally, 'Poor Jill's inside you,' he also said, 'You're mourning her.'

A pause, as he observed the boy.

'I guess that's it.' Ponce said. from under the floorboards.

'You might feel pretty low for some time,' now Tiger said, 'That's normal.'

The boy shook his head. 'I know I won't sleep tonight. I know I won't eat. I know that,' he said.

'It's been a kick in the teeth, alright,' Tiger said.

76

'Oh man, *it has*,' said the lad.

'That's life, Ponce,' Tiger now said, very gently, 'That's how it is sometimes.' He paused, then added, 'Lots of times,' more quietly than ever.

'I guess so,' the lad said, mumbling the words, and then sitting quietly looking down still.

They sat in silence.

'You know what, Ponce?' Tiger suddenly said, after a while.

'What?' Ponce asked, more or less.

'You know that T-Fifty-four Decoy Line Buck Left And Cross Right On Three – ?'

The lad looked up.

'Yeh, Tiger?'

Tiger leaned forward, flipping through his file until he found what he was looking for. He spread the diagram of the play before him on the desk. He tapped his finger on it.

'You know that shift you suggested – between left tackle and left guard – involving the quarterback and their line backers – you know that – '

The boy was looking at the diagram.

'Right, Tiger – ' he said.

'Well, that's the one I really want to work on next Practice – I don't want any of them to know until we actually start scrimmage – I want to spring it on them – see what I mean?'

'Right, Tiger –' the boy said.

'No one knows about it, do they, Ponce?'

'Not that I know of. I haven't mentioned it. Not to anyone,' the lad said.

'Great! And that's how we'll keep it. Don't mention it. I think it's a great one. I can't wait to spring it – '

Ponce nodded his head. He was grinning. He was emerging from under these floorboards.

'It all depends on the quarterback. The quarterback, Tiger,' the boy said.

'I know it does.'

'If he gets it – '

'Down pat, you mean – '

'That's what I mean – '

'I can't wait to try it! Ponce.'

Tiger said.

Ponce was nodding, grinning, still studying the diagram. . . .

Surcher returned to the school after leaving the Fairbunns. He had that packet of letters and he would browse through them later on today, possibly this evening, at home, at his leisure. Right now he wanted to see how his other assistants were getting along with the mass screening of all the students, and also he wanted to talk to some of Jill's closest girl friends, whose names had been given him by her mother. He had displaced Proffer from his inner sanctum and arranged through him to see and talk to the following – today, if at all possible: Yvonne Mellish (a Senior), Sandra Seymour (also a Senior), and Alice Patmore (again, a Senior). Tomorrow, he would talk to a few more. And by then – who knows ? He would have read through the letters. . . .

At the moment, the Captain had before him Yvonne Mellish, a fine figure of young womanhood if ever there was one. She had brown hair and brown eyes. She was healthy and positive. A beautiful smile. Of course, today, under the circumstances, she wasn't oversmiling. In fact, just now, she was solemn. She listened to the Captain's questions and tried her best to answer them. She spoke earnestly, though not without a certain charm. She had a frank, open face, and this indefinable young charm about her. Surcher liked her. It was an honest charm, no doubt of it. And he was beginning to construct a picture of Jill Fairbunn, as she had been, in his mind, no less.

'When did you actually last see Jill, Yvonne ?' He asked now, in his quiet way, notebook at the ready.

'Well, let's see,' the girl answered, 'Just let me see – ' The Assistant Head Cheerleader, no doubt in line for promotion now, responded, 'Well – it was just about the time of Assembly – yes – just about then – Captain – ' She halted.

Surcher nodded.

'That was when – Captain – ' Again, she halted.

'Was she actually *in* Assembly ? This is important, Yvonne – '

The girl shook her head, 'No, definitely. That is the absolute truth, Captain. It's a fact. I swear it.' She paused, lowering her voice. 'And that's when it happened – isn't it – Captain ?' She added.

Surcher nodded.

'We think so.'

Yvonne flew on, 'That's what I heard – what everyone's saying –'

The Captain nodded.

'*Poor Jill* –' the prospective Captain of the Cheerleaders choked, '*Oh that poor kid* –' She gasped and choked.

Surcher waited.

'So you never actually saw her in Assembly,' he said, finally.

'That's right, Captain – None of us did –'

'Did that seem odd to you?'

'No, it didn't,' Yvonne sobbed 'If we'd only known! If only we'd known!' She sobbed, profusely, yet quietly, 'See, sometimes you might have something special or important to do, and so you skip Assembly. It doesn't happen too often, because Mr Proffer doesn't like anybody missing Assembly – No, it didn't seem odd, not at all – Oh Gosh! I wish it had Captain!' The tears cascaded.

The Captain watched her, patiently, and compassionately.

'How did she seem to you when you last saw her, Yvonne?' He asked finally, quietly.

'She seemed fine, perfectly fine, same as ever!' Yvonne answered, through a fresh burst of tears.

'You don't remember her saying anything to you?' The Captain queried, gently.

Yvonne shook her head, 'Nothing out of the ordinary, Captain – she was just the same old Jill, the same as ever. Honest.'

Surcher nodded.

'Yvonne –' he said now, 'I'd like to ask you to think about yesterday, and the day before yesterday, and weeks and months before yesterday –' He paused. 'Did Jill ever talk about anything, anything at all that seemed to be troubling her? Did she talk about boyfriend trouble, for example? Or anyone, for instance, anyone at all, in a way that made you feel there was something troubling her? I'd like to ask you that. It's important.'

The girl gave a good think to it, dried her tears, sighed, and answered, 'She didn't, Captain. That's the truth. Honest, she seemed real happy to me. She had this terrific personality. It was really terrific, Captain. She was the most popular girl in the whole school, I know. Ask anybody –'

'Did she go steady?' Surcher queried.

'No, she didn't.'

'But she had boyfriends?'

'Oh, sure – a few of them.'

79

'Who were they?'

The girl reflected.

'Well, gee – I don't know that you really could call them *boy-friends*, Captain – I mean, they just took her out, that's all – ' she answered.

'It might be important though, Yvonne. Who were they?'

'Well, honestly, it *couldn't* have been one of them – Captain – '

'I'm sure you're right, Yvonne. But will you give me their names?'

A pause.

'Do I have to?' she asked.

'I wish you would,' Surcher said.

The girl's big brown eyes showed all signs of concentrated thought on the issue. Surcher searched them.

'Well – ' she announced, finally, 'Let's see – ' she went on, quietly, 'I'll try my best, my very best, Captain – ' she paused, and Surcher nodded, 'Well, there's Dean Morgan – Phil Potter – ' she began.

'Hold it – go a little slower if you would, Yvonne – '

She gave a little laugh, 'Oh, you want to write them all down – '

The Captain nodded.

'Go on – ' he said.

'And, oh – Dink – Dink Reagan, Captain – he's our quarter-back, and also a *terrific* basketball star – oh, you probably know all that, don't you, Captain?' She paused, as Surcher wrote down the name, giving a little nod at the same time, 'And then – Art Lever – and Buzz – Buzzy Bozink – he's so cute – and Lennie Almot – I think – '

'A-l-m-o-t?' the Captain spelled out.

'That's right. Cute name, isn't it?'

'Go on,' said Surcher.

'And Petie Smith – ' She halted, profoundly concentrating, 'And that's all, right now, well, really that's all I can think of, I mean. There may be one or two more, you know, who took her out sometimes, but I just can't think of them – I know for certain the ones I just gave you took her out quite a lot – dances, movies – things like that – well, we used to double date a lot, as a matter of fact, Captain – ' she said.

He nodded.

He waited.

'You can't think of any more?' He asked her. 'Take your time, there's no hurry about it,' he said.

She shook her head, 'I really can't. Not one more.'

Surcher perused the list of names.

'Did any of these boys, as far as you know, Yvonne, want to go steady with Jill ? Think about it.'

She did just that.

And she said, 'I don't know. As for that, I just don't know. Not that I was told about, or that I heard about, anyway.' She paused. 'Though I guess just about any boy would have *wanted* to go steady with her. Really,' she added.

The Captain nodded, slightly.

'Do you go steady ?' he asked now.

Yvonne seemed ruffled, slightly, she even seemed to blush, so very lightly. 'No, I don't, Captain,' she said.

'Do you date any of those boys you've just mentioned, Yvonne ?'

'Not really.'

'Do you or don't you, Yvonne ?' he pressed, gently.

'Well – Dink's taken me out for sodas and stuff – Lennie walks me home sometimes – I've been to a movie or two with Petie Smith – ' She paused, 'That's about all.'

'What do you think of them ?' Surcher asked.

'Oh they're fine! They're really fine boys, Captain, all of them! I see what you mean – ' she told him quickly.

Surcher nodded. He sat quietly. The girl touched her hair, sat back in her chair. From time to time, she turned her big brown eyes on him.

He said, finally, 'Is there anything else you want to tell me, Yvonne ? Anything. Anything at all that you might have on your mind, or that you may have forgotten, or overlooked, that we should know about ?' He paused, looking at her, 'Think about it.'

The brown eyes were on him, she seemed to be breathing a little quicker, or catching her breath a few times. She swallowed, quickly. He felt the youthful vigor and sensuousness of the girl. The warmth of her. It filled the office. A fine figure of a girl, blooming with life, fragrant with it. No doubt of it. A winner of an All-American girl, if ever there was one. Surcher couldn't help admiring her. He thought of his own girl, fondly.

'Gosh, Captain, honestly, there just isn't anything not a thing, oh how I wish there was, I'd tell you,' she told him.

He nodded. He waited awhile.

'Yvonne, who do you think did it ?' he asked, very quietly.

'I wish I knew! I really do!' she blurted at him.

'Do you suspect anyone? Do you have any ideas?' he went on.

'I'm just – *baffled*,' she told him, finally, finding the word. 'I just hope – ' she added, 'I hope you find him – Captain – ' she told him.

Surcher nodded.

'Alright, Yvonne,' he said, 'That's all now. Thanks for your cooperation.' He got up, she got up, he showed her to the door. 'If there's anything else you want to tell me or talk to me about, anything at all you might recall or think about, please don't hesitate, Yvonne. It might be important. Very important. Can I count on you?'

They were at the door.

'Oh, I'd come to see you right away, Captain, don't worry. You can count on me.'

She told him.

He was about to open the door.

'By the way, Yvonne – ' the Captain said, his hand on the handle.

'Yes?' she asked, standing before him.

'Did any of those boys you mentioned have the habit of calling Jill "*Honey*" – that you know of?'

The brown eyes were really on him now, almost asking him to fall head first, into them.

'No,' she replied, 'Not that I *know* of – '

She stood still near him. He heard her breathing. He could almost feel her heart pounding.

'Alright, Yvonne,' he said, opening the door for her, 'Thank you.'

'Thank you, Captain,' she told him, in a very soft voice, a whisper almost, and smiling.

She departed, smiling.

18

Ponce, departing finally from the Guidance/Counseling office, turned left into the hallway and walked up it with something like his old steady confidence and grip on life again. He knew that would happen. That's what a talk with Tiger would do, always no matter the circumstances. And the long discussion, examination, and analysis of football plays had engaged him and stimulated him, profoundly, as always. He had even devised two new ones based on the special left and right decoy 'I' formation. They excited him. He knew Tiger had been excited by them and would try them as soon as he could. He always did. All in all, therefore, Ponce didn't feel too bad. *Not wonderful* – of course – but definitely, certainly, *not bad*. At all. He walked up the hallway, now deserted, to all intents and purposes, since the schoolday was over and certainly there wouldn't be anything in the way of extra-curricular activities going on tonight, of all nights. Ponce remembered his very different journey along this very same hallway earlier in the day. He cringed at the memory, though he had thoroughly discussed it with Tiger. He hadn't been able to mention Mummer though, no matter how close he came to it several times. He just hadn't been able to. That he was sorry about, and he resolved to tell him one day, without fail, possibly tomorrow even. He hoped secretly though he wouldn't have to, that Surcher would have cornered the culprit by then, or before then. He hoped fervently for that. He heard his footsteps, very soft ones now of course since he had changed into a pair of suede shoes whose soles and heels were made of thick, soft rubber, or facsimile thereof, at any rate. He could creep along like a cat on them, almost. Like Peppy, almost. He grinned thinking of his funny cat. He just loved it. What a cat. It was a cat-and-a-half or more and who didn't know it ? He thought of Tiger he heard his voice he saw his morale-boosting, confidence-inspiring face before him, he saw the whole of him before him, in short, Tiger internalized. He saw his mother, also, and felt her warmth, her love for him, inside him. He saw his father. And brother. That cute little Rusty Joe, what a sweet little brother, shooting questions at him a million a minute, and sometimes more, and always trying to be like him. He saw Peppy. How he loved her. Was there another cat like that in the whole world anywhere ? he wondered. She could sit on the kitchen doorstep for hours, watching something, watching him, he saw her sitting there, watching him. Those big, yellow-green eyes, watching him. She loved him. He knew that cat loved him. What a purrer ! The whole kitchen shook with her purring, especially at night, when he fed her, or his mother did. And held her. And stroked her. He reached the lavatory. He would have to walk past that lavatory. Where were all the Troopers ? he wondered. Where had they got to ? He wondered and wondered. Maybe there were some inside. That could be. Ponce's heart started pounding, he half-expected somebody to come tearing out of there like a space shot, running, screaming, down the hallway. He braced himself, and pushed himself, hanging on to Tiger, his mother, his father, Rusty Joe, and Peppy. He heard her purring. He hung on now, to all of them, as he started to walk past that awful door. That *unavoidable* door. He saw Miss Smith, suddenly.

She was up ahead, just coming out of her Home Room. She had her coat on, but unbuttoned. She was about the last one to leave tonight, Ponce supposed, quivering slightly, watching her. She would go down the stairs, to her left, she probably wouldn't even see Ponce, as a matter of fact. He could be lucky. His heart pounded hard, but in a different way now, he was very embarrassed, he just didn't want her to see him. Though he loved her. Madly. So madly in love with her. Her heels tapped in the hallway. His quivering increased. He wished he could just sink through the floor. Disappear. Anywhere. She didn't turn to the left, she turned right, surprisingly enough, mortifyingly enough, and headed toward him. There wasn't any way in the world now he could avoid her – unless he took a fast dive into that lavatory, lightning fast, no less. Like the quarterback would have to dive on that new 'I' play –

'Why, Ponce! Hello!' He heard her fabulous voice, and he halted, not that he had ever started, and nearly fell over, wishing suddenly and powerfully that he could fall into her arms, marvelously, and be swallowed up by her, completely. She approached him.

'Ponce, how are you ?' she said to him, coming up to him, a fragrance like roses hitting him, all the roses in all the rose gardens of the world, plus lilacs, at least. 'Oh, Ponce, you sweet kid, honestly – ' she said to him, near him, in fact before him, as he stood there, paralyzed, yet throbbing. Where was his voice ? He fought for it.

'H-h-H-H-Hello, Miss S-S-Smith,' he said, at last.

'What a terrible thing, oh you poor kid, I've been so worried about you – ' she said.

'I'm – I-I-I-I'm – oooo – O.K. – Miss – Smith,' he told her.

'Are you sure ? Are you alright ? Oh, how awful! They sent you home, didn't they ? Did you come back ? Are you alright ?'

'I-I-I – think – ' he faltered.

She examined him, she laid a royal hand on him.

'You poor kid, she said, softly, passing her hand fantastically tenderly over his face, leaving roses on it, as he staggered, 'Oh you poor kid, you dear kid, what a terrible thing, you poor kid, my heart goes out to you,' she murmured, looking at him.

'G-G-G-Going – H-H-H-Home – Miss – S-S-S-Smith – ?' he managed.

'I was just leaving, yes,' she answered, 'What about you, Ponce. What are you doing here? May I ask?' she added, so softly. What held him up?

Ponce stammered, 'Talking – with Tiger – *Mr McDrew* – ' he said.

'Mr McDrew?' she asked him, 'Is he still here, Ponce?' she also asked him, 'I'm sure he helped you, he's a wonderful person, isn't he?'

'S-S-S-S – He – sure is – Miss – Smith – '

She kept her warm eyes on him, he was aware only of them. Where was the rest of the world? 'Feel better?' she asked.

'Sure do – M-M-M-Miss – Smith,' he told her.

'I'm glad you do. That was a terrible shock, wasn't it? It's going to take quite some time for you really to get over it. You don't know how I've been thinking of you,' she said, tenderly.

'*R-R-R-Really*, Miss Smith?'

'Yes. That's so.'

'I – ' he said, 'I-I-I've been thinking – a l-l-lot about you – too – M-M-M-M-Miss Smith – ' He halted.

She smiled at him. That beautiful mouth those lips, those perfect teeth – *smiling at him*.

'I'm glad, Ponce,' she said.

He stood there. Never again would he move from there. How could he? One day he would nail a plaque here, when someone finally hauled him away from here. He still felt her magnificently marvelous hand on him, and would, forever, though she had taken it away, of course. He was enveloped by the warmth of her, as they stood there.

'Well – ' she murmured, finally, 'I've got to be running along now, Ponce – ' she said.

'O-K-K-K-K – Miss Smith – ' he managed.

'Are you going home now?' she inquired.

'Y-Y-Yes – Miss Smith.'

'Well, take care, won't you, Ponce?' she said.

'You – Y-Y-You – too – I mean – I-I-I will – Miss S-Smith – '

She still stood there, looking at him. He watched with astonished eyes as her hand reached out again for him, and touched him. He closed his eyes.

'You poor kid,' she murmured.

'I'll be – *alright* – ' his voice said.

He opened his eyes.

'Are you reading?' she asked.

'Always – M-M-Miss – Smith – ' he said.

'How do you like *Paradise Lost*?'

'Great – ' he said.

'I'd like you to write a theme on it – '

'For when – M-M-M-Miss Smith?'

'Oh – say next week – alrighty?'

'All – right – y – ' he said.

'Are you coming to school tomorrow?'

'I – think so.'

'Well, fine. I hope you do,' she said, 'And if you want to talk with me about the theme, don't be shy, Ponce – please do so.' She paused, tenderly surveying him, 'Do you want to come over to my place to do so?' she asked. 'You know where I live, don't you?' she said. 'In fact, Ponce, I *would* like to talk with you about it.' She stopped.

Ponce stood there.

He felt a tremendous roar, he was blasted off, no doubt of it, he was outside the building now, high above it, soaring. Where was he soaring? He tried to see, he had to –

'*Really?*' he said, hearing a strange noise, his own voice, no less.

'Yes, really,' she said, as he soared and soared, heading far into space.

'W-W-W-When?' he said, or thought that he said.

'When would you like to?' she said.

'T-T-Tonight?' he said.

'Yes, alright,' she said.

'T-T-There's n-n-no Practice – It w-w-w-would be *f-fine*,' he said.

'That's fine,' she said.

'I'll s-s-see,' he said, 'I'll t-t-try hard to *m-make* it ' he said.

'Alright then. I understand. Come about seven or so, if you can.'

'O.K.'

'Sure you know where I live?'

'Elmwood Avenue – '

'That's right.'

'O.K.'

She smiled again. Her hand left him.

'Don't forget now,' she said.

'I won't – *Miss Smith* – '

She stood there a moment looking at him. He was there, but a few million light years away, also.

'Alright, Ponce,' she said.

'Bye, Miss Smith – '

'See you later – ' she said.

'O.K., *Miss Smith* – '

She walked away, down the hallway, her heels tapping away. Ponce, trembling violently now, watched her.

She disappeared down the hallway.

19

Somehow, Ponce left the building, soon after, but the English Literature teacher didn't. She got as far as the Guidance/Counseling office, stopped, touched her hair, and tapped gently on the door, twice. She waited a moment, then entered. She closed the door behind her. She looked around the office, she looked at the desk, she looked at the chair behind the desk – she looked at Tiger.

'Hi,' she said, feeling a distinct, warm flush.

'Well Hi ' he said, lifting his head from a mass of papers, 'You look great,' he said, 'You *are* the greatest,' he said, 'know it ?'

She laughed softly, moving deeper into the room.

'That's what you tell them all,' she said.

'Don't I,' he chuckled.

She approached the desk. He grinned now, sitting back in his chair, surveying her.

'What a day, what a day,' he said.

'*Wasn't it !*'

'Ever been through such a day ?'

'I haven't.'

'Sit down. Want to ?'

'I think I will. Yes. I will. If you're not too busy – '

'Take your coat off,' he said, 'In a hurry? It's warm in here –'

'O.K. – I will,' she said.

Tiger got up from his chair and moved toward Sawyersville High's outstanding Literature teacher. She smiled at him. He stood behind her and helped her slip out of her coat. Her unique, fresh fragrance came to him, already, in fact, it was starting to fill the office. He loved it. As the coat slipped away from her, he saw her marvelous profile, all the way down. She had on one of her sweaters. He stood there a moment, looking at her. He put the coat on the coatrack, beside his own. Then he returned to his chair behind the desk. She took a chair near the desk. She sighed. She opened her bag.

'Cigarette?' she said, pulling out a fresh pack.

'Don't mind if I do,' Tiger said, grinning, and reaching for one.

'You don't inhale much, do you?' she said, lighting them up.

'I try not to,' Tiger said.

'Of course that takes all the fun out of it,' Miss Smith said, with another soft laugh.

'True, true,' Tiger said, 'But what can you do?'

'You want to live too long, Mr Tiger McDrew, that's your trouble, I think –'

Tiger shook his head, slowly, 'Oh, man, man, have I got troubles –'

'Haven't we all –' Miss Smith told him, taking a long drag on her cigarette, 'Ummmm – so good –'

'So – what's new?' Tiger asked, admiring the view, 'You're working overtime tonight, my bonnie lass, aren't you?'

Miss Smith blew out a long cloud of smoke, slowly. Tiger caught it as it came drifting by him. He loved it. It smelled good, doubly good, having been inside her.

'I could say the same for you – *Mr McDrew* –'

'And – in view of the circumstances – my lass –'

'God! The circumstances! Tiger, did you ever think we had a lunatic loose in the school?'

'*Psychopath*, Miss Smith. That would be the correct appellation.'

'Well, *whatever*. I'm glad those State Policemen are all around the building anyway. I never thought I'd be one to be grateful for their presence! Let me tell *you*.'

'There you are –' Tiger said, 'A place for everyone, in life – Didn't Plato say that?'

'Sounds more like the Founding Fathers – ' Betty Smith said, with her soft laugh.

'Any particular one?' Tiger asked.

'I wonder – '

'Those Founding Fathers – ' Tiger murmured, chuckling also.

Betty Smith crossed her legs. Tiger noticed. She pulled again on her cigarette. Tiger noted. The sweater was a pale, pale blue. Gorgeous. Without a doubt, *a gorgeous one*. He couldn't help admiring it. He dragged on his cigarette, inhaling almost.

'How are you?' Tiger asked, in his friendly way.

'Very very upset about this whole thing,' she confided.

Tiger nodded, 'And so am I. Believe me. It's a hell of a thing. What a thing.' He was gazing at her. 'A real piperoo of a thing, a hell of a screwy thing, if ever there was one,' he added, quietly. 'How was she in Lit?' he asked her.

'Well – ' Miss Smith replied, 'I couldn't honestly say she was *outstanding* – however, she certainly took an interest in it – '

Tiger nodded, 'She was very good in Languages, and Social Studies, that I know,' He told her, still looking at her, 'I'm going to miss that kid. No kidding.'

'Her poor parents!'

'What a thing.'

'I'm impressed with this State Police Captain – what's his name?'

'Surcher – '

'I'm certainly glad he's handling it. I was afraid *our* – esteemed Chief of Police – '

Tiger nodded, grinning.

Miss Smith continued, 'It's an awful feeling, Tiger, in front of a class now – wondering if this – *psychopath* – is sitting there, in front of you, laughing at you, inside himself. It's not going to be the same around here for a long while – certainly, not until they've found the creature – '

Tiger nodded.

'I couldn't agree more.'

Miss Smith pulled on her cigarette, held the smoke a long while, then blew it out, finally, slowly. She touched her hair. Who had such gorgeous hair? Tiger stared at it.

'No practice tonight?' she asked.

'Canceled.'

'Is Saturday's game canceled?'

'We're working on it. We'll know for sure tomorrow. I think it will be,' he answered.

Silence. Their eyes met. And held.

Now, 'How's Hilda?' she asked, softly.

She meant his wife, Looby Loo, of course. He shrugged, looked to the left a moment, the right, then back at her.

'Same as ever,' he told her.

'Poor old Tiger,' she said, placing her smooth, white hand on the desk, near him. He looked at it.

'What does it matter?' He told her, placing his hand on hers, 'You make up for it,' he told her, *You honey* –

'Do I?' she queried.

'And how you do,' he told her, moving his hand over her wrist now, and upward, inside her arm, traveling, slowly, *'But do you.'*

'I'm glad I do – '

'You do, you know it – '

'Poor Tiger – '

'Lock the door. Want to?' he murmured.

'Of course I want to,' she murmured.

'O.K.,' he told her, caressing her arm, his fingers lingering inside her elbow, stroking gently there, it was so warm.

'O.K.,' she whispered, blowing him a little kiss, and some smoke also, and he loved both. She rose and walked to the door. She set the lock. He was observing her. That gorgeous form. What a form. Who else had such a warm form?

She turned, faced him, walked to him. She put out the cigarette. She sat on the desk, near him. She looked at him.

'How did you ever marry her?' she murmured to him.

'Don't ask me. God, don't ever ask me – O.K.? Honey?'

She leaned toward him, she placed her arms around his neck.

'Honey – ' she whispered, *'Oh you honey – '* she also whispered.

His hands touched her waist, he pushed his chair back and brought her in one deft movement onto his lap. She gave a little sigh, and made a cooing sound. He moved his hands up toward her breasts, he stroked them, gently, he fondled them, through that soft sweater. He loved them.

'Darling – ' she said, *'Tiger – '* she said, searching for his mouth with her open lips, her eyes closing.

'Don't ever talk about her,' he murmured, kissing her, 'Will you – '

They kissed a long time, she sighed, she murmured and

moaned, softly, she caressed his neck, his face, she held close to him.

She felt his arms about her, now one of his hands was straying under her sweater, her blouse, and upward. She felt his hand on her breasts, her brief bra pulled away from them. He fondled them, marvelously, stroking their firm tips. . . .

She came up for air, finally. 'Let me help you,' she murmured to him, '*Will you let me*,' she told him. . . .

He murmured, 'I want you to – '

20

At home in his little den, Captain Surcher was having a very interesting, though so far unfruitful, time with the late head Cheerleader's ample package of letters. She certainly was an avid correspondent, if the letters she had *received* were anything to go by. They came from points far and wide, including Morocco, no less. There was actually a letter from some individual in Morocco, yes. And how had she ever met him ? A pen pal ? Purely ? Out of her early girlhood ? Surcher felt a fond surge, thinking of his own twelve-year-old, who had pen pals, gleaned out of some kid's magazine or other, all over the globe. This particular letter was in French, actually, and in an almost indecipherable hand, to boot, and so of course meant absolutely nothing to him. Or next to. He looked at the date of the postmark, which fortunately was legible, and concluded that the fellow could most probably be eliminated, unless he had hopped a couple of supersonic jets. And worked fast, at that. Not that Surcher seriously considered this. It just didn't look like the work of a French Moroccan to him. No, he mused. He just couldn't consider this. Though such was the nature of the blank wall he was up against that he was ready to consider anything. He thought back now to his interviews with Jill's closest friends today. None had helped him much in any way. Sandra Seymour cried just about the whole interview, and though Alice Patmore had certainly tried very hard to be of help, she just had nothing much to tell. Jill had simply been too much of a healthy, wholesome, yes, All-American girl. Surcher shook his head, slowly, thinking now about the abusive phone calls he had received during the day from certain quarters. He was used to such calls, of course, for they cropped

91

up during any investigation. He thought of the one he had taken just a half hour or so ago, here in his own home. The caller had identified himself as 'an active member' of the John Birch Society. He had thereupon launched upon a vituperative assault on the lack of police activity in the matter, with special reference to their apparent failure to focus their inquiries on the most obvious immediate suspects, to wit, the 'black boys' in the school. Surcher wasted no time talking to the man, of course, but before hanging up he was presented to boot with a sermon on the inherent stupidity and evil of even this kind of token 'mixing of the races,' a mixing which was 'against all nature,' according to his caller. Surcher was polite to him, however. He said 'Thank you for calling,' before hanging up. He knew that was the way to handle such crackpots. Polite, but firm, and ignore them. It was the only way. If you handled them like they really should be handled. that is, a swift kick in the rump, they would only keep phoning, and phoning, and organize all their friends too – to do so. Surcher sighed. musing poignantly, as he often did, over the trials besetting even the most honest and dedicated policemen, in this day and age. Perhaps any age. As if the immediate task, and problem, weren't enough. He certainly was grateful though for the excellent caliber of help he was getting from the authorities up at the school. He was particularly impressed with that Assistant Principal, Mr Mike McDrew, who of course was known throughout the entire State for his football-coaching activities, his amazing teams. The Principal himself, Mr Proffer, wasn't anywhere near as impressive. but at least he didn't create any problems, and certainly cooperated, in every way. Surcher felt sorry for him. He certainly had a mess and a half on his hands. Imagine some of the phone calls *he* would be getting tonight – from parents. mainly. Surcher sighed again, and opened a letter. It was from a magazine.

Dear Jill,

Thanks a lot for telling me about the plans for the Carverton game. It was awfully nice of you. I want to do the nicest article on you and your Cheerleaders for the next issue, as you know, and so I'll certainly be there to meet you. It will be a tremendously popular article, I'm sure, for there is great interest, as I'm sure you know, in the extraordinary football teams of Sawyersville High School, and naturally, in the wonderful Cheerleading squad that so loyally and effectively supports them. I'm going to be bringing along a really first-rate photographer to take a lot of shots of you and the rest of the girls, in action. They will make a wonderful splash beside the article. The Editor has already told me I can have at least four pages. And I'm telling you now!

Looking forward to seeing you,

Janet Lance
(Features Writer)

Surcher sadly laid that one aside. How many similar ones would he have to read through? He tried another one. His eyes were getting a little blurry and tired now, for it was his forty-fifth one, at least, some of them ten pages long, no less.

– Honey –

It began.

Surcher sprang to attention.

– You honey you, let me tell you, I'm true blue, and I'm sold on you. *How about it?* Coming through soon? When? You peachy honey. You're the top of the charts! All the charts! You know it. What's up? Hup? You don't like my *color?* See you in class, lass. So long for now – honey. . . .

– Kid

Surcher was riveted. His head was spinning. His eyes came to life again, he could see perfectly. *Could it be true?* He poured over the letter again, ecstatically, almost. *Was it really true?* It was one of those rare, rare occasions which set his heart pounding, his temperature rising. *Pure Gold. Discovery.*

'Ding dong!' he said out loud, clapping the desk with his hand. 'Diggidy dong!' he also said, slightly rephrasing it.

So long . . . Honey . . .

His eyes nearly burned a hole through it. He didn't know quite what to do with it. He had of course been very careful handling all the letters, not wishing of course to smudge up or otherwise mess up any and all possible fingerprints. In fact, he wore gloves. A thin, white pair, specially made for the job. Now he handled the letter as if it were the world's most fragile, priceless piece of glassware. He hardly dared breathe on it.

'Son of a pup,' he murmured, two or three times aloud, from a high, billowing cloud.

Now, the next move. What a move. Who best to get hold of? Who, up there at that school, would help him most? Who had the best, the most intimate knowledge of all the kids in the school? It might be a good idea to get hold of the three young maids he had interrogated, so to speak, earlier today, they might well be able to illuminate things, right away, or – *McDrew !* That sharp fellow would probably be his best bet. On the other hand, Surcher's mind clicked, why not just interrogate the twelve or thirteen Negro kids in the school ? *And tell nobody a thing !* That might just be the way. Certainly, *Kid* was among them – unless he came from another school. *And if he was among them –*

That was the course the Captain decided on. It was, in his studied view, far and away the best. Now he had two choices before him on how to go about this. (1) Have all the Negro kids picked up tonight and start working on them, or, (2) Hold everything until tomorrow morning, when he arrived bright and early at the school. His first impulse leaned toward alternative (1), but on reflection, in spite of the risks, the circumstances, he considered (2) would be the best way to tackle the problem. Certainly it would mean he would be getting very little sleep tonight, itching as he was for action, and worried about the culprit taking off or even pulling a carbon copy. For he was capable of it. Surcher was quite convinced the criminal, however young he might be, was certainly capable of it. Nevertheless, he decided on that course, he would just have to risk it. And he hoped to God he wouldn't regret it – later.

He still held the letter, very carefully, one might say exquisitely, in his gloved fingers. He read it over and over again, six times at least, and finally put it down all on its own, on his desk, so very carefully. He would carry out tests for prints himself – later.

Meanwhile, there were still some half dozen letters to investigate, and though he didn't have much heart for them, Surcher knew he had a duty to them, and he got to them, however reluctantly. He knew, or was almost sure, it would be all anticlimax now.

The first one was from a girl friend, obviously. He noted the feminine paper and handwriting, the slight trace of fragrance, perfume, powder, or similar item. It came from New Jersey.

– Jill Honey –

Surcher halted, jogged by it! Then he smiled. He had after all run across this sort of opening on a few other letters, mostly from girl friends or female relations, far and near. All perfectly innocent, innocuous, to a fault, in fact. He kept on smiling, and read on:

– And how's everything with you, lovely? Still cheering on that fab, that mad, Sawyersville club? Are they a club! Listen, hon, next time you come over to see me, next summer will it be, I want you to tell me all about them. I mean: How do they do it? (Oh, I know you'll be graduated by then!) Is it *Tiger?* (Don't tell, but I go for that throbber!) (Oh Harbor!) Seriously, though, what fun is it to be Captain of the Cheer Leaders at a school like *mine?* Oh Gee! Do you know how many times, no, how many games (pardon me) we've won in the past *two years?* I won't tell you! Listen, nobody *goes* to the games anymore. Know that? It's heartbreaking! I tell you! What's the news? Any news? How's the love life? (You'll make a *fine* wife!) I'm a poet! Listen, Jilly. who was your favorite, really, at Asbury? I mean, every time I saw you on the beach I wondered who it would be – today, that is *That* day, I mean. See what I mean? (English was never my strong point!) Did I tell you I just *about* made the grade? I prayed. Old man Bane. On what a pain! Ha Ha! Am I funny? Be a bunny: I'm on the hop – blame me? And which was your favorite group? I mean the dances on the jetty, the *dance hall* there, that is! I mean that one. Well, I liked *The Giggles.* Oh, they were great. Great! I thought honestly I would find them all kid stuff, but I was in the mood, and the rhythm is just terrific anyway – isn'it it? And . . .

Surcher halted there, observing there were ten more pages of this. He wasn't a martyr, after all. He felt he could in all fairness and without any prejudice or damage whatsoever to his cause – his reputation, his profession, skip the rest. And he did. He just turned to the last page, which was written in a sloping, cockeyed, downhill and uphill manner, as if the writer had just had a fix, or was profoundly sleepy, at least, and the signfiture, illegible. alas. Though, hazarding a rough guess, Surcher mentally wrote down: 'Ribby.'

And on to the next one:

My Dear Jill,
   I'm so glad you were accepted. I think this is a piece of news all of us can't help but be very, very happy about. I know you will be very happy here, and of course we shall be only too glad to see you. . . .

Surcher skipped the rest, four pages of it, though he made a mental note to possibly inquire just what it was about, this acceptance. It was signed, '*Martha.*' Simply.

Taking a deep breath, thinking of Dolly, his wife, wondering if she had yet gone to bed, he went on to the next.

And the next.

His eyes starting to burn again, he gazed at the heap of letters beside him. He turned, he looked at the single, solitary, glittering scrap of a letter on the corner of his desk –

He blew a kiss at it.

21

Ponce, pedaling through the streets of Sawyersville, was as spruced up as a bridegroom – almost. He had shaved, electrically, he had combed and brushed his rather short brown hair, carefully. He had examined his face for a long time, in that mirror. He wasn't handsome, he knew, but he wasn't ugly either, that too he definitely knew. He found his face very interesting, in fact. It looked different from each side, and, on the whole, he preferred the view from the left side. It had always struck him as a very interesting fact, how faces looked different from each side, and each angle, too. Head on, for example, he looked real good. He had made a note to look at her squarely, as much as he could. He had chosen his clothes with care. He looked very good. And he had told his parents that he was off to see Tiger. He hated doing that, but he felt he had to. He knew it was his only chance of being allowed out – tonight, of all nights. Incredulous, but ever patient and full of adoring parental faith in their Ponce, they had let him go. It hadn't been all that easy, of course. He had to argue awhile, and insist, in his quiet way, for quite a while. In the end, he had won out.

He chose the most direct route to Miss Smith's apartment house, but he was going to be a little late in any event, due to the prolonged negotiations and preparations. Rusty Joe, his little redheaded brother of course, had stared at him with big questioning eyes, aware as he was that some momentous event had transpired in Sawyersville that day, but not quite one hundred percent in tune with the exact nature and/or significance of it, just yet. Peppy had hung around him, and tagged after him, meowing, tripping him up, for he had forgotten to feed her, of all things, and so had his mother, extraordinarily. Peppy gave not one damn about the event, or any event, she wanted to be fed, and on time, come what may. And he had done so, finally, apologizing profusely to her. She had only purred, and devoured her meal, selfish beast as usual.

Ponce had a copy of his Eng. Lit. book and a notebook on him. He was going over in his mind certain aspects of the work in question which would possibly be of use as the subject of the proposed theme. At any rate, he was trying very hard to go over these aspects, for to tell the truth they all led to one aspect, and that was Miss Smith. His mind and body were dominated by a certain general bewilderment and an associated spectrum of feelings ranging from sheer, brute lust to dark, stark terror. This was one of the reasons he had in fact chosen his bike as the mode of transportation to the house of his dream. It would give him time to think and work off some of the more potentially dangerous, wild uncontrollable impulses surging all through him, like a house on fire. Even though it would get him there somewhat late. He could have gone on his cute little motor scooter, or, if he had talked long enough and hard enough, his mother's car, of course. But he had chosen his bike. And he was glad of it. It was a brisk November night. It wasn't cold though. Just perfect for cycling. . . .

What would her place be like? *he wondered.* His heart pounded and shuddered at the mere thought of it, actually stepping inside it, actually confronting the supreme being that divine dream, *that honey.* He had only seen the apartment house on Elmwood Avenue once or twice before, from the outside, whizzing past on his scooter. It was a fairly large brick apartment house, and to tell the truth he didn't know anyone who lived in it – except the goddess. *Would they talk in the parlor?* Talk, Ponce wondered, how would he be able to talk he wondered and wondered. He assumed a parlor, for he had in his fantasy a vivid picture of what the place would be like, or should be, at any rate: it included a warm, cozy parlor, suitable for small, intimate parties, and similar get-togethers, or gatherings, for two, for example, preferably. Would she sit beside him on a sofa? Or would she have a couple of easy chairs or other chairs and each would occupy one? Where would they be? he wondered. Would there be a table? A card table? Would he lay his book on the table? And notebook? Where would he lay that notebook? It needed some space, opened up, that is, especially. Would there be room for the notebook? On a *card table?* Ponce pondered the matter, and other matters, which now were leaping up in his mind like lightning flashes as he pedaled on through the cool night air. He sensed in a sense, even as he was answering them or trying to answer them, that they were irrelevancies – such was the nature of one part of this young lad's extraordinary makeup. He sensed that. He knew that the real question. *the only question*, was and could only be: *What would happen?* In a way, he realized. he stood at a cross-roads in his existence: *How would he handle it?* Or. *Would* he handle it? Ponce wondered worried. for the possibilities were trying. Would *he* be handled? That was worrying. Ponce pedaled. Above all he hoped that when he got there he wouldn't walk in through an open door and find another one, like this morning. That was a worry. He drove it off though, it was one he couldn't bear keeping more. At any rate. he tried very hard to. . . .

He was getting near the place. All he had to do was take a right at the next corner, Tenth Street. go down about one hundred yards or more, the length of a football field of course. turn left at Elmwood, and –

Ponce faltered, he almost fell off his bike. How would he ever do it? What about when he got to the door? Would he just raise his hand, hold it out, knuckles toward the door, and let the quivering of his body take care of the rest? What kind of a rap would that be? A rat-a-tat. He hoped she had a doorbell. Maybe he could guide his finger to it and actually in one wild burst get the strength and courage to press it. He slowed his bike down to a crawl. His body hammered. He began to plunge, within himself, a gross despair overtaking him. He would never make it. No.

He thought of Tiger. Suddenly, that internalized bedrock stirred in him, and sustained him. pumping courage, life, and hope – through him. As he had seen him do so many times with the foot-ball team, during halftime, when they had been taking a beating. He saw him, before him. He was there, counting on him. Could he let him down? How could he? Who ever did? Who would dream of it? It was true, it was a fact, it was interesting, Ponce suddenly mused, how many games Sawyersville actually won in the second half. No matter what had happened in that first half. He saw him. At football practice. At the games. In the classroom. In the auditorium. *In the Guidance/Counseling Office.* . . . He saw him everywhere. Effective, Formidable. Calm. *Human.* . . . He saw Peppy. He saw his mother. Rusty Joe. His father. . . . He broke his plunge, he headed upward. He felt himself heading upward. The bike moved faster. He turned the corner. He pedaled. . . . Another corner. . . . If nothing else, he had hit Elmwood. . . . He pedaled into it. . . .

'Hello! Come on in!'

The voice, in the doorway, obviously belonging to the warm, sweet-scented, gorgeous body, also there, came to him.

Ponce fought hard, like a tiger. He fought to control his violent trembling.

'H-H-Hello – Miss – Smith – ' he managed.

She was wearing a pale-green dress Ponce somehow noticed, not the same skirt and sweater she had on in the school today, Ponce, observant as ever, noticed. The dress clung to her with a warmth and fondness which only a dress on her could conjure, it outlined her form, heavenly. Ponce, inside, was hammering. He saw the way it dipped toward her astonishing treasures. He thought he caught a glimpse of the soft, round, white tops of them, just peeking out of the dress, when she moved. He hammered more, hanging on to a slim thread of consciousness, no more.

She let him in, or rather, he almost fell in.

'Well, I'm glad to see you Ponce,' she hummed in that divine voice, 'We can have a nice talk, can't we, about the whole matter – ' The voice flowed through him.

'Right – Miss Smith – ' he got out, astonishing himself.

He saw a room that wasn't all that far removed from his fantasy though it was somewhat larger. It was softly lit, there was a sofa, two easy chairs, and a table and chairs around it. Also, at the end of the room a desk. A pretty little desk. Where she corrected exams, and themes, and papers, Ponce thought, warmly. He made 'A' on most of them.

'Come in and sit down,' she said to him, crossing to the sofa.

'Yes – Miss Smith – ' his voice answered.

He sat down on the sofa about two and a half feet from her, a wild man, throbbing inside, and terrified.

Silence.

Miss Smith was moving around on the sofa, making herself comfortable. Casually comfortable. Ponce, though not looking, knew it. She seemed to be reaching for something, though Ponce still did not have the courage to look. The next thing he heard was the flick of a lighter. Then he saw and smelled cigarette smoke. It floated, billowed, enveloped him, he was part of that floating now. *Now –*

'You don't smoke, Ponce, do you?' the dream of a voice, he was aware, was asking him.

'N-No – Miss Smith,' the lad answered.

'Well, I hope you don't mind if I do' she told him.

She could have fired twenty shots at him, he wouldn't have minded, of course.

'No – Miss – Smith –' the boy answered, 'I mean – I-I don't mind at all, Miss – Smith – ' He paused now, 'That's what I mean – ' he added.

'It really is an awful habit, in many ways but I just love it,' he heard her say, as she took a long, long drag, out of his way.

'Comfortable?' she asked, sending out another billowing cloud of heaven-scent.

'Yes, Miss Smith – ' Ponce politely told her.

'Now you just relax, will you – ' she said to the lad. 'You've been through a *terrible* day – I know – You poor kid,' she said, 'I'm glad you came tonight.'

Ponce got out, 'So am I – '

She pulled on the cigarette as Ponce continued staring straight ahead, at eternity. There was also a wall. And a painting on it. He saw the painting. It was a reproduction, a fine print really, of a Degas. A group of young ballerinas on the stage, rehearsing. It was beautiful, especially in the soft light. He kept on staring at it.

'Like it?' he heard, from somewhere.

'The painting?' he asked.

'That's right.'

'A lot.'

'Lovely, isn't it?'

'It's just perfect.'

'Genius *shines* through – '

'Right.'

'The painting *envelopes* one – doesn't it, Ponce?'

'It does.'

'That's the secret of any great work of art, Ponce – did you know that?'

'I had – an idea about that – '

'I'm sure you did. Yes. That's why most modern art is so awful. Oh God it's awful! It just makes *attacks* on the viewer. I hate modern art! Do you know what, Ponce? Ninety-nine percent of it at least is rubbish. *Pure Rubbish*,' she said.

'Is that right, Miss Smith – ?' the lad asked.

'I'm afraid it is.'

'I – didn't know that.'

'Please take my word for it.'

'I don't know – much – about modern art. Haven't really seen – much of it – it – Miss Smith – '

'Please take my word for it.'

'I will, Miss – Smith – '

He didn't dare look, but he felt she was smiling now.

'You know I went to Italy last summer, don't you, Ponce?'

'Yes – Miss Smith – '

Could she speak Italian? he wondered –

'What a marvelous, marvelous place Florence is! Oh, Ponce, I had a most breathtaking week there. I've never known such pleasure. Such joy. Such delight! There just isn't a city like that *anywhere*. It's perfect, Ponce. Why those sculptures by Michelangelo in the Medici tombs alone are worth the journey! And that's just the beginning of it! Ponce, the priceless treasures in the galleries the Uffizi the Pitti – I wish I could have borrowed one or two of the masterpieces – for example, the *Madonna and Child*, by Filippo Lippi – or his portrait of a fellow monk – that one's *fabulous!* Oh, Ponce, what have you got me started on? Once I start, I just never stop – on this subject – did you know that?'

'I – didn't know – that,' said the lad.

Silence. Again.

He heard her move around again, probably making herself even more comfortable. He heard her fingers tap the cigarette, over an ashtray, probably.

'So I'd better stop,' she said, 'After all, you didn't come here tonight to hear a lecture on Art!'

She laughed, softly. Ponce throbbed away, constantly.

Silence.

Miss Smith was definitely reaching over the ashtray again, this time to stab out the cigarette, Ponce knew. Also, he had found the courage to peek – out of the farthest corner of his eye – and of course what he saw made him throb all the more, filling him in addition with a wild impulse to tear out of the room, through the walls, if necessary – somewhat – *much as* – He drove it away. Would it plague him the rest of his life, that memory? As soon as she sat back, or started to sit back, Ponce's gaze once again jumped straight ahead.

'Well,' said the dream, 'What about Milton?' she said.

Ponce sprang to attention.

'He was a great poet,' he said.

'That he was,' Miss Smith agreed.

'His – early poems show – a characteristic mingling of Renaissance and Puritan influence,' the lad said.

'Look at me,' said Miss Smith.

Somehow, after a mighty struggle, and very slowly, the lad turned to face the dream.

'Don't be shy with me,' she said, *and who else in the world had a voice like that?* 'Just picture yourself in class, will you, Ponce – ? It's the same – ' She smiled at him, while he hammered away, *somewhere*, not there. She lifted her hand to her hair a moment, 'You don't think I'm going to eat you, do you?' she said.

'N-N-*No*, Miss Smith – ' the lad bravely lied.

'Alright then – ' she said.

Ponce tried hard to imagine he was in class. But it didn't really help all that much of course, for the closer he got to realizing that fantasy, the more pronounced became the phenomenon associated with the actual reality of being there i.e., in his dream's class. And no matter how hard he tried to control it. He was mortified

'Are you alright, Ponce?' the divine creature asked.

'S-Sure – Miss Smith – ' Ponce said, lying again.

She snuggled around on the sofa, before him, making herself very comfortable. She pulled out another cigarette. She lit it, waiting to hear more from her top student. 'Go on then,' she said, very softly.

Ponce plunged on, getting in stride, in spite of everything, 'In the early poems, for example, *Il Penseroso*, Milton meditating in the cathedral expresses no aversion as a Puritan should for the beauty of the lofty arches, the stained-glass windows, and the music – '

'Especially the music – ' murmured Miss Smith.

'Yes,' Ponce said, 'Milton's love of organ music, so well described in the poem, continued throughout his life. and its tones and its dignified rhythms are reflected in the music – of his lines – Miss Smith.'

'Absolutely, Ponce,' Miss Smith purred at him, absolutely delighted with him, 'And where does that take us?'

Ponce's organ, at this juncture, despite all efforts, was going somewhere. Definitely. He did his best to camouflage the mortifyingly and supremely embarrassing development, with his book and notebook, no less. He only prayed his teacher-hostess would not ask him to stand up – *under any circumstances.*

'Well – ' he said, still in stride, 'I just mentioned that because it seems like a good way to approach *Paradise Lost* – '

Miss Smith nodded her head, obviously more than delighted with Ponce, the best, without the slightest doubt, the most receptive, and perceptive, of all her Lit. students, by far. She had certainly done the right thing asking him over tonight. It was always the case that one, just one student like this made all the sometimes dreary effort worthwhile. She pulled an extra long pull on her cigarette, her eyes shining.

'That's a good idea, Ponce,' she said, exhaling a cloud of smoke, slowly, as she spoke, part of it touching Ponce, and thrilling him, no end.

'Take – ' said Ponce, soaring on, 'The masque *Comus* – and the elegy *Lycidas* – ' The lad paused, 'Here again, in both of these works, you can see the effects upon him of both Renaissance and Puritan – ' He paused, for a breath, 'Influences.' He stopped.

'That's right, Ponce,' said the dream, 'Absolutely – and what an interesting, interesting approach to it – ' she said, 'Exciting almost – ' she added, 'and accurate – ' She paused, 'And when did you think of it ?'

Her warm eyes surveyed the lad's face. He only wanted to plunge, head first, into them, lose himself, forever, in them.

'Ever since – just since – ' he faltered.

'This morning ?' she offered.

Ponce shook his head, forlornly, at the mere thought of *this morning*, 'No – ' he told her, 'Since – well – after you met me in the hall, to tell you the truth, Miss Smith – It all started then – and developed I guess quite a lot between then and now – no doubt – ' he informed her.

'I inspired you!' she smiled.

'I guess so – ' he murmured, also smiling, shyly.

'Would you like a cup of cocoa ?' she inquired.

'That would be – great – ' Ponce answered.

'I'll get it in just a minute,' Miss Smith said, 'O.K. ? Right now, what about telling me more, in general terms, about *Paradise Lost* – ?'

The lad thought, and answered, quietly, finally, 'Well – it's an epic or heroic poem – and – Milton had more or less planned and prepared for it since his youth, to tell the truth. It was part of a trilogy, actually. *Paradise Regained* and *Samson Agonistes* are the other two parts – ' He paused – 'They explore the mystery of God's dealings with those who dwell on earth – in short, human beings – mainly – which was of great interest to the Puritan Age – ' He paused again, casting his eyes on her, 'They reveal the vastness of Milton's learning, the loftiness of his language, the stately music of his lines – ' He paused once more, his eyes glued on her – 'In short, his genius. *Paradise Lost* actually tells the story of the – temptation of Adam and Eve and their expulsion from Paradise – ' He halted.

'Go on – ' she murmured, encouragingly.

'Well, more than that, and on top of that, it describes the origin of the Devil, or Satan, and the War in Heaven, from which he was finally expelled and evolved into the Devil, taking his revenge on God by corrupting his finest, his most unique creation, *Mankind*, I mean.'

'Yes – ' she said, obviously affected – she almost whispered. 'The poem is divided into twelve books,' said the lad.

'How is the imagery ?' she asked.

'Vivid,' he answered.

' ". . . eagerly the Fiend o'er bog or steep, through strait, rough dense, or rare, with head, hands, wings, or feet pursues his way, and swims, or sinks, or wades, or creeps, or flies too." ' she quoted, partly closing her eyes, as Ponce admired the astonishingly beautiful eyelids and eyelashes, of his dream.

'Book Two,' he said still admiring her.

'That's right,' she said, looking at him.

'And so –' the lad said, 'And so – that's what I have in mind to do, Miss Smith, that's it –' he said.

She nodded and smiled at the boy, 'And I think you can do it – I know your theme will be the best, the most original in the class –' She paused, adding, 'As usual.'

'I always try my best – ' the lad said modestly.

'I'm glad you do.'

'Because I think – I think – *You're just about the most terrific Lit. teacher a guy could have* –' Ponce heard himself say.

'Well thank you, Ponce! Well isn't that nice. That's awfully nice of you to say. It's so nice, Ponce,' she responded next.

'I think you are.'

Silence next. They were looking at one another.

'And who is the hero of *Paradise Lost* ?' Miss Smith in that soft voice, unexpectedly asked.

'Man,' answered Ponce, without losing his pace.

'I'm really looking forward to this theme,' said the dream, pulling on her cigarette, as Ponce stared.

'How long –' he said, 'should it be ?'

She shrugged, in an exquisitely gentle way, maddening him, 'Don't write a book,' she said, 'Oh, say – five typewritten pages ? Double spaced – '

'O.K.' Ponce said.

'By the end of next week – '

'O.K.'

'Now, some cocoa – ' she said, stirring herself, rising from the sofa, Ponce's eyes glued to her, evermore.

'Come in the kitchen,' she said, in the friendliest way, smiling also.

The moment Ponce dreaded most had come, no doubt of it, and he sat there, going numb.

'Come on then,' Miss Smith repeated, standing, patiently waiting for him.

How could he get out of it ? Ponce, turning all colors, on fire within, tried desperately to find a way. Oh for Aladdin's Lamp! Should he pray ?

'O.K. if I wait here ?' he tried, feebly.

'Oh, come and watch,' she said, 'It's a lot of fun.'

He knew it was.

He sat still.

'What's the *matter* ?' she said, genuinely concerned, 'Frightened again ?'

He made no move.

She moved, toward him. She stood just before him. She leaned over and touched his cheek with her fantastic hand. He felt the soft warm treasure-hand.

'What's the matter ?' she inquired so softly.

He made no answer. No word could possibly emerge from him. He sat and stared.

'What ever's the matter ?' she said, passing the glorious hand over his cheek in short, caressing it, 'Come on, come with me,' she murmured, taking his hand now, gently urging him up.

He felt himself going up, up, up. He was up. Before her. In all his shame – and glory. She didn't seem to be offended. In fact, Ponce suddenly and alarmingly thought, Had She Noticed ? *How couldn't she have noticed ?* Ponce was in despair, pondering, trembling hard there.

The goddess's warm hands were still on him, she stood there, before him. He was just slightly taller than her.

'You're shaking like a leaf, my goodness,' she said to him

'What's the matter?' she asked again, in that softest, warmest, most enchanting voice – in the whole universe, ever-increasing his despair.

'I guess – ' he said – 'Must be – ' He also said – 'It – ' He then said – 'I think – ' He said – And stopped dead.

He stood there.

She spoke gently and tenderly, 'You've just been through too much today. Yes. I'm sure that's it. I'm not feeling all that wonderful myself – ' she said – 'So, imagine you – ' She still held his hand. 'Maybe I shouldn't have asked you to come tonight, Ponce – ' she said – 'That really wasn't all that considerate of me, maybe – ' She paused again – 'Well, if you want to go – '

'I don't want to –' he said, definitely.

She smiled, he was almost sure he felt an increase of pressure from her hand, '*Alrighty* – come and have some cocoa then,' she sang.

He nodded, and she led the way. All the way to the kitchen, and in his condition, she held his hand.

'A shock like that's going to take us all some time to get over,' the angel said, flipping a knob of her electric stove, 'I'm not so sure I'd even be *conscious* tonight – if I had – found her,' she said.

Ponce, saying nothing, just fought hard to subdue his shame.

'Let's just hope they soon find the fellow,' she told him.

Ponce, astutely, sat on a kitchen stool, silent, watching her.

'So you think my idea for the theme is alright?' he finally managed, from that perch.

'Oh – ' she said, facing him, 'I think it's marvelous!'

Ponce nodded, feeling good about that. He knew she meant it. She poured the cocoa into cups. She popped marshmallows in each cup. He watched them, fascinated, as they floated. The cocoa smelled great. Like his mother's –

'There you are,' she said, handing him a cup.

'Thanks a lot,' the boy murmured, taking a sip, right away.

'Ummmm – ' she said.

'Real good,' he told her.

'It'll calm you down,' she said, taking over another stool, not far from him. She was made for it.

'You're from New York, aren't you, Miss Smith?' the lad ventured.

'That's right,' she told him, 'Syracuse, in fact.'

'Like it there?'

'Oh, it was alright. I went to school there. Oh, but I'm very happy here. I love this town,' she enlightened him.

'I like it too,' Ponce tried, 'I get bored sometimes though, no kidding, Miss Smith –' He paused, further trying, 'A lot of the time – ' He halted.

She smiled. He treasured that smile.

'What do you hope to do with yourself, Ponce? Next year will be your last at Sawyersville – '

He sipped his cocoa, slowly. It was so delicious.

'Gee this is good – ' he said, and continuing, 'Oh, I'm not really too sure about that yet, Miss Smith – ' He paused, and looked around. It sure was a cute kitchen. 'I want to be a writer –' he said, quietly, 'I guess you know that – '

'And I think you'd make a good one – ' she said.

'But I have to find some way to make a living, don't I, Miss Smith?' he said, intelligently.

'Why not teach?' she said.

'Well – I get real scared in front of people – no kidding, Miss Smith – I'm not so sure I can take it, in front of a class – all the time – ' he confessed.

She understood.

'Well, we all get scared, Ponce, let me tell you – ' she said – 'I can't tell you how scared I was during my practice teaching! *Golly!* I get scared even now, sometimes.' She paused – 'It's something you get over – or learn to live with – at any rate – ' she said, reassuringly.

Ponce nodded, and sipped more cocoa. The marshmallow bumped his lips. He took a nibble.

'What does your father do, Ponce?' she inquired, watching him.

'Oh – he works for the V.A. – ' Ponce answered – 'In Kitston – the big V.A. building there. You know?' he said – 'Do you know him?'

'I met him at a P.T.A. meeting last year, to tell the truth. He seems awfully nice, Ponce,' she told him, 'How do you get along?'

'Oh fine – We get along fine,' Ponce said.

There was silence. He finished the marshmallow.

'I like Mom best,' he confessed.

Miss Smith gave a little laugh, 'And what boy doesn't?'

Ponce sipped the cocoa.

'I like Peppy too – '

'Peppy?' she asked.

'My cat – boy, Miss Smith, what a cat – '

She laughed again.

'I ought to have one.'

'Well, I can get you one.'

'Oh, would you?'

'Sure, Miss Smith.'

And more silence.

'That would be nice.'

'Oh, they're great.'

'I always had a cat – at home – growing up – ' she said.

'Aren't they great?'

'They really are great.'

'I'll get you one.'

A pause,

'I have a little brother, you know – ' Ponce said.

'Isn't his name Joe?'

'Well how did you know?'

'His teacher up at the elementary school is a friend of mine – ' she smiled.

'Miss Tyler?'

'That's so.'

'What do you know.'

'She says he's awfully cute – '

'Aw, he is – The things he comes out with!'

'I'll bet – '

Ponce grinned, 'I call him Rusty Joe – '

'How cute!'

Silence again.

Ponce sipped cocoa.

'What do you think about Vietnam?' suddenly, he asked.

His hostess didn't seem to have at all expected that one. For a moment, she looked baffled, almost. Then she took a sip, and looked warmly at him.

'Well, why don't you tell me what *you* think of it?' she said.

Ponce held the cup in his hands. He liked the warmth that came to him from it.

'Well – I don't know – I don't think it's too good of an idea though – ' he said.

'How do you mean?'

'I don't much see what the point of it is supposed to be – ' he said, 'Do you?'

'To tell you the truth – I don't,' she answered, 'No, I don't.'

'And yet try telling that to just about anybody in this town!' he said.

'Well, actually, Ponce,' she said, 'you'd be surprised how many teachers feel the same way. I mean, like we do. *And* I'll bet a lot more people than you think – ' she also said.

Ponce sat quietly.

'Just like integration?' he said.

Miss Smith was thoughtful. 'Now that's a very, very difficult problem,' she said.

Ponce nodded, 'I know it is.'

'At least,' she said, 'we're making some attempt to solve the problem – in a decent way – ' she paused, 'Unlike other places, those horrible South Africans, for instance – ' She paused – 'Aren't you proud of the worthy contribution Sawyersville's made? I mean, it's something, anyway – '

'I know it is.'

'Shall we go back to the front room?' she said.

'O.K.' Ponce said.

'I want to hear more about your theme – the ins and outs of it – I just don't know how you came up with such a good idea – ' she said, getting up now, 'Bring your cocoa with you.'

Gazing at her, Ponce got up, somehow.

'O.K., Miss Smith.'

She smiled, taking his hand.

'*Come on*,' she said.

22

Tiger, arriving home much earlier than usual, due to the cancellation of one of his activities, i.e., football practice, surprised Looby Loo.

Walking in the front door, he found his loved one in the hallway, on the phone. She turned to him as soon as he closed the door. He looked at her, admiringly, awaiting her first words of the evening for him. He wondered what they would be, for she always had a unique way of saying the same thing, it was a matter of combination, and innuendo, subtle as can be. That was part of the fun of being married to her. She gave a little wave, and a smile at him. Her eyes were full of love for him. The party on the other end of the phone, whoever it might be, appeared to be talking a steady stream. It was obvious she wasn't listening. Finally, shrugging her shoulders, she covered the mouthpiece with her palm and said to him, 'How's everything?'

Tiger also shrugged his shoulders, and advanced toward her. She took her hand off the mouthpiece.

'Well, thanks much, Elaine, and I'll speak to Sally Ann as soon as I can – Yes, I will – And now I've got to run – So – *Bye for now* – Elaine – '

And she hung up.

She sat there, looking up at her man, now very near her.

'Hello, Sugar Plum,' she said to him.

'Hi, Bun – ' he greeted her.

He was grinning, he touched her face, he passed his hand over her face, gently, toward her blond hair. She moved her face slightly sideways, into his hand, she kissed the palm of his hand, she gave at least a half dozen little kisses to it.

'What's that school turning into?' she said, finally, softly.

'Don't ask me,' he replied, raising his face upward, tenderly, 'I just work there.'

She smiled.

'Well, they better find the guy – ' she said.

'The State Police are doing a great job,' he said.

'I'll believe it – when they find him – '

'No practice tonight – ' he said.

She stood up, she was in his arms, looking into his face. She rubbed her nose against his, once, twice, a number of times.

'That's what I thought – '

'Game's been canceled Saturday, also – '

'I'm not surprised.'

'We've got it lined up for Wednesday afternoon – next week. We were lucky enough – '

'Away – or home? – '

'Home. No less.'

She sighed, 'It's all very sad.' She paused – 'But I hope you win – '

'We have a good chance – '

'Unless – ' She paused.

'Unless?' he asked.

'– The guy turns out to be a star of your team – '

Tiger started kissing her around the eyes, he strayed to her ear, and down to her cheek she caressed his face.

'I sure hope not – ' he said – 'I'd be mighty, mighty surprised – ' he also said.

'Hungry ?' his wife murmured, as Tiger pressed on, gently kissing her neck, 'Are you hungry, *you* ?' She was all warm, '*You Tiger you* ?' Tiger's lips kept up their work.

'You make me hungry,' he said, murmuring too. '*Looby Loo* – '

Her head was arched upward now her lips parted, she was near his ear with her lips, she brushed it, tenderly.

'*You're really hungry* – '
She said.
'Expecting anyone ?' he asked.
'No one.'
'Where's Jane ?'
'At Aunt Lucy's – '
'Let's go upstairs.'
'O.K.'
'*You honey you* – '
'You're going to wear me out – you are – *I love you you* – '
'I won't – I won't – No I won't – ' Tiger said, sweeping down her neck with his kisses – 'Oh no I won't – ' he added, reaching her breast with his kisses. She arched her head back, ever more, giving a little cry, sighing –
'*You Tiger – you* – '
'*Looby Loo* – '
'*I love you* – '
'*You're great* – '
'Carry me – '
'I'll carry you – '
'Please do – '
'You're a feather to carry – upstairs –
'*My Tiger man* – '
'Your only man – '
'*Oh man* – '
'How are you ?'
'Kiss me – *you* – '
Their lips met in a long, long kiss. Sweet, soft tongues, intermingling.
'Ummmmm – ' she moaned – 'Ummmmmm – ' she moaned and moaned. 'How do I seem ?' she said, finally, surfacing.

Tiger was unbuttoning her blouse, that treasure house. His hand reached her breasts. She had on no bra. His hands were full of her breasts.

'*Upstairs –*' she whispered, barely, 'Honey – *wait –*' she only whispered, kissing his lips.

The blouse was completely unbuttoned now. He was kissing her breasts now, wetting their lovely tips, lingering a long while there, as she held him, stroked him, whispered to him, her eyes closed.

'*Upstairs –* ' she urged him.

He stood up, took her in his arms. He lifted her. He started walking. . . .

'Been a good boy at school ?' she murmured to him, gazing at him, her arms clasped behind his neck.

'I always am,' he told her, kissing her eyes, nose, and forehead too. . . .

They lay in their bed, naked. They had been kissing petting, a long while. His hand was between her thighs, playing, wonderfully. It was drenching wet. He loved it. She held his phallus in her right hand, gently stroking it.

'I'll put the record on,' she murmured, her voice husky.

Tiger nodded, murmuring something, as she slipped away from his caresses, and out of bed, a moment. She crossed to the phonograph, and flipped it on.

'Darling – ' she said, in bed again, kissing him, straying over his chest and stomach, and downward, ever kissing, at times licking, '*Darling, Darling –* ' she murmured, over and over.

The record started. It was poetry. It was in fact, an excerpt from Clough's 'The Bothie of Tober-na-Vuolich,' and the voice was Hilda's, no less. They had cut the record some time ago at her suggestion – she had always loved the poem. She loved it now even more, and Tiger concurred. When the moment arrived they played it, without fail. It was always there. Now, as her voice began speaking the first lilting lines, her lips parted and her mouth slipped over her Tiger's throbbing organ.

– Yes, I don't know, Mr Philip – but only it feels to me strangely like – to the high new bridge they used to build at, below there, over the burn and glen on the road. . . . You won't understand me. But I keep saying in my mind – this long time, slowly, with trouble, I have been building myself, up, up, toilfully raising, just like as if the bridge were to do it itself without

> masons. . . . Getting myself upraised one stone on another – all
> one side I mean. . . . And now I see on the other just such
> another fabric uprising – better – and stronger. . . .

Her mouth glided, all the while, her tongue was sliding,
caressing her Tiger's hot, huge formidable – the whole while –
Now, his hand moved out from between her thighs, and gently,
murmuring, he urged her on her back. His phallus slipped out of
her mouth, drenched. The record went on –

> . . . close to me, coming to join me – and then I sometimes
> fancy – Sometimes I find myself dreaming at night about arches,
> and bridges. . . .

Tiger was over her, and mounting her, he slipped in masterfully, yet tenderly, magnificently, as she gasped, and moaned,
knees high, loving it. He penetrated easily, gliding deeper, ever
deeper, slowly –
They heard the record –

> . . . A great invisible hand coming down, and dropping the
> great keystone in the middle –

She was moving, arching her flanks fabulously, upward, downward, as Tiger plunged, and lunged, beautifully, into her, thrilling her, rocking with her. She was a volcano. A sheen of sweat
spread over her body, they rolled slowly, over, and over, plunging, rocking, dangerously near the edge of the ample bed – and
the record played on –

> . . . There I feel the great keystone coming in, and through it
> feel the other part – all the other stones of the archway, joined
> into mine with a strange happy wild sense of completeness. . . .

'Oh! *OH!*'
Looby Loo cried out, convulsed in spasms, clinging, part of
her Tiger's spasms, fiercely, her mouth on his now, wildly, as he
jolted and jolted in her, massively, driving her out of her mind –
'*TIGER! OH!*'
She cried, and cried.
'Honey – my own – '
He murmured – to her.
'How could – *I tire of you* – ' she gasped, finally.
'You never will – '
Tiger, caressing her breasts, murmured to her.

'Stay in me – *my wonderful one* – '

She murmured, over and over, kissing him, dozens of times. . . .

23

The first thing Chief Poldaski heard from his wife Mary when he got home that night was, 'Get the butter?'

John, having had a very hard day, perhaps the hardest of all the many long crime-busting days in his entire career was in no mood for such pleasantries, no matter how much he loved her, and how hungery he was, incidentally.

'What butter?' he growled, forgetting all about what a mean fuck she threw, without a doubt of it.

'*What* butter?' Mary fired back, definitely riled, 'Are you being funny? *Boy?*'

The Chief a dim recollection in the back of his mind, was aware of himself wondering, at the same time: How would this finish up? He was apprehensive.

That part sank from view as he answered, with another growl, 'What in hell you talkin' about?'

'Christ! Oh *Kee*rist!' His wife's response was to that, 'Didn't you even *open* your dumb book today? Huh? Boy? Didn't you *see* it on the very first page? *The First Page! Hey? Plain as your monthly pay?*'

'*What The Hell's Wrong With My Pay?*' John blasted off, stung to the quick by that one.

'You could be pulling in more just sweeping the floors up at the Electronics Plant – *that* for a start – if you want to know – But You Don't Want To Know! *Do you*, Bo? You just want to play big – Big BIG – Big John The Frig! *Oh You Frig! FRIG!*' she handed him, in one go.

'ARE YOU KIDDIN' ME?' John roared.

And Mary belted him across the face with the long, damp rag she had in her hand. It made a resounding smack. What a blow.

'*YOW!*' The Chief cried out, stunned, and in pain.

'Don't holler at ME – YOU BUM!' Mary made herself heard, and belting him once more, 'I'll pound you black and blue, I'll

kick you all over the floor, I'll mop the house up with you –
AND MORE! YOU CRUMMY BUM!' She belted him more.
It was a steady downpour.

The Chief tried to cover up, dance around, duck, and otherwise evade the blows, now raining in from all directions, it
seemed. He felt he had twenty wives, or more.

'Christ!' he yelled, 'Holy Christ!' He yelped and yelled, 'Hey!
Knock it off! For Christ Sake! Jesus Christ! Wo! What's Up?
What The Hell's Up? What's Up With You? Don't You know
– WHAT HAPPENED TODAY?'

'*You Didn't Get The Friggin' Butter Today!*' she told him,
definitively, bombarding him more.

'LISTEN! GODDAMIT! HEY! LISTEN – WILLYA!
Where Ya Been? What You been DOIN' Today? LISTEN
HERE! HERE! HEY!' The Chief tried, in vain, performing
quite a dance.

'When I say *Butter* – I mean BUTTER! Mo. I'm SO god-
damn sick of you! GO! Your Whole crummy family – TOO!
How'd I ever get MIXED UP with you? GODDAMN POLAK
YOU! Bunch of NO GOOD DUMB POLAKS. All of you!
YOW! YO! OH MO!' She maintained her assault.

'*A GODDAMN SCHOOL KID WAS MURDERED TO-
DAY!*' Poldaski roared out, shaking the house.

'Who?' Mary asked, slowing down her barrage.

'That Fairbunn girl – you know the girl – *that gal* – Hell, *you*
know the girl – *That Cheerleader Chief – Jill*, that's her name –
Know her? *Now?*' John shouted out, taking advantage of the lull
and springing a brilliant tactical surprise, to wit, snatching the
rag out of her hands.

'*Gimme that rag!*' she cried out, infuriated by what looked like
a ruse, 'Are you kiddin' me? What the hell are you talkin' about?
GIMME! You Crummy Cop! YOU POLAK! *You Dumb Crumb
Of A Polak!*' She hurled herself at him, wrestling him for the
rag.

'Where the hell you BEEN today?' Poldaski fired, hanging on
for dear life.

'YOU MEAN ME?'

'Didn't ya see the papers? THE RADIO? You always hear
the RADIO! What about TV? Jesus, you been under the
FLOORBOARDS? *Hey?*'

She delivered him a terrific blow, to the side of the face. It sent him staggering back, against the chair, which he fell over. He hit the floor like a ton. She stood over him.

'*YOU STINK !*' Mary roared, '*YOU ALL STINK !*' You Friggin' Crumb! YOU BUM! SELMO BUM!'

She picked up a loaf of bread from the table nearby and threw it at him. He got it in the face.

'OWWW!' the Chief roared. 'WOW!' he went on to roar. '*You Whore !* I AIN'T KIDDIN' YA!' he implored.

'WHO'S KIDDIN' WHO ?' Mary asked.

'This kid was MURDERED Today! HEY! Turn on the NEWS! GO ON! You *whore* of a WHORE! *You busted my Nose !*'

'Don't bleed all over the floor! GET OFF THE FLOOR! *Go in the bathroom* – CRUMB! Get Your Hankie Out – YOU POLAK BUM!'

'*Her head was stuck down the head* – LISTEN – *Don't Think I'm Kiddin' You !*'

'*Who ?*'

'I TOLD YA ALREADY! This FAIRBUNN gal – I'm TELLIN' ya!'

'HOLD THAT HANKIE TO YOUR NOSE!'

'I'M NOT KIDDIN' YA!'

Silence. At last. John daubed his nose.

'What's her name ?' Mary asked, ten tones lower.

'*Jill* Fairbunn – I think – '

'*I know her !*'

'Well *sure* you know her! Well, they found her – '

'What didya do ?'

'That's what I'm trying to *tell you* – '

'What ?'

'*I'm not kiddin', you shoulduv seen it* – '

'Who did it ?'

'Who knows ?'

'*Murdered ? Jill Fairbunn ? That Fairbunn girl ?* She's a *beautiful* girl! You better not be *kiddin' me around*, no kiddin', *Boy* – '

'*Listen.* I'm not *kiddin' at All !* Well Just turn on the News! Go on! Paper come yet ?'

'I'll get it – Mustuv – by now – '

'You'll see if I'm kiddin' or not! *And Your Friggin' Butter !* HUH!'

'Jesus Christ! *It takes a lot less than a murder to make you forget my butter !* That's *All !*'

'Well Stop Writin' In My Goddamn Pad!'

'LISTEN, I'LL MURDER YOU!'

'Get the goddamn paper – Go on –'

'Did you do it? Crumb?'

'HUH?'

'You're about the only guy in Sawyersville who could do it! I know! Tell the truth, Polak! I don't give a frig! Think I'd turn you in?'

'You ain't funny!'

'Who else could do it? Where's The Paper?'

She searched around the room, she left the room, she banged a few doors, he heard the front door, she came back, she had the paper, she was just opening it up. Her eyebrows shot up a mile. She whistled.

'Didn't I Tell Ya?' Poldaski said, triumphantly, the handkerchief still to his nose.

'It's got your name in here –' Mary said.

'Yeh?'

'Don't tell me you're workin' on it!'

'What's wrong with that?'

'Oh man! How come you didn't call me? You coulduv put in a phone call to me! No? Hey –'

'Listen –'

'Who's Ponce de Leon?'

'Don't it say? The kid that found her –'

'I'll bet he did it? What a name!'

'Naw. Uh Uh. I got some ideas –'

'You shoulduv called me –'

'Take a look at my nose –' he whined at her.

'Get up – you stayin' there all day? Look at what it says – the whole front page – And You Never Called Me! Or Got The Butter! Listen, Safeway's still open – Get Down There!'

'With my nose like this?'

'Get up –'

'Take a look at it –'

The Chief got to his feet. He stood before her. She glanced up from her paper, cursorily examined his face.

'It's alright.'

'Where'd ya get that hard loaf?'

'Don't worry. It's alright.'

'Look at it bleedin' though –'

'Just hold the hankie to it –'

'I had a rough day. Rough. No kiddin', Mare. What a day.
And you bust my nose –'
  'You should of phoned me –'
  'Jesus, I thought sure you'd heard it –'
  'Who did it?'
  'I got some ideas –'
  'Yeh?'
  'Can't tell ya yet though –'
  'Who's this *Surcher?*'
  '*Aw –*'
  'What ideas?'
  'Can't tell ya, Mare –'
  'Waddaya mean? *Why not?*'
  'Can't – that's all –'
  'Want your supper? Bo?'
  '*Aw – Mare –*'
  'Better tell me –'
  'I was kiddin'. That's all.'
  '*C'mon –*'
  'Honest! I was!'
  'Alright! *No supper!*'
  'Want the butter?'
  '*Tell me –*'
  'Jesus Christ!'
  'Did *you* do it?'
  '*No!*'
  'What ideas?'
  'I'll tell ya later.'
  '*Now.*'

Chief Poldaski, still holding the handkerchief to his nose,
looked down at his wife. She waited to hear from him, the newspaper in one hand, her other hand on her hip.

He spoke, finally –

'One of them Jigs.'

Mary stood quietly, taking it in. She kept her eyes on her husband, letting it sink in. Looking at her, he wondered if he would
get anything tonight. He touched his ear, which was flaring red.
She had teased the hell out of him – last night.

'Get the butter.'

She said, finally.

Very quietly.

24

Tiger, after supper, which was delicious, as usual, for Looby Loo certainly could cook, and a browse around in his den, left the house, for although he had had a full day, more or less, he wasn't quite set to turn it in. He told Hilda he was just going to 'check around,' which meant, as she knew, he was going to visit the various high-school hangouts in town, juke joints, pizzerias, and the like, and see what his athletes might be up to, if anything, after their curfew hour (imposed by Tiger). He kissed his sweetie of a daughter Jane goodnight, admiring her pretty face, which was a lot like Looby Loo's, and her steadily developing elegant little body (she was eleven), and her cute personality and character structure, to boot. He certainly was fond of her. He said, 'See you later,' to Looby Loo, and set off, not without a little kiss for her too. He loved them both. He glanced at his watch as he climbed into his Mustang, for he had an appointment at nine-thirty of course with the most interesting, in many respects, of all those on his interesting list. *Rochelle Hudson.* No less. Tiger smiled, warmly, thinking of her, almost seeing her, before him. The back of his neck and head tingled, his shoulders and back, his arms felt a certain surge in them. Without a doubt, he was fond of her. He started the car and rolled away from his house on Maple Avenue, one of the nicest of Sawyersville's very nice avenues. His car radio was on, in fact it came on automatically, and a soft tune was playing for him, it was a soft jazz rendering of "Georgia" and it was great, just perfect and great, it had the smoothest beat. He and Looby Loo liked to dance to that tune, played this way, sweet and slow, low. He remembered their courting days, they used to dance a lot, they would hold close, and drift around the floor, their arms about one another. It was out of this world, dancing that way, to a great tune like this. They didn't dance all that much nowadays of course, but in his mind, right now, hearing the tune, Tiger was dancing with Looby Loo, holding close, loving it, loving her. He had never known anyone who could dance like her. It was just one of the reasons he had married her. On that dance floor they were one. Warmly, he thought of his loved one. She used The Pill to contracept, and he loved her for that too. It was great. She always had a plentiful supply on hand. In fact, more than enough. Just now, before coming out, Tiger had filled up a number of little bottles. He did this about twice a week. He had a few of these bottles in his pocket right now, as a matter of fact. Though, before the evening was over, he might well have one less. He had to check. He grew warmer, thinking of Rochelle, that unique girl. All in all, he felt good. Pretty good. For of course there was the matter of that tragic disastrous event of the morning nudging its way in, from time to time, in fact, a good deal of the time. It saddened him. He felt bad. *But that's life,* Tiger thought, sadly driving on, his headlights cutting the night. Korea. That had been life. To date, probably his saddest, hardest experience in life. Looking back now, to what seemed a long time, a far-off time, tucked far away, in time, he could definitely say it, and see it: the saddest, the hardest – bar none. And all through it she had waited. That sweetheart, that darling, that only one. . . . He would love her, treasure her forever. *Looby Loo.* When had he first given her that pet name ? She had loved it, right from the start. It was part of her. Sometimes, signing checks, he knew, she had told him, she almost wrote it down. They laughed over it. They had soft little laughs over it. He loved her blond hair. It was natural. He couldn't stand blond hair that wasn't natural. He could spot it a mile off – anytime. Any old time. In Korea, all through it, her picture was in his pocket. During lulls, when he wrote to her, he would take it out, and lay it down, before him. His Company knew all about her. She was there, when he got back, waiting for him. She loved him. Who else had so loved him ? And loved him ? His mother, passed away now, had loved him. But a different love, certainly, wasn't it ? This was complete love, total, wasn't it. *For him,* all of it. He adored her. He drove through a patch of light mist, thinking of her, warmly, he drove down Maple Avenue, along Tenth Street, across Linwood Drive, down Sawyers Avenue, the main business section of Sawyersville, lined with neon-lit stores, two moviehouses, bars and grills, and into Twelfth Street, cruising easily, steadily, thinking, as always, looking out at a group of kids hanging around Jimmy's Juke Joint, glancing at another group walking along possibly toward Giannari's Pizzeria & Jump Joint. Certainly, their activities didn't appear to be curtailed tonight. It surprised him, slightly. He wondered if any of his star athletes might be among them, hoping not, hoping if so they would have sense enough to get themselves home early, as per his curfew, for tonight would be pretty much of an impossibility for him to check up properly. *That's life alright*, Tiger thought, sadly, driving along, listening now to the next great tune coming out of the radio, introduced incomparably smoothly and soothingly by Bill somebody or other, Night Owl, and Prowler, self-styled. *There's no explaining it*, Tiger thought, *the tragedy, the disaster, the sheer hell that all of life essentially is, look around you.* Tiger thought, sadly, *and especially for kids, for any kid, my kid, my own sweet kid, that kid and the kid I once was, I was a kid, long ago, hell I'm getting old, long. long ago, running around, in the summer sun, that good Sawyersville summer sun, what a sun, who else has such sun, thinking it was all one long summer sun, I hated winter, that was an intrusion and a half in my life which I couldn't understand, long ago, no matter how often I saw it, it was all such a long time ago, my mom, my pop, Mom, Pop, on the porch, the summer sun. . . . For kids are full of hope and life and dreams, most kids anyhow, I rarely have met a negative kid, a genuinely antisocial kid, rarely, in all my long experience working with kids, and beauty and truth and good, most of all they want to grow up and fulfill all their dreams. . . . For there,* Tiger thought, ever more melancholy now, *there is the essential heart of the greatest disaster and tragedy on earth bar none, this Hell-Earth,* Tiger thought, *the utter fiasco, the fraud, the bitter mouthful of ashes it all turns out to be, for these kids, any kid. . . . All parents, well most parents, certainly, hope that for their kids it will turn out differently, another way, in fact, it's what they mainly work and sweat and go through sheer hell for, another way, as if there ever was or ever could be another way. What way? I myself, looking at Jane, that little doll, feel the same way, it's only natural, it can't be helped, that's how we are, watching her, loving her, hoping for her, working for her, it's all part of that sad, mad game. . . . For it turns out the same. . . . Only the same. . . . Poor Jill, that sweet kid, that lovely, luscious, honey-kid. . . . Think of her when you think of the timeless moment of truth, suspended, cold, forever more, for all of us in store, think, I knew her so well, so well . . . That kid. . . .* Tiger shook his head, sadly, the closest yet to tears, filled with the heaviness of the loss. . . . *Gone, she was gone, and really gone and never again never not ever again. . . .* How could he balance it accept it? *Where was the perspective?* Figure. Ground. *It was all ground.* . . . Tiger's thoughts hit a bleak terrain. For a while, he merely drove, like a zombie, thinking nothing at all. He passed the Episcopalian church, his church.

Something was going on in the hall, all the lights were on. Was it a dance? He wondered. *How could it be? Looby Loo hadn't mentioned it to him. Tonight? Just how could it be? It couldn't be.* Maybe the electricians were working in there. He would ask Looby Loo. He slowed down, he didn't see any kids . . . . *Kids are my life,* the voice in Tiger went on, alive again, *through them I live, I know. My football teams. My classes. My work. My own kid. I know it's the spirit of kids that keeps me alive. Just as in Korea there, Looby Loo kept me alive. I know. It wasn't until I hit thirty that I began to feel the full impact of the disaster that life in the adult world, our world, really was. It was then that I started going through the crisis which nearly took me out of it all. It lasted several years. I know. I came close, so close, to saying goodbye to it all. Until I found the way. I found my way. The only way, so far as I know, or can tell, to hang on, to stay around, for a while, anyhow. For, anyhow, you never know, you just never know – who ever knows? Did those guys in your Company know? Did Jill know? That warm, wonderful girl, that tremendously vital, living girl. What did she know? Ten, fifteen seconds –. and no more. Nothing more to know. No. Do you know? The brutal core of life. That's it. The dark forces swarming around, all around, within, and out there, only waiting to put out the light. And yet – and here's the most agonizing part of it – part of the light, yes, that's it, absolutely, and mocking it, ever attacking it, insidiously. brutally. . . . In myriad ways. . . . Yet always, essentially, the same way. . . . This is life. The tragibeauty, Life. . . . Never would I talk this way to Jane. I couldn't bring myself even to mention any of this to Jane, I couldn't bear it. And yet – there she is, before me, my own, my very own, given me by Looby Loo, the best a fellow could ever hope to have, how did I ever land such a gem, how could she be my own. . . . IN FOR IT, my Jane, the grotesque world of ADULTS. . . . What am I supposed to do? As I watch her play, and grow up, I have this dark, stark truth hidden away, pushed out of the way – What can I do? Does it show through? When? At what point? When she's especially happy and thrilled about something? In the way that kids are and only kids can ever be? I don't know. Maybe. I feel it, certainly. I try not to show it. I don't show it. I play the game. It's all a game. To the end. . . .* Tiger sighed, turning up Schooley Road and slowing down to a crawl, just at its intersection with Sycamore Street on or near the corner of which, if all went according to plan –

He saw her, just running toward the corner, and he began to climb out of his deep, dark melancholy, as soon as he saw her young form, that exquisite form, running, easily toward that corner.

He pulled up beside her, and opened the door. The fresh, sweet fragrance hit him and filled the car, almost at once. She sat beside him and pulled shut the door.

'Hi,' she said snuggling up to him.

'Hi,' he said, pulling away from the curb, aware only of her, the wonderful fragrance of her, beside him, near him, her hand, her fingers now playing with his ear.

'Maybe tonight's a bad night,' she said. in her low, astoundingly beautiful voice, that unique voice, which he loved, 'But I just couldn't wait anymore.'

'I know,' he told her, murmuring to her, and placing a hand on her lap, where her hand promptly clasped it, eagerly, yet tenderly.

'You're great,' Tiger said, 'You're always on time,' he said, already beginning to feel fine, in fact quivering a little inside, at the thought of what lay ahead, with his breathtakingly unique Rochelle, that astonishing maid.

'That was just awful. wasn't it ?' she said, raising his hand, the hand, to her cheek, and her lips, caressing it with a kiss.

'And how,' he said, driving ahead. He was heading out of town, he would take the road up to the hills which overlooked the town, and the valley From there they could see the whole valley. It was marvelous, the view was unbeatable. At night, in particular.

'It's really scared everybody,' she said. continuing to caress his hand, 'That poor kid ' she said, cuddling the hand.

'You like that hand ?'

'I love it.'

'That's your hand.'

'Ummm – I know it – '

Tiger turned into the highway. The traffic was very light tonight. It usually was – around this time. Tiger was thinking about the girl beside him. Rochelle had two more years at the high school, this year, and next. She was, as a matter of fact, in the same class as Ponce that great kid, Tiger's unofficial right-hand man, his future full-time assistant and eventual successor, he hoped, fondly. She was seventeen, and terrific. Really uniquely terrific, Tiger knew murmuring it to himself, within. That first encounter in the Guidance/Counseling office had truly astonished him, putting it mildly, and he had then and there created the new category of stars, blue, i.e., especially for her, and no other. He had also decided, then and there, that she was to be catered for in the car on all future encounters. It was the least he could do. He knew it. He had missed her most of all, the truth be known, during the long summer vacation, which Tiger, each year, dreaded more and more. He suddenly recalled, for she had gone out of town, away to some seaside resort or camp, was it, and he hadn't 'had one single opportunity to contact her, the whole while. It was a spectacular affair, their reunion, Tiger recalled, warmly. She was certainly a great kid with a phenomenal intelligence, second only to none, well, to Ponce, maybe. On the Stummper, the truth be known, they were level. Somehow, though, Tiger felt Ponce was ahead – by a shade, only. He had no objective proof of this. It was intuitive, purely. For when he had first administered the Stummper to her last year, in the middle of her sophomore year, when in fact he had first met her, face to face, there in the Office, she had soared spectacularly, truly amazing him, for the blunt truth was: he hadn't expected it. She had, up to the time, seemed so normal. Truly amazing. It had amazed him, and taught him a lesson he would never forget, one each and every Guidance Counselor should learn. Not unlearn. In some instances. He had mentioned it in one of his papers. Since then, of course, subsequently, as a matter of course, having had the opportunity to really get to know her, thoroughly, more or less, he had come to realize the girl's performance in other life-areas was little short of phenomenal also. He had, in short, come to realize that he had on his hands in that school a genuine phenomenon, of no mean order, no less She was, for example, probably the finest natural actress Tiger had ever encountered in all his years as Adviser Director, Coach & Teacher of the school s Drama Department & Club. She had fine presence, a natural ability to fall into each role, however diverse or difficult indeed, she did this with vigor and zest, and passionate intelligence, to boot. She was a gem. He was not only proud of her he was crazy about her, and she knew it. With her intelligence, Tiger mused, and had always mused, how could she help but know it. She was great. *Great*. She astounded him. They were out of town now and heading into the hills. All around them was darkness, except straight ahead of course where the lights played. Yes, Tiger thought, feeling her snuggling beside him no doubt dying for him, her face just against his shoulder and from time to time lifting and kissing him all about the ear. Yes, Tiger thought, as he had on many previous occasions, this was the girl he would most like to have by his side, his partner in life, should anything ever happen to Looby Loo, his true blue. Out of the blue. For it could, well he knew, in this uncertain life, this tragic, and utterly baffling, this only life. It was true –

'Tiger,' the girl murmured, 'I forgot to tell you –' she went on to murmur – 'Oh, don't get scared, Darling, are you scared?' She paused, smiling, he knew – 'It's not too bad.' She paused once more, teasing him, he knew – 'I'm running a little low, that's all – *Lovely* –' she told him, sweet and low.

Tiger grinned, turning his head quickly to give her a little kiss. He was a careful driver. He kept his grin, looking ahead again, this was one he never had to worry about in any way, shape, or form, or remind, at all, she was so much on the ball. He adored her.

'My coat pocket,' he said, giving her one more peck.

'Ummmm –' she said, dipping her hand into his coat pocket, as instructed. She found the little bottle and curled her fingers about it, withdrawing it, finally.

'How many?' she murmured.

'Enough,' he told her.

'Hold them for me.'

'O.K. – Lovely.'

'*You're so lovely* –'

Her head on his shoulder.

'How's everything?' he murmured.

'You'll find out –' she told him, snuggling up to him, dropping the bottle back into his pocket, 'Aren't they marvelous –' she murmured, 'A marvelous development –' she told him.

'I can tell you,' he told her.

'Yes, you'll find out,' she murmured.

'I'd like to find out more often –'

'You're so busy – busy busy – my Tiger –'

'What have you got on?'

'No bra –'

'Lovely –'

'They are lovely –'

'They must feel comfy –'

'They're waiting for you, Lovely, comfy and lovely, all for you – let me tell you –' she told him, murmuring.

'Tell me –'

'Ummmm – comfy –'

'What are they doing?'

'They're under my dress, you haven't seen my dress – it's a new one – '

'What color ?'

'Orange. A dusty orange. They call it.'

'Sounds lovely.'

'You'll love it.'

'I'll have a good look at it.'

'Oh you'll love it.'

'Have a slip on ?'

'Pretty one.'

'And they're under it.'

'They are, Lovely, comfy, waiting for you, just for you, oh you *Tiger you my wonderful you Tiger under it –* ' she said.

'Silkies ?'

'*Awfully pretty ones –* '

'We're almost there – '

'*I love it there.*'

'The view's great – '

'*Isn't it –* '

'Working hard ?'

'You gave *so much* Civics homework – *Honey –* '

'Don't you like it ?'

'I've got a theme to do for Miss Smith – you know Miss Smith, don't you, Lovely ?'

He grinned, at the same time wondering. He couldn't help wondering. For her intelligence was phenomenal. But he let it ride, for the position was laudable. Laudable. He was lucky.

'When did you first wear a bra ?' he asked her.

'Oh – ' she murmured.

'They start at nine nowadays – don't they ? Lovely ?'

She laughed softly, 'That's a billion-dollar market, isn't it, Tiger honey, *to be exploited* – ask Uncle Brucie – '

'He earns more than the President – doesn't he ?'

'He does – doesn't he – '

'He ought to run for President – '

'He'd make it – '

'A Reagan-Uncle Brucie ticket – ' Tiger chuckled.

'They'd make it – '

'You know it.'

She was still laughing softly, near his ear. Her warm sweet breath, in his ear.

'America – ' she murmured.
'The Beautiful – ' he told her. . . .

Tiger turned off the road when he hit the top of the hill and pulled into their favorite hideaway. It was a nook completely screened from the road, over which little traffic passed at this time of night, in any event. Yet, they had a magnificent view of the lights of the entire valley, spread out before them, far below them. It was perfect. Tiger was in a warm, light, frolicking mood now. The height. The night. The unique Rochelle. It always did it, and in fact kept him in it for a couple of days afterward, at least. It was his favorite mood. He wished all of life could be journeyed through in that mood. She was a tonic. Just the mere proximity of her. Just now they were nestled in each other's arms, having just completed their first, marvelous, deeply passionate kiss. It was a kiss and a half, as only she could give. She was caressing his face, neck and back of his head. She sighed, as only she could sigh. He was quivering within. Gently, adoringly, he brushed her sweet ear with his lips, and caressed her lovely, full breasts, unencumbered by any manner of trappings underneath. He loved caressing them. For a long while, through that new, lovely, dusty-orange dress, he did just that. He found the intoxicating tips. He lingered there, as she arched and moaned, clasping him ever closer to her.

'I could never marry anyone – ' she murmured, in her remarkably lovely voice, 'My only one – ' she went on, 'No one – ' And on, 'Not after you – Darling Tiger you – ' She kissed him, *'Except you – '*

'I'm sorry I'm tied up, Lovely, I really am – ' Tiger murmured in a brief moment of disengagement *'I'm crazy about you – '*

'Anyway – ' she moaned, kissing him, wonderfully.

'How are you ?' he said to her, continuing to fondle her breasts, through that exquisite dress.

'My Darling – ' she moaned, huskily, clinging to him. Her warm, sweet breath in his face.

'Someday – ' he murmured to her, 'What a day – ' he told her.

'My day –' she whispered to him.

He unbuttoned her dress. She slipped out of it, smoothly.

'It's a nice dress,' he told her, laying it down, carefully.

'Like it ?' she murmured.

'Love it,' he said, 'Love your slip – ' he also said.

'Yes, that's nice too – ' she said.

'Love it – '

'So glad – you love it – '

'You lovely honey – '

'*Oh I love you, Honey* – '

His hand was inside her slip, caressing and fondling her breasts. Softly she moaned, seeking his mouth.

'*Tiger* – '

'*Lovely* – '

She was growing warmer and warmer. her hands caressed him, gliding over him. He slipped her breasts out of her slip, which itself was half off her, and slipping ever more. He kissed those superb treasures, all his. She fell back slowly onto the ample seat, taking him with her. He kissed her breasts, his mouth closed over the tips, wetting, suckling them. His hands glided over her, caressing her, searching for her – She helped him slip off what remained. Already she had discarded her slip. She was ever warmer, her body burned under his hand, though he was on fire as well, he felt her pounding heart, his own matched it, she moaned and whispered to him, over and over. Her hands found him, she fondled him. . . . A long while he, kissed her thighs, her belly, he glided his tongue over her stomach, her belly, her thighs, he smothered them with his kisses, she was more than on fire, he realized. Her knees were rising. She was calling his name, again, and again. His head was between her thighs, he was kissing, gliding, tenderly, he murmured and whispered to her, constantly, she trembled, moving, moaning, near ecstasy at his exquisite caressing – she was ready – waiting – she was trembling – He mounted her, he glided into her trembling body. marvelously, deeply, stroking her tenderly, she pulled him on top of her she was trembling violently, moaning his name. constantly, they kissed, their tongues intermingling, wonderfully, a long while. he stroked and stroked her, she was a hot river, deep, flowing, ever more opening – They were burning hot, drenched – both of them –

'Now Tiger – ' At last she said – '*Now My Tiger* – ' she gasped and said, trembling more and more.

'Alright, Lovely – ' Tiger said, withdrawing his shaft, exquisitely, slowly, as she moaned, murmuring – He eased himself downward, gliding over her form – His entire body pounded at the impending, approaching, spectacular finale, the most unique and glorious he had ever heard of or know, unfurled for him by her, only, this unique one – and only –

'*Now Lovely* – ' she gasped out, barely, ready, totally.

'*Wow, Lovely* – ' he told her, making his hand into a fist and easing it between her divine thighs, and upward, slowly, ever upward, gently, entering her, marvelously, sliding upward, ever, deeper, seeking her, as she groaned, and moaned, trembling violently –

'*Yes Lovely* – ' Her voice came to him, somewhere near a scream, it seemed, as a hot, white spinning haze began enveloping him, '*Yes, YES, LOVELY* – ' she said – His arm was gliding, penetrating, he was almost up to his elbow, he was drenching wet, nearly out of his head, he began to stroke, he stroked and stroked, she was writhing under it, it was a pumping stroke, he stroked more rapidly, feeling the very depths of her meeting his loving fist, each time it thrust home in her, he stroked and stroked, she began to scream, he was in a wild dream, the sweat poured off him, she couldn't have been drenched more, he plunged and stroked, up to his elbow.

'*TIGER!*' she screamed, wildly, reaching for him, clutching him – He withdrew his arm, fully – '*OH – TIGER!*' She pulled him onto her, he plunged his throbbing shaft into her, she clasped him tightly, a fiery vise, she kissed him, passionately, her legs wrapped around him, her body jerked and jerked, fabulously, he plunged massively, all the way, wildly jolting, spilling within her, violently, a tributary to the vast, convulsing, flowing hot river she now was . . . totally – They rolled off the seat, rapturously jerking spasmodically. . . . They were on the car floor, still entwined. . . .

'*Tiger* – '

She moaned, over and over, in his ear, kissing it – she was still twitching.

'*Lovely Honey* – '

He murmured to her, in her ear, a long while, coming back to this world, gradually, caressing her, tenderly. . . .

25

Ponce, floating on clouds at least ten miles high, got back home about eleven that night, just about the time Rochelle, and Tiger, and seventy-seventh heaven, were parting. Ponce had passed a truly inspiring, exciting, breathtaking evening at his dream's apartment. They had talked and talked, Ponce never knew he had so much to talk about, that there was so much two people together could talk about. How had he done it? It just seemed to flow out of him, all sorts of things, subjects, topics, intoxicating him. He was intoxicated. She had inspired him, without the slightest doubt of it. Sitting there, especially after they had finished their cocoa, he was aware of a definite, gradual, most gratifying and welcome melting away of the powerful forces which had, up till then, to all intents and purposes, paralyzed him. His dream had probably smoked about a pack of cigarettes, at least, Ponce reflected, thinking back on it, attentive to detail, as always. She had made toasted cheese sandwiches with olives and pickles as a side dish and potato chips too, to boot, for both of them. It was delicious. And more cocoa too. Before the evening was through. She made him feel right at home. It was wonderful. He still saw her, sitting there, on that sofa, not all that far from him. Her fragrance surrounded him. Even though, Ponce floundered, dipping downward, he hadn't kissed her, or caressed her, or laid a hand on her, as much as he had been dying to. Screaming within to. He loved her, he was utterly and desperately in love with her. Even though, Ponce further floundered, she had held his hand, on that walk to the kitchen, and back again. Even though, Ponce really floundered, crestfallen, she had stood before him, and touched his face, with that heavenly hand, that hand . . . so tenderly . . .

But how they had talked! At least they had established a rock solid relationship there, in that sphere, no doubt of it. First, of course, Milton. They had gone up and down, and across and down, and in and out, all the lanes and byways, not to mention highways, of that great English poet. Ponce had learned more in one evening from her than he would, he knew, from all the reading he could do in the next five years, at least, on the subject. It was great. She had gone right to the heart of it. He had felt right in tune with it. His theme would show it. Would such a theme, at Sawyersville, ever be seen again? Ponce doubted it. He was excited about it. Perhaps they would publish it. Yes, it could well be, possibly, his first published work, he thought of it. Inspired as he was, aware of his abilities as he fully was, the idea seemed not too far-fetched at all to him. Ponce pondered. He'd be thrilled no end. His mother would. Certainly, Miss Smith, and of course Tiger, would. What about Peppy? Ponce grinned. . . .

Then, Democracy. Passing over, somehow, into the realm of Social Studies, they had thoroughly explored the cherished ideals and practical practices of that much bandied and living concept. They had come to the conclusion, more or less, and however reluctantly, that in the great and powerful country in which they after all did happen to reside and were part and parcel of, the concept, in fact, up to now, had been, and was, somewhat of, or something akin to, a fiasco. More unkindly, and only mentioned in passing, a *floperoo*, a first-class one. Miss Smith had pointed out how in fact the great democracy was almost totally, and purely, in the control of, and hands of, 'The Industrial-Military-Right,' as she termed it, and Ponce, on reflection, concurred in. A vast, banal complex, it ran the show. In fact, banefully, it was the show. That was the cruelest fact. The hardest. Who disputed it? Miss Smith, for the life of her, couldn't imagine anyone trying to. Ponce didn't try to. The nation was a monolith, one hundred percent, *almost*, behind it. How couldn't it be? *It was it*. It saddened him. And really they didn't know or have in mind anything that could replace it. For they agreed that it was the characters and personalities of the vast majority of citizens that needed replacing. *Or altering*. And how could that be accomplished? Could it ever be? Caught as they were in the vicious cycle of heredity-social-personal-intra-and-inter-personal pressures, factors, and processes. all interrelating and interacting relentlessly, what possible chance did they have? *Could* they have? Plus intelligence, Ponce certainly was aware how that was distributed. Totally undemocratically, and unalterably, at birth no less! What was the answer? It was baffling. Perhaps, one day, The Bomb would take care of it. Though of course they hoped not. Certainly. For when it came to that, they knew the side they were on. Life, imperfect, flawed, general floperoo or fiasco though it might be, was the *only* one, to be on. They knew it. They agreed. Completely. For there was *hope* in it. . . . Next, integration. Civil Rights was the only and proper approach to the matter, and it would take a long, long time for the Negro citizens to reach their goal. The problem, Miss Smith had told him, was in fact a psychological one, based on the equation of black citizens in the minds of a very substantial majority of white citizens with *feces*. That was exactly how she had put it to Ponce, and though startling at first, on reflection it made a good deal of sense to him. He accepted it. This vast majority, Miss Smith had gone on to tell him, had never really evolved or developed beyond an early anal structure, rooted in infancy. Their characters, however mature in many ways, still were under the influence of powerful split-off parts of themselves, anal totally. They were made sick, in short, they were horrified by the thought of (though they weren't in the least bit aware of it) having to rub shoulders on equal terms, in short, *to mix* with what were, in their primitive minds, chunks of living, walking, talking *feces*. In short, *shit*. This vast majority would certainly have to grow up, integrate those split-off parts of themselves, before the Negro really had a chance in this country. And the Negro would have to haul himself up by his bootstraps also, somehow, so he could help these primitives by showing them that certainly he wasn't at all what their minds equated him with, despite his color. It was a two-way process, without a doubt of it! Ponce had been fascinated, in fact almost staggered, by this revelation and interpretation of the sad situation. And the high esteem in which he held Miss Smith rose even higher, if that was possible, for clearly she was sophisticated in areas other than Literature, and without a doubt of it. Ponce had expressed his concern that possibly in the present circumstances of the tragic situation which had hit Sawyersville square in the eye, i.e., the demise of Jill Fairbunn, there would be strong pressures brought to bear in support of the theory that the culprit must have been one of the handful of Negro students not so long ago introduced into the school system – unless, of course, the real culprit was quickly found. And, Ponce had added, wistfully, he certainly hoped to God *that it didn't* turn out to be a colored boy! Miss Smith had agreed, sharing his anxiety, adding only that in view of the apparently high caliber of the person handling the matter, to wit, Captain Surcher, the culprit would be found – for how could such an undoubted monster remain undiscovered for very long? How? Just how? How could he? She pressed it. And she assumed, she added, with a little laugh, it *was* a *he*, naturally. Ponce shared the little laugh, briefly, unexpectedly. . . .

Next, Education. And Miss Smith had let it be known how terrible in her view many of the present trends and so-called developments in that area were. For example, the encroachment of mechanization into the teacher-pupil relationship, in the shape of, just for example, teaching machines, computers, TV classes. Miss Smith said it was very bad, outrageous, and based principally on the desire to attack the very heart, the essence of the educational process, viz., the teacher-student relationship. The answer was to supply more teachers, more classrooms, not mechanical gadgets, she emphatically stated. She happened to have known some of the characters who had played a part in 'developing' certain of these gadgets, in particular, the Teaching Machine, that blatant horror, and she could tell Ponce categorically what perverted souls they were, to a man, of no mean order. Ponce believed her, for he couldn't agree more, regarding Teaching Machines, and Computers. A number of the former had been installed at the high school on an experimental basis, and he hated them. He hoped it would flop, dramatically. Certainly, he would do all he could, toward that end. He told Miss Smith. She smiled at that. Tiger, he knew, didn't think of them. Who did? *Mummer*. That queer of queers, that possible murderer. Ponce once again had run into it. He resolved to build up the guts to talk to Tiger about him. Or Surcher. Maybe Surcher. Certainly. And that would take more than guts. He knew it. He mused over it, painfully. He veered back to teaching machines. He saw them for what they were. He agreed with Miss Smith, completely – they were part of an attempt to dehumanize the whole process of Education. The goal was to break the links, destroy the *very essence* of Education. Would it happen? Ponce, for one, vowed he would do his best to see that it didn't. . . .

Then, Foreign Affairs. Vietnam, of course. Miss Smith's view was that America was too unsophisticated a country to go around trying to decide and act on moral issues in remote parts of the world whose problems were quite beyond our comprehension. It was all pretentious. So far as she could judge, as a matter of fact, it would be no great harm at all if the whole of Southeast Asia was turned over to the Communists. They could have it. Certainly they had the required energy and drive and organizational ability if nothing else to get things moving and all those millions and millions off their hopeless behinds. Certainly they would awaken them. That part of the world had a vast potential. If left alone. Look at China! Just what in God's name we were doing in Vietnam, other than giving the Industrial-Military Pots something to do, she never knew. Bombing, burning, uprooting that already miserable people – back to the Stone Age? To quote someone. In Aid Of What? She wondered. Ponce, growing unhappier, also wondered. He certainly agreed with her when she put out the unique suggestion that if Uncle really wanted to act on a genuine moral issue he should pull out all those troops and planes and what have you and send them along down to South

Africa – and Rhodesia – plus a few other such places – there was an Issue! A real issue! What were we doing with it? On the other hand, what could we do with it? Since a substantial majority, or certainly a large enough minority plus armies of silent followers, of good Americans shared the hateful Apartheid doctrine totally. Sharpsville and all, and more even. Here was the paradox, the essential core of hyprocrisy which was the reality behind the facade of Wholesome American Democracy, of course. It was a highly *undemocratic*, conservative bordering on reactionary Society, the Great American Democracy, on the whole, no less. And corrupt to the nth degree, more or less. Who didn't know it? All intelligent people, outside of America, certainly knew it. Those within, fogged as they were, conformism, cowardice, all the rest ... It was a sad affair. No doubt of it. How would it end?

Then, Culture. Miss Smith had said that the appreciation of Culture would always of natural necessity be restricted to a relatively small proportion of humans, since this appreciation and understanding required a certain level of intelligence and intellect and emotional maturity and character structure – and certainly this level could not be reached by very many, in the present context of things, and not *ever* by too many, in view of the highly unequal distribution of certain basic gifts at birth, by the Maker, she smiled, wryly. ... Ponce, reflecting, certainly had to agree....

And other subjects, and topics, and areas, of course. God how many of them! One of them hitting him in the face now as he entered the house and saw his beloved little brother Rusty Joe glued to the radio in his room listening to that latest innovation in the National Escalation toward Total Lunacy, all in aid of Exploitable Markets, *Uncle Brucie*. ... *He's a lunatic*, Ponce thought, glumly, hearing the manic voice. He gazed at his brother.

'Rusty Joe – '

'Shhh – Ponce – I'm listening – '

'Aren't you supposed to be asleep?'

'C'mon, Ponce – let me listen – '

'I think you better go to sleep.'

'Mom and Dad are asleep – '

'I know it.'

Ponce crossed over to the transistor beside the boy's bed and turned it off. He knew Rusty Joe at that moment hated him.

'Are you going to bed?' The boy asked, not in the friendliest way.

'Yeh.'

'Well, take Peppy.'

And reaching under the covers he hauled out Ponce's favorite cat, the purest joy of his life, outside of Miss Smith. He wondered how that crazy cat had managed to survive under all those blankets, anyhow. They really did have nine lives, Ponce fondly pondered. He took the gray-and-white darling in his arms and stroked her, murmuring to her. She started purring. Rusty Joe smiled. He too loved that cat, without a doubt of it. Now he doesn't hate me, Ponce thought, grinning at him. That cat was a bond, alright.

'Where you been, Ponce?' the boy asked him.

'Out.'

'Got a girl friend?'

Ponce didn't answer that. He was aware of the *agent provocateur* lurking behind that one.

'Don't put Peppy under the covers again,' he told the boy.

'She won't die.'

'Don't do it.'

'She likes it under there. No kidding. Read me a story.'

'How many did Mom read you?'

'None.'

'Liar.'

'I'm not a liar.'

'And Dad?'

'Read me *one!*'

'I'm tired.'

'Got a girl friend?'

'Aw, good night.'

Ponce started to withdraw from the room with his Peppy draped in his arms, purring away, loving it. Rusty Joe jumped out of bed.

'Where you going?' Ponce asked.

'To the toilet.'

'And then right back to bed. Don't forget it.'

'Aw, Ponce, gee, you're as bad as Mom, *no kidding*. Uncle Brucie – '

'Hurry up now,' Ponce interrupted, stiffening at the mere mention of the name.

'Boss Ponce!' Rusty handed him, scooting into the toilet. Ponce went downstairs with Peppy and deposited the little darling of a creature, still purring, in the kitchen, where she slept in a comfortable foam-pillow-lined basket. He spoke to her for a few seconds, petting her, sweet nothings, really. She loved them. He gave her a final caress and took off, heading for bed. He peeped in his brother's room to make sure he was in bed. He was.

'Good night, Mike,' Ponce kidded him.

'Good night, Spike!' called out the boy, 'See you at breakfast!'

Ponce nodded, grinning. He loved the boy.

In his room, Ponce lay in bed, and all he could think of was Miss Smith. He had knocked gently on his parents' bedroom door, then gone in. His mother was still awake, and she had hugged him and kissed him good night. His hand had accidentally brushed her breast. It was so soft. She didn't mind. She wore a light nightdress. He had felt her breast under his hand, he had been excited by it, for his mother had beautiful breasts. If there had been more light in the room he might even have seen them, as sometimes he did, through a light nightdress. They were nice, soft breasts. *Like Miss Smith's* Ponce reflected, thinking of that dream, the dream of all his dreams, forever more. He grew warm, lying there, in bed. He thought of her, and couldn't get to sleep. He felt such a tremendous longing for her, there just was no one else in the world he had ever longed so much for. If only he were older, and working, Ponce thought, he could date her and get engaged and marry her. He knew she liked him. He would give just about anything and everything he had or ever would have to be married to her. He tossed and turned on the bed, utterly unable to sleep. His heart pounded, he was in some state. He would see her tomorrow, she would be there in front of the class, she would be there, smiling, talking, moving. He saw her moving. He saw her near him, in that dress she had on tonight, moving. He clenched his fists, angry that he hadn't been able to do a thing, *anything*, over at her place tonight. She had held his hand and stood near him and caressed his face. He had seen her breasts rising, he had seen the whiteness of them just rising out of the top of that dress, before him, as she leaned toward him. That had thrilled him. He had done nothing. *Well why hadn't she done something?* Suddenly, Ponce found he was angry with her – a little. Certainly, she had seen the state he was in, his organ protruding a mile and nearly bursting out of his pants, no less. She had seen it! She hadn't even *mentioned* it! Ponce's anger faded quickly though. For he was aware that although she thrilled him physically and he would give just about everything to be able to

136

relate to her physically, she meant much much more than that to him, of course. Even in the lavatory, at school, when he jacked off over her, he knew. He always knew. Now he knew. He would always know, no matter what finally became of her. He was blue. She would probably be meeting some guy one of these days and marrying him, Ponce thought. How long could a dream like that keep from being snatched up? Maybe she even had a boyfriend now, Ponce thought – he should have asked her. How could he ask her? *Why hadn't he done something?* Lying there, once again growing warm, he felt sure he could have done something. Would he ever again get the chance to? He was sure she wouldn't have stopped him, in fact, probably, maybe, there was just the chance, yes, *she might have liked it*. Certainly, she liked him. What other kid had ever been up there? Ponce didn't know of any. He just couldn't sleep, pondering all these things, seeing her, before him, *Beside him*. He was dying for her. He was just about *burning* for her. His organ was stiff and large throbbing, screaming out for his hand. Should he stroke it? There was certainly plenty of it. enough to satisfy anyone, *anyone, anyone.* Ponce murmured her name. '*Betty – Darling –* ' He was murmuring. He throbbed with longing for her, he was dying for her. He fought the wild desire to move his hand to the organ. He didn't want that. He wanted to go beyond that. *The real thing.* Tonight, he had muffed the golden opportunity, he hadn't done a single thing. *Not a thing.* What good would this do, knowing what he had missed? *It didn't matter though. The golden day would come!* Ponce was throbbing, starting to sweat now. He could smell his dream. Without a doubt, her fragrance was in that bed, with him, and smothering him. He didn't mind, it could smother him. Ponce fought. He closed his eyes. He forced himself to lie still, though his whole body hammered away. He saw her there. He could almost feel her, under him, there. Ponce sweated. His clenched fist pounded the bed.

His hand was dying to meet, to stroke, to stroke and stroke, his red hot. He fought. The fragrance of roses filled the room. *He kissed her.* . . . Ponce, in a state of supreme anguish now, fought and fought . . .

26

Tiger didn't get back home all that late that night, despite all. It must have been around twelve or a quarter to twelve not much later than that. He felt pretty good. The world and life seemed not only tolerable again, but fresh, even somewhat challenging, once again. Like they used to be all the time, Tiger mused, or practically all the time. *Once upon a time*. He mused and mused. *Long ago. How long ago? When, though?* He roamed around the house. He didn't feel like going to sleep right away. Not right away. Still poignantly aware of the presence and fragrance of the unique Rochelle, he walked through the house looking for something to nibble on – an apple, anything at all to nibble on. An apple, in fact, would do. And he found one. A big red one. He took a big bite out of it. Absolutely delicious. Was it Italy Betty said grew apples even bigger than this? She had been there. He would like to have seen them. She had raved about them, and only was sorry she hadn't brought back at least one for him. He remembered. He grinned. He certainly was fond of her. An apple always brought her to mind for him. He stood there in the kitchen eating away at that apple and looking out into the night through the big kitchen window. He hadn't put the light on in there, it was a pretty clear night and wasn't necessary. There was a moon somewhere, though he couldn't see it. Not from there. He liked to stand there sometimes in the darkness especially on such a night and look out that kitchen window. Anytime, in fact, he had been out late at night, on the prowl, checking up on his athletes, such things. Rochelle had remarked on the moon. From there, they had seen it, not too long ago, suddenly emerge out of the clouds as the night cleared. Now Tiger could see how it lit up the back yard so softly, and the woods beyond the back yard, for Tiger's house was situated in that part of town which gave an unobstructed view of them. It was some view, alright. They stretched for miles, part of the hills. It was a great part of town, and Tiger loved it. As a kid, he had often played in those woods, though he had lived in another part of the town. He moved here not long after he got married, when his teaching career began. He had been lucky enough to buy this great little house. He loved it, as did Looby Loo. It was perfect. All they wanted, and perfect. He remembered a moon like this in Korea. One such night, looking out he suddenly saw what seemed like the whole Chinese army pouring out of the hills. In the moonlight, which had broken through. His Company had been over-run. Their sector of the front smashed. It was the end. How had he survived? *Everything?* To this day, he couldn't understand. Was it luck, purely, that handled such things? What was he supposed to do with that medal – upstairs? At any rate, he thought that's where it was. Somewhere, upstairs. He had lost track of the thing. He stayed there quite a while, looking out that window, until he had completely eaten the apple, and thrown the core away. Then, giving the fabulous scene one last look, and thinking once again of Rochelle, that unique and wonderful girl, and Betty Smith, thrown in, he left the room, and headed upstairs. He thought of Jane. It was too late probably to go into her room and tuck her in and say good night to that cutest kid. He headed for his den. Looby Loo probably would be asleep, or pretty nearly asleep, certainly. The door to their room was slightly ajar, and as he walked past he heard his wife's voice murmuring to him, out of the night.

'That you, honey?'

'Yeh, hon.,' he replied, softly.

'Everything alright?'

'Right,' he replied, into the opening of the door, 'I'm gonna read a little while – O.K.?' he said.

'O.K.,' she replied, murmuring drowsily, he could see her drowsy smile almost, which he loved so much.

'Don't be too long,' she added, falling away.

He nodded and left. He walked past Jane's door. He peeked in and could just see her form in the bed. She was asleep. He entered the room and went up to her bed. He leaned over. He heard her breathing. He saw her pretty face, her mother's face, and her blond hair spilling over the pillow. He kissed her on the lips, lightly. She gave a little sigh, but otherwise did not stir. Tiger felt warm, and good, toward her. He loved her. He was smiling, as he left the room.

Reaching his den, he flipped on the light and looked around. There was some schoolwork to do, a batch of Health Ed. test papers to peruse, some Guidance/Counseling stuff. But there was no great hurry, he could take care of that tomorrow. He picked up the latest *Time* magazine. It was open at the page he reached earlier in the day. He sat down in his comfortable easy chair, near the desk, and began to read. He wasn't exactly in love with the magazine, but sometimes it had useful information in it. Without a doubt. That was it.

He read –

– *The Need For Laughter* –

What Tiger was reading actually was a review of a book in the Education pages, a book in the field of Education, that is, by one Kenneth Eble, a Professor of Education somewhere, Tiger noted. It seemed interesting. It was something like this that made the subscription worthwhile, he knew, even before starting to read the review. He just knew. The letters weren't all that bad either. Often, he was amused. Other times, intrigued. Once in a while, bewildered, also. Were they made up ? Was some editor charged with the task ? Tiger grinned, wondering. One of these days they'd be doing a little article on Sawyersville, the fabulous team. He knew it, without a doubt, they'd do it. He read –

– *A Perfect Education*, by Kenneth A. Eble.

– *Love, learning and life are what education is all about. Yet somehow, US schools never get involved in any of them.* Tiger halted, nodding his head, musing, smiling a little bit. He couldn't agree more. From one end of the country to the other, he knew, and up and down, to boot, the situation was exactly like that, absolutely. It was sad. Here and there, of course, there were isolated patches to the contrary, those wonderful exceptions that always occurred, no matter how grim a situation. Tiger knew. He hoped Sawyersville was one of them. He liked to think it was. Certainly, it was his goal. He agreed, and completely, with the Professor's wise words.

– '*to learn*,' writes Eble, '*is to love.*'

Absolutely, Tiger thought. delighted. *Of course it was.* That was a remarkable truth to read in this magazine, and no doubt of it, even if it was only quoting. Did everything, but *everything*, after all, serve a purpose ? As Hetty Nectar so often told him ? Tiger chuckled. She was so fond of saying it. He read –

– *Students ought to revel in discovery, Eble says, but educators from grade to grad school* – Tiger loved that – *have a knack for taking most of the joy out of learning.* . . .

Still grinning at the cute turn of phrase, a specialty of the magazine, true, he knew, Tiger nodded his head. Who was this Eble ? Tiger wondered, did he know him, perchance ? He kept on wondering. The name was vaguely familiar, but then that wasn't enough. He examined the photograph of the man on the page.

140

He could have known him. Through one of the corridors of learning somewhere their paths may well have crossed, possibly without their knowing it. Some conference perhaps, or other, it could have been. It was the smallest of smallest possible worlds, he knew. *How right he was*, Tiger mused, knowing or not knowing him. He read –

– *Pupils should be in love with their teachers. . . .* 'It is no joke,' says Eble, 'it's the way of learning.'

Certainly it was, Tiger knew. Anyone with any understanding of the human condition knew, and it certainly was a condition, well he knew. It was built into every good teacher, it was what made him or her tick, this love, this ability to elicit it. It had to be there. If it wasn't, the result – *Mummer*. Tiger shook his head, over that one. Well, we couldn't all be perfect. Once he got rid of him, he would certainly hold nothing against him. Maybe Proffer would take him on in the TV business. They could start a new line, selling Teaching Machines – to the public. Tiger grinned, over that one. Yes, Educators had to have this innate trait, the character and personality structure that went with it, to elicit love, to make pupils fall in love with them. Eble had hit it. *Warmth*. So many educators lacked it. Too many more were afraid of it. What was wrong with it ? It was, basically, Mummer's trouble. And Crispwell's. Tiger reflected further, on the former, the very teacher Ponce had apparently bowled over that morning in his flight from the lavatory. He certainly fell in that category. Tiger knew the kids just hated to go to his classes, they were bored stiff by them. How well it tied in with the man's fanatic belief in Teaching Machines, and other similar 'educational aids', so called, ironically. And the next paragraph –

' . . . *that is the advantage of live teachers and live books – they can be fallen in love with, possessed – That is the whole secret of real education,*' Eble says. . . .

The article concluded, leaving Tiger highly delighted, and contemplating writing a letter even to the fellow, Eble, congratulating him on his efforts. Maybe he would even send him reprints of some of his own papers, in case he hadn't ever seen them. They had appeared for the most part in the State Educational Journal, which he may or may not have taken. They were specialized articles, in the sphere of Guidance/Counseling, for the most part. Certainly, he would be interested in them. Tiger also made a note to get a copy of the book, through the usual channels, Hetty Nectar, that sweetheart of a Librarian, of course. She was a marvelous Librarian, the best Sawyersville had ever hired, no doubt of it. Tiger mused, over her. The kids loved her. They made full use of the Library. . . .

Tiger flipped through the rest of the magazine, all anticlimax, of course, and threw it aside, finally, after tearing out the page which had interested him. The magazine itself he had thrown in the wastepaper basket.

He sat back in his chair, thinking, a warm smile on his face. What would Rochelle be doing? Sleeping? Dreaming? How did she feel, that astonishing girl, and what was she dreaming? Tiger wondered. He hoped she felt wonderful, he had done his best to make her feel wonderful, he knew it. He always did. What more could he do? He didn't know it. She was a dream, he hoped she was dreaming of him. . . . Tomorrow, in Civics class, he'd be seeing her. She and his Ponce as usual sparking the class. He smiled warmly, thinking of his two bright stars of the class. Often they tangled head-on, on certain issues, and how the sparks flew. It was neck and neck, nearly always, Tiger knew. Sawyersville was lucky, having *two* intelligences of that order, in *one class*, no less. Lucky. He was proud of them, as who wouldn't be. . . . Tomorrow would be *Jill plus one* also, now Tiger mused, suddenly, sadly. The great search for the culprit would be swinging into high gear, if he knew. He felt it, and the very best of all possible luck to the man in charge of it all, Captain Surcher, that sober, earnest, intelligent, in short, definitely competent man, Tiger felt sure. He sat in his chair awhile longer. He was thinking of Jill. Of it all. Of Rochelle. He found himself wondering, suddenly, did that dream ever caress her own breasts? Just what was it like, having such marvelous breasts? *Perfect*. The only word for them. In bed, perhaps, sometimes, did she play with them? Tonight, maybe? Lying there, before going to sleep, thinking of him – maybe? He knew that he would, he mused, certainly, if he had them. . . . *Poor Jill*. . . . She wouldn't leave him. He shook his head, he sighed. That variation by Ponce on T-Special Twenty-four Pass On Four Decoy Left And Center was something. Something. Tomorrow, he'd try it. He couldn't wait to try it. . . . He felt sleepy. He yawned. Time to hit the hay, definitely, he mused. . . . Looby Loo. . . .

27

Surcher arrived at the school bright and early the next morning, with his assistants, all of them. He had briefed them, even earlier. To his relief, there had been no further murder. Now, speed, and efficient action. For he really had something. On that letter he had found not only the deceased Head Cheerleader's prints, but also a perfect set of others. All he had to do now was find the fellow who matched them. It shouldn't take long – provided he showed up. And Surcher definitely felt he would be showing up. He would be that kind of character. *Kid.* The name suited him, whoever he was, without a doubt of it. He and his corps of assistants tried not to betray their excitement, but it was difficult alright, no doubt of it. For they were hunters closing in on their quarry, a team on their opponents' one-yard line – how not to show it ? Surcher pictured the signed confession, for of course that's what it would have to be. Though the letter of course was the golden clue. They had no evidence that would stand up in court, so far, at any rate. A confession, the only way. Certainly, they'd get it, once they got him, he knew. State Police techniques were highly refined, and irresistible. Every criminal knew it.

He cornered Proffer and told him nonchalantly to rearrange all the previously worked out arrangements and schedules just a little bit if he would, by sending in all the colored students one by one this very morning, no less. He and his assistants would talk to them. He had decided that last night, mainly to eliminate them from further involvement in the matter, for reasons he could well appreciate. Proffer concurred. He put Miss Craymire, mostly recovered now, on to it, right away.

'We're having a special Assembly this morning, Captain, by the way,' he told Surcher, 'Will it be o.k. if you see them after it ? Or do you want them during Assembly ?' he asked.

Surcher thought it over.

'How long does Assembly last ?' he asked.

All the doors to the school, all possible exits, were well guarded, he knew. The Troopers had been briefed too.

'Ten, fifteen minutes,' he heard.

The Captain mused.

'O.K.' he finally said.

'You and your men are welcome to attend, Captain, if you want to,' Proffer said.

'Thanks – but I'll have to say no, Mr Proffer,' Surcher said, 'I have a few little things to take care of,' he also said.

Proffer nodded, wondering what these things might be. . . .

Teachers, pupils, the entire school filed silently into the auditorium. Ponce found himself sitting next to Rochelle Hudson. As always, he admired that gorgeous girl, her long dark hair. Her brain. There was a girl with a brain. He said Hi to her and she smiled at him. He knew she liked him. They got on great. Then Proffer walked onto the platform. He had a Bible in one hand. He opened it up and began reading from it. Ponce couldn't exactly place what it was he was reading, for Proffer had a way of reading that was more like mumbling, really. Maybe those right up in the front rows heard. Of course, he knew it would have to do with death, and mourning, and so he could narrow it down, for it would be among a certain select number of passages. Only. Ponce played his guessing game. Proffer read on. Five minutes later he closed the good book and started to address the Assembly. Now Ponce could hear him. Only when he was reading something did it come out mumbling. It was interesting, Ponce mused, as always, noting it. . . .

'And so we are gathered here today to pay a silent tribute to that wonderful, wonderful girl who was Jill Fairbunn, that wonderful girl whose fresh smile and wonderful personality used to make our day, the girl who was cruelly taken away from us yesterday, only yesterday. Let us bow our heads and pray. First of all.'

Ponce, not knowing why, bowed his head with everyone. And so did Rochelle, he noted. He stole a glance at her, that brilliant, beautiful girl. His heart started thumping. He felt a hot flush. *What a girl.* He thought of Jill. *What a beautiful girl that Rochelle was.* He wondered where Miss Smith was sitting. He hadn't seen her, to tell the truth. Tiger was up in the front row, he had seen him, just near the platform. Rochelle's eyes were closed. What long lashes they were.

Proffer went on, and Ponce tagged on, ' . . . Words are very hard to come by on so tragic and sad an occasion. Nothing I could say would bring back that wonderful girl, the one thing all of us want most of all. I can only say, and I'm sure the entire faculty would join with me in saying, let us remember that wonderful girl, as she was, let her be our standard, our guide, our ideal, in our minds, as we remember her and knew her. Let us try to emulate her love and loyalty and hard work for Sawyersville High, and community, as a whole. Let *this* be our memorial to her. . . . '

Ponce was moved by this passage, and in fact definitely felt tears welling up in his eyes, and all around him he heard sniffles, quite a few. Proffer went on. . . .

Surcher thought it would be a good opportunity to take a look around the school while the Assembly was going on. He especially thought it might not be a bad idea at all to have a peek in that lavatory, for who could tell. He and a couple of assistants, Lieutenants Grady and Follo, strolled along the hall toward that destination. As they strolled, they took a quick look in the classrooms they passed, all empty now, of course. They slowed down as they approached the lavatory and in fact walked so carefully and ingeniously that hardly a trace of their footsteps would be heard, even in that echo chamber of a hallway, no less. When they actually reached that door they stood outside for a few moments, listening. Then, they opened it.

'Let us all bow our heads therefore once again, let us pray, each in his own way – ' Proffer was saying, solemnly. . . .

The lavatory was spread out before them, and appeared deserted. There were the cubicles, their doors closed, most of them. There was the one. No feet were visible in the space between the doors and the floor, in any one. Of course there was the one at the end, near the far wall, which was in a sort of secluded spot and might just be hiding a pair of feet. They started toward that cubicle. . . .

Ponce wasn't praying. He tried to find some way to pray for poor Jill, but just couldn't. The truth was, he found his thoughts going in a crazy circle, touching here, there, finding Rochelle, Miss Smith, and Jill as she was, always there. . . .

They were almost halfway down that line of cubicles when the door of the last cubicle burst open and a figure plunged out, catching them by surprise. They hadn't even drawn their revolvers, and certainly they needed them now, for the figure before them was formidably armed.

'*Don't Make A Move!*' They heard him shout.

It was Chief John Poldaski, with a drop and a half on them. . . .

'Now let us all silently rise and file out of the auditorium,' Proffer was saying, finally, 'Just let us go back to our classrooms, and carry on, as that wonderful girl would have wanted us to. . . .'

'What the hell are you doing here?' Surcher asked, sharply, after a moment or two of rattling silence.

'Put that thing away,' Grady said, not too kindly.

'C'mon, do that,' Follo chimed in.

The Chief did so, slowly, fumbling around with the holster a while.

'Well?' Surcher said, eyeing him.

'Well –' the Chief said, shifting around, eyeing them, patently unhappy with everything, 'I had an idea – '

'What idea?' Follo asked.

'Well – goddamn it – ' the Chief said, 'It's this way – ' He also said, 'I got the idea – ' He then said, 'What about this guy, wouldn't he just maybe give it another whirl?' he finally said. 'See what I mean?' he said.

'With you here?' Grady said.

'How long you been here?' Follo said.

'Aren't you supposed to be out there?' Surcher said.

'Seen that traffic? Take a look out there,' Grady said.

Poldaski stood there. The questions had staggered him.

'Listen – this is *my* town – ' he said, finally.

'And *our* case,' Surcher informed him.

'So get out there,' Grady told him.

'Listen – ' the Chief tried, narrowly.

'Out of here,' Surcher said, definitively.

'*No kidding,*' Follo added, quietly.

They stood there.

Poldaski finally said, in an angry mumbling tone, 'O.K. – O.K., you guys. – O.K., O.K. Yeh. You guys,' He paused – 'But wanta put a bet? Huh? *I bet I find the guy.* I'll show you smart guys. Put that bet? Huh? Wanta?' He eyed them all. Nothing at all. He started to leave. Muttering. 'Smart guys,' he muttered, at the door. 'I got my leads – You'll see – ' He was halfway out the door. '*Wait and see.*' He was out, the door closed.

The three State Police officers looked at one another, then grinned. Then, they had a little laugh. Surcher shook his head.

Grady said, 'Oh man.'

Then they finished looking around. There was nothing to be found. Surcher glanced at his watch.

They left.

On his way out of the auditorium, Tiger passed Marjorie Evanmore, and smiled at her, saying a friendly good morning to her. Her eyes sparkled and a slight flush distinctly spread over that honey of a face, as she smiled and said Hello. She moved on, with her class. He was on his way to the Guidance/Counseling Office, where he had two appointments this morning, one with Mona Drake, a Junior – a colored girl – and Hetty Nectar, that excellent Librarian, if ever there was one, who wanted to talk with him about that new list of Guidance/Counseling publications which had just come out – she needed his advice and final O.K. He would take the opportunity to have her order Eble's book, he reminded himself, nearly out of the auditorium now and nodding here and there to students, in his way, saying good morning to some, hi, and hello, to others, there was Rochelle Hudson, whose smile now really perked up his morning, and there was Ponce, that great kid, looking a little better, though still of course under the weather, Tiger taking the opportunity to remind him there would be Practice tonight, definitely, and to pass the word along to all the boys, which of course Ponce would, without fail, and there was Jim Green, and he nodded to him, also reminding him, that really fine Right End, one of the finest he'd ever had – And Betty Smith, that sweetie sweet, a cheery good morning to her, just for her, what a smile she had – And Kathy Burns, that petite sweet, that honey, she was absolutely and without the slightest doubt one of the sweetest of little bunnies – Now there were Dink Reagan and Petie Smith, great kids, true blue, and feeling mighty blue, sort of boy-friends as they were, in a way, of the late Jill, he knew. He said a serious good morning to them. And there was Anne Williams, that cute sophomore who was coming up, on the up and up, without a doubt, a cutie if ever there was one about, he smiled at her, she caught her breath, he saw that, she smiled, she said hello, in her way. What a way. Jeannie Bonni with that nice dark hair, not unlike Rochelle's, greeted him, she said hello and smiled at him, walking by, in her way. That girl would go places if no one else did, she was terrific out there with those majorettes, and when Marjorie finally relinquished her post, upon graduation, or possibly sooner, for who knew, he was sure she would be in line for the job. When was she due for her

147

Brooder? Soon, he thought, pretty soon, he thought. He would check. Alice Patmore and Yvonne Mellish, probably Jill's best friends, he knew, passed by, looking lovely, despite all, they smiled and said hello to him, he said a compassionate hello to them. He could tell they were pretty blue. And up ahead, just entering her Home Room, was Marie Amis, he just caught a glimpse of her red hair. He loved red hair, there was this something special about it, though he couldn't put his finger on it. Tiger chuckled to himself, coming across a special section of warmth, of good humor, all concerned and connected with red hair. Everywhere. He was chuckling, within, walking on, greeting still more students, thinking Proffer hadn't done too bad a job, at least he had kept it short, as Jill would have wanted it, he knew. He greeted fellow teachers, feeling a special camaraderie for his colleagues, as ever, of course. And there was that little lynx Peggy Linski, a pure Polish blond, a delightful kid, weren't they all though. What a sweet kid. Down in Molbie, all those little Polish sweeties, blonds, most of them. Some of the best football material came from there. There was his full-back Fifi Gaudi, now saying hi to him, he asked his Coach if there would be Practice tonight. Tiger told him. Feef, who was going to Notre Dame next year, having decided upon that one out of the dozen or so offered to him, coast to coast, nodded happily and buzzed off to his classes. There was nothing he liked more than football. Tiger knew. He was fond of the boy, powerful line-bucker that he was. Tiger saw him as All-American without a doubt, maybe his first year, even, with the Irish. He grew warm. How many All-Americans had he turned out? He grinned, within, mighty proud. Of all the high-school coaches in the country, he must hold the record. *Must.* Though no one, as far as he knew, kept such records. He made a mental note to check into that. He thought of his team, all his teams, feeling good. He thought of Dink Reagan, his quarterback, whom he had passed just a little while back. What a lad. Where was he headed for? A batch were hot after him. He hadn't decided yet. What a sparkplug he was. All he or Ponce had to do was give that kid the gist of a new tactical switch and he would do the rest, even if there were three or four minutes to go, and they might be behind. He would get it through to the team just like that, what a lad. How many times had he got them across in the last minute or so, racking up another one yet for old Sawyersville? Yes, Tiger mused, feeling pretty good, despite all, the sad event, what a crew, what a lucky guy to have material like that on his crew. He was grateful for small mercies, aware of the sad circumstances hanging over the school like a pall, thankful indeed for the quiet and happy life in many respects that he led here in Sawyersville, and the High. It made it easier to cope with the downward curve of his life, always on his mind. That was where he stood, of course, he wasn't one to kid himself about that, the years couldn't be held back or dispersed or reversed, he was only too poignantly aware of that, he would go forward, undirectionally, to his end. Nothing could halt that trend. But he was entrenched happily here, in his own little sphere, and he did what he could, to help everyone. How many could say that? He mused over that. He turned a corner and headed down the hall on his last lap to the Guidance/Counseling office now, where Mona would probably be waiting already for him. He knew. They had a lot to do, to get through, he mused. Affluence was a phenomenon of this century, its base being precisely that which any self-respecting cultured intellectual or at least individual would acknowledge, right off: Technology. At least in great parts of the world. For that was the rub, the irony, wasn't it – the rich got richer and the poor poorer, despite everything, speaking of nations, that is, the have and have-nots, that is. The developed and under-developed countries, so to speak, grew further and further apart, no doubt of it. It was that vexing, trying, most difficult question of getting them to that taking-off point. *Taking off*. Tiger mused. They had to take off, or never get there. And while in fact what was there was something to ponder thoughtfully about, at least it was something, certainly not starvation, pure and physical, he knew. Or misery, through and through. He had arrived, practically.

'Good morning, Mr McDrew,' Mrs Mortlake, that happily married and humanely fanatic school nurse called out, almost bumping into him. She was on her way to work. And Tiger wondered, as ever, benignly of course, just what work? True, she was only part-time, but it cost a pretty penny anyhow. He made a mental note, while admiring her, warmly, to thoroughly explore that situation, that position, that job description, as soon as he got the chance. He wouldn't be able to do much in the way of acting on it until he had taken over, of course, the reins fully in his hands, more or less, but of course. But it was best to prepare. Get ready. Of course. She wasn't on his list. He had explored that situation some time ago with a view toward a slot, but had concluded, for the time, that it wasn't the time. In this matter, that was the most crucial, indeed the most difficult and challenging judgment to make – it took the greatest talent and insight to make. The wrong judgment, he knew, could lead to disaster, only, he knew. How well he knew. He mused. *No, not yet, at any rate –*

'How's my favorite nurse?'

She smiled at him, clinically warm. He wondered how things went with her husband. Pretty good, no doubt. He was an Insurance man. Tiger was all for Insurance men, their social function was high. She had a pair of thighs. He could almost see those glistening white thighs. Would he? he wondered. Within, he sighed.

'Very well, thank you, Mr McDrew,' she said to him, a perfect set of teeth staring him in the eyes. He stared at her. Was it time, he mused, to reexamine the judgment he'd made? He wondered. He thought of those thighs.

'Well, don't work too hard,' he offered her, a tentatively exploring shot. Tiger thought. Certainly, her treasures were jumbo size grapefruit at least, and ten times as soft. Tiger watched thoughtfully. Her white uniform fitted so well. Crisp, white. She smelled cleaner than white. For him, she was a virgin in white.

'I'll try not to!' she smiled, and continued to smile, taking off. He smiled.

He entered his office.

28

Captain Surcher began interviewing the Negro students as soon as Assembly ended. He was told they were all present and accounted for, and that was good. Very good. One of them, Mona Drake, was in the Guidance/Counseling office for a testing session this morning, he was told. He said she could stay there, he would see her last on the list. Though he knew, of course, it didn't matter. Certainly, it wasn't she he was after.

The interviews proceeded smoothly, simply. He and his assistants asked each of them a few preliminary, innocently routine questions, such as their names, and grade, and home address, and occupation of their parents, writing it all down, carefully, and then, with regard to the boys, took their fingerprints, casually. So casually they hardly knew it had happened. After that, one simple question was asked of them –

'Who's "*Kid*" ?'

'What ?'

'Do you have a friend nicknamed "*Kid*" ?'

'Here ?'

'Here, anywhere – '

'Let me think.'

'Sure, think. Don't worry about it.'

'That's Jim – '

'Who ?'

'Jim Green.'

Five of them said.

29

Tiger, entering, saw the attractive brown girl. He grew warm, and he was aware, for just a fraction of a second, or two, of that odd snatch of nursery rhyme, in his head, once more. It disappeared, as he spoke.

'Well, Mona, how are you this morning ?'

She looked at him. She looked good.

'O.K., Mr McDrew, thank you.'

He grinned, 'That's fine.'

She looked great.

He sat down behind his desk, looking at her, that warm grin on his face. She smiled at him.

'Nervous ?' he said.

'Yes,' she said.

'Don't be,' he said, 'It's not that bad.'

'I hope I pass it,' she said.

'Well, I know you will,' he said, 'Anyway, it's not really a matter of passing – this test.' Tiger sat back, observing her, warmly. She certainly was a lovely young nubile maid. 'We're just going to see something, a little something, of what you're all about, and what sort of a career you might profile into – fit into – as a result of us, together, here, finding out this little bit about what you're about.' He paused. 'See what I mean ?'

She seemed fogged, lost in thought. Fraught with thought. Tiger mused. The colored races certainly have the most physically handsome specimens in them, without a doubt, Tiger thought, particularly when mixed with white. The intermingling of races, which he was all in favor of, produced the most wonderful results, time after time. What pure beauty the human race would be if all the races freely crossed! It was the only answer to the problem of course and would have to be adopted sooner or later, as a matter of course. It was a question of time, he knew. As everything was –

'I – think I do,' she said, sweetly, relaxing, just a little bit. She liked him, he knew. It was part of the road.

'Well, where shall we start?' Tiger asked. And paused.

'I don't know,' the girl replied, after a pause.

Tiger reached for a folder, opened it, and glanced here and there, through it.

'Hmmmm?' he now said, humming it out.

'Isn't there a place to start?' she asked, somewhat perplexed, and possibly a bit distressed. Tiger noted her breasts. Under her dress. A very pretty little dress.

'That all depends on you,' Tiger grinned, aware of growing rapport.

She shrugged, and, if Tiger thought he could really tell, flushed a little, and smiled, 'What do you want to know?'

Tiger, warm, supremely poised yet relaxed in his chair, was well aware. He cast caressing glances on her, positively sure he could tell.

'Well,' he said, finally, gently, Eble's book popping up in his mind, 'Tell me about yourself.' He paused. 'Anything at all that comes to your mind about yourself,' he said, tenderly. 'Don't be bashful.'

She said, suddenly, 'I'm scared of you.'

'You are?' Tiger said, 'Of *me?*' He grinned.

She gave a little smile, 'I don't know why I am.'

'Let's find out.'

She gave a little laugh. How Tiger loved that laugh.

'How can we do that?' she asked, at last.

'What are you scared of – ' he asked, 'About me?'

'Well – I don't know – ' the girl said.

'Because I'm white?'

Mona stared at him. He sat calmly, letting her stare at him. He continued observing her. They had marvelous uplift. He had first noticed in Civics class, at the beginning of the new school year. Certainly, Tiger mused, contemplating them, in his mind, unbared before him, they were something. He had never seen a brown pair before. It would be something. Uplifted, he gazed warmly.

'I –' she said, definitely flustered, 'That could be.'

'I know it.'

'I never have felt too good with whites,' she told him, hesitantly.

'And I can believe that,' Tiger said, softly, 'and understand that,' he also said, quietly.

'So that's what mainly comes to my mind,' she said.

He nodded, slightly.

'How old are you, Mona?' he asked.

'Seventeen.'

'Just?'

'Two weeks ago.'

'You're very attractive – you know that?'

She smiled, she shifted in her chair, they shifted with her. Tiger loved it.

'Thank you,' she said.

'Do you know that?' he repeated.

'Well –' she said, trying not to look at him, 'I guess I'm not bad –'

'Oh, you know it.'

She smiled again, looking at him, 'I'll take your word for it.'

'Are you happy here?' Tiger asked.

'Sawyersville, you mean?'

'That's right.'

She thought about that. Tiger waited patiently, watching her think about that. He glanced at her legs. His eye traveled upward along those well formed legs. The knees were together. And above there –

'On the whole –' she said – 'Yes.'

'You're doing pretty well here. You've been making good grades in just about everything –'

She had brains, certainly.

'I try my best.'

'What do you think about what happened yesterday?' he suddenly asked.

'Awful, just awful. Really *bad*,' she said.

Tiger nodded his head.

'Do you mix much with the white girls?'

'Well – ' she said, 'I don't live in Sawyersville – naturally – and I think that's the main trouble. See? Because the girls really are nice. On the whole, I mean. I'm pretty sure they would mix.'

Tiger nodded.

'Hill was awfully nice – ' the girl said, very quietly.

Tiger nodded.

'Was she a friend of yours?' he asked, very quietly.

She was looking at him. Without a doubt, he saw loss in her eyes.

'She was,' she replied, softly, 'and that was very nice of her, because she didn't have to be – being a Senior – and everything – ' Mona paused. 'We used to talk together a lot – we worked together on the school paper – did you know?' Tiger didn't know. 'I was planning on asking her over to my house – ' She paused – 'Sounds crazy, maybe, but – that's how sincerely friendly she was.' She paused. 'I mean, you know, a lot of white girls – *and* boys – are just plain insincere when they're "friendly" to us – ' Again she paused, as Tiger nodded.

'Is that why you're scared of me?'

A pause.

'It could be – ' she said, finally, very quietly.

'Well – ' Tiger said, 'I thought that was it.'

Silence. He sat calmly, patiently, waiting for more, meanwhile feasting his eyes on her. Those magnificent hips. The thrust of those young hips. Her slim waist. She was divinely formed.

'Do you have a boyfriend?' Tiger asked.

'Well – ' she replied, looking at him, 'Not a steady – '

'Date a lot?'

She waited a bit.

'Oh – I go out maybe once a week. Not always on dates though.' She paused. 'I sometimes go to dances and things with girl friends – ' She stopped.

'Where do you go when you date?'

'It – depends – ' She paused, still looking at him. He could sense the ever-growing rapport, that phenomenon without which human life would be very poor. In fact, it was its core. He felt warm. He wondered if she was warm. Her eyes were deep brown, full of contact and warmth. She was still scared, somewhat, though. But – at this stage – that wasn't uncommon – of course. He had seen it often before –

'Sometimes a movie – ' she said, her eyes on him, and pausing to catch a little breath, while he admired her lips, her pink tongue, 'Sometimes just to dance, or to roller skate – oh, all kinds of things!' She paused, smiling at him. 'One boy takes me to motor-cycle racing. I don't like that very much.'

Tiger nodded, and smiled too.

'How are they?' he asked, casually.

'How do you mean?'

'Are they good to you?'

'My boyfriends?'

'That's who I mean.'

A pause, her eyes stayed on him. What warmth in them.

'Oh – they're alright.' she said.

'Are they all colored boys?'

'Yes,' she replied, 'I've never been out with a white boy,' she added. Somewhat shyly.

Tiger nodded, feeling ever closer to the maid.

'Do any of your boyfriends go to school here?' he asked.

'Well, I've been out with Jim Green a few times,' she informed him, with a smile.

'He's a good kid,' Tiger said.

'Oh I like him a lot. He's lots of fun. And smart.'

'I know he's smart.'

'But it's nothing serious,' she sighed, 'I'm too young for that.'

Tiger grinned.

'You feel you want to wait before getting serious – ' he said.

'That's right,' she said, nodding her head, and relaxing in her chair a bit more, entering a new stage of rapport, Tiger noted, 'Because after all there's plenty of time for that – isn't there, Mr McDrew?' She paused. 'I mean, you're only young once.'

Tiger, saying nothing, only nodded warmly. He couldn't agree more. Of course. He felt all those years – behind him. He saw Mona – before him.

'Your father works in a restaurant, doesn't he, Mona?' he asked.

'He does,' she answered, somewhat surprised, it seemed.

He grinned. 'I know because it's on your records, I just took a glance at them, before you came in,' he explained.

'He's a cook,' Mona said.

Tiger nodded.

'Mother works too – ' she said, 'in an office – ' she also said, 'Did you know that?'

'Secretary?' Tiger asked.

'Something like that.' Mona smiled. 'She types an awful lot!'

'Does she bring it home sometimes?' he asked.

'What?'

'Work – officework – ' he grinned.

'Oh, just once in a great while – '

'I'll bet you're glad of that.'

'I'll say I am. Oh, but don't worry I help quite a lot in the house.'

'I'm sure you do.'

Silence now. Tiger kept on looking at her. She wasn't afraid of his gaze. She met it openly, warmly. He was aware of the warmth in her.

'What do you think you'd like to do – When you finish school?' he asked.

'Well – I'd really like to go to college. I'd really like that, I'm not sure what I'd study, but a lot of the time I think I'd like to be a teacher. I like teachers,' she said.

Tiger nodded.

'I think you're an awfully good teacher,' she said, softly, almost shyly.

Tiger was moved by that. It was the sort of remark that always moved him, he appreciated it. He had heard others tell him that, but he was especially moved to hear her say that. It drew him closer to her, he felt a great deal of warmth toward her, more and more. He was sure she felt the same.

'Thank you, Mona. That's a very nice thing to hear. It's made my day.'

'I mean it, too.'

He knew she did.

'I know you do,' he said, quietly.

'I always thought civics would be so boring. I really did. Not with you though. I love it, Mr McDrew.'

'I try to make it live,' Tiger modestly said, 'I'd hate to be sitting there being bored by it. I always try to put myself in the student's place. I can remember my high-school days!'

They were piperoos.

They had a little laugh. Again, Tiger found himself in love with her laugh. It was soft, and warm, and this young maid, it was a lovely, human laugh. He certainly liked this young maid.

'The colleges are getting pretty crowded these days,' he said, 'But I'm sure you'll get in. Where would you like to go? State?'

'Oh, I'd love State – '

'I went there.'

'I'd love to go there!'

'You'll like it there,' Tiger said, 'Of course, it's changed a lot since I was there – the campus is filled with new buildings – I think now there must be about twenty thousand students there. Five times as many as when I was there!'

'Is there a quota there?' she asked.

Tiger knew what she meant, what was on her mind there, and he felt sorry for her. And angry, also, at the whole rotten business of race.

'They're not supposed to have,' he answered, gently, and truthfully, 'You'll see when you fill out your application form they don't ask anything like that – ' He paused, 'As far as I know, they don't have anything like that,' he said. 'You get that rotten business at private schools, and of course down south. I guess you know that though. Don't you?'

She nodded. She was a bit blue.

'Well, I'd really like to go there,' she said.

Tiger nodded. He gave a warm smile. He wished her all the luck in the world, certainly, he'd do what he could for her.

'Well, when the day comes that you fill out your application, just let me know, I'll help all I can.'

'When should I do it?' she asked.

'Oh, about the beginning of your Senior year, next year.' Silence, now.

'Are you from Sawyersville, Mr McDrew?' she said.

'You can call me Tiger – in here,' he said, warmly, aware of the marvelous rapport enveloping them.

'I can?'

'Sure you can.'

She gazed at him. She looked beautiful gazing at him. Was her heart pounding? He thought he knew.

'Are you?' she said.

'I am. I was born and brought up here. Of course, I've been around a little bit,' he chuckled softly. 'Here and there.'

'I'll bet you have.'

'But most of all – I like it here.'

'It's so quiet – so nice and peaceful here.'

Tiger grinned, 'It's not a bad town.'

She sat quietly, continuing to gaze at him. She smiled. She touched her hair. She looked away a moment from him. She sighed.

157

'What would happen if my family moved in?' she asked, suddenly, looking at him once again.

Tiger admired the girl. He thought about it, not knowing exactly what, as yet, to say. For the citizens of Sawyersville, in truth, weren't all that advanced in their views – if he knew. And he really thought he knew. They even had their share of John Birchers, true. A tiny minority, true. But, there they were. He thought of Crispwell, and felt blue. Did she have any classes with him? He didn't think so. She was in the Academic course. He sat there, gazing at her, admiring her, wondering how he could answer that one. He didn't want to hurt her, or lose her, for certainly it was fabulous rapport. On the other hand, he never liked kidding anyone around. In the end, it shattered rapport. And he loved truth. He felt sure all the troubles in the world, here, there, anywhere, could in the long run be attributed without a doubt to a suppression or distortion of truth, somewhere along the line. The human line.

He told her, gently, quietly, 'I think a certain number of people would raise a lot of cain about it.' He paused. 'Also, a certain number, including myself and just about all the teachers in the school, would be happy about it.' He paused again, watching her. 'Then, as always, a certain number in between wouldn't know one way or the other.' He paused once more. 'There'd be quite a tussle. I don't know how it would all end up.'

And he sat quietly, watching her, admiring her. He wondered if her family had been thinking along those lines. He wouldn't mind. He wondered what her family was like. They sounded alright. She had two older brothers – in their twenties. He knew.

'Would this certain number against it try to hurt us –' she said – 'I mean, throw bricks through our windows, maybe even blow up the house – or try to – Do you think they would?'

Tiger pondered. She had foresight, alright.

'They might,' he said. 'Those types exist.' He paused. 'You know it, don't you, Mona?' he also said. 'The country has its fair share of them, without a doubt.' He paused. 'Look at Kennedy –' He stopped.

'Yes –' she said, quite blue, 'Yes – I know. I know alright – *Tiger* –' She stopped.

'That sounds nice.'

'Why did I call you that?'

'Well, I asked you to.' He paused, and smiled. 'Didn't I, Mona?'

158

'Why do they call you that?'

He shrugged, still smiling, 'I used to be called that when I played football, a heck of a long time ago. I guess I was pretty fierce! Or something. I don't know. Anyhow, it stuck with me.' He paused. 'Don't you like it?'

'And is the team named after you?' She meant *Tigers*, of course. Sawyersville High's *nom de guerre*, in full.

'No,' he said, tickled pink, 'They got that name long ago. It's just pure coincidence – that's all.' He paused. 'Lots of people wonder like you!'

Silence, again.

'Don't you like it?' he asked again.

She smiled, warmly, 'Well – if it was anyone but you – ' She paused – 'Since it's you – ' It was the warmest smile. She paused.

'You're very nice,' Tiger spoke softly, to her.

'Are you married?' she asked, quietly.

'I'm married,' he answered, very softly.

'I knew you were – '

'How are you?' gently, he asked.

'I'm alright – '

'What kind of music do you like?'

'All kinds – '

'No favorites?'

'I like to dance – I like dance music. A lot.'

'I'll bet you can dance – '

'Oh, I like to – '

'Are you a good dancer?'

'Depends who I'm dancing with – '

'How would you dance with me?'

There was silence. Her eyes never strayed from his in that silence. Could rapport be more pure? He felt sure.

'I don't know – ' she replied, finally, very softly, 'I'd have to try it – '

'We can't try it here – ' he murmured.

'I know it – '

A pause. Eternity lay beyond.

'What can we try here?' he asked, warmly.

'I don't know – '

'How are you?'

'I feel good – '

'Get up – ' he murmured – '*Lovely*.'

She sat there a moment, just gazing at him. He felt great. He knew she was warm, and thumping inside, under that bundle. She got up, slowly. He adored her.

'Walk to the door – '

She did so.

'Lock it,' he murmured.

She did so. She turned, facing him, after doing so.

'*Tiger* – ' she murmured, somewhat tremulously. She stood there.

'How are you ?' he asked, softly, across the way to her.

'A little scared – truthfully – '

'Come back here.'

She walked to her chair, slowly. His warm gaze followed her.

'That's a very nice dress,' he told her, 'I like your dress,' he informed her.

'Thank you – ' she told him.

'Let me touch it – '

'You – can touch it – '

'What can we do ?'

'I – don't know – '

'Like me touching it ?'

'Yes – I do – '

'Would you like to ?'

'*Tiger* – '

'Have you ever ?'

'Once or twice – '

'Enjoy it ?'

'It – can be nice – '

'How are you ?'

'You keep asking – '

'You're a beautiful girl – '

'Am I ?'

'You know it – '

'I think you're nice – '

'What have you got on ?'

'*Tiger* – '

'Come over here – '

'Alright – '

He pulled her gently onto his lap. He had pushed his chair back from the desk.

'*Beautiful* – ' he murmured. '*You're just beautiful* – ' he murmured, embracing her, aware of her pounding heart, the slight trembling of her warm form now, in his loving arms.

'Is it alright?' she said, quietly, her voice shaking a little bit, 'In here – I mean?'

'Perfect,' he replied, '*Don't worry.*'

Her face was turned to his, she was breathing softly, yet quickly. She closed her eyes, and kissed him. It was a luscious kiss, delicious, he loved it. His hands caressed her body, gliding over that sweet dress. They found her breasts. She moaned softly.

'When did you have your period?' he asked, gently, finally breaking the kiss, his hand inside her dress, fondling those breasts.

'*Don't worry –*' she told him – her lips seeking his, hungrily.

'O.K. –' he said, 'That's just great –' he said, pressing his mouth to hers again. His hands strayed around her back, they found the hook on her bra straps. He released it, deftly.

'You're a beauty,' he murmured, '*A beautiful beauty,*' he kept on murmuring.

'*I'm going to enjoy it –*' she began whispering to him, between kisses, so warm and luscious. She caressed him. His hands held her treasures, and played with them. Tenderly, he fondled them, and stroked the tips. She sighed, she moaned, against him. Her legs parted. His hands strayed to her legs, and up them. Gently, lovingly, he caressed her thighs, which were lovely, exquisitely, he found the moist, soft terrain. He caressed it. More and more she moaned. Her kisses were frantic. He urged her to get off him. He stood up, he held her in his arms, kissing her. She was a lovely.

'*Tiger –*' she moaned, murmuring low. She was pounding and trembling against him. He caressed the dark skin, loving it.

'How do you want it?' he murmured.

'*Up to you –*' she barely moaned.

He slipped her breasts out, he turned her around. Her back was to him. His organ touched her magnificent buttocks. He played with her breasts, a long while, and then down, ever down. He was between her thighs. Her dress was above her thighs. She was loving it, whispering and murmuring to him. He helped her slip out of her things. Last of all, the silky underthing. Neatly, he draped them over a chair. He turned her around again. She was gasping, in his arms, against him. Her hands strayed all over him, they found his organ. She trembled.

'Unbuckle my belt –' he murmured.

She did so. She helped him off with his trousers. Now, his organ was in her hands. Tenderly, she guided it, and it was wet by her, as it pressed against her. His hand encountered hers. He caressed and stroked her, his fingers gliding, parting her, gently. She moaned even more.

He had an idea, suddenly. An inspiration, actually. She had said it was up to him.

'Here – ' he murmured, leading her to his chair. He sat on it and guided her onto his lap. Gently urging her, helping her, she straddled him. Finally, marvelously, he entered her.

'*Tiger* – ' she cried, softly, with delight. She kissed him.

He murmured, between kisses, caressing and fondling her. He was deep in her. He reached the depths of her. She moved, with him. She moaned, tropically wet.

'Ever try it this way?' he asked.

'*No* – ' she gasped.

'Nice, isn't it?'

'*I love it* – '

'I thought you would.'

Her magnificent buttocks were in his hands, as she rocked with him, exquisitely. They could go on all day. He loved her. He was kissing and suckling her breasts, those brown lovelies. The tips filled his mouth, he suckled and suckled them. He thrust upward vigorously, ever upward, into Paradise, and she moved divinely, with him, crying out softly, to him. . . . She was great. *Great*. He felt great. *When had he last felt so great?* he wondered. . . .

30

Surcher had Jim Green before him. This lad was a handsome young Negro if ever there was one. He was tall and powerfully built, an athlete, without a doubt, as well he knew. He starred in basketball, as well as football, he knew. Looking at him, he reminded him very much of that other Negro athlete, the internationally renowned Cassius Clay, or Muhammad Ali, as of course he preferred to be called. Physically, only. There the resemblance ended. Jim was a quiet-spoken, apparently modest boy. In marked contrast, Surcher mused, to the ebullient former Heavyweight Champion, for whom he had a certain respect, but, in truth, did not like. He felt sorry for him. He felt he would have a tragic end. Sometimes, he even wished he would.

'How are you, Jim?' Surcher began.

'O.K.,' the lad said waiting for more.

'Well, that's fine,' Surcher said, 'I'm just going to ask you a few questions, that's all, like I did the rest – '

'Uh huh,' the boy said.

'So – ' Surcher said, 'Your name is Jim Green – you're a Senior here – and – you live with your folks at Thirty-eight Franklin Street, East Caxton – Right?' He spoke quietly, mildly, as he always did.

'That's right.'

Surcher was busy writing now.

'And your father works at the typewriter plant – is that right, Jim?'

'Right.'

'What's he do there?'

'He's a janitor.'

'Does your mother work?'

'She cleans a few offices – couple hours each day – in town.'

'Uh huh. You have brothers, Jim?'

'Three.'

'How old are they?'

'Uh – one's fifteen – other two are older than me.'

'How old are they?'

'Twenty-two, twenty-four.'

'Where do they work?'

'At the plant.'

'Doing what?'

'On the line.'

'And where does your younger brother go to school?'

'East Caxton – still.'

'Uh huh. You came here last year, is that right, Jim?'

'Right. Beginning of my Junior year.'

'Like it here?'

'Yeh, it's alright.'

'You're doing pretty well here, I hear – '

'I try.'

'You've got quite a name for yourself – I mean especially on the sports side – football, basketball – '

'I try.'

'I've seen your name in the papers lots of times – sports pages – Remember that Kitston game last year? Basketball, that is – '

The lad grinned. And nodded his head.

'How many'd you plunk in?'

'Oh – I dunno.'

'Thirty-eight?'

'Something like that.'

'That was some show.'

'D'you see the game?'

'I saw that one.'

'Uh huh.'

'I saw the football game, too – ' Surcher said.

'Kitston?'

'Yes. I'm from there, my kids all go to school there.'

'Uh huh.'

'Two TD passes you caught – right, Jim?'

'I think so.'

'That's alright.'

'Well, look who threw them. Anyhow, Tiger – Coach McDrew – deserves all the credit – He's great.'

'Pretty good coach, huh?'

'Aw, the best. Listen, he's the best. He can get anyone to play – really play – '

'Is that the secret, then?'

'I think so. Ask the guys on the team. Lot of those boys, they're nothing great. He just gets them to play their best, he gets the best out of them, all of us. That's it.'

'That's right?'

'Right.'

'Sawyersville's sure lucky to have him.'

'You're right.'

'You don't do too bad on the scholastic side either, Jim – '

'Well – I'm no brain.'

'Not bad, though. You're up there, alright.'

'Well, if I try hard maybe I can nail down a little scholarship – '

'That's right.'

'I wouldn't mind going to State.'

'There's a place.'

'Tiger went there.'

'So I heard.'

'He was a pretty good player, I heard.'

'Quarterback – right?'

'That's right.'

They fell silent. Surcher gazed at the boy.

'Got any girl friends, Jim?' he asked, casually.

'Well, a few – '

'Where? Here at the High School?'

'Uh – well, one or two – '

'Care to tell me their names?'

The boy looked him over.

'What for?'

'Oh, I don't know. Just to fill up this page.'

The boy grinned. Already, Surcher had grinned.

'Couldn't say they're really girl friends – here at the school, I mean – Just gals I kind of – hang around with, take out sometimes – know what I mean?'

'What are their names?'

'Well – there's Mona Drake – '

'Uh huh.' The Captain was writing it down.

'And – uh – Sandra Lane – '

'Uh huh.'

'That's about all.'

A pause.

'Are they both colored girls, Jim?' Surcher asked.

'That's right.'

'You don't have any white girl friends, Jim?'

'You kidding, man?'

Surcher paused, looked up from his writing.

'Not here at the school?'

'Oh *man* – '

Another pause.

'Sure about that?'

'I'm sure.'

Surcher again paused, his eyes on the boy.

'You like white girls, Jim?'

The lad's eyes hit back. He didn't answer this time.

'You don't like white girls, Jim?' Surcher tried.

No answer again.

'Which is it? You like them – or you don't like them – Jim?'

'You're kidding me.'

'No, I'm not kidding you.'

'What you trying to prove?'

'It's a routine question, Jim.'

'I'm not answering it.'

'Why not?'

'I'm not answering it.'

'You said that.'

165

'Right, I did.'

'Want to know something, Jim?'

'Just don't kid me – '

'I think you like them a little bit.'

They sat quietly, eyes on each other.

'Jim – do they call you "*Kid*"?' Surcher asked, finally. His tone was innocuous.

The boy didn't move.

'Is that your nickname Jim?'

Nothing.

'I'll tell you, Jim – Quite a few of your friends say it is.'

'What of it?' the boy said, suddenly.

There was a knock on the door. Surcher called out, 'Come in,' and Grady walked in. He said, 'Here it is,' handing over a folder to Surcher, and walking out, without as much as a glance at the boy.

Surcher opened the folder and perused its contents, for a little while. He nodded his head, finally. Then, lifted his eyes and looked at the boy.

He said, 'Know what I've got here – Kid?'

'Uh uh,' said Jim.

The Captain sat back in Proffer's comfortable chair.

'Your fingerprints, Jim,' Surcher said, 'Remember we took them when you came in? While you were waiting out there to be called?' He paused, watching the boy slowly nod. 'We took everybody's, you know – ' Once more he paused. 'I've got yours here.' He surveyed the lad, who sat quietly.

'Kid – ' the Captain went on – 'Jim – What did you think of Jill Fairbunn?'

He watched the boy as he answered, 'She was alright.'

He hadn't faltered, delivering that answer.

'Just alright?' Surcher inquired.

'I liked her.'

'I guess she was a big help to the team all the time – at all those games – '

The boy nodded.

'Talk to her much?'

'Once in a while.'

'She was a real friendly girl, wasn't she?'

'She sure was.'

'Ever try dating her up?'

Silence.

166

'She went out with your quarterback, Dink Reagan, once in a while, didn't she?'

'I guess she did.'

'A real quarterback that kid, isn't he – ?'

'He is.'

'Wouldn't she give you a date, Jim?'

The boy stared at him.

'How many times did she turn you down, Jim?'

'What's your angle?' the boy said.

Angry – *or rattled?* Surcher tried hard to tell.

'Angle?' he asked.

'What are you driving at, man?'

'Listen, did you ask her?'

'What if I did?'

'What was her answer?'

'You got something on me?'

'Like what, Kid?'

More silence. Surcher's eyes remained on the lad.

'She said maybe,' Jim said.

'Did she, Jim?'

'That's right. She did.'

'And what else did she say?'

Again, silence. The boy kept on looking at him.

Surcher said, quietly, 'That was a cockteasing answer, wasn't it, Jim?'

'She was no cockteaser, man.'

'Wasn't she?'

'No, man.'

'What was she?'

'What you after?'

Silence. Only.

Now Surcher said, quietly, as always, 'What else did she say, Jim?'

The boy answered, 'She said she'd like to. But it would be pretty hard to. Pretty rough on her – if she did.' He paused. 'You know how it is.'

Surcher nodded, barely.

'You really liked that girl, didn't you, Jim?' he asked, in his way.

'She was great.'

'I think you really were stuck on that girl – Jim.'

No answer.

'Ever try any other way to get a date?'

'Like what way?' asked the lad.

'Oh – I dunno. Phoning her up.' He paused. 'Writing her a note – maybe.' Surcher stopped.

No answer. Surcher waited patiently.

At last, the boy said, 'What's up, man?', his eyes on the Captain.

Surcher lifted something out of the folder. It was the letter.

'Jim, listen – ' Surcher said, holding it up for the lad, 'ever seen this little letter before?'

He watched the boy studying it. He waited to hear something. But the boy said nothing.

'Did you write that?' Surcher asked, very quietly.

No answer.

'Jim, guess what – ' Surcher said, 'I think you did.' He paused. 'I'd put all the gold in Fort Knox that you did.' Again he paused. 'Know why?' A pause. 'Your prints. Your prints were on it, Jim.'

'My fingerprints?' the boy said.

'Right.'

The boy moved around a little bit in his chair. Surcher's eyes stayed right on him. He still held the letter. The brief little letter He had plenty of copies of it.

'Did you write it, Jim?'

The boy said 'Captain, I better get hold of a lawyer.'

'A *lawyer*?' Surcher said. 'What for, Jim?'

'I smell a frame.'

'A *frame*?'

'Quit kidding me.'

'Did you, Jim?'

'You know I did.'

'That's all I asked.'

Silence. Surcher placed the letter back in the folder. He sat back, quietly, observing the lad. In the outside office, Miss Craymire's domain, a phone just could be heard, ringing. It sounded far, far away. It stopped, finally.

'O.K. if I go now?' the boy said, after a few minutes had passed.

'You want to go? No kidding, Jim?' Surcher said.

'Yeh, I do.'

'Well, I can't stop you.' He paused. 'But I'll tell you what – I think we have a few more things to talk about.'

'Like what ?'

'Well – take for instance – ' And the Captain leaned forward slightly, 'Take for instance, Jim – ' he said – 'Just exactly where were you during Assembly yesterday morning ?'

The boy's eyes dug holes in him.

'Jim ?'

'*In Assembly, man.*'

'Is that right ?'

'Damn right it's right.'

'Where were you sitting ?'

'With my home room – where I always sit.'

'Is that right ?'

'*Right.*'

'Next to who ?'

'Hell – Dink – uh – Dink Reagan, yeh – and – Lennie Almot – for two – '

'Were you between those two ?'

'Yeh – I was.'

'Sure you were ?'

'Well ask them, I don't care.'

'What's the difference if you were ?'

'That's what I'd like to know!'

'You think I'm nuts ?'

'You're on the wrong trail.'

'Know what your Home Room Teacher said ?'

'Crispwell ?'

'That's the one.'

'What'd he say ?'

Surcher answered carefully, laying on each word, 'He wasn't sure.'

'*Not sure ?* Hell, ask Dink! Ask Lennie! Ask anyone!'

'I will – I'm only telling you what Mr Crispwell said – '

'That guy's nuts!'

'He might be.'

'I was there.'

'What if you were ?'

'Listen, say what you wanta say – '

'What would I have to say ?'

'Aw – I'm going, man.'

The boy got up from his chair. He walked to the door.

'Jim – '

Surcher calmly said. . . .

31

'Mmmmmm – ' Mona moaned '*Ohhhh* – '

Tiger couldn't agree more, and he told her so, murmuring to her. What a great kid. What a girl. What a hon bun. He kissed her again and again, gratefully. What a throbbing girl. What a reward. Long months patiently thinking of her, watching her, wondering about her. Marvelous reward. Triumphantly, gloriously, mutually – patience's reward. He viewed the situation in bliss, in all its exquisite glory. Warm. She was so warm. On his lap, still. Tiny pulsations still. He loved the warmth, the last tiny pulsations of bliss. The embers of that great bliss. What bliss. How deep had he probed? Embracing her, giving her face whisper kisses, Tiger wondered that. He thought of her stars. He would be generous and how. Two at least. Tiger mused. With a kiss.

'You liked that?' he murmured low.

'*Ohhhhh* – '

'I loved it, hon – '

'Mmmmmmm – '

'Deep enough?'

'Ohh – Were you deep – ' She kissed him.

'Like that way?'

'It's *quite* a way – '

'It's a way – '

'Hope I don't have a *baby* – '

'Not much chance – '

'Hope I don't – '

'You won't – ' He kissed her again. They gave little kisses to one another's lips. 'Next time – ' he said, 'we'll try another way – ' he said – 'and – I'll give you a little something – to take – ' The little kisses flew – 'You take them like I say – then – everything – *will be O.K.*' She sighed, she moaned. 'O.K.?' She nodded her head. '*No worries no more.*'

'Tiger – Ohhhh – ' She embraced him.

She was all set again, Tiger couldn't help note, amazed, almost, but, as always, open-minded, and ready for all things. He stirred, taking her warm, wet lips in full form. *What lips. What marvelous lips.* Her gorgeous tongue probed –

'*Let's go on the floor –* '

He murmured low. . . .

32

'I didn't touch her!' shouted the boy, whirling around to face Surcher, who sat absolutely unruffled, in that comfortable chair.

'Who said you did?' he asked, calmly.

'Well quit screwing around – ' the boy said.

'Who's screwing around, Jim?'

'You are.'

'Jim – listen – ' Surcher said, quietly, calmly, as ever, 'Sit down, let's talk awhile – '

'What's there to talk about?'

'Well – Jim – we've got a problem – ' Surcher said, 'Quite a problem – ' he also said – 'Look at it – Somebody, somewhere around here, probably yesterday morning, probably during Assembly, we think, killed that girl. You know that.' He paused. 'This guy is *running around*, somewhere, we think *around here*.' He paused again. 'See the problem?'

'I'm not that guy.'

'Did I say you were?'

'You don't have to, man.'

'Jim – put yourself in my shoes – '

'You talked to the others only ten minutes – maybe.'

'Did they write the letter?'

The boy stood still. Then, he moved a few steps toward Surcher.

'That letter can't prove a thing,' he said, quietly. 'You can't pin this on me.'

'I don't want to, my boy,' Surcher said, in all sincerity, 'I just want to find the guy.'

'I don't know about that.'

'You'll have to believe that.'

'Why should I?'

'Well what good would it do?'

171

'Make a hero out of you.'

'Are you kidding? A monkey, you mean.'

There was silence. The boy stood there.

'Sit down, Jim,' Surcher said.

Slowly, the boy did so.

'Now,' Surcher said, leaning forward slightly, over his note-pad, 'Let's start from the beginning again – '

33

'*Tiger!*' Mona moaned, beside herself, once more.

'Aren't you a hon – '

'*Ohhh – what fun – *'

'You bun – '

It had been even more spectacular on the floor, Tiger mused, finally withdrawing from her. She continued to sigh and moan, she held him close. It had been superb, without a doubt, and he was more than ever in favor of a free and complete mixing of the races, all the races, particularly white and colored. *Particularly*, Tiger mused, feeling her warm form pressed close. That marvel-ous form. Milk chocolate, really, that's it. What a form. He perused and admired her form, he fondled her marvelous orbs, cupping them in his hands. The uplift was a sight to behold, a gift of the gods, he tried to think just who had more. It was much more than he had bargained for. A class of its own. The sweet tips sang. Truly they sang. Forever more. He thought of those two stars. Was he being generous enough?

'How long can we stay?' the girl said, cuddled on his shoulder. She murmured low.

He was impressed. He thought: *More than two. Definitely.*

'Better break fairly soon,' he murmured, 'Fairly soon – Honey.'

'*Mmmm – *' said the girl, '*Mmmmm – *' she moaned.

'I feel the same,' Tiger said, helping her up.

'Look at me,' Mona said.

Tiger did, grinning, admiring her naked form.

'You're a beauty. You're beautifully formed. I could pet you all day. Know that?' he murmured.

She snuggled up in his arms, making soft little sounds, rubbing herself exquisitely, against him. Tiger chuckled, and urged her away from him.

'No more for now.'

'*You're a tiger you are –* '

'Ah ha – save some for next time – '

'When will that be?'

'Soon as I can.'

'Let me know?'

'Don't worry – I'll let you know.'

She was fondling his love tool again. Gently, Tiger drew away. Without a doubt, it could go on all day.

'Let's get dressed,' he said, tenderly.

'You're spilling out of me – '

Tiger grinned, nodded at her.

'There's a box of Kleenex over there.'

'Help me get dressed.'

He did just that, in gradual steps, giving her a little kiss, a nip, a caress, now and again. She loved that.

Finally, they were both dressed. She was smiling happily, dreamily, at him. She looked great in her dress.

'Well – ' she said, 'What's the result of my test?'

Tiger grinned, she was a good-humored lass. A touch of wit, no less.

'We'll discuss that next time,' he said.

'Promise that?'

'More than that.'

'I hope I passed.'

Cuddling her, Tiger said, 'Now look – let's just keep this our own little secret – O.K.?'

'But *O.K.* – ' she said, her hands gliding downward again.

'Uh uh – and look – Here's this little bottle for you – '

She looked at the bottle he held. She smiled. She took it from him.

'See, it tells you on there how to take – '

She nodded, gave him a little kiss.

'The little darlings work wonders – no kidding, hon – '

'Are they The Pill?' Mona asked.

'That's right.'

'That's *wonderful!*' she said.

'I think they're great. Just do as it says on the bottle. O.K.?'

'O.K.'

173

'Promise?'

'Sure I do.'

'That's the way. Then – no problems. Only fun.'

'*Let me kiss you – Mmmmmm –* '

'Let me know – when you run low – '

'I want *one* little kiss – *Whitey* – ' she murmured.

Tiger chuckled.

'You're some lovely honey,' he said, giving her a little peck, loving those lips.

'See you soon.'

'How do I look?'

'Good as new.'

She laughed her soft little laugh, he walked her to the door.

'*Bye – for now –* ' she murmured to him.

'Be good – ' he grinned at her.

She left.

Tiger, feeling very good, returned to his desk. . . .

34

'Jim – ' Surcher said, in his quiet way, 'What I'm trying to do is get at the facts. In other words, the truth. I'm not after you.' He paused, observing the lad. 'If you didn't harm that girl, there's nothing for you to worry about. Not a thing. Believe me.' Again he paused. 'That's a fact.'

They sat silently.

The Captain shifted around in Proffer's chair. He put his feet on one of the desk drawers, which he had slightly pulled out. His hands were linked across his stomach.

'See, Jim – or Kid – I'll call you Jim – The real problem here, as far as you're concerned, is that note.' He paused. 'I mean, *both* notes – the one you wrote to Jill, with your prints all over it, and – the one that was pinned to her.' He paused, keeping his eyes on Jim. '*By somebody*.' He paused again. 'I guess you heard about that.'

The boy nodded, 'Yeh, I did.' Then he said, 'Whose prints were on it?'

Surcher waited before dealing with that. He was impressed

with the shrewdness of the lad. He was no dumb kid. He wasn't, in truth, sure about the boy. It could – or couldn't be. He was only maneuvering now, trying to find out. And he wasn't going to let himself be outfoxed. Prints or no prints he could be his man. So he played his cards as close as he could, answering now.

'Whose do you think, Jim?'

'Not mine, man.'

Surcher watched the lad.

'That would look pretty bad.'

'Were they?' the boy asked.

'Jim – why do you think you're in here with me so long?' Surcher tried.

'*The hell they were*,' the boy said.

'Did you wipe them off?'

'You make me laugh!'

'But what if you didn't get them all off?'

'What a load of crap!'

Surcher sat quietly, unruffled, as ever. He had all the time in the world. If no more.

He asked, finally, 'Is there football practice tonight, Jim?'

'There is.'

Surcher moved from his comfortable position and leaned forward on the desk. He looked at the folder's contents again. He made a few notes on his pad. He finally spoke but didn't look up at the lad.

'You might have to miss it – Jim.'

He said.

35

Ponce was in Trigonometry class, and he was feeling bad. If there was anything by itself, not to mention everything else, it was Trigonometry that could make him feel bad. He had to take it, for it was part of the Academic course, of course, and Mummer was the teacher. He could never hope to get into State if he didn't pass it, either. Or anywhere, for that matter, that he knew of. He had always had a pretty rough time with Mathematics, especially that end comprising Algebra, Geometry, and Trigonometry. Was it a coincidence they were all taught by Mummer? Could he have made out better if the teacher had been another? He wondered. He often wondered. When he got to college, maybe, he would know. He knew he would have to take Algebra, his first year. At the moment, he was in anguish. That queer Mummer was babbling away up there – about something. Ponce was baffled. He couldn't latch on to it. How had he ever got through Geometry? Algebra? True, he had just scraped through, but in Geometry, especially, he knew *nothing*. From time to time, even now, looking back on it, he wondered just what it was all about. He had once discussed his Mathematics problem with Tiger. He had been very understanding, in sum telling Ponce it didn't matter. His talents lay elsewhere. Ponce knew it. *Did Mummer?* Would that creep give him just one more break now? *Especially now?* he thought, forlornly. He tried hard, he studied, he listened. Sometimes, he was sure he was just about to break through that solid wall and find himself on the other side, in the golden sunlight, basking and at last understanding the gibberish that was Trigonometry. Then, suddenly, the wall held, and he was back where he was, *Nowhere*. That was the moment of darkest despair, always. For then he felt he never would, no matter what he did. It just wasn't in him. Definitely, he would have to see Tiger again about it. For somehow, he had to get through this course. It didn't particularly matter to him how he did – short of letting Mummer blow him. There, absolutely, he called a halt, and how he did. He'd rather die first. Sighing, he looked at Mona Drake, in the seat alongside him. She seemed to know what was going on. She seemed with it. She followed Mummer's incomprehensible patter without a tremor. The rows and rows and columns of utterly mysterious figures apparently meant something to her. In fact, right now, she looked dreamy-eyed, almost in love with it. How could that be? Ponce was mystified. He stared at her. Maybe he could get her to help him with it. He wondered about that. He would ask her. She was a dark beauty, without a doubt of it. She was warm, just the sort of warmth that could help him get it. That queer Mummer – he could forget him. Ponce felt resentful. What the hell was it all in aid of, anyhow? Was he going to be a stupid engineer or something? Why did he need it? Why did the colleges require it? He smoldered over it, knowing there was little he could probably do about it – except try and get through it. Definitely, he would approach Mona. She had come to class a few minutes late. She had been tied up in the Guidance/Counseling office, with Tiger, she had explained. Was he testing her?

What test had he sprung on her? Ponce wondered. He would ask her. That damn Mummer. If he was anything but what he was Ponce could have a heart-to-heart talk with him, about the thing. He might get that break. As it was – *a talk with him*. Suddenly, Ponce got an idea. What if he cornered him – unless he gave him a break? For a moment or two, Ponce was excited about the idea. It sounded great! Poetic justice – almost! But then – he knew it was something he couldn't do. Besides, it was stupid. It just wouldn't do. Again, he was blue. Mona, Tiger – somehow, between them, he'd make it through. What a gorgeous girl she was though. Ponce mused about her, that curvaceous, gorgeous colored girl. What a girl. He thought of Jill. Suddenly, hitting rock bottom again, he saw that poor girl. He missed her, he felt an empty spot alright, without her around. *When was the funeral?* Saturday, he had heard. Practically the whole school would be there. He knew. He didn't look forward to being there. Funerals were bad, this one was appallingly bad, he'd never get over it. The mere thought made him feel numb, and heavy, so heavy – and a little sick. Would he have to look at her – in the coffin? Would he have to do *that*? He felt scared, on top of everything else. He was right under the floorboards, with that. 'Page one-sixteen – ' Mummer said, and Ponce flipped to that page, woodenly. *Tonight – football practice.* And Ponce felt better. He had already passed the word on to most of the boys, after Assembly, where Tiger had told him. *And next period – Eng. Lit.!* Now, Ponce soared. He saw Miss Smith. He was way, way above those floorboards. There were only ten minutes to go. He looked up at Mummer. He would have to make a move soon about him. He couldn't walk around forever with that on his mind, definitely. If Surcher didn't soon crack the case – He looked around the room. There was Jeannie Bonni. That cutie. Sally Swink. What a sweetie. They were both trying hard to follow what was going on, but the fog was thick. He could see it almost enveloping them. He grinned, to himself, knowing only too well what they felt. He saw their breasts outlined under their clothes. They were both stacked. *Was that the tips?* Jeannie had on a cute yellow blouse. Pale yellow. Sally a pink sweater. A very light pink. It looked great on her. Her breasts pointed right out at the world. Ponce stared at them, imagining the glory of fondling them, or at least *seeing* them, *bared*. He was growing warm. He saw Peggy Linski. He saw his Trig book. . . .

36

Tiger, in his office, was thoughtfully perusing his list and making little amendments, here and there. He mused, lovingly, doing it all with great care. His interoffice phone buzzed and he picked it up, hoping it wouldn't be Hetty to say she just couldn't come. He was looking forward to seeing her, so much. She would make his day. Sometimes she did cancel out, involved as she managed to get from time to time, in that library, between the stacks. He prayed.

'Hello – ?' he said, in his gentle way.

'Mike – ' the voice said.

It was Proffer – again. Ironically enough, he was relieved.

'Listen, I'm sorry to bother you, boy – '

'That's O.K.'

'I just wanted to tell you – ' Tiger heard the banal voice, dropping down to a low, confidential tone, 'This Surcher – ' He held.

'Yeh?' Tiger urged, completing the artwork beside Mona's name.

'He's had the colored kids down to see him this morning, you know – '

'I know – '

It was an extra half-star, in fact, she wound up with.

'Well – ' Proffer's voice went very low, 'He's had Jim Green in there with him for a hell of a long time now – '

'How long?'

'Over an hour – at least – '

Tiger had put the pencil down. His forehead wore a distinct frown.

'Where you calling from, Harry?' he asked.

'The Teachers' Room – '

'Uh huh.'

Tiger checked his watch. Any minute, the Librarian was due.

'Well – what can we do?'

'Nothing – I guess – ' Proffer said.

'Don't worry about it,' Tiger said.

'I was *surprised* – '

'And so am I – ' Tiger paused. He was. 'But don't jump to

conclusions – It may mean nothing – ' He paused. 'Nothing at all.' He hoped.

'It's going to raise *Holy Hell* – '

'Wait awhile – '

'I just have that feeling – Wow – '

'Harry – just wait awhile – '

'I thought things had been going too well! Boy, that School Board's gonna clobber us! Did I tell you the talk at the Legion last night ?'

Tiger tried hard to imagine the lofty heights it had reached. It staggered his efforts.

'Uh uh, Harry,' he said to the prospective TV/Radio retail outlet.

'Well – let me tell you – you'd be *amazed* at the anticolored feeling it's generated.'

'Generated ?' Tiger couldn't help venture, however aware it would bounce right off Proffer.

'And that was before this development – ' the banal voice went on in his ear.

'What development ?'

'Well – Jim Green, I mean – '

'Listen, it's not yet a development – '

'Yeh, but – listen – '

'Is it ?'

'O.K. It isn't – ' and – 'I know how you feel – '

Tiger just had to smile at that.

'You'll just have to wait and see – Harry boy – '

'Right – we'll see – ' Proffer said.

Tiger glanced at his watch again.

'Well, Harry – We'll see – Sit tight and see.'

'I'll keep right on top of things, Mike – I'll contact you as soon as anything breaks – Be there ?'

'Until noon.'

'O.K., boy.'

And he hung up.

Tiger sat back in his chair. He was hurt. Was Surcher really chasing Jim Green ? How had he got *so* fogged ? Was *he* a Bircher too ? Dumbhead Proffer had sounded happy about it, underneath it all. He pictured him last night, at the Legion, assuring them that *he* had never wanted to bring that bunch in. The wizard. The pure dismal wizard. Well, luckily, the whole town wasn't that way. So, even if something was up – if the boy *was* a suspect

– Tiger winced, dumbfounded now at Surcher's blunder – or, more precisely, apparent blunder. For, as he had told Proffer – *Proffer!* The Wonder, Sawyersville's own Wonder. Tiger ruminated, contemplating an even earlier retirement, for the wonder. He sighed, not exactly chipper. He would have to check with Surcher. He shook his head, slowly. He certainly was disappointed in him.

Hetty Nectar walked in.

She looked superb – as usual.

'Hi – ' she greeted him.

'Well Hi – '

'Am I late?'

'Never.'

'Whew! What a day! Brother!'

She sat down on a chair, near the desk.

'Rough one?'

'Listen – *Just Imagine* – Those detectives have been around me all morning – more or less. Questions, questions, about a whole sheaf of pupils' reading habits – *and* other habits. *Imagine!*'

Tiger nodded, imagining.

'What an awful affair!' she said to him, pulling out a cigarette. 'How can anything be the same again?'

Tiger nodded.

'You said it.'

'Well, how are you?' she queried.

'Not too bad.'

'Busy?'

'I try to be.'

'*You one-man show.*'

Her eyes twinkled. Tiger always loved the way her eyes twinkled. They made his want to twinkle. Was it the Irish in her? Her personality was exuberant. She was a positive creature. The life force registered in the highest reaches, it bubbled over in her. He had rarely encountered such a positive person. She had the fiercest grip on life. His feelings toward her were utterly positive. Would this delightfully positive redheaded creature ever wind up with a husband? Already she was pushing twenty-four, wasn't she? Didn't she want one? Certainly, he knew quite a few who would want her. Would she want them? Maybe – all of them. He grinned, within. Certainly, she could handle them. She had a catalog with her. She wore a pretty fawn skirt, a pretty open-necked blouse, a soft cardigan. Cashmere? It was something. It looked very soft. Tiger wondered. It went so well with her hair. Perfect. Tiger wished he could touch it.

'Don't you look pretty.'

'Thank you! *Tiger*.'

'How's everything?'

'I miss you.'

'You know how it is.'

She crossed her legs. Tiger admired them. Who was the genius responsible for stockings? Once again, for the hundredth time at least, he found himself wondering that. What legs she had for those stockings! He kept on admiring them.

'Well,' Tiger said, 'What have you got for me?'

Hetty smiled. He could have grinned. He studied the warm, yet partly mischievous smile on her. The mixture was fascinating. Irresistible. He grinned. 'Well –' she said, plunking the catalog on the desk, 'Here's the list.' She paused. 'Formidable.' She opened the catalog, to a certain section.

Tiger took a look at it. Page after page of new Guidance/Counseling/Career stuff. Just published. Tiger grinned.

'They really churn it out, don't they?' he said.

'Don't they! It's getting big as a whale – each month it's bigger – it's crowding other fields out, Tiger, I'm telling you,' she said.

'Um Hmm,' he said.

'How's Hilda?' she said.

'Same as ever.'

'So it's a problem. I wouldn't know where to start.'

'Good thing you came to me.'

'Don't they have anything else to do with their time?'

'Well, it's the way up, you see –'

'Amazing, isn't it?'

'Wait till computers take over –'

She laughed, in that way he just loved, 'I'll just give up then – *period*.'

'Can't see you doing that.' He grinned again.

'Look –' she said, placing a loving finger on the page. Tiger admired the nail, an intriguing pink, well cared for, she had lovely white hands, warm, too, *the absolute temporary crazy utterly transient fleeting nature of things*, Tiger mused, out of the blue, 'Look at this one –' she said, '*The Average Response Pattern And The Perpendicular Theory Of Rest*,' she read out, from the page, looking at him afterward, befuddled and mis-

chievous, those bright big blue eyes right on his. He loved her
lipstick.

'Sounds great, doesn't it?' he said.

'J. Kimona –' Hetty read, 'Know him?'

'Never heard of him.'

'I mean, just what are they getting at?'

'Guess.'

'Ha Ha! Yes.'

'We *need* rest.'

'*Tiger*, honestly –'

'How's the best?'

'Are you stuck with her?' she asked, softly.

'Looks that way.'

'How can you take it?'

'I try my best.'

'I know you do.'

'You help a lot.'

'Ah, that's sweet of you,' she said, warmly, laying her hand on
his.

'It probably has something to do with computers – to tell the
truth –' Tiger told her.

'I'll bet it does,' she said, stroking his hand. Tiger loved her
warm, soft hand.

'I'll tell you one book I'd really like you to get for me –' he
said, telling her about Eble's gem. She nodded, jotted it down.
Her hand came back.

'I'd like to read it,' she told him, 'I think I'll order two copies.'
He nodded assent.

'It sounds great – let me tell you.'

'Whose hands are like mine?' she murmured now.

'Nobody's.'

'*Ah – sweet –*' she murmured, warmly, to him.

Tiger grinned, and nodded, and started patting her hands.

'I do all I can to keep this teaching-machine and Programmed
Instruction and computer racket down to a minimum,' he told
her, speaking low, 'You know that –' She nodded, her eyes were
on him, tender and warm, as she listened to him, 'But those guys
are shrewd little operators, let me tell you. They go and work on
the individual School Board members, maybe even offer a cut, I
don't know. That's the latest. Once they sell them, the fight's
harder than ever. See?' He paused, caressing her lovely, slender

arm. 'They don't bother at all coming to see me or Proffer any-more – How about that?'

'What a racket – ' she murmured.

'We'll beat them,' he told her, 'I get along pretty well with the Board, due to factors, the team, other factors. He grinned, 'At least the key members, I mean – ' He was up to her elbow now, caressing tenderly, just inside. She gave a sigh.

'I'm glad of that – '

'How are you?'

'*I love you – *'

'How's everything?'

'*You'll see – *'

'Will I see?'

'*Always – *'

'Let's check the catalog.'

Tiger's favorite Librarian came around to his side of the desk. She laid her hand on the catalog. Tiger glanced admiringly at her red hair. He loved her fragrance.

'Here's one – ' she said, softly, '*I locked the door, my love – *' Tiger nodded. '*Patriotism and Counseling – *' she read. 'P. T. Johnson – ' she said.

'Pat Johnson!' Tiger grinned – 'I know him.'

'We'll get it – '

'Sure, get it – '

'But what's Patriotism got to do with Counseling?' she asked, touching his face.

'Don't sell it short – ' he murmured, 'Check his namesake – ' he also murmured, touching her lovely soft hair, 'What have you got on?' he murmured now, kissing her sweet nose.

'Just cologne – ' she murmured, 'Like it?'

'Love it.'

'Like my lipstick?'

'Gorgeous color.'

She smiled warmly, she brushed her lips against his.

'*You angel – *' she said.

'I try – ' he said.

'*Touch my breasts – *'

He did so. He found them free.

She laughed, very softly, in his ear.

'That's terrific,' he said, 'Really terrific,' he also said, fondling those warm, full, joyful things.

'What about Patriotism?' she said, kissing little kisses all around his ear.

'It has its place,' he murmured to her, loving those soft breasts, stroking their tips now, gently, 'There's nothing perfect in the world – ' he said, 'Except you, of course – ' he also said, as she slipped her arms about him, and looked at him, her sweet warm breath in his face, 'You – of course – ' he reiterated – 'But – there's a lot to be said for the USA – ' He kissed her eyes. What an exquisitely feminine creature she was. Tiger idolized her. He could play all day with her. Time permitting. *Time, time.* The master of all destinies. It was Tiger's archenemy. 'Imperfect as it is – in many ways – ' he said, gliding his right hand down her side, reaching her flanks, caressing them, tenderly, and around the back. She would have purred, he knew, if she could. Her breath was a purr, stirring him, more. Tenderly, he caressed. 'No intelligent person would deny it's imperfect – ' he murmured, continuing to brush her ear with his lips, dozens of little kisses falling there, as her eyes closed, and she moaned, 'But of all the many many imperfect countries in the world – and they're all imperfect, of course – I, personally, prefer this one – ' he said, 'In many ways,' he also said, gently slipping his hand under her skirt, and upward, as she let him glide, ever upward, and sighed, making way for his hand – 'England, for instance – ' he went on, murmuring low, 'I wouldn't live in a class-ridden place like that – for anything – anything – What a rotten setup they have – and – as far as I can see – always will have – that's their trouble – that's why they're always in trouble – who's got a chance?' He kissed her lips, which were moist, and warm, and opening for him. His hand reached silken skin, just above her stockings now. He stroked and caressed, quite awhile, before venturing farther on. She kissed beautifully, giving all to him. He loved her. He surfaced for air. 'It's in the Educational area of course that the worst injustices are perpetrated there – ' he told her, soft and low – 'In that country – ' he said, as she licked his lips, gently, her warm, sweet tongue gliding tenderly, 'They separate the kids with a vengeance, way back there, right at the beginning – almost – ' He gave her tongue a little nip, and she gave a little cry, and a quiver – 'The poor kids of the community get a slum education, except those with the *very highest* intelligence – *and* drive – However, if the family has dough – or is titled – any of *their* dumbheads can get the best education – ' She sighed, in his arms – as he went on – 'A rotten setup – ' He kissed her tongue, letting it slide into him. He kissed her, fully. They clung a long time. They surfaced, finally – 'Very few get to college – ' he went on – 'The so-called "intellectual elite" – and the rich, of course – only – ' he murmured, stroking her, his right hand lovingly on its goal, as she moaned softly, in his arms – 'Result – ' he said – 'A moronic country.' He paused – 'An uneducated mass of class-ridden *and* dominated nincompoops. No kidding – ' he said – 'What a country.' She whispered something, he couldn't make out what it was, she continued moaning. He went on, murmuring – 'Then all the rest – ' He paused, his hand stroking Paradise – 'Germany – just marking time until the next Nazi Lunacy – or whatever they'll choose to call it then – ' He paused – 'France, Italy – Russia – ' he murmured – 'All of them – ' He kept on murmuring – 'Not to mention South America – ' He paused – '*And the Far East* – '

'*God The Far East!*' Hetty cried out, softly, and moaning, holding so close to him.

Tiger unbuttoned her blouse. He bared the white, soft treasure breasts. His breath was taken away. He kissed them. He buried his head in them. She caressed him, sighing, murmuring. He suckled her tips –

'*Where?*' he said, tenderly.

'*Anywhere* – ' she gasped, beside herself.

Her skirt was up to her hips. He admired her thighs, he stroked them, gently, just below that moist zone of Paradise. She moaned. . . . He picked her up. . . .

She was on her back, her knees raised, on Tiger's ample and comfortable office couch, where he had carried her. He murmured to her all the while. His head was between her thighs, which he lavished with marvelous kisses, gradually approaching the drenched golden rise. She moaned ever more, and moved, murmuring his name, over and over, she caressed his head. . . . He reached the rise. . . . She cried out, finally, urging him upon her. . . . He complied. . . . She moaned and cried. . . . His phallus throbbed, poised on the wet edges of life. . . .

37

Word had already started making fairly good progress around the school regarding Jim Green and his long session with the State

Police when Ponce finally emerged from the Long Agony of Trigonometry class – blank, as usual. It was when Ponce hit the hallway just outside the classroom that he first heard about it. Amid that swarm of fellow students, it was Kathy Burns, of all kids, who broke the news to him. She was a good pal of his, as a matter of fact, actually living just two doors away from him on Britfield Avenue, that shade-tree-lined thoroughfare. She was a friend of the family, of course, a cute kid in her sophomore year. She had a turned up nose. She was small, but neat, really sweet. Ponce was fond of her, she was like his sister, almost. Or at least a close cousin. It was that way. He literally bumped into her, in that babble and swarm.

'Whooops!' she cried out – 'Ponce! I'm sorry!'

He gazed at that cute kid. She was well formed. Two soft mounds stuck out at the world. He certainly was fond of her. He grinned at her.

'Gosh, I'm sorry, Kathy – '

'Oh it was my fault – I'm sorry, Ponce!'

'What class you going to?'

'Algebra,' she said, wrinkling up her nose.

He grinned again, he knew how she felt. He wrinkled up his nose too. They both laughed.

'Hear about Jim Green?' said the little lass. Her cute face was staring up at him. Ponce jumped a little, he started guessing already, as was his way.

'What?' he asked her, anyway.

She came closer, in the melee.

'He's been in with the State Police a *long* long time,' she informed him, confidentially.

'Oh yeh?' Ponce said, fully rattled.

'Do they think *he* did it?' the girl asked.

'Gosh I don't know,' Ponce answered.

'I thought he was *awfully* nice,' she confided in him.

'He is,' Ponce agreed.

'I hope they're not hurting him – in any way!'

'Aw, they can't hurt him, Kath – ' Ponce said.

'Can't they?'

'Well – thanks for telling me – ' Ponce now said, sensing the time to break it off, 'I gotta run now – Lit. class – ' he also said, turning, 'So long, Kath – see you – say hello to your mom for me – '

'O.K., Ponce. Bye. Probably be seeing you – '

He disappeared in the crowd, bumping along in it down the hallway, on his way to his favorite class.

'Hey boy – ' Dean Morgan, suddenly beside him, greeted him.

'Say, Dean –' Ponce answered him.

'Hear about Jim ?'

'Yeh, I heard it.'

'Sure hope it isn't him!'

'Aw, it wasn't – '

'Don't think so ?'

'Heck no.'

Ponce pushed on, really rattled, wondering just what was developing down there, in Proffer's office, no doubt. He was making up his mind, then and there, to break out of his shell, *what the hell*, and tell all – to Surcher. But he was going to wait awhile, to see just what developed – with Jim Green. He vowed that if they took him in, he would move, but fast. Or as fast as he could. Certainly. He shuddered. Could it be true, though ? Could it ? *Jim ?* How could it ? He was the tops, he was all there, he wasn't even a *minor* nut case. Ponce knew full well the culprit was far, far out there, a first-class kookeroo, no doubt of it. What were they trying to do ? He still looked forward to Eng. Lit. class, of course, but he would be glad, for the first time in his life probably, when it was all over. He also would be glad to talk with Miss Smith – about everything. If he got the chance. What would happen ? His buddies and friends passed him by the dozen, they greeted him, but he hardly saw them. If he stopped and talked with them, however briefly, he knew what they would have to say, there was only one topic now, wasn't there, and he didn't feel like hearing it again. *That damn Mummer !* He pictured himself confronting Surcher – *no – Tiger.* He would see Tiger. He would hold fire of course until he knew what exactly was happening – but then – no delays any longer. He thought of Miss Smith. Last night he had had about a hundred dreams at least – all of her. In one she was purring. It had started out with Peppy walking into the room, purring. Then, there was Miss Smith, sitting on the bed, looking at him, reaching out her hand to him – and purring. He thought of football practice. What kind of a practice would it be tonight, he wondered ? If Jim wasn't there – especially! What would Tiger do ? Ponce wondered and worried, on top of everything else, a whole series of key plays was built around that Right End. He was getting close to his classroom. *His dream's room.* There was Miss Nectar, the red-headed Librarian, just coming out of Tiger's office. Ponce had a little bit of a crush on her too – though of course nothing like what he felt for Miss Smith. She was carrying something, a thick magazine, or book, or something. Maybe a catalog. She looked glowing. That's the only word Ponce could think of at that moment to describe her, his eyes falling on her. She was sure nice. What eyes. What a honey. He began to feel all warm inside, watching her. Next to Miss Smith, she was the only other faculty member who really gave him the hots, without a doubt of it. The *love hots*, and no doubt about it. She would be his number-one dream – if Miss Smith wasn't handy.

'Hello, Miss Nectar – ' he greeted her, shyly, as she passed near him. His heart was thumping.

She looked up, and smiled, though she was somewhat pre-occupied – Ponce could tell. He heard suddenly in his head the verse of one of those sometimes appealing songs the pop groups sang, was it *The Cleaners* – 'What The World Needs Now Is Love, Sweet Love . . .' And so on.

'Why hello, Ponce – ' she said to him, singing it out, clearly pleased to see the lad. He knew she was fond of him.

She was gone. He walked on, for obviously they both had things to do. Maybe later, in his Study Period, he could drop into the Library and have a talk with her. It was always nice talking with her. She was up on everything. Not only was the Library one of his favorite retreats, but he learned a lot from her.

As he got nearer to his Lit. class, there was one thing Ponce was really very grateful for: No one, so far, had made any fun out of his screaming run. He was more than grateful for it. He began to hope he might even get away with it. He kept his fingers crossed, hoping hard, feeling ashamed of it, and aware of the tactical brilliance of it. . . . *So far*. Because he was only so far. Time would tell. He was at the door of Miss Smith's classroom. Already, he thought he had caught the scent. His heart started jumping on top of the thumping Miss Nectar had triggered off. He almost didn't make it any farther, thinking of confronting Miss Smith. Today, sure as hell, he vowed, he would control himself. He would put up the stiffest fight ever heard of – he didn't feel like visiting that lavatory again – *under any circumstances* . . . for one thing. Besides, *he was more than in love with her*. Last night, between them, something powerful, and beautiful had sprung up. He had to control himself. No more of that kid stuff. It was with her, he knew, that he had to prove himself. If nothing had happened last night, it was his own fault. Did he expect her to rape him? Ponce felt embarrassed, even thinking that. It had no place in the thing. His view, his image – of everything. He saw Yvonne Mellish, and Rochelle, entering the classroom. They smiled at him. Somehow, he smiled back. He followed them. . . .

38

After having spent most of the morning with Jim Green, employing just about every subtle device he could muster, Surcher was still nowhere. It could be – and it couldn't. The boy puzzled him. If he were the one, he was a tough nut and a half, and no doubt of it, shrewd way beyond his years, on top of it. On balance, things in Surcher's mind were evenly balanced. He would like to work some more on the boy. Possibly, and preferably, over a period of days. Sometimes, that produced wonders. Confessional wonders. How could he hold him? The moment his people, and the civil rights people, got hold of it – Surcher felt grim. What a prospect. Should he just release him? And watch him? Surcher didn't like it. Matters were urgent. For one of the very few times in his professional career, the Captain was troubled. He needed someone to talk to – and not a Policeman. He thought of Tiger – or *Mr McDrew* – as Surcher still called him. He seemed like someone eminently qualified to talk to – Not only was he obviously smart, and sharp, but he knew the boy through and through. He must do. Certainly, much more than he did – or could hope to. And so, leaving the lad with his key assistants, Grady and Follo, he emerged from the office, walked through the outer office, encountering Miss Craymire's ravenously curious stare, and others', and went to see Tiger, after first buzzing him to make sure he was there and not too entangled.

Tiger, as a matter of fact, was there, and not at all too wrapped up in things. He was on his own and would be for a half-hour or so, at least, musing, sort of resting, ruminating over things. His schedule, that sort of thing. It was a very full schedule. When Surcher buzzed, he wondered what he could want, and then quickly remembered Jim Green's plight. And his own plight too, Tiger mused, thinking ahead to Practice. No doubt that's what the good Captain would want. In Tiger's mind, as he continued perusing his schedule, there was no doubt. He still was disappointed, not to mention baffled, utterly, over Surcher's incredible blunder. He shook his head at it, sighing. What could he do about it? He would see, that's all. Next period he had Civics class. He looked forward to it. He loved teaching. In fact, if his interests weren't to catholic, he wouldn't mind sticking to teaching and nothing else, period. But it wouldn't work out. It couldn't. He couldn't kid himself. He would get bored. In a rut. He needed activities of a wide and varied nature. That was a fact, and he knew it. Then after Civics, and after a break for lunch, Kathy Burns coming to see him here for her weekly session. Tiger smiled fondly. She was like his own daughter almost, she was the cutest thing. He had watched her coming along, over the years, from the pre-bra set. Now of course she took a pretty-fair-sized one. He grinned, warm at the thought of her. Then there was Drama class, or play practice, or tryouts, which it amounted to, just now. They were casting for the new production scheduled for December. *Flowering Cherry*, by Robert Bolt, of course. It was a terrific little play and Tiger looked forward to doing it. Rochelle really had been the one to choose it. Everyone had agreed enthusiastically, including Tiger. He mused over the male lead. Ronnie Swann might do it. He didn't know for sure, he would have to hear a few of the boys give it a whirl. Rochelle would help him decide. He grinned warmly, thinking of her, that supreme kid. She of course would take the female lead. Who else could? Perfect. Of course, she could do just about any role – perfectly, such were her talents, up and up. He grinned more warmly, sensing her unique presence. Then, he mused, after that, which would not doubt take up just about the rest of the afternoon, Football practice. And Tiger braced himself for it, suddenly troubled, wondering just what the hell he was supposed to do if Jim Green really didn't show up, due to that policeman's unbelievable maneuverings. He was still wondering, when the good Captain himself strolled in, after knocking.

'How are you?'

'Fine, Mr McDrew – well, pretty nearly fine, I guess I should say – ' He grinned. He sat down. Tiger waited. He saw clearly that the man was unhappy.

'What can I do for you?' Tiger asked, finally, in his best Guidance/Counseling manner.

Surcher searched him, and said, 'What's the story on Jim Green?'

'Story?' Tiger asked.

'I'll tell you, Mr McDrew, I've got him on my list as Number One Suspect.' He paused, as Tiger took this in. 'But – I can get nothing out of him.' He paused again, as Tiger sat calmly, waiting for more. Surcher looked around the room. He pulled a cigarette out of a pack, and lit up. 'Smoke?' he said, offering Tiger one.

'No, thanks,' Tiger said, and, 'Jim Green? What's led you to Jim Green? May I ask?'

'You sure may,' Surcher said, grinning, wryly almost. 'You'll have to pardon me – I've been going all morning, working on him. It takes a lot out of you. Maybe you know – ' He paused, as Tiger understandingly nodded, watching him take a long puff – 'It takes a hell of a lot. Well – this is strictly confidential, O.K.?' Tiger nodded again. The Captain went on, 'We found a letter he had written to the girl – ' Surcher paused. 'It was pretty suspicious. I'd have to show it to you to make you see what I mean. So here it is.' And he hauled out one of his copies of the letter and passed it to Tiger, who read it, thoughtfully. 'We know he wrote it,' the Captain said, 'because his prints are all over it. Also did you know his nickname was *Kid*?' In truth, Tiger didn't. He shook his head. 'Well, maybe his own kind just call him that – ' Tiger, wincing slightly, nodded. He sat calmly. 'Anyhow, that's the only damn thing we've really got. Nothing else. Not a thing. That's the whole thing.' He paused. Tiger took it all in.

He said, calmly, 'You can't convict anyone on that – check?'

'Double check,' the Captain said.

'So – now?'

Surcher puffed his cigarette and blew out smoke. Tiger watched it. He would, at this rate, stink out the place. But Tiger wasn't worried. He could air it out quick.

'That's the question,' Surcher said, taking another long drag, 'Lots of things could happen now – ' He paused – 'For example, he could confess – ' Tiger nodded, but totally doubted it. 'But that could take a long time – a lot of time,' the Captain said. 'I could just turn him loose, of course – ' he went on – 'Keep an eye on him – or try to. But – I just don't like to,' he said. 'He worries me.'

'What else could happen?' Tiger couldn't help ask.

'Well – all kinds of side developments could take place – the race problem, for example – ' He paused, taking another drag –

'The parent problem – ' he said – 'All kinds of things.' He stopped.

Tiger nodded. Was the Captain waiting to be prodded? He ventured, 'I see what you mean.'

'I thought you would,' Surcher now said, 'And that's one of the reasons I wanted to talk to you – ' Tiger nodded. The Captain talked on, 'You know Jim Green pretty well, Mr McDrew – '

'I hope I do.'

Surcher said, not without the hint of a grin, 'I'm pretty sure you do.'

Tiger waited.

'What do you think of him?' Surcher asked.

'In what way?' Tiger answered.

'Well – in a general way – first of all.'

Tiger answered, carefully, 'I have a high opinion of him.' He paused, keeping his eyes on the Captain. 'He's a good student a fine athlete – I hope you don't lose me an athlete – ' He grinned –

'I don't want to,' Surcher told him, also grinning, in his way.

'And as a person, I like him. All in all, I think he's a fine kid. A credit to his race.'

Surcher nodded, slightly. Then he said, 'What do you think – could he have done it?'

Tiger shook his head, slowly, 'I'd say no – ' He paused – 'Unless proved otherwise – of course.' A pause – 'You'd have to show me ironclad proof, I'll tell you though.'

Surcher nodded, and waited. He had finished his cigarette. He put it out in an ashtray. He looked up from it, at Tiger.

'I'd like to ask you to do me a favor, Mr McDrew – ' he said.

'What's that?'

'Have a talk with him.'

Tiger nodded, 'Sure – I'll be glad to.'

'I mean really talk with him – ' Surcher paused. 'See what he tells you.'

'Sure. Any time, Captain. I'd be glad to.'

'I appreciate that.'

'Tell you what – ' Tiger said, 'Send him over during lunchtime – I'll pick up some sandwiches from the cafeteria – we can have lunch over it.'

'That sounds great.'

'O.K.'

'I'd like to know what he says.'

'I'll let you know.'

'I'll send him over.'

'Lunchtime.'

'O.K.'

There was silence.

'Get him back to me when you're through – O.K.?' the Captain said.

'I'll bring him back to you.'

'That's great.'

Silence, again. And Tiger sat there, thinking about the development in fact thinking a whole host of things and wondering what to say. Right now he was hoping the Captain wouldn't drag out his visit too much longer, for he didn't want to be late for his Civics class. He glanced nonchalantly at his watch. Five minutes to go.

'I'll let you know, don't worry – Captain,' he said, finally.

Surcher stirred, 'It might be a big help to us. Just might be, Mr McDrew. That kid likes you, he thinks the world of you – it's all a hell of a thing, in a way – but – this thing is too serious to play around with. You know how it is.' He paused. 'I have to try everything – even if I hurt somebody a little bit, along the way.'

Tiger nodded, surveying the man, 'I know – ' He paused – 'So everything else is a blank?'

Surcher said, 'Right now it is – I don't mind telling you.'

'A hell of a thing.'

'You know it.'

'Well – don't worry. I'll let you know what he says.'

'You having Practice tonight?' Surcher asked.

'Right.'

Surcher grinned his grin, 'Tell me something – how do you do it?'

Tiger also grinned, modestly, 'It's the material here.' He paused. 'I mean it, Captain.'

Surcher replied, 'Yeh – I'll bet it is. They could sure use you at Kitston – let me tell you – ' He still grinned.

'Joe Palone is a fine coach – ' Tiger said.

'Except when he bumps into Sawyersville – '

'Well, we've been lucky – that's all – ' Tiger grinned broadly.

'How lucky would you be without Jim Green?' Surcher asked.

Tiger still grinned, 'Don't tell me that's your game – '

The Captain got up, not making Tiger too unhappy, of course.

'Could be – ' he said, kidding, of course. He looked around, starting to leave, 'Nice office you've got here – ' he said.

'Not too bad,' Tiger said.

'You're a busy man,' Surcher said, opening the door, 'I'll see you – and thanks.'

'So long,' Tiger said, watching him leave. He sat back in his chair a few moments, wondering, musing over things. He thought about Jim, that poor kid, who wouldn't be coming to Civics class today, probably. *Or football practice.* Tiger felt definitely irritable now, at that, and Surcher, that bungler. How long would he screw around with that kid ? he wondered. A *confession.* He could laugh, under any other circumstances. It was something. Would he be able to use him in the game with Carverton ? That was something to think of, as if things wouldn't be tough enough. Tiger grew more irritated, at the bungler. He hoped Looby Loo would give him a call, during lunch hour. That would cheer him up, if nothing else did. It would be one job and a half, he mused, for Ponce and him to find a replacement for Jim. He hoped it wouldn't come to that. He hoped that by tomorrow, at any rate, or the next day, the latest, Surcher would have come to his senses. Once the civil rights people and their lawyers got into this, he wouldn't be long in his clutches. Should he call them ? No, Tiger decided, better stay out of it – for the present. He pushed himself back from the desk and got up. He put his folders and other things away. It was something he always did. He said 'Ho Hum – ' and yawned, and stretched a little. He stood still a moment, then grabbed a few books, and walked out of there. He was well on his way to his Civics class, without a doubt one of his favorite classes. . . .

39

'Here we go – ' Tiger said, as usual, detaching himself from a small group of students he had been talking to, and striding up to the front of the class. He deposited his books on the desk there and looked over the class, as usual, a moment or two. Jill's seat, where she usually sat anyway, was unoccupied, he noted. He couldn't blame them.

'Dink – ' he said, addressing Sawyersville High's brilliant

quarterback, 'What were we saying last time about referendums?'

The boy stirred, looked around, then at Tiger. 'Well – a lot of things – ' he said. 'Everybody seemed to be saying a different thing.'

The class giggled, and Tiger grinned, at that one.

The boy went on, 'Some said the referendum was the logical and most perfect method for the people to express themselves in a democracy – in fact, I think a majority of the class said – or *felt* that way – ' He paused – 'Some said just the opposite, that is, the referendum had no place in a true democracy, because – uh – it meant – well – uh – it meant that the people elected to decide things and formulate policies weren't to be trusted – they said, what was the point of electing representatives of the people and other officials and then not trust them to know what's best to do, in situations, in issues – in other words, how could they do their job, what they were elected to do –' He paused – 'It was a – contradiction in terms, I think they said – '

'What do you say?' Tiger asked.

'I haven't decided.'

That brought another round of giggles, and laughs, which Tiger joined in, heartily.

'Well – we'll come back to you – ' he said, going to the board. He picked up a piece of chalk.

'Right now, let's have a little referendum here – O.K.? I'd like to get it down pat – just how many are for, and against. *Referendums*, that is. O.K.? Or "don't knows" – like my good friend Dink here – ' He grinned, writing three words on the board in capital letters – YES – NO – DON'T KNOW. 'Let's give it a whirl – all systems Go? How many YES? Raise your hands – ' About half the class of thirty had their hands in the air, including, he noted, Yvonne and Marjorie. He counted them and entered the number. 'NO?' he said, and noted that about a quarter of the class felt that way, including, among others, Rochelle, Mona, Ponce, Sonny Swingle, Jeannie Bonni, and Lennie Almot – He wrote down the figure. 'DON'T KNOW?' The rest of the hands went up, including Mary Holden, Peggy Linski, and Sally Swink – among others. The score was 15-8-7.

'Well – ' he said, facing them, 'Looks as if it's a kind of tie – '

There were cries of protest.

'What's the matter?' Tiger asked.

'Well – you can't lump the DON'T KNOWs with the NOs – Mr McDrew –' Someone, Jim Rossi, he believed said.

'Why not?' Tiger asked.

'Well – Jeepers – that's altogether a different category – '

'Is it?' Tiger asked, 'Dink – what do you say?' He returned to the quarterback.

'Wow – ' the boy said, 'This is getting over my head – ' He also said – 'But I wonder about that too.'

'About what?' Tiger asked.

'Well – mixing up the two categories – '

'In other words,' Tiger said, 'The question we really want to know the answer to is: Are DON'T KNOWs really NOs? Or aren't they?' He paused, talking to Dink – 'That's why I picked on you.' He turned away – 'Rochelle?' That unique girl had her hand up.

'I think they are NOs – Mr McDrew,' she said, as only she could say, 'The very fact that they can't express themselves *positively* indicates a certain negative attitude to the whole thing.' She was caught under a swell of protesting voices, but she talked on, despite them, '. . . and that really is just one more argument against the whole theory and practice of the referendum – ' she said.

'It isn't!' John Campbell said, 'The ones who answer DON'T KNOW in any kind of a poll do so because – uh – well they just *don't know* – that's it! They may not have the information to make up their minds, one way or another – for instance – '

'And how does that explain the DON'T KNOWs we got today? I'd like to know – ' Rochelle said, 'Everybody here has all the information they could possibly ever want or hope to have on the matter – '

'That's right!' A small chorus called out, as Tiger gazed admiringly at the astute girl.

'I want to change my vote to NO,' Peggy Linski called out, amid laughter, and clapping too. Tiger readjusted the figures.

'Where do you stand on this!' Dink asked Mr McDrew.

'I'm not going to tell you – ' He was told, followed by a chorus of 'OHHHs' – 'Not now, anyhow – ' The teacher added – 'It wouldn't be fair!'

'Will you tell us after awhile?' Dink pressed.

'Sure I will – ' Tiger said, looking here and there, 'Ponce, what do you say?' He asked that smart boy, who was on the verge of speaking in any event.

'Well, I think Rochelle is right, without a doubt – How could anyone here today, for instance, say they *don't know*? I'd sure like to know what they mean – *I don't know* – '

'Ask them – ' Jim Rossi, and a few others, said.

Tiger called on Sally Swink, 'Sally, why did you say DON'T KNOW?'

That sweet honey blonde attired in a pale blue sweater, and things, said, looking here and there, 'I don't know.' And the class laughed. She blushed. Tiger left it at that.

'There are other factors – other factors – ' Rochelle now said, about to tread, Tiger sensed, where everyone else absolutely feared to, '*Intelligence* – ' She said, as Tiger looked on, admiring her more – 'For there's where the real heart of the argument against referendum lies – ' She went on – 'We all know we weren't all blessed with an equal amount of intelligence, there's no disputing that *fact* – ' She just barely paused – 'And so to throw a complicated moral issue, say – or any other issue, let's say – out to the general masses for a free vote, a *decision* on – is absolutely ridiculous!' She paused – 'And how!'

'That's antidemocratic!' Fred Ripak, in the back row, said.

'No it isn't!' That fascinating girl said.

'Why?' Ripak said.

'Well, I was just about to tell you that – ' She said.

'O.K. – tell us that – ' Some other lad said.

'Tell us that!' A small but vigorous chorus said.

She said, 'It isn't antidemocratic because in the final and realistic analysis it's a very, very tiny minority of intelligent, sane, and sophisticated people who keep any democracy going – define the term as you will – That's Why!' She astonished Tiger, as usual, and perhaps even more than usual, with her acumen.

'Good Point – ' cried out Ponce, suddenly aware of it too.

'My eye!' Someone, and then someone else, said. Voices were flying around fast.

"Hold it – Hold it – ' Tiger said. And, more or less, the class did just that.

'Rochelle – ' he said, to that fabulous girl, 'Care to elaborate on that?'

'No,' she said, with the trace of a smile for him, 'I've made my point clear.' That was that.

Tiger nodded, and looked around. 'Dink?'

'Well, there's no getting around it – I think what she says does make a lot of sense – '

'Are you swaying toward the NO column, Dink?' Tiger asked.

'If this keeps up, I will – ' the lad said.

'Don't do it, Dink – ' John Campbell said, 'What she's talking is a lot of antidemocratic bunk!'

'Ponce – ' Tiger said, 'What do you say?'

'She's opened my eyes.'

'Elaborate – ?' Tiger said.

'Well – it's a fact. I agree with her. An absolute fact,' the lad said, 'I just haven't thought about it much, in that way. That's all. When you stop to think about it though, it's an obvious fact.'

'So, as far as you're concerned,' Tiger said, 'Getting back to our original quest – No specific issues per se should ever be put before the general public for a decision on?'

'Right. Let the elected officials and representatives do it.'

'Dan – ' Tiger said, turning to another lad, 'You were a DON'T KNOW – '

The lad nodded his head.

'Why?'

'Well – ' Danny Moss said, 'I think it depends – '

'Depends?'

'Yeah, well, I mean – sometimes yes – sometimes no – it depends on what's coming off – '

'The issues, you mean – '

'Right, I mean, some things I think it would be alright to have one on, a referendum I mean, and other things I don't think so – ' He paused. 'That's why I said I don't know.'

'I see,' Tiger said, 'It was the only category you felt you could fall into – '

'Right.'

'Actually, we need another category for you – YES and NO!' There was some laughter at that.

'I guess so – ' said the lad.

'Well, I'd like to change my vote to NO,' Mary Holden said.

'So would I – ' chimed in Sally Swink.

Tiger, nodding, and grinning too, made the adjustments on the board.

'We're going to wind up with a real tie!' He said, 'If this keeps up – anyone else want to change their vote?'

'I want to change to DON'T KNOW,' The one and only Marjorie called out.

'Oh NO!' Tiger exclaimed, in mock pain, provoking more laughter now.

'Well I've a right to!' The maid said.

'You certainly have – I was only kidding – ' Tiger said.

'What would Jill have said?' Joe Fletcher, out of the blue, suddenly said.

Silence reigned, and Tiger almost bowed his head. He looked around. Everyone seemed profound. There wasn't a sound. Ponce coughed, a brief, subdued cough. Rochelle looked at Ponce, and then across the room, out of the windows. Marjorie was playing with her pencil, scribbling little things in her notebook. Peggy Linski looked straight ahead. Joe Fletcher, Tiger knew, felt like a fool. He just sat there. Tiger felt for the boy. For a few moments, Tiger just stood before that silent class and said nothing, nor made a move. Finally, he crossed to the desk. He flipped open his main textbook and examined a page. Silence. Only.

'Would you hand in your homework now,' He said, finally, quietly, to the class. . . .

Ponce, passing his homework forward, wondered how the class could go on. Joe had really dealt it a blow, though he didn't know. How could Tiger possibly get it rolling again? Everybody felt bad. And things had been going so good. Almost as good as last period, in Eng Lit., where he had confronted his dream. What a class. He had soared in that class, *he had controlled himself*, *admirably*, too. And he had talked a little bit at the end with his dream. He didn't know what he was exactly saying of course and he nearly fell over himself, to boot, but he knew they had talked a little bit. What a dream. She had said, *this* he knew, *he could drop by to see her anytime*, she didn't mind. He couldn't really remember anything else after that. Or before that. Next thing he knew, he was here, in Tiger's class. He hadn't forgotten what he had to do. It was just a question of hitting the right moment and telling all to Tiger, true. As far as he knew, they were still holding poor Jim. He glanced over at the empty place. Only the day before yesterday, incredibly enough, she had been sitting there, beautiful and lively, a flower in full bloom. Who could have dreamed it? Ponce felt so blue. He turned away from the empty place and the silent class and just looked down at his book. The homework had reached the front of the room now, and he could hear Tiger collecting it from the front of each row. Now what would he do? Just give a reading assignment, kill the rest of the period that way? If he were in his shoes, Ponce felt, that's what he would do. What else could he do? What did Joe have to shoot his mouth off for? Ponce tried thinking of other things. He thought of miniskirts. They were something. As yet, you didn't see much of them in the States – certainly, not this area. He saw them only in magazines and movies and TV. England of course was the place for them. In a certain part of London, he knew, they wore them the shortest of all – in fact, there hardly was a skirt at all! That was Chelsea. He knew. That was the name of the place. They sure looked cute though. Different. Ponce wouldn't mind seeing them in Sawyersville. Like Majorettes, actually. Even shorter! He thought what must happen when a girl wearing one, the shortest ones especially, bent over. Or leaned over. He pictured it. What about sitting down? That must be something. He pictured Miss Nectar in one. Miss Smith! She would look terrific. With those legs of hers – those legs – Ponce could see it, not his book. He started getting hot. Maybe though they wear something special under the mini-mini ones. What? It could be. But what? What would his dream wear? He got hotter, it started happening again. He thought of opera. Now, he started very hard thinking about opera, which he loved, as he loved all music, of course – or most of it, certainly. As a kid he had taken guitar lessons, and later, clarinet lessons. He still had those instruments in his room, and once in a while, when in the mood, he would play them. If he had more time he would really concentrate on them. Anyhow, he knew that throughout his life he would have them around and when he felt like it play them. Ever since his eleventh year, as far as he could honestly say, he had loved opera, especially. Before that, back even to his earliest memories, he had been exposed to opera, for it was one of the things both his father and mother loved – they had records of all the important operas, or at least highlights from them and major excerpts. Perhaps it was the Southern European origins of his father's family, in the dim, remote past, far, far back, that accounted for it, or had something to do with it. In any event, Ponce loved it. Most of all he loved Italian opera, though of course nothing could beat Mozart, which wasn't strictly Italian, after all. His tastes were eclectic. For instance, he was crazy about

Carmen. He had in fact seen a wonderful production of the Bizet masterpiece in New York two years ago, with Victoria de los Angeles, who in his opinion sang the role best. He had gone with his mother and father. He had been absolutely swept out of this world by it, the music to this day intoxicated him, when he heard it. The strength, the vigor, the sheer beauty of it, like a Turner painting, *The Fighting Téméraire*, for instance, just overwhelmed him. He loved it. Now, Ponce heard it, and he was aware of Miss Smith materializing once again in his reverie. He saw her. The music rose and swelled all about her. She had on a miniskirt. He was near her, the aria of love was being sung to him, by her. He responded. He was aware of the most powerful and formidable erection, responding to her. He was dying for her. He loved her miniskirt. . . . *La Traviata.* . . . *Rigoletto.* . . . Those two operas. *Marriage of Figaro.* . . . That most delightful of operas. . . . *Pagliacci.* . . . Now a whole torrent of operas fell all around him. . . . On him. . . . His dream disappeared. He watched her, looking so terrific, disappearing. He was heartbroken, still dying for her. He waved to her, from the dark depths of *Lucia de Lammermoor.* . . . A Wagner crescendo swept him off his feet. Where was it taking him? He tried to see her. . . . He thought of *The Teatles.* . . . That phenomenon of the times intrigued him. And grounded him. He was thinking, clearly. He couldn't say he completely hated that kind of so-called music, he grinned within, descending, because whenever he did hear one of their silly records he just felt good, at least the first time, jumping around inside with the beat of it. Really, it was kid stuff though. Most of the kids in the school, from Freshmen on down, generally, Ponce had noticed, wide-ranging and intelligent observer of the human condition that he was, were crazy about them, and got into a state of near-hysteria over them. It started petering out when they hit their Sophomore year. Ponce pondered it. He saw a million kids shrieking their heads off at a Teatles 'concert'. He saw them breaking the barriers and ripping their clothes off. Or trying to. Would they stop there? Now they were ripping all the cops' clothes off. Now suddenly and once again Miss Smith entered. She was wearing no skirt at all. What was that she had on? She was jogging around, yelling *Yea, Yea, O Yea Yea Yea*, all over the place. What was she up to? Ponce's organ was up too – once again. He thought of Practice, struggling hard with his predicament. It would be great tonight alright seeing the boys out there and

Tiger putting them through the ropes again. Even if Jim didn't show up. A lot of plays would have to be revised, if he didn't. *Special T Pass Seventy-three And Fake To Left On Three From Quarterback Spin And Handoff With Lateral Decoy*, for example, would have to be completely rethought. Ponce fixed his thoughts. He saw the diagram of the play, clearly before him, in his head. He remembered the first time he had outlined that gem of a play for Tiger. A winner and a half if ever there was one. He didn't even know how many TD's had been scored with it. He could reshuffle the swing to right and cut off the pivot. But who would pivot ? It was absolutely essential that someone step in and take over the pivot. Slim Elkins could decoy alright and spin without any trouble, but when it came to the pivot – and the ensuing snarlup in the defensive secondary that could always occur on that one without the split second timing called for – Ponce pondered, wondering, getting worried. No doubt Tiger was pondering over it, right now, in his office. . . . Ponce checked himself, surfacing suddenly, remembering where he was, and where Tiger was, right up there, in front of him. He thought of his Uncle Phil, who lived in Kitston. He was a lawyer. Once in a while, he went to see him. The poor guy was so busy though he just about saw his family these days. *The funeral*. Ponce suddenly found himself face to face with that again. *Mummer*. And that again. He would have to act. But *when* ? Ponce was agitated. As soon as he could, without a doubt. As soon as he heard. He was sinking again, seeing the funeral. She would have a nice one, he knew. She came from a religious family, she was pretty religious herself. They would all go to the church. It was a nice church, a nice old church, the Methodist one, on the corner of Spring Avenue and Cherry Street. Miss Smith would wear black. A *black miniskirt*. He suddenly saw his dream, in that black miniskirt. . . .

'Well – ' Ponce heard a voice, Tiger's, speaking very quietly, 'If nobody has any objections, we'll move on to another topic – He paused, and Ponce looked up, and then he went on, 'No objections ?' Another pause, and then, 'Well – let's see what we can do with the principle of voting in a democratic election. I'm thinking of the election of officials and representatives by *majority* verdict, as we practice it of course in our own country, as opposed to election by *Proportional Representation*, a method of course practiced, for instance, in several European countries.' He paused, Ponce saw him look around. Then, 'Yvonne – first of all, how about telling us the difference ?'

'Well – I *hope* I can – ' That sweet girl, smiling, said. . . .

40

Tiger found Jim Green waiting for him when he returned to his office after Civics class. He had picked up some lunch at the cafeteria, for both of them.

'Howdy – ' he said to the boy, setting his books and the lunches on his desk.

'What's new ?' he said, sitting down at the desk and starting to open the package. He noted how unhappy the boy looked. 'Hungry ?' he added.

'Not too much,' Jim answered.

'Want a sandwich ?' Tiger inquired. 'I got us some lunch.' He mentioned.

The boy took one, slowly.

'What's been going on ?' Tiger asked, munching his sandwich. He was sitting back in his chair with his feet propped on one of the open desk drawers. He was thinking, *some Surcher*.

'Search me,' the boy said, glumly.

Tiger was enjoying his sandwich. They always had pretty good sandwiches up there, on top of everything else. It was a good cafeteria, Miss Eccles was a Home Ec. grad. from State, it ought to be. She ran it. He took another bite, thinking about her. She had often, in the past few months, caused him to think about her. He would see. He waited for the boy to say something. She wasn't exactly *a beauty* – but – there was – something –

'You know they've been working on me all morning ?' the boy said, 'Do they have any right to do that ?'

Tiger thought about that.

'Have they accused you of anything ?'

'Not directly.'

'You didn't do it – ' Tiger said, taking another bite out of the sandwich, 'Did you ?'

'Heck no, Tiger,' The boy answered, a little hurt by it.

'Go on – eat your sandwich – ' Tiger said.

The boy hesitated.

'I'll try – ' He said.

'If you didn't, you *didn't* – ' Tiger said, munching away. He had an appetite. He took a sip of milk now, through a straw. *That fool Surcher*, he thought. 'Trouble is,' he said. 'They're up against it.' He paused. 'They haven't got a single clue to go on, from what I've been told, and so they're pretty desperate.' He paused. 'Like the sandwich?'

'Yeh,' the boy said.

'Couple more here,' Tiger munched away, 'Have some milk – ' He said. 'So – ' He went on, 'They're hitting at anything they can find – or think they find – in that darkness.' He paused. 'What I'd like to know is, why have they picked on you? That's what I'm wondering.' Again he paused. 'You have any idea? What have they got on you?'

The boy was munching listlessly at the sandwich, however delicious it was. He answered, finally, 'Well – see – ' He paused. 'I liked Jill a lot – maybe you know or don't know – I guess though you don't know – ' He paused – 'And, well – couple of weeks ago, after that Lansdale game, I was feeling so good – heck, high I mean – I wrote her a crazy note, no kidding – ' He paused. 'And, well, this guy Surcher latched on to it – in her house – see – ' He paused – 'Yeh, there it was, she kept it, and my fingerprints all over it – ' Tiger absorbed it. 'And that's about all, far as I can see. That's what they've so-called got on me – ' He paused – 'One thing, they been real cagey about that – other piece of paper – you know the one I mean – ' He paused, as Tiger, munching on, took that in – 'I mean, they been kind of hinting around that maybe my prints were on that – just hinting around, being real foxy about that – ' He paused – 'But that's crazy, Tiger – because they just couldn't be. I don't know what their game is, I'm telling you – if my prints are on there, I sure as heck didn't put them there!'

'I wouldn't worry about that,' Tiger said, 'If they had found your prints, by now you'd be up the creek. Don't worry. I think they're playing with you.' He paused, taking a sip of milk, and surveying the boy. 'What was in that note you mentioned?' he asked, just to hear what he'd say.

After some hesitation, the boy told him. It coincided exactly with what he had read. Tiger nodded, and finished his sandwich.

'I don't think they can do much with that – except worry about it,' He told the lad.

'They sure been trying.'

'Well, sure, as I said, they're up the creek. I guess they'll keep on trying too – ' Tiger said.

'I oughta have a lawyer – right, Tiger?'

'If they take you away from here, certainly. If they just turn you loose, after they're through with you here, I don't know as I would worry about that – unless of course they keep on bothering you.'

'That Surcher sure acts like he's got his man – ' The boy told him.

'Oh – I don't know. Never can be too sure with those guys, who knows what's on their minds? Maybe he's just foxed, and ready to try anything – Maybe he hopes you'll tell him something – if he works on you long enough.'

'I've sure got nothing to tell him.'

'Well, I believe that.'

A pause. Tiger started eating a piece of apple pie.

'Boy they sure make nice pie up there though,' he said, enjoying it, 'So you never got anywhere with Jill?' He asked.

'Nowhere,' the lad said.

Tiger nodded, taking due note of it. He finished the pie.

'Have a piece of that pie, Jim – ' He paused, pushing a good-sized portion toward him. 'One of these days, we're going to be living in a civilized world, and you won't have any problems with that kind of thing – I don't mean you literally, Jim, because it looks like it's going to be a long time away. That's the way things move.' He paused again. 'The more I get to know human beings, Jim, it's a miracle things move at all, no kidding. That's how we are. How we've always been. From time immemorial.' He paused once more. The boy was trying the pie. 'Immemorial.' He said again. 'You really were stuck on that girl, weren't you?'

The boy nodded. He said, 'I don't mind telling you.'

Tiger said, 'She was a fine girl.'

'You know it.'

Tiger nodded. He said, 'She used to drop in to see me once in a while. I can tell you, I used to enjoy those talks.'

The boy nodded.

'Did you talk with her much?' Tiger asked.

'Oh – yeh, I guess. I talked to her quite a lot here in school – around the school – that's all.' He paused, looking very downcast – 'I always wound up trying to take her out – ' A pause – 'And it was always no go – ' Another pause – 'That really made me feel bad, let me tell you. I hated her whenever she turned me down – *the whole setup* – that's a fact.' He paused – 'Also, funny enough – Tiger – I felt sorry for her – '

Tiger nodded.

'I know,' he said, 'It's that way. I understand that.' He paused. 'She was a fine girl, Jim, like most of the girls around here. But – well – like most of us, I guess – she was a prisoner of *her culture*. That's right, Jim.' He paused. 'You understand what I'm saying? Her culture.' He paused, surveying the lad, he saw it had registered. 'That's a powerful, powerful force, Jim – ' He went on – 'It takes one hell of an extraordinary person, in the USA, to buck his culture, Jim. That's why it's going to take so long. Long long. Any progress in any area of human social activity always does. And I said, it's a wonder it ever does. Look how long it's taken us to get this far!'

The boy nodded. He finished his pie.

'And how far is that?' Tiger asked. '*You said it!*' He added.

'What did Surcher send me to see you for?' The boy asked, after a silence.

'Oh – I guess he wanted me to work on you.' He grinned. 'I guess that.'

The boy nodded, and grinned a little bit, too.

'I don't think he's a bad guy – ' Tiger said, 'I could be wrong, but I don't think so.' He paused, thoughtfully. 'He's just up against it.'

'Those other two guys, Follo and Grady I think are their names, they're pretty mean-looking – '

'I agree with you.'

A pause.

'What did she used to talk with you about, Tiger?' The boy asked.

Tiger thought about it. Memories were flooding back. He sat there looking around his office, giving quite a lot of thought to that. Finally, he turned to the boy again.

'Just about everything,' he said.

'She was great to talk with – ' Jim said.

'She sure was.'

'Did she ever talk about me?' The boy asked.

Tiger thought hard about that.

'I'll tell you the truth, Jim – she didn't.'

The boy shook his head.

'That's what I figured,' he said.

'She never talked about any boys, for that matter – come to think of it – '

'She didn't?'

'Uh uh. She didn't.'

Another silence.

'Did she ever tell you what she wanted to be?' Jim asked, finally.

'She had a few ideas – ' Tiger said – 'Mainly, I think she was interested in Journalism – '

'That's right. That's what she told me.' The boy paused – 'Like Mona – '

'Mona?' Tiger inquired, 'Mona Drake?' He also inquired. 'Is she interested in Journalism?' It was a piece of news to him. Certainly.

'Well – it's one of the things – I know it's one of the things – ' The boy said.

'I thought she was mainly interested in schoolteaching, Jim – '

'Yeh – maybe you're right – '

'She a girl friend of yours?'

'Well – yeh – in a way – I guess – ' He paused, looking at Tiger – 'I take her out once in a while.'

Tiger nodded.

'She's a swell girl – '

'You said it.'

And they fell silent. They had both finished their lunches. Although the boy looked a little better to him Tiger still felt very sorry for him. He would of course do all he possibly could for him, for he hadn't touched the girl, certainly. He would have some rough hours to go yet with the misguided Captain, he knew, and his band of stalwarts, he also knew. But – in the end – of course – they would spring him loose. They had to. Still, he felt sorry for him. He had a pretty good idea of the ordeal he would have to go through. And why should he have it to go through? What effect would it have on him? Certainly, when he saw Surcher he would tell him bluntly just how he saw things. Would it matter? Probably not. The man after all had a police mind, and a job to do, and he was jammed up to boot. He was doing his best, and he wanted to show it. What kind of pressure would build up from all corners, all around him, if he didn't show it? Tiger, in short, had compassion for him too. A situation like this was a hell of an affair, and scared everybody. He had to explore every suspect, or possible suspect, pretty carefully, thoroughly, Tiger knew it. And unfortunately, Tiger mused, that very unfortunate letter made Jim a sort of suspect. No doubt of it. *Most unfortunate*. Tiger, within, sighed at the injustice of it.

'Tiger,' the boy now said, 'What do you think – Who could have done it?'

Slowly, sadly, shaking his head, Tiger told him, 'I wish I knew. I'm telling you.' And he stopped there.

'There sure is some nutty jerk running around loose in this place – ' The boy said, '*Man* there is.'

'You know it,' Tiger told him.

'I sure wish old Surcher knew it!'

'Don't worry about him.'

'I'm in for it.'

'Well – maybe – but they can't touch you.'

'Sure of that?'

'Positive.'

The boy sat quietly.

Tiger said nothing.

What could he tell the boy? Nothing. Reassurance got nowhere, essentially, especially in a situation like this, he knew it. His years of work in this field had taught him that, perfectly, and totally. The boy had a rough experience ahead of him, Tiger knew it, what was the point of trying to kid him? He would just have to go through it, for it was unlikely that Surcher would pay too much attention to him, unless he had somehow stumbled across something else, in the interim. Tiger almost shuddered to think what that might be, on his present form. Certainly. He kept on looking at Jim, feeling for him. It would be a unique experience in any event, Tiger thought, trying to find the bright side of it, he could look back upon it later on in life as part of the grand fabric and design of his life. Certainly. Involvement. Tiger knew it. How well he knew it. The human personality was a plant that thrived only in the rich terrain of contact and involvement with other humans, and concern for them. It would always be and had always been. Man hungered for contact. Humans were profoundly *social* animals. Though, of course, sometimes bizarre ones. Who ran away from this contact, this involvement, this concern, did so at the most terrible cost to his soul, his life, his entire being, in toto. That was the main force, this hunger for contact, which Tiger in fact always tried to stimulate or at least harness whenever he encountered a student with a few problems. Not that all students, in fact, all *humans*, didn't have problems. Some, however, could face them, or at least tried to, and just needed some help to. That was it. And it was all really Tiger could do, for to probe deeper, to uncover the depths of some of these problems would take about half a lifetime, at least, and some luck to boot. Such were these complicated, sometimes brutal, always complicated creatures, redeemed solely and uniquely and only by love. *Only that*. Human beings. *Homo sapiens*. Tiger mused, his eyes still on the boy. Here was this young boy, this fine young colored boy, and he would have to endure the pain and the humiliation of the next few hours, that's all there was to it. No matter how much compassion Tiger felt for him. . . .

'Well, listen – ' he said, suddenly, 'Don't let them keep you too long, will you, Jim ? We need you.' And he grinned.

The boy grinned, for he loved football. He said, 'I'll see what I can do.'

'Thought any more about those offers ?' Tiger now said – 'The one from State seemed pretty good to me – ' It wouldn't do any harm, cheering up the lad.

'What about UCLA ?'

'That wasn't bad – '

'State's not been doing too well – '

'Yeh, they did run into some trouble this year – '

'Six-Three so far isn't too bad though, considering all those injuries they had – look at Palmer – and Carlucci ! Wow !' The boy said.

'That was bad – '

'Watch them next year though. When did they last have a bad year, Tiger, anyhow ?'

'Heck – I don't know – !'

'When do I have to let them know by, anyway ?'

'Well – I think by the first of the year – Jim – '

The boy nodded. And was quiet once more.

Tiger thought about the boy playing for some top university – State, he hoped – He would make the grade anywhere, of course, but Tiger had a soft spot in his heart for his old alma mater, no matter how much it had grown and changed. Tiger gazed fondly at the boy. He would be a pretty good bet for All-American, just one more started on his way by him. Chalk it up. Yes, Tiger mused, he would be chalking him up, sure enough. He could pull a pass out of the air like an angel, no less. And run – like a halfback, almost. Tiger admired the lad.

'You could play basketball too.' Now Tiger said. For the boy was great at that too.

'I'd want to.'

'Not a bad little team they've got there – last year they hit the NCAA Finals – I guess you know – '

'Yeh, I know.'

Now Tiger felt the boy should go. After all, what could he do further for him here? He was a strong lad, he could take care of himself. Surcher had asked him to 'get him back' to him, but that didn't worry him. He would just let the boy go back by himself, of course.

'Well, Jim – ' He said to the boy, 'I guess you'd better go back to our friend.' And he grinned. 'Unless you have something more you want to talk over with me.' He paused. 'Do you?'

The boy shook his head, 'No – ' he said, 'I don't.'

'O.K. – ' Tiger said, nodding, and giving that friendly grin.

The boy got up. He looked a lot better, Tiger thought. Without a doubt.

'Thanks for the lunch,' the boy said, 'I hope I'll be seeing you soon – ' He paused – 'I sure hate missing practice tonight – the guy said I might – '

'We'll see you soon. Don't worry about it.'

The boy grinned, and left the office.

Tiger sat back and relaxed, and thought about things, after Jim left. He had about twenty minutes to go before young Kathy Burns was due to show up. Tiger reflected on things, all sorts of things, including of course the boy who had just left. Certainly it was news to him to have heard of his interest in Jill, not to mention the letter, of course, he had written. Even more interesting, in a way, though not all that much news, in another way, was his dating that peach of a Mona. That hon. He wondered what went on there. He would see if he could find out next time, from Mona. Of course it would have to be a very subtle approach – but, he thought he could swing it. He was good at that, and knew it. What a terrific couple they would make! Tiger suddenly thought of it. Jim and Mona! He could recommend her to him, that young lad would have to travel pretty far and wide to find someone more eminently suitable, whatever angle you looked at it. What a girl. That girl. Tiger mused, over her. And the boy. He thought of the many years and many trials and experiences ahead for that young colored lad. Luckily, he was intelligent, and a gifted athlete. He would go to college and if he didn't play pro ball afterward, which he didn't necessarily have to, due to the quality of his gray matter, he was sure to land a pretty good job somewhere, in whatever area, more or less, he chose to specialize in. What was he interested in? Tiger thought of his Brooder. He recalled that on that Profile he had scored heavily in the Scientific Humanities area, if he wasn't mistaken, and Tiger very rarely was. So maybe he could go for Medicine, which was a great field, or something similar. He was sure someone would put up the dough. Tiger liked the lad, it was certainly one hell of an inane shame for him to have to go through this show. But then, Tiger mused, glancing quickly back at his own life, Look what I've been through! When would Surcher contact him? Tiger wondered. It was hard to predict what that guy would do. When he did, he would certainly tell him just what he thought of his suspicions. . . . Some Policeman, he mused, regretting again the initial rating given him. Well, they were essential, though. Unfortunately essential, Tiger mused, turning his mind to that problem, for a few moments, at least. The innate destructiveness and aggression in *Homo sapiens* made them essential, of course. *Old Cornpone*. He sighed and opened up another one of his desk drawers, hauling out a book he had recently acquired, through the good offices of Hetty Nectar, of course. It was a very interesting book, in many respects, and he was finding it not only readable but enjoyable, to a certain extent. Since obtaining it, he had spent at least fifteen or twenty minutes each day, working on it. He opened it and browsed here and there through it, it was his way of reading it – when he hit a part that appealed to him, he would start taking it in – and concentrate on it. It was an admirable book, the product of many years' scientific research on the subject by a highly qualified team of medical scientific research workers, of course. He read: *The vagina of Human Females in the age group spanning puberty to the mid-thirties, at the minimum, is ready to receive the engorged, fully tumescent, erect penis within a minute, at the maximum, of commencement of a suitable form of sexual stimulation* . . . On the whole, Tiger would concur with that finding, though he had not actually ever utilized a stop watch, as the research workers, somehow, obviously had done. . . . *Regarding The Breasts* . . . He read on – *The nipples definitely become erect when the human female is sexually aroused* . . . Tiger acknowledged the phenomenon, having long been aware of it, and admired the astuteness of course of the reasearchers' recognition and detailed observation of it. . . . *See Chart 52-C-1 (a)* . . . He would, one day. . . .

Definitely. He browsed on: *Knee-Chest Position, Secondary* . . .
He preferred primary, and would recommend it, any day. He
flipped on, though he would look more closely into that, one day.
Supine . . . Lateral . . . They were self-explanatory, practically . . .
THE SEX BLUSH. Tiger halted. And concentrated . . . *The
extremely interesting, uniquely human, and almost universal
phenomenon of the Sex Blush has not received significantly
meaningful attention heretofore* . . . Tiger was only too well aware
of that. . . . *Without a doubt, it is now more than clear that the Sex
Blush may take different forms and patterns in different Human
Females* . . . He could vouch for it. . . . *Generally speaking,
however, it can be different only in clearly defined ways, though it
can be definitely stated that it is directly related to the amount and
type of Response to sexual stimulation on the part of the particular
Human Female* . . . Certainly, it was so, Tiger knew, and what a
unique way of putting it. Like a gas law – almost. On he read. . . .
*The Sex Blush tinges the breasts a very delicate rosy pink, and it
affects the anterior and superior surfaces first – (See Table 99-II-a).
By slow degrees there then occurs a diffusion of the rosy hue to the
(1) undersurfaces of the breasts and (2) the anterior chest wall –
just as the phenomenon of Orgasm is on the brink of manifesting
itself – in the Female* . . . Tiger took note of it, for he hadn't
ever noted this, so far as he was immediately aware, in any event,
and certainly it was something to take note of, carefully. In due
course of time and circumstances, for in actual essence it was a
matter of circumstances, he would explore it. He noted it. . . .
The Blush is not confined to the aforementioned areas, however . . .
Tiger was wondering about this. . . . *All of the following areas, in
one way or another, are affected: The shoulders, the ante cubital
fossae, the lower abdomen* . . . Tiger nodded. . . . *the entire back, in
fact, and the thighs and buttocks* . . . those MAGIC AREAS, Tiger
murmured, almost . . . *The literature in the past has vividly
described the state of the Human Female zeroing in on Orgasm* . . .
Tiger nodded. He himself had on occasion considered making a
modest contribution on the matter. . . . *The post-orgasmic
Human Female generally regains conscious contact with her
external environment by degrees which can be more carefully
perceived by studying Table 52-X-11 (z), as amended* . . . *The
following areas at this stage are generally covered in perspiration –
(a shimmering sheen, in fact, it can best be described as): The back,
the anterior chest wall, the thighs* . . . HEAVENLY THIGHS,
Tiger interjected, SILKEN SKIN PARADISE, he suggested.

. . . He flipped pages, browsing here, there. . . . *Masturbation in the Human Female has not been satisfactorily documented before* . . . Tiger thought about it. It would be a gap, and no doubt of it. . . . *Hundreds of Human Females were involved in our investigation of this phenomenon, under widely varying conditions and situations, from mechanical to manual* . . . *A vast spectrum of orgasmic experiences, falling into the normal curve pattern* . . . Tiger chortled . . . *resulted and were carefully annotated and studied. [See Table 24-Q-VII (p)]. Two main avenues of investigation were paramount and can now be seen to fall under the salient headings: HOW? and: HOW MUCH? Definitively* . . . He didn't doubt it, not a jot of it. He was aware how widespread the phenomenon was – Rochelle, that astonishing girl, had very considerably enlightened him, surprising him, he had to confess. Always, there were things to learn. . . . Now he was examining Figure 16-2 (c), having somehow arrived there. *The Penis.* It showed several views, not all of them conventional, actually, and extraordinarily well done, no doubt of it. Tiger noted . . . *Detumescent (Side View)* . . . *Tumescent (or Excitement) – (All Views)* . . . *Peak (or Total) Engorgement* . . . Tiger studied them. . . . *Cowper's glands in action* . . . He noted . . . The artwork was of the highest caliber. He flipped pages. . . . *The main function, in fact the only validly authenticated and historically implemented function of the tumescent (or Fully Erect) penile shaft has long been known* . . . Tiger paused there. He had to. It wasn't anything he could turn a blind eye to. . . . *Penetration* . . . He read . . . *or Mounting of the Human Female is sometimes attempted in the early phases of sexual play* . . . Tiger winced, openly almost. . . . *This creates a problem, for the Female may not be in fact ready at this particular stage to comfortably accommodate the fully tumescent penile shaft* . . . And only a brute would attempt that stupid move. Monumentally stupid, Tiger knew. . . . He flipped pages. . . . *The Human Vagina* . . . Tiger lingered, briefly, then turned more pages, leaving that for the moment, reluctantly, for another day. He glanced at his watch. It wouldn't be long. That cute Sophomore. That class had a batch of cuties this year, and she was about the cutest, hands down. He had always thought so in fact, since he had first spotted her on a visit to the elementary school a few years ago, when she was just finishing up eighth grade. That was it. He recalled thinking at the time, How could anything be so cute? *Could it?* Now, here she was, a Sophomore, no less. . . . Tiger found he was at the back of the book, leafing through the last few pages of it. *Mount*, he read, *the initial penetration (or thrust) of the erect penis into the vagina at the commencement of coitus (see Erect Penile Shaft)*. Certainly, it was one way of putting it. *Os*, he read, *mouth or orifice, e.g., the Os of the Uterus*. Tiger took note, it was a useful term, in the next Health Education class he would make use of it. *Perineum*, he read, *the area between the thighs*. He stopped, almost with a sigh. *Paradise*. He sighed. Where in the whole of the Universe was there an area so sublime? *Divine*. It was divine. He checked the time. *Gluteal*, he read, *pertaining to the buttocks* . . . Automatically, almost, he gave a thought to Mona's absolutely glorious ones, those superbly supple ones. . . . The phone rang.

Still perusing, he picked the phone up with his free hand.
'Hello?'
'Hello.'
It was Looby Loo. He grinned warmly, into the phone.
'Hi, Hon – ' he said, lovingly.
'How's everything?' She said, in her loving way.
'Oh – O.K. – ' He informed her – 'Considering things.'
'Ummm, I know. Have a nice lunch?'
'Uh huh.'
'Janie's just gone back – I took her.'
'Not a bad idea, bun.'
'What about tonight, honey?'
There was a knock at the door.
'There's Practice, hon.'
'Alrighty. See you around the usual time?'
'Maybe earlier. Might cut it short.'
I'll have something nice for you.'
'You always do.'
'Uh huh – '
He chuckled warmly. He adored her.
Kathy Burns walked into the office. He gave her a little wave.
'You're the best – ' He murmured, into the phone.
'Ah ha – ' She said, murmuring low.
'See you – '
'*Si si* – ' She said, transmitting a warm little kiss.
He hung up, grinning warmly, still.
'Hello, Mr. McDrew – ' Kathy Burns, in her usual sweet way, that cutest of ways, greeted him. . . .

41

Surcher took his decision. He took it while still in a state of gross indecision, and a creeping frustration, to boot. He took it while in the middle of his two-hundredth question at least to Jim Green, after lunch, after having welcomed him back from Tiger's office, unescorted, he had noted, and after having had a talk with Tiger, over the phone, about him. He took it in spite of what Mr McDrew had said, to wit, that as far as he was concerned, the boy couldn't possibly have done it, and he had, from said boy, furthermore, elicited nothing. Not that he hadn't taken due note of what Sawyersville's Head Coach, among other things, had told him. He had the highest respect for him. But – he was frustrated. And not at all sure yet about the boy. And he had his duty, and his golden clue, which of course pointed straight at the boy. And so, in all conscience, he couldn't, at this point at any rate, having weighed all the factors, let the boy walk away from him. He just couldn't. And wouldn't. He had decided, at the two-hundred mark. He would see what developed down at Headquarters. He said to the boy, after that one, in his usual mild and unhostile way, 'Jim, I'm going to ask you to come down to Headquarters.'

The boy stared, definitely shaken at that.

'What for ?' He asked.

'See what we can discover.'

'Well I want a lawyer.'

'Don't worry, you'll have a lawyer.'

'You're sure screwing me up, man,' the boy said, *'for nothing* too.'

Surcher nodded, only, and prepared to leave – with the boy, for Headquarters.

Thus, shortly after, walking between Grady and Follo, but not handcuffed, and following the Captain, Jim Green walked out of the high school toward a waiting State Police car. Before reaching it, however, the party encountered quite the little number of local citizenry, including of course the sturdy Selmo contingent, and a sprinkling of media men, photographers as well. They were well controlled by a cordon of Troopers, not to mention Chief John Poldaski, of course, who strutted back and forth before them like a minor Polish-American Duce, no poke.

'Didn't I tell ya, John?' Joe Grotto, one of Selmo's called out to him, as the party passed by him. 'The Fuckers!'

'You dirty Jig!' Abe Muvitz, another stalwart of course, called out, loud and clear.

'Take them all, the black bastards!' Someone else, Jake Dalton perhaps, shouted out. Other utterances were made, here and there.

The boy looked them over, and Surcher looked them over, and Poldaski mumbled something to them. They fell silent, miraculously. Meanwhile, the reporters were trying to get near the Captain, and in fact two or three of them were practically tripping him up.

'Are you arresting him, Captain?'

'No comment.'

'This is a matter of great public interest, Captain – I represent – '

'Nothing to say.'

'What have you got on him, Captain?'

'You guys deaf?'

'Listen – Captain – '

'Out of the way.'

'Hey – who the hell are you? You'll be sorry for this!' One of them said, actually elbowed aside by the Captain.

'I'll issue a statement in time – don't worry – ' Surcher said. And that was that.

'So it wasn't the other kid – De Leon – after all – Right, Captain?' One shouted out, as some Troopers and Poldaski pushed the rest our of the way, amid loud protests.

The party climbed into the car, under a small barrage of camera flashes.

As they drove off, the following comment was made by one of Selmo's best, in stentorian tones, or just a little less.

'You Sonuvabitch! Black Prick!'

There was a flurry of media men heading for their cars. They would follow the Captain, no doubt heading, they correctly assumed, for State Police Headquarters, District 'A'.

At about that moment, or thereabouts, in the office of Guidance/ Counseling, Kathy Burns, that cutest of cutest kids, was saying to Tiger McDrew,

'*Mr McDrew –*' as she still would address him, despite his

clear intimations that certainly she was free to call him by his more familiar style, '*Who do you think did that awful thing to Jill Fairbunn?*'

'I don't know,' Tiger murmured, thrusting his formidably erect penile shaft into that cute maid's well-lubricated and wonderfully receptive vaginal barrel, noting the rapidly spreading sex blush on the supple young body, and the widespread filmy sheen of perspiration on that utterly delightful cutest young form, 'I just don't know – ' He told her, in short, mounting her. . . .

She gasped and cried out with sheer delight –
'*Mr McDrew – I love You – !*'
He murmured. '*You little sweetheart – *'

Ponce, along with most of the students having classes at that time on that side of the school building, watched the departure of Jim Green, and entourage, in the State Police car. He watched it with a sinking, sick feeling, and a growing resolution to speak to Tiger as soon as the class was over, or as soon as he could get hold of him. This was it. He would wait, he could wait, *no longer* – period. Mr Hinkle, whose History class he was in at the moment, was trying as calmly as possible to get the students back to their places. Ponce stared out that window feeling just awful – *about everything*. . . .

42

When Captain Surcher arrived at Headquarters with the boy he took him back to the Interrogation Room. Formally he merely booked him for 'questioning.' Which in fact was the case. He wondered how long it would be before all the lines to Headquarters were jammed up with callers – all kinds of them. He pictured the place swarming with civil rights people and lawyers not to mention reporters. Of course they would all be kept under control. It didn't really worry him. He was only interested in one thing Jim Green: Had he or hadn't he? All the rest of the complications and developments which no doubt would be cropping up all around him were secondary things, they would take care of themselves or be taken care of in due course, and order. As far as he was concerned. He hoped. For if the boy hadn't done it, if he could really convince him he hadn't, that would be that, the end of it, as far as Jim Green was concerned. Sawyersville could have back its star Right End, all cleared. And – he would have to start over, and keep hoping. He had been disgusted by that mob of jerks hanging around outside the high school, so much so that he had issued instructions to the Troopers to keep them well away from there, at all times, in the future. They certainly had abused the boy. They would only be too glad, he knew, to see the boy burn for the thing. And it might have been one of *them*, for all he knew. That too he knew, and it made him blue. It could have, alright, only he had nothing at all to connect any of them with it. And in any event, he still stuck to the theory that it was someone *inside* that school. Part and parcel of the school. The question was: Was it Jim Green? In a few days, if he could somehow hold onto him that long, he would know.

In the Interrogation Room, Jim found things slightly different than they had been in Proffer's inner sanctum. For one thing, it was plainly, even austerely, furnished. There was a desk, and a few chairs, and they were all wooden. For another, Grady and Follo hung around, as well as Surcher. And there was a Trooper sitting on the sidelines, taking everything down, in shorthand. And, if Jim had known, there was also a tape recorder, the microphone cleverly concealed, of course. Jim sat there on one of those wooden chairs and waited for Surcher to start again. He was also waiting for his lawyer to turn up, or phone up, or something. This lawyer in fact was none other than Phil Marlowe, from Kitston, Ponce's uncle, no less, a very energetic and active civil rights worker, and well known. He had played no small part in the token integration, so to speak, that had taken place in Sawyersville High School and other schools in the area, including G.A.R., of course. Jim wished he would hear from him soon. And what about his parents? Who was going to break the crazy news to them? He wondered.

It was Grady, however, who began. The others sat there, quietly, observing the lad.

'Jim – ' Grady said, right off the bat, 'I'll tell you something – Don't think you can get away with it – if you did it.'

The boy sat there.

'Because I'll tell you – ' Grady paused – 'I think you did it.'

The boy said nothing, though aware of the new track.

'All you've got to do,' Grady said, 'Is go through the whole thing, step by step, and tell me just how you did it.' He paused. 'That's what I want to hear, right now, primarily.'

Nothing.

'When did you first get the idea?' Grady tried now.

'Where's my lawyer?'

'Don't worry about your lawyer – Just answer that –'

Nothing.

'Listen – don't jazz me –' Grady told him, sharply, 'We're not going to play any little games down here – got me?'

'What about my lawyer?'

'You're going to need a platoon of lawyers –'

'You mean *you* will –'

'Are you threatening me? Kid?'

'Show my lawyer.'

'Just what did you mean by that?'

'I want my lawyer.'

'What's a coon like you doing chasing a white girl? That nice white girl? Huh?' Grady shot at him.

'You're the coon, buddy.' Jim told him.

'Yeh? Look at my face. *Am I?*'

'Get my lawyer.'

'When's the last time you tried making out with Jill? Yesterday? Just before the whole school went to the auditorium for Assembly? Is that when?' Grady fired now.

'Go to hell.'

'Want a rap in the mouth?'

'Wouldn't that be great. Man, great.'

'Think we can't do that?'

'Sure. Great.'

'You got a real lip, Blackie – don't you?'

'Hey – go to Mississippi – you'd be great –' The boy said.

'What a lip!' Grady said, 'Hey – hear this blackball of a mother's lip?' He was apparently addressing the others in that room. 'Christ, take his clothes off and bring in the strap!'

'What about South Africa?' The boy said. 'There's a place! That's more your place!'

Grady stared at him. For a moment or two there was silence. Surcher sat quietly, just looking at Jim.

'You're hot stuff –' Grady finally said, 'Real hot stuff – an *Integrated Boy* – Right? Hot Stuff? You think so?' He paused –

'You think I think so? Know what? *I don't give a damn!* Who the frig gives a damn! Know what those whiteys in that school think of you? These white gals wouldn't give you a tumble, would they, Hot Stuff? They wouldn't be seen dead with you! So you decided to take care of that, didn't you? *Right*, Hotshot? Some Hotshot! What about Jill? You really had the hots for her, huh? Boy, didn't you! And what did she think of you? Hell, she wouldn't look at the best part of you! So you sure took care of that – Right, Bright Boy? Like they take care of them in East Caxton once in a while – that right, Hot Stuff? Come on, quit wasting our time, we *got* you by the balls!'

The boy stared at him, for half a minute at least.

Then he said, 'You make me laugh.'

'Like Jill laughed at you? Listen, she just about split her sides laughing at you! Know that? That's a *fact*! A coon like you – '

'She'd have puked on you.'

'Where were you during Assembly, Kid?'

'I told your Chief.'

'A lot of crap!'

'Ask anybody. Ask Dink. Ask Lennie – '

'They don't remember.'

'*That's* crap.'

'You're a big strong boy – it wasn't any trouble at all dragging that girl in there – where did you knock her off? In *there*, or *where*? How'd you get her head down there? You thought you'd taken care of the prints, that was a bright move, wasn't it though – Where'd you learn that? TV? *Or maybe you got a record – huh?* Right now, we're checking up on your whole damn family for records – Know that?'

'Buddy, I believe that.'

'Whaddaya mean by that?'

'That.'

'You black crap! Holy Crap! I have to take this crap? One more flip of that lip – listen, you're flat! Flat, flat! We'll have a little session with that strap – see what a hotshot you are then – How about that? Like that?'

Jim sat quietly.

Grady went on, 'Did she used to drive you nuts out there, on that football field? Is that who you played for? You used to see her, all sexed up, leading those cheers – what did you think of that hot cheerleader's uniform, huh? Some outfit and a half, huh? What about her honey pot? She must have had you off your nut! Holy Hell, How'd you ever *play* a game? I'd like to know that! Ever take your eyes off her?

The boy said nothing.

'Who were you thinking of fixing next time?' Grady went on – 'Who's next on the list? How many more notes did you write?'

The boy sat quietly.

'I'm talking to you, boy!' Grady threw at him.

'I know you are.'

'How'd you get her head down there?'

'Where?'

'I'm warning you – '

'My lawyer should be here – '

'What about that note you pinned on her? How'd you get that bright idea? Think it was pretty cute?'

'Were my prints on there?'

'You'll find out in court!'

'You didn't find a print of mine on there – '

'Wanta bet?'

'Any bet.'

'You think you wiped them all off?'

'Oh Man!'

'What did you use? Prints aren't that easy to wipe off – know that? I'll bet you didn't know that!'

'Christ! I'll laugh!'

Grady stood there.

At last he said, 'Was she already dead – when you shoved her head down there?'

Jim said nothing. He sat there, feeling funny. The way Grady said it, that last one sounded like the title of some weird song. He thought next he would sing it for him. The guy had talent. No doubt. He wanted to laugh, in a crazy way, at the guy. And maybe shout. But he sat there, as Grady pressed on. He glanced at the Captain. And Follo. They just sat there, taking it all in. It was all weird. He wondered when his lawyer would show up. He wondered how he had thought Surcher wasn't a bad guy. He was nothing but a white prick. Like practically all of them were. What would he try when his turn came up? Jim wondered all this, sitting there, utterly unresponsive now to Grady's barrage of questioning, flying thick and fast, from all directions.

Surcher listened attentively, and unhappily, not to mention forlornly, to the proceedings unfolding before him. It would be Follo's turn next, and then, again, he would take over. What the boy wasn't aware of was that he was being subjected to the special State Police Interrogation Technique known among its practitioners as 'Change Up' and also, though not as popularly, 'Chinese Indoor Polo.' This technique had been developed some time ago at the State Police Academy, though its origins could probably be traced to much more esoteric sources, somewhere along the line, geographically, and historically. It consisted mainly of a period of 'soft questioning' followed by a period of 'hard questioning' followed then by a period of 'mixed questioning' or 'no questioning,' depending on circumstances. It had proved highly successful, especially since its perfection through a long period of use and refinement, by the State Police force. Surcher was all in favor of it, though the 'hard questioning' always disturbed him a little bit, especially if the suspect was someone he was in sympathy with, to some degree at any rate. This disturbance however was more than offset by his awareness that the technique worked. Sometimes *wonders*, even. Provided of course they had enough time. So far, in Surcher's experience, the record was five days, no less. He sighed, within, knowing he would be lucky to have one day with Jim. He wondered how they had ever got anywhere before its development, the days of crude approaches to the problem, such as a bit of clubbing or way before that a touch of hot irons, long over, of course, buried in the dim sad past, he fervently hoped. Would he have time enough? That was his main worry. The boy was obviously a tough nut, done or not done it. He would be jerked out of his hands before too long, he knew, unless he got something out of him, or on him. For Surcher just didn't know. He was in that quandary. He wanted to hold him, and work on him, and if Jim but knew, which obviously he didn't, much to the Captain's distress, it had nothing to do with his color. He could have been green, yellow, or any color. The only point was, as far as Surcher was concerned, he happened to be – at the moment at least – his Number One Suspect. Of course, if his other assistants, still busy at the high school, happened to stumble across something else – that would be something. He would release the boy happily, nothing could make him happier. Not even a confession. For he admired the lad, not only for his athletic prowess, but also for his deportment under questioning, especially. Change Up Phase Two, now going on. . . .

'How many times have you jacked off over this girl?' Grady asked, and Surcher winced, within. The unfortunate necessity of the whole thing. . . .

'Where's my lawyer?' The boy asked, for probably the thirtieth time. Surcher glanced at his watch. He felt a little hungry, to tell the truth, for he had only eaten a very light lunch. Grady had been going for over an hour now. Was it time? This was always a delicate point to judge. Surcher decided to stretch it.

'What really beats me, Green, what really beats the hell out of me, is why in hell you didn't lay her – or anyhow, try ramming it into her, when you had hold of her, even after you fixed her – know what I mean? Hell, she must have been still *warm*, man! *Wasn't she?* How come you didn't?'

The boy said nothing.

Surcher got up, intending to leave the room for a while, see what was doing up front, and grab a cup of coffee, and some food, to boot. A sandwich, at least. He was just opening the door, very quietly of course, when he encountered a Trooper Clerk who as a matter of fact was just about to do the same, from the outside. Surcher stepped out into the hallway with him and closed the door.

'His lawyer's here,' said the clerk.

Surcher nodded. That was quick. He would see him, talk to him, put him in a good frame of mind – if possible – and stall for time. *Time, Time.*

'And a lot of other people,' the clerk said.

'What people?' Surcher asked, though of course he knew.

'Reporters. Other people. Couple of his brothers.'

Surcher nodded. And murmured. Something. . . .

43

'O.K., Johnny, let's hear you read that again. Just once more, boy – ' Tiger said, though in truth he had already practically decided the lad just wasn't right for the part, no matter how hard he tried. That was his trouble, actually. He only *tried*. In acting, Tiger knew, it was much more than trying. It had but very little in fact to do with trying. For either it was there – or it wasn't; either you had it, or didn't. If you did, you fell naturally into it, effortlessly achieving the maximum identification with the character, and the project, totally. In fact, it was a lot like football, Tiger mused, looking around the room and noting Ron Swann, that nifty natural of an actor, if ever there was one, in conversation now with Rochelle and Sandy Seymour, whose light red hair was tied up in a bun. She was certainly another natural, though of course, Rochelle topped them all. *All.* There was *an incomparable.* Without doubt. Tiger grinned, within, thinking of another thing, Ponce, that great kid, as a matter of fact. He wasn't here, of course. Dramatics wasn't his line. Though from time to time Tiger had mentioned it to him, attempting to encourage him. No, it wasn't that. He was just thinking of what Ponce had told him, about a half-hour ago, bursting in on him to do so. It had been a revelation and a half, and Tiger certainly intended to take action on it. He would of course see Surcher, as Ponce had requested. And though of course it would be just another dead end for the man, he would do it. For it fitted in beautifully with his primary aim: getting rid of the creep, Mummer. *Beautifully.* He could barely restrain himself now from chuckling, thinking of what Ponce had told him. It had surprised him, totally. One of the few times in his entire life, so far as he could immediately recall, Tiger had been surprised at somebody, especially that kind of thing. He certainly had kept it hidden. Well hidden. Poor creep. No wonder. Now, Tiger did chuckle, so softly though nobody really noticed. The Teaching Machine Wonder! Tiger felt good, though not entirely discompassionate either, anticipating the early departure of Mr Mummer. A windfall, if ever there was one. First of all, he would get on to Surcher. Tomorrow morning. There was no hurry. Jim was alright. Unlike Ponce, he wasn't worried. He continued that soft chuckling, to himself, only. It *really was something.* In the room also sitting here and there about Tiger were Sonny Swingle, that very promising Junior with a special flair for tragicomedy, how she could swing such roles, Marie Amis, another quasi-red-head now in her Senior year and certainly very useful to Tiger in her capacity as Student Director, what production could ever materialize without her, Dick Traugot, a terrific little actor now in his Junior year, lively as a firecracker, he would go somewhere, Judy Johnston, only a Freshman really, unbelievably, and only just admitted to the Drama Society, a black-haired charmer of a girl, a winner, bursting with life and warmth and talent, to mention some things, and of course Anne Williams and Sally Swink, those adorable things, though the truth be known Sal looked down in the dumps today. That time again? And others. Here, there, listening, or taking a hand in things, a few others, Alice Patmore among them, that very talented blond, natural of course, and, as was well known, a close friend of poor Jill's, and understandably *way down* in the dumps, under the floorboards, in fact, as Tiger noted. She was brave though. Tiger treated her with the greatest consideration, even more than usual, which was very considerable, of course. . . .

'Alright, John boy, thanks a lot, that's enough for now – ' Tiger called out. The lad looked up at him hopefully. He was extremely sensitive, this youngster, and Tiger wondered just how to break the news to him. Wasn't there *some* part for him? Maybe it would be best to let Marie handle it. She was good at such things. He thought of Ponce again. He certainly had been embarrassed, agonizingly so, making that revelation to him. He almost hadn't. Only Tiger's gentle encouraging had finally toppled him into it. Was that what Ponce had kept to himself all this long time, the something Tiger had *long* felt was on his mind? It must have been. What a lad. Certainly, if Jim hadn't been foolishly picked up that way, if – Jill hadn't gone that way – he never would have heard of it. Tiger sighed, within, aware once again, as so often, of the truly ironic paradoxes of things, practically all things, always. . . .

'We'll let you know a little later, Johnny – I have to have a little powwow with Marie – ' Tiger told the lad, who nodded, still hoping, but somewhere of course aware of his fate. Tiger felt sorry for him. What could he do? There weren't any one- or two-line parts he could shove him into. Not even walk-ons! That was the trouble with such plays. One day he'd do a light light comedy, and stick him in it. But – as for this one – they had wanted it, Rochelle and Ron especially, who would of course play the leads, spectacularly. Maybe even Shakespeare could be next on the list, he mused. There was the stuff – parts for absolutely *everybody*! He even had to reach outside the Club sometimes, in fact, for that one. In a corner of his mind, that notable playwright was known to Tiger as the Democratic One.

'Alright, Sonny – ' Tiger said now to that young actress, 'How about taking a shot at Scene I, Act II – O.K.?

'Sure Mr McDrew,' she told him.

'Dick, you get in there too, will you – ' he said to that boy.

Sandy Seymour detached herself from Rochelle and walked over to Tiger. She sat down near him. Rochelle glanced their way, then sat down over there, near the door, near Anne and Sally. She was saying something to Johnny, Tiger noted, hoping she was setting him up for the blow. Next time, Shakespeare, definitely, Tiger thought. . . .

'O.K. – go ahead – ' Tiger said.

Dick and Sonny started reading their lines. Tiger listened, as did everyone else, more or less – Anne and Judy were softly giggling about something.

Soon, Marie murmured to him, 'He's perfect – '

Tiger nodded, 'I think so.'

'Sonny isn't quite there – '

'But she'll make it.'

'You know what we ought to try one day ?' Sandy said to him.

'What ?' he asked her.

'*Six Characters* – ' she told him, not entirely surprising him. She was gone on Pirandello. 'Oh that would be *great* – ' she said.

Tiger nodded, being himself very pro that fellow. 'We'll talk it over.'

'Might be over everybody's head though – ' she said to him.

'We still could do it.'

She nodded. And they fell silent, listening to the rest of the reading. Those two kids really were pretty good, mused Tiger, taking it in. Dick was a natural and if he wanted to and worked hard and got the breaks through some right contacts, he could get somewhere, definitely. Professionally. Would Dick try it ? He was a funny boy. Very funny. He wondered what he would do. On the Brooder his profile was spread all over the place, as a matter of fact. Tiger grinned, looking at Sonny. She was certainly one of the sweetest of honeys. There was something special about the way she held herself, and walked, and *her carriage*, it reflected her character. But then, thought Tiger, didn't everyone's walk ? He remembered the way Jill used to walk. That had been a walk. She certainly intoxicated him with her walk. Her talk. Right up to the last moment he heard it. . . . He remembered a dream, suddenly. From last night. He should have written it down. Nowadays he rarely did so. At one stage in his life, some four or five years ago, he used to write down most of them. They used to fascinate him. Certainly, they were the golden key. He had quite a number of notebooks filled with dreams, tucked away in a certain corner of his den at home. He used to study them.

Nowadays, busy as he was, he rarely took a look at them. He felt blue about that. *The dream:* He was walking on the high-school grounds with Looby Loo, Ponce, and Hetty Nectar. It was strange, because with the exception of Ponce, that unique lad, they were all naked. Fortunately, it was a hot summer day. And that was the other strange thing, because out on the grounds there were at least several hundred kids milling about, and also teachers, and of course the school should have been closed, completely, for the summer. For example, he saw Betty Smith, *Naked*. Every single person on those grounds, in fact, was naked. And it was then that Looby Loo, interrupting a conversation he was having with Hetty and Ponce too it seemed about Vietnam, Violence and American History, suddenly said, 'Why does Ponce have clothes on, Honey?' A good point, at that point, Tiger thought, noticing also. 'I don't know – ' he had answered, turbing to Looby Loo, lovingly, 'I just don't – ' He had added, putting his arm around her, fondling her, 'You know what a bright kid he is.' And it ended. As far as Tiger could immediately remember, that was the end of it. Sitting there now, admiring Sonny, he mused, and wondered. . . .

Marie murmured, to him only, 'Tomorrow, Tiger?'

'Tomorrow morning.'

'What time, Tiger?'

'Ten-thirty.'

She nodded, gazing at him, warmly. He gave her a grin.

'Ten-thirty – ' she was murmuring. . . .

Dick and Sonny had finished.

'O.K. – Great – ' Tiger said, to them.

'Is the part mine, Mr McDrew?' that brown-haired maid asked him.

'Sure it is,' Tiger told her.

'Oh gosh! Thank you! *Thank you!*' she said, beaming, smiling, happily. Dick gave her a hug.

'She'll be fine,' Tiger murmured to Marie, quietly.

She nodded.

'Rochelle – Ron – ' Tiger said, looking over there – 'Let's hear your opener once more – O.K.?'

'O.K.,' that lad said, moving to the front of the room, Rochelle following.

'Now we'll hear something – ' Tiger murmured to his Student Director.

Marie nodded, and said, 'You know it.'

They sat back, as indeed Sandy, and everyone else did, waiting for it.

Suddenly, Tiger thought of Jill, in her casket. The funeral would be day after tomorrow. Ron and Rochelle began. He and Looby Loo would pay their respects tomorrow. He thought: She must look beautiful, like a princess, sleeping, in her casket. . . . He was filled with sorrow. . . .

44

Surcher was having a rough time with the lawyer. Although he had been extremely courteous and friendly, as indeed he nearly always was, Phil Marlowe just wouldn't see things his way, or even remotely his way, to be blunt. For example, he kept exclaiming, 'I want to see him *now* ! The hell with that crap!' Of course there was really no way for Surcher to make him understand, that he knew. How could he communicate to him that his great fear was the possibility of another Boston Strangler situation developing right here, in the area, with Sawyersville its ground zero, and epicenter ? He wouldn't understand that at all, he wouldn't buy it. To him, Jim was no potential Strangler. He only saw a Negro boy, victimized. And he wanted to see him, and release him. Right away, now, as he kept reiterating, before they had even had much of a chance to work on him. It was a problem, Surcher wrestled with it. How could he keep him away from the boy, at least until tomorrow morning ? By then – with some luck – within, Surcher sighed. He would try.

'Mr Marlowe,' he said, patiently, calmly, 'Believe me, I'm going to arrange for you to see him as soon as possible – '

'Right now, I said!' the response came.

'We're *talking* to him – '

'What have you got on him ? Have you booked him ?'

'For questioning – '

'What have you got on him ?'

And, for the tenth time at least, the Captain explained, carefully.

'That's nothing! What the hell's that ? *Nothing !*' Marlowe said, waving his arms around, in front of him. 'You can't hold

228

him! Listen, I'll raise holy hell! You'll see, you'll be worth nothing! I'll get a writ slapped on you in no time flat – '

How much time? Surcher wondered, as the lawyer talked on. If he got hold of Judge Flannery or one of that breed tonight, that's how much time, probably. He observed one of Jim's brothers – the older one. He was in the room, along with the lawyer and others. He had been introduced to him, by Marlowe, in fact. He looked a lot like Jim. Surcher was more unhappy. What a mess.

'Mr Marlowe – ' he said, 'I really would appreciate it a lot if you could wait until tomorrow. There's a lot we want to talk to Jim about. We're not going to harm him. We just have to find out a few things.'

'Listen, I'll get through to the Governor – how would you like that?' Marlowe threw back.

And so, for another ten minutes at least, on it went. At last, Phil Marlowe stormed angrily out of there, through that small mob, many of them trailing him, out of Headquarters. In front, before that imposing white colonial building, on the sidewalk in fact, he gave a press conference, impromptu.

With another sigh, and after a cup of coffee, and some brief consultations with various and sundry Headquarters men, and a glance at the teleprinter, Surcher returned to the Interrogation Room.

As soon as he walked in, he gave a signal to Grady, who stopped his questioning and walked away from the boy. In fact, he walked out of the room. He looked like he had been working hard. The last question Surcher had just caught as he was entering the room had been the roughest yet. The boy hadn't answered. Now, slowly, looking up to see what was going on, he met Surcher's gaze. The boy looked sullen, angry, ready to knock him down. Surcher studied him. He was in control of himself.

'Hello, Jim,' he greeted him, in his friendly way.

'Where's my lawyer?' the boy said.

'Listen, you'll see him anytime.'

'Has he showed up?'

'Not yet,' Surcher, much to his regret, had to say.

'You oughta let me go – ' the lad said.

'Jim, I'd sure like to. You know that.'

The boy stared at him.

'You're gonna look great – Real Great – Ever think of that?' he said.

Surcher didn't reply to that.

'What happens now?' Jim said.

'Oh – few more questions – '

'Few hundred, you mean – '

'How are you?'

'Ha Ha!'

'Want a cup of coffee or anything?'

'Just my lawyer, that's all, man.'

'I'm sorry you're going to miss football practice – '

'Yeh, I know you must be.'

'Jim, were you in Assembly yesterday morning?'

'Brother! *Yeh!*'

'How come your home-room teacher doesn't remember?'

'Listen – you're like a record, man!'

'When did you write that note to her, anyhow, Jim?'

'About the same time I wrote you one.'

'You're sure giving me a rough time, Jim. Put yourself in my shoes – '

'What size are they?'

'You're not helping at all, Jim – I mean that.'

The boy said nothing.

'Let's go back to yesterday morning, Jim – '

'Take your buddy boy Grady with you – ' the lad said.

'Was he rough on you, Jim?'

'Listen, he's a sweetie, man.'

'He's tired, Jim. He works too hard. I don't know when he last saw his wife – ' He paused – 'I'm sorry he was rough on you.'

The boy stared at him.

'When's the first time you asked her for a date, Jim?' Surcher asked, quietly. . . .

45

Tiger walked along the hallway toward the Guidance/Counseling Office, after Drama class, and play tryouts, which were one and the same today, of course. He was very satisfied. It would be alright. There certainly was a lot of talent in the school, good old Sawyersville, it was some place, and no denying it, Tiger chuckled to himself, proudly. Rochelle alone would one day without a doubt rank with the greatest of them, of all time, if she wanted to. Already, that astounding girl was halfway there. Watching her, listening to her was a spellbinder, alright. He couldn't wait to see the show produced, that first night would be something. That wasn't a bad idea at all of Sandy's about *Six Characters*. It was powerful, dramatic stuff. If done right. And he was sure Rochelle as the daughter would be absolutely right. She would do her as she had never been done before, he was sure of it. What a perfect peach of a part for her. What a part. Yes, Sandy certainly had a great little idea there. He would start seriously looking into it. Who would they get to play the little boy and the little girl though? Tiger wondered. Maybe somebody from the grade school. That was it. Jane, his own Jane would do! What a chance for her! Tiger chuckled again. Looby Loo sure would get a kick out of it. Ronnie of course would be the father. That would be his toughest role yet, but he knew he could count on him. Tiger kept musing over it. He was actually on his way to football practice now, the schoolday being over. He just wanted to stop by the office to drop off some books and also to check this and that. He thought about Anne Williams. She had read those lines just a little bit too fast, that was the trouble there. He would tell her, next time he saw her. He was surprised Marie hadn't mentioned it. She usually did, on those things. Football Practice. Tiger felt a little low suddenly thinking about that. How would the boys shape up tonight? What about Ponce? Would they be able to do anything at all? Somewhat glumly, he hoped so. At the moment he didn't feel too wonderful, but as soon as he got out there, with them, on the practice field, he would start picking up, he was pretty sure. The old Tiger of old would come out again, as he always did, face to face with the team. *Even under the circumstances*. The sad circumstances. . . . He loved the game. He loved his football squad, as he had all of them, all his squads, back to the days he had first taken over, after the demise of that great old coach, the one and only Hink Henderson, that terrific old guy from whom Tiger had learned plenty. Wouldn't old Hink be proud of his record! He hadn't done too badly himself, of course – but, since Tiger – Year after year, undefeated! One or two ties, only. Incredible. Tiger, feeling pretty good, and proud, of his efforts, knew it was that. And who didn't? The material. What material! Tiger thanked God for it. He thought of Mrs Mortlake. How much patience was the world made of? There was a fabulous piece of material if ever there was one. What a specimen. What thighs. Would his eyes ever alight on those thighs? Would they? It was absolutely essential to be patient though. It was the essence of life in the adult world, without a doubt. For where would all movement, perpendicular or otherwise, find itself without it? *Could* it find itself? The forces of inertia, ever beckoning life back to its primal, dead form, were formidable. Incredible. What could surmount them – if only, of course, and tragically enough, *for the moment, temporarily?* Life was a temporary, *temporary* affair. . . . When had he and Looby Loo last danced? Tiger suddenly felt like taking that sweetheart, that one and only wife of his, that honey bun, out somewhere nice and romantic, dancing. *The Spinning Wheel?* He would check into that. Definitely. The loving honey, how had he been lucky enough to land such a bun? He longed to hold her close and sway across the dance floor, dreamily, with her. What a partner. His life partner. He was utterly for her. And she for him. As far as he knew. She too was a Sawyersville girl. The wonderful letters he used to get from her in Korea. Now the boys were having a time in Vietnam. That was just about the dirtiest war ever fought anywhere, and Tiger, for one, was glad he wasn't there. What would it do to all those basically decent kids shipped over there? Sons of mothers, one and all, and what was happening to them? When they got back, what kind of members of society would they be? After *that?* What would human life mean to them? In that dirtiest of dirty wars, it meant nothing at all. Fry them one and all, that was their motto, he knew. What a dirty war, Tiger sighed. What was he supposed to tell the kids? In Civics class, where it inevitably came up from time to time, a thorny side issue which somehow always managed to get in, he let them slug it out, and it certainly was surprising to hear some of the remarks, those kids weren't dumb at all. Not just the bright ones, like Ponce and Rochelle, but on down the line. They realized, most of them anyway, what a dirty show it was. Again, within, Tiger sighed. The messes Uncle could get into. *Cornpone, take a walk, will you?* He thought of scrimmage. He and Ponce would have to do some fast reshuffling and rethinking, in view of Jim's absence. What would happen? What kind of shape would the team be in? He reached his office. He opened the door. He was surprised to find Yvonne Mellish inside, waiting for him. . . .

Ponce walked down the stairs toward the basement of the school and the locker rooms. He walked with Dink Reagan. He felt a hundred percent better since having told Tiger all. He wondered if he had contacted Surcher yet. With some luck, if he had, Jim might even be around tonight. He and Dink had talked about Jim of course. Dink was really worried, though Ponce couldn't tell him what was going on.

'Gonna be rough without him, Ponce – ' Dink said.

'We'll try.'

'Using the same plays ? What should I call ?'

'Wait until Scrimmage tonight – you'll be surprised – '

'Yeh ?'

'I'll bet Tiger already has a few new ones worked out – '

'I hope so – ' Dink said, turning his curly head to say hi to some majorettes going out to the field for a practice session too. 'You have any ideas, Ponce ?'

The lad grinned, 'Maybe.'

'Not Bob Britko! You're not thinking of sticking him in! Are you, Ponce ?'

'Bob ?' His grin widened, where did Dink get crazy ideas like that from he wondered, 'I don't think so.'

'Hope not!'

'He's coming along though, Dink – no kidding – ' Ponce said, 'I think he's better off at tackle though – '

'He's great there – '

They walked along the basement hall now toward the locker rooms. A few more majorettes walked by, smiling broadly.

'Hi, Dink!'

'Hi!'

They greeted Ponce also.

'What about T-Twenty-one Buck Decoy Left And Pass Right On Four, Ponce ?' Dink said, 'How we gonna work it ?'

Again Ponce grinned. He had in fact thought of it. If Jim in fact didn't turn up, he would certainly ask Tiger to try it.

'Wait till Scrimmage,' Ponce said.

'Give me a rough idea, Ponce – it beats heck out of me – no kidding – '

'Well – I'll tell you what – ' the lad said coyly. 'Think of the number three and subtract ten – ' He clamped up, and Dink stared . . . though he wasn't worried. He was sure Ponce and Tiger could be counted on to pull them out of anything. Even this one. He would do his best, and cooperate with them, one hundred percent. He always did. He wanted to finish up his high-school career in a blaze of glory – and keep that fantastic Sawyersville winning streak soaring. In spite of everything, he felt strong, and good, he couldn't wait to get out there. He couldn't wait to see what Ponce and Tiger had cooked up. They could do it. He knew it. . . .

'Well, hi – ' Tiger said to Yvonne, closing the door behind him. Certainly he was surprised, but he didn't show it. He grinned at her, she was sitting on the chair near the desk, just waiting for him. She smiled at him and said hi, though it seemed to Tiger she wasn't her usual glowing self tonight, or very late afternoon. Actually. Her usually warm and sparkling brown eyes seemed a little dull, maybe more than just a little. Was it her time? Tiger usually remembered. No, it wasn't. He wasn't unhappy to see her of course, though the visit was totally unscheduled, and unexpected. However, he was curious, and possibly even the slightest bit rankled, nothing at all, barely registering. How much time could he spare? At this time of year, there wasn't all that much time between the end of the school day and practice. The team was waiting for him. He took a quick look at his watch. Just may be. . . . She had the loveliest brown hair. There was hair. She wore a skirt and a sweater. And who could look nicer in a sweater? Would she be taking over as Captain of the Cheerleaders? Today? Is that what she had come to tell him? He walked up to her. He put a hand on her.

'What's up, Honey?' he asked, stroking her soft hair.

'Tiger – ' she said, and he saw the tears in her eyes. She put her arms around his waist.

'Hey – tell me – ' he said, murmuring to her, so low. 'Just tell me – ' he said, deciding the team would wait – this once.

'*I want to marry you* – ' she said, giving a few choking sobs. The tears were rolling now.

Tiger heard it and viewed it in his mind's eye in a perspective akin to distress, though he did understand, completely, or tried to. It was the circumstances. For after all, it wasn't the first time in his career he had encountered such a declaration.

He continued stroking her, aware of a growing need to.

'You do?' he said, humoring her.

'Yes I do,' she said, looking up at him. Her face was a mask of tears. It distressed him.

'Well – ' he said, urging her up and putting his arms around her. He could feel the warmth vibrating in the maid, a warmth directed toward him, definitely. She kissed him, with those marvelous lips. He caressed her breasts, through that soft sweater. His face was getting wet.

'*I really do –* ' she said, breaking it, but remaining in his embrace, and looking into his face. He admired those brown eyes. What lovely brown eyes. Spilling tears –

'I wouldn't mind,' he said, caressing her. It was more than perspective now, whether or not he was humoring her. She was growing warmer. Maybe no longer part of it. He pressed against her, definitely stirred.

'Do you mean it – Tiger?' she murmured now.

'Sure I do.'

'Because I really mean it, Tiger – '

'I know you do.'

She kissed him again, as only she could. His hand slipped into her sweater. He fondled her treasures. Of course, no bra. He found their sweet tips, already they were waiting for him. He caressed the firm things. He feather stroked them.

'Tiger – ' she sighed.

'You honey you – '

'That's why I waited for you – '

'How are you?'

'I wanted to talk with you – '

'I love you talking with me – '

'I really mean it, dear' she paused, giving little faint gasps in his arms, tilting her head back, her eyes closing now, he loved that nose. 'I really do mean it –' she said, barely getting it out, 'I just – I – Tiger – I can't go on like – this – ' she said, and Tiger almost paused – 'I love you so much – my darling Tiger – mine –' she said, quickly now – '*Oh my Tiger –* ' In one breath.

'I know you do,' he murmured to her, removing her sweater, and unbuttoning her blouse, 'You think I don't know it? Hon? *You honey hon –* ' he said, his hands full of her treasures.

'So – darling – I've – decided – ' she said, '*Oh poor Jill –* ' she said suddenly – 'Well I've decided – ' she said – 'Darling, *we just have to get married –* ' she said.

Why? Tiger wanted to ask, saying nothing instead, merely nodding, helping her slip out of her skirt, admiring her slip, and her form. He caressed her form. He murmured to her, kissing her around the ears.

'*I'm going to tell everybody about us –* Tiger – *if you don't marry me –*' she gasped – '*I love you so –*' she said, throwing this little problem in Tiger's lap, as he moved on, along her fine neck, for his need was great, and she was one of the top eight. He caressed her thighs, still murmuring to her, his hand slipped between, parting them, gliding over silken skin. There wasn't much time. How long could a team wait?

'Are you?' he asked, stroking her between those fine thighs, heading for Paradise, while she sighed, and let him stroke as he liked.

'*Everybody* – ' she said, falling back – back, back – slowly – with him – supported by him – '*But everybody* – ' she barely said.

'*When?*' he said, easing her gently onto the floor, on her back, on the carpet of course, slipping off the rest of her things, the silky things, and throwing his trousers off, deftly, reflecting for the moment and in passing the merits and possibilities of the knee-chest approach, and abandoning it, almost at once, in view of the pressing reality of the time factor, without a doubt the greatest plague of all factors and preparing to mount her, conventionally. She was ready. He gazed upon her momentarily. Admiringly. She was moaning, beckoning. *What a treasure.* Obviously dying for him. *Sweet treasure.* He adored her.

'*Right after* – ' she said, whispering, hoarsely, and just barely, 'Unless – *you promise* – ' she added, as he mounted her.

Without a doubt, he was aware of her problem, as well as the need upon him. He thrust home beautifully, into that open way. Her legs rose higher, though her feet stayed flat on the floor. Tiger stroked, she moved wonderfully, under him.

'*I promise* – ' he uttered, hardly aware of uttering it, as he stroked, exquisitely, thrilling both of them.

'*You do? You do?*' she said, on fire, streaking upward, on her heavenly way. Where *was* seventh heaven? She'd find the way –

'*I sure do* – ' he said, at the very height of things –

'*OH!*' she said. '*OH—OH!*' she said, crying out to him, clutching him, as they jolted, and pulsated, simultaneously, massively and stupendously. . . . She raised her feet and wrapped her legs around him, tightly. . . He gasped for breath. . . .

'I'm sorry – ' she said at last, releasing him. Her feet glided to the floor, and rested flat again. '*You really do?*' she said, kissing him, her tongue gliding marvelously into him, meeting his.

He reiterated, quietly, almost sorrowfully, in fact feeling a great wave of sorrow now, without a doubt. Of course she was so young. And magnificent. And Beautiful. She was a beauty. Perfectly beautiful. That was the sorrow of it. For she meant it. He was aware she meant it. Tiger, arriving at the moment of decision, felt such sorrow for her he could barely speak her name anymore. He felt her tongue so incredibly lovely and delightful, profoundly skilled in all the arts, within his mouth, as if all the ages had done nothing but teach her the art. She did mean it. She really did. He knew it. He had always tried to deny it, but she was a staggeringly imaginative maid. That was the pity of it. The greatest pity of it. Hot on the heels of it. *Why, so hot on the heels of it?* He was puzzled, as well as sorrowful. He couldn't deny it, he had always had to bear in mind that she would pull this play. He had carried her. She was too beautiful. *I'm growing old.* The words echoed, within him, increasing his sorrow, twofold. Unfortunate play. Tiger, pulling slowly away from her exquisite lips, gazed down on her face. Her eyes were opening, she looked in such bliss. *What a shame.* He couldn't find a name. There was a name – His hand slowly moved to her face, slowly, he caressed that young, glowing face. There were tears almost in his eyes, it was a fight to hold them back. Certainly, she meant it, he knew. *Hot on the heels of* – The tears, hotly pressing, nearly broke. A *real shame.* He caressed her face. She gave his hand tender little kisses. She caressed his back, beautifully, so soothingly.

'Are you in trouble?' he murmured, almost hopefully.

'No,' she told him, smiling beautifully.

'No?'

'No, Tiger – ' she told him, murmuring, '*No.*'

He sighed, loving her little kisses, and caresses, continuing to stroke her face. It was a catastrophic shame. Statistics had let him down. One in ten thousand, *yes* – he had been prepared for that. *But now.* It would have shattered another man. Sorrowfully, he had to act. Bizarrely, the rhyme came back. It flitted in and out – an instant, and gone. And then he thought: What was Sawyersville coming to? Could it be true? *Incredible.* He knew. The tears barely could be restrained. He kissed her, so she couldn't see. He stroked and caressed her, the warm, young lovely –

'Going to tell your wife?' she asked, blissfully.

'Tonight,' he had to say, sealing her lips with a kiss, the tenderest kiss, as his hands slid away from her face, and found her neck, pausing there, caressing it. Her head fell back.

'*Tiger* – ' she said, with a sigh, all set to fly, '*Darling* – ' she said, as he kissed her white throat, exquisitely lovely, beyond any doubt. Lovingly, he caressed her neck, both his hands now doing so. She loved it so.

'*I love it – Oh –* ' She told him so. Her voice let him know she was ready for more. Her warm form. Her heart pounding hard in that form. He gazed on her. *Too lovely*. That's all.

'Nice – *you're paradise –* ' he murmured to her, a million years, more, of sorrow in the tone. . . . His loving hands continued their caress. . . .

'*Darling –* ' she gasped, near a divine state. . . .

Ponce, in the locker room with most of the team, walked around to each of the boys, checking them out. They were all getting their gear on, jazzing around, as they always did before going out on the field, though a little less than usual tonight, of course, in fact, not much at all, to tell the truth. Though things weren't funereal. Of course. Out of respect for the late Head Cheerleader, things were subdued, though the fire burned. She was missed and mourned, by one and all. Without exception. Ponce knew. They were getting ready and Ponce was glad to see that only a handful of the third team was missing, three or four at most, he noted. There was even a chance they might still show up. He hoped. He had just about stopped hoping for Jim Green though. Well, it would be tomorrow night then. Certainly not later than then. Tiger was a little late getting here tonight, as a matter of fact, but that was understandable, Ponce mused. Was he tied up with Surcher – right now? Ponce was still a little scared about the whole thing, though Tiger had absolutely assured him there was nothing to worry about. He hoped not. He didn't want to be in the center of all Hell breaking loose – over him. As far as he was concerned, the world never would have been told, no one would have known, the guy could have continued teaching here the rest of his life, as far as he was concerned – if the thing hadn't happened – that way. And Jim – taken away – What else could he do? Tiger had agreed, *totally*. He had no choice. . . .

'How's that shoulder pad, Beep?' Ponce asked a square, monolithic lad, Ralph (Beep) Satchell, that granite lad, their most formidable linesman, a Tackle, and the very best.

'Uh – O.K., Ponce – ' the lad replied, in that always surprising high tiny voice, like a little boy's, 'I think,' he said.

'Let's have a look at it.'

The lad leaned over a foot or so at least to reach Ponce's level, and that lad checked over the massive shoulder armor carefully. It looked alright.

'Looks alright,' he said, 'They did a good job on it.'

'Yeh!' Beep grinned.

Ponce grinned, and slipped on, after slapping him on the elbow, encouragingly. He stopped at the next locker, where another linesman, a massive youth named Al Bartholomew, Right Guard, though on occasion Left, was making progress.

'Show me your helmet, Saint,' Ponce asked the lad, who fished it out of his locker without a word and tossed it over to that lad. He examined it.

'Aw – I think you better have another one – ' Ponce said – 'See that crack?'

Saint took a look at it. 'Yeh – guess so.' And then he said, 'Hey – how'd you know about it?'

'I noticed you were having trouble with it last practice, Saint,' the boy said.

'Geez, I was!' Saint grinned.

'I'll get you another one,' Ponce grinned, heading for the Equipment Room, where that young Freshman, Billy King, Ponce's first assistant, was sorting out a pile of stuff.

'Helmet, Bill,' Ponce said to him.

'Another one?'

'Yeh, Saint cracked it. Same size, of course.'

The youngster found what he needed and handed it over to Ponce. He took the old one from him and threw it in the corner.

'Hey, Ponce – ' then he said.

'Yeh?' the lad said, examining the new helmet, carefully.

'Jim gonna be here?'

'Search me,' Ponce said, 'Don't think so though,' and he was off.

'Where's Tiger?' the youngster called after him.

'He'll be here soon,' Ponce assured him.

He handed the new helmet to Saint and resumed his tour. He was thinking of Mona Drake, strangely enough, just at the moment. He had spoken to her about his Trigonometry problem, having cornered her, finally. And she had been real nice to him, agreeing to help him. Tomorrow in the Library they would start, first Study period they got. He was grateful to her, for now, he knew, he would make it. Even if Mummer wasn't faded. He grinned warmly, within, thinking of Mona Drake. She certainly had been nice to him. It was real nice of her. She was warm and nice.

'Get that shoe fixed, Feef?' Ponce asked Al 'Fifi' Gaudi, that ramjet of a Fullback, who could carry half the defense on his back, third-highest scorer on the team, no less. He would get Notre Dame, Ponce knew. Tiger had told him.

'Yeh, Ponce – ' said the dark-haired, powerful lad, 'Billy took care of it – before you came.'

That was alright.

'O.K. then,' Ponce responded, 'Let's see it.'

Grinning, Fifi handed it to him. Ponce checked it over. He handed it back to him.

'You could have killed somebody,' Ponce told him.

'Yeh, I know it,' the lad said.

'How's your brother?' Ponce asked.

'Aw, he's getting along o.k. *O.K.*,' the Fullback said, 'He'll be back in there next week, you'll see.'

Ponce grinned again, glad to hear it. Fifi's brother was a Senior at State and not doing too badly. He had hurt his arm last game though. Ponce moved on and checked Slim Elkins. He was alright, anyway. Ponce moved around, checking everybody. 'Pope' Poker, that classy left half, was o.k. Ponce checked them all. It was something Tiger had taught him to do, long ago. It was the first thing he asked when he arrived, 'Check everybody?' Ponce grinned, moving around, he'd sure hate to ever say 'No!' He never would, of course. He loved the game, and the squad. Even the two real solid dumbheads on the squad, no names mentioned of course, good only for plugging a hole once in a while, or warming the bench most of the while. He checked everybody, except Jim Green of course, whom he thought about sadly now as he passed his closed locker. Jerry Konski dressed forlornly near it. His was the last locker.

'What about Jim?' that ace inquired, after Ponce had checked him over. He had a loose hip pad.

'Wish I knew,' Ponce told him, 'Maybe Tiger'll know.'

'Geez, I hope so.'

'Better get a new hip pad,' Ponce told him, moving on.

Tiger hadn't arrived yet. Ponce walked back to the Coach's room just a little bit concerned. Some of the boys were already starting to file out of the locker room on their way to the field. Dink, just pulling his sweatshirt on, stuck his head in the room.

'Tiger here?'

'He'll be here soon.'

Tiger, walking along the hallway, reflected on the innumerable and indecipherable, not to mention inescapable, paradoxes of life, in particular human life, ironical to the nth degree, all of them. He couldn't get over it. What exactly kept them from utterly annihilating all life, once their full propensities were realized? Was it *love*, that divinely mitigating force, *only*? It must be. For every human being, Tiger mused, every single solitary human being with any kind of mentality at all beyond an idiot came to realize, sooner or later, somewhere within himself, the power and presence of these stark, awful paradoxes, propensities and all. *Even Cornpone.* For example, Tiger mused, he loved Looby Loo not a jot less than the most happily hitched-up man could ever hope to, in fact he adored her. He was madly in love with her, had always been and very likely always would be, till death did them part, without a doubt. He remembered that line from their marriage ceremony in her own church, that sweetest church in all of Sawyersville, a dozen or so years ago. It had a special flavor about it, that church, being in the colonial style, which Tiger was especially fond of. In fact, it was his favorite style. And yet, Tiger mused, and yet, madly in love as he was with that dream, and, with the possible exception of that exceptional girl, Rochelle, utterly inseparable from her, he had to contend with a thoroughly bizarre dream he had just recalled from the other night. It was the other night. He was holding their pet cat up before her beloved face, that ever-loving face, he was holding it in such a way that its hind end was directly in front of her face. Clearly, an unloving act. Further, as if that weren't enough, he was asking her, in a most unloving tone, *'What the hell's this?'* Waving it right in front of her face. But possibly, now that he reflected on it, *her answer* was the most bizarre part of the dream. It was, *'The cat's ass.'* Loud, clear, delivered in an extremely unloving way, in fact, a coarse way. Definitely. And that was that. The dream had faded, or certainly he couldn't recall any more of it. He mused over it, heading for the climax of his full day, Football Practice. The nearer he got to it the more everything else began to slip back into a valley of ever-deepening shadows, no matter how hard he mused. By the time he got there, the shadows had enveloped everything, in fact, the valley itself had disappeared. There was only Football, his mind solely and singularly concentrated on it. As always. It always happened. Whatever the circumstances. Just before he got to the locker rooms he passed that Captain of the Majorettes, Marjorie Evanmore, of course, on her way out to the field with a few of her entourage, and he barely noticed her, returning her greeting automatically, almost. She understood, of course. When he reached the locker room, he was Tiger truly, Sawyersville's renowned one and only, fabulous Head Football Coach, intensely, singularly. Nothing other. They all knew it, and that was it, in a nutshell, the true secret of his phenomenal success. He knew it. Not now though. Right now he was strictly a walking concentration of power, strategy, and tactics – and more. Possessed and blessed with that rare ability to project this concentration into every single member of his outstanding football squad, down to the dimmest block, including Beep Satchell, that irreplaceable tackle. How much did he weigh now? Tiger wondered, entering the locker room. . . .

46

Mary Holden was feeling blue. So blue that she had made the unprecedented move of skipping Majorette practice. Marjorie would be pretty mad at her, but she couldn't do it. Not tonight, at any rate. She just felt too blue. She had walked home from school with Sandy Seymour, who as a matter of fact lived her way, just a block from her. She had really been hoping to walk home alone, because she felt so blue. But she had bumped into her, just coming out of the door. She had just come from Drama class. And that was that. Mary admired her red hair, and her personality. She had the right personality to go with that hair, always bubbling over with life, and talk, and high spirits. She was full of fun. Mary couldn't help coming out of the dumps a little walking home with Sandy. She was that kind of girl, she got into you. But once she got home and said so long to her and closed the door she began to sink again. No one was home. She went to her room. . . .

She put her books and things down listlessly, and sighed. She looked around the room, that pretty, feminine room, decorated here and there with photos of pop idols, for she loved them still, especially Tim Clean and *The Cleaners*, that terrific group, zooming fast to the top, without a hop. She thought *The Pigs* were great, but – on their way down, definitely. Of course *The Teatles*, that group of groups, would never go down. Down. She sat down. Her gaze swept slowly around the room. She saw them one and all. Since she was in seventh grade at least she had collected photos of the idols. Unlike most of her girl friends, she still did. She loved them all. They gave her great comfort, here, in her room, when she was on her own. Often, she was on her own, here, in her room. She liked to be. Her gaze settled on the one who at the moment inspired her most, Tim Clean, of course. What a beautiful smile. She sighed, staring at him, his golden locks, his pure but rugged face, *Angel Face*, as secretly she thought of him. But she turned away from him, and sighed again, looking out the window, hoping Marjorie wouldn't be too mad. She was feeling so blue, uninspired even by that terrific view of the hills she had from her window. She didn't know what to do. She had plenty of homework to do, including Civics, she knew, feeling even more blue, thinking of Mr McDrew, *her Tiger*, who she loved so much, and, she knew, *so hopelessly*. Her hopeless love. . . . He was wonderful. She had never dreamed she could ever have been treated so nicely by so wonderful a man. And he kept her out of trouble. She took the pills just as she was supposed to, as it said. And they kept her right out of trouble. They were great. Fabulously great. As her Tiger himself – just – *that terrific man*. That man. She felt so low. She drifted over to her mirror, she glanced at herself and could see just how low. It had been this way for a couple of days now, actually, even before the awful thing. *That* thing. She hit a new low. *Jill*. Was she there? She closed her eyes, she didn't dare stare. . . . It had started then and it hadn't been helped much by *that*. If anything, it had been made worse. That. But it had started somehow after a night of tossing and turning, wanting and burning, and not having him near her, next to her, the man of her dreams, let alone Tim Clean. For she knew her Tiger was worth twenty-five Tim Cleans at least. She wanted him, now, and forever. She had never wanted anything so much. She felt so blue, knowing it could never be. She had started knowing somehow after that agonizing night, that restless, tormented night, all alone, here, in that very bed. She couldn't even *possibly* have him, more than she had him. And later? What about later, when she had finished high school and got out on her own – what about then? She grew ever more blue. She needed him. When had she last seen him? Last week, and that could have been years ago. Slowly, she opened her eyes, she saw herself in the mirror again. When was she scheduled again? *Not this week.* Gently, so gently, he had told her he just couldn't see her this week. She had cried openly, even though she knew what a busy man he must be, all those activities, she was lucky she had him as much as she did, she had sobbed away, in his arms, as that wonderful man that very wonderful that – *oh* – *what* – his – of his – slipped right into her, so deep. . . . *She loved it.* She closed her eyes again, suddenly seeing it, and feeling it, almost, *in there.* . . . She grew warm, her hands glided there, she touched herself, near there. She murmured his name, caressing herself now, her hand gliding over her dress, there. She grew so warm, she began feeling less blue. Her heart beat with some life again, as she caressed herself more, now whispering his name, over and over. She caressed herself much as her Tiger did, those wonderful hands of his, over her. She opened her eyes again. In the mirror she saw her face, flushed. She saw her figure, outlined under her dress. She was proud of it, he loved it so much. The breasts he loved so much. . . . She gazed at herself, she liked her pretty face. Her lips. She leaned toward the mirror, slightly opening her lips. 'Honey,' she sighed, 'Oh Tiger Honey –' she sighed. *When would she see him again?* She had asked him that, and he had assured her he would do his best, probably next week. *Next week.* It was a century away. She would be *dead*. Mary, again, felt so blue. She managed a last sigh at the mirror, turned, and drifted across the room. What would he be doing now? *Her man.* Football practice, no doubt. At least if she had gone to Majorette practice she might have caught a glimpse of him, if nothing more. She didn't want that though. That probably was why she didn't go. She couldn't stand that, it was just agony. She wanted more. *More.* So much more. . . . The worst kind of agony was just seeing him, *and no more*. . . . She sat down on her bed, and then rested back on it, and finally lay flat on it. Almost crying, she turned her head, and saw Tim Clean. The photo was just next to her head. There he was, grinning at her. She liked him too, and blew him a kiss. Then she sighed, and turned away from him. She thought of her Tiger, only, again. She murmured his name. Her eyes closed, her hands drifted to her breasts. She caressed them, second best. It didn't feel so bad. With her eyes closed, murmuring and murmuring his name, he was almost there, caressing them. She grew warm again, and her hand slipped inside her dress, there was no bra of course, and she played with her breasts. They were so soft. She brushed the tips, just as

244

her Tiger would. He could brush them for hours, if he wanted to. She caressed and fondled herself, she began to feel really warm. ... She moved. ... she slipped off her dress. She caressed herself more, her hands gliding all over her. Her heart began to pound hard, she slowly raised her knees. ... She caressed her thighs, she moved, and moved, gently undulating. She was very warm, her heart hammered loud, shaking the bed, as she caressed and played with herself. ... She was perspiring. She was hot. She raised herself and slipped off all her things. Now her warm, almost burning hand glided there. Gliding, and gliding it settled there. She was drenched there. Opening her legs, slowly, exquisitely slowly, she caressed herself there, her hand gliding, sliding, forever and ever it seemed, thrilling her. She thrust herself upward, in rhythmical movement now, accompanying her hand. Her Tiger was before her, on her, caressing her there, he was marvelously kissing and doing everything there ... his tongue glided, right in there ... the way her hand her fingers her burning fingers drenched as they were now were sliding in there finding their sweet way into her, she breathed quickly, she was panting now, actually, thrusting herself upward frantically, urgently, rocking with her one and only her Tiger only terrific Tiger in her so deep so marvelously thrusting deeper and deeper into her thrusting a million miles an hour now deeper than ever oh ever in her. ... Her legs were in the air, she thought she would touch the ceiling, she was drenched from head to toe, her hand had quickened its pace, reaching a frenzied rate, deeper, ever. ... She was on fire. ... She was a streaking fire. ... She cried out his name ... again ... again. ...

She lay on her side, her breathing gradually slowing. Her heart still hammered, but was trying to return to normal. She opened her eyes, slowly. She saw her breasts. She was alone. How white they were. '*White –*' she whispered. Her legs were drawn up, her hand still between her thighs. The pulsations were fading, gradually. Tiger loved those pulsations. He told her so. *Beautiful*, he murmured to her. '*So beautiful*,' she murmured now, though all alone. She saw her thighs, and the drenched nest there. She lay still. She felt sleepy. The drowsy afterward, as usual. Dreamy drowsy, usual. ... She wished her Tiger were truly here. He wasn't there to talk to her. Pet her. When he petted her – they would start again. How he could pet her. He never tired, nor did she, petting her. ... She was blue. What could she do? Somewhere, downstairs, she heard a door. Mother had come in, and closed the door. She had come home. She would call her name, as she had always done. . . . She lay there, so blue. . . . She should answer her mother. . . . She should. . . .

47

'What time did you get up this morning, Jim?' Surcher asked, quietly, patiently. He had been at it for quite a while now, since taking over from Grady. He thought another twenty minutes or so would do and then he would hand over to Follo. Not Grady. Save him for Operation Midnight Oil, the Graveyard Shift. . . .

'Seven,' the boy answered, obviously beginning to show signs of weariness. *Good.* Surcher reacted, noting this development. He felt a certain profound regret as well, needless to say. For no doubt about it, he admired the lad.

'Seven, I said,' the boy repeated to him.

'I know you did,' Surcher said, 'And yesterday morning?'

'Seven,' Jim said again.

'Sure about that?'

'Positive, man.'

'How did you get to school, Jim?'

'Same as I always do.'

'You caught the bus?'

'That's right.'

'What time does it start running, Jim?'

The boy looked at him.

'What time, Jim?' Surcher asked again.

The boy didn't answer.

Surcher studied him, calmly. . . .

'Let's Go!' Tiger called out, soon after coming on to the field. He blew his whistle also, as usual. The whole team began whooping it up and trotting smartly toward him, gradually crowding around him. Ponce was there, of course, near Tiger, as well as a crowd of young kids and a scattering of local citizens who always turned out to watch their favorite and fabulous team practice. Now the squad had formed its circle around him, leaving enough space in there for him to pace around in, as he always did, while talking to them. He looked at them. He touched his cap. He walked around inside that circle and looked at them all. He halted in front of Dink Reagan, finally.

'What are you here for?' he asked, firmly.

'To win!' Dink replied.

'What?' Tiger asked, snapping it.

'To win!' Dink replied in a much louder tone.

'That's Right!' Tiger said.

'*Right!*' the players roared.

'Why do we win?' Now Tiger asked Dink.

'We're the best.'

'What?'

'*The Greatest!*'

'Right!'

'*The Greatest! Right!*' the squad roared.

'Who can beat us?' now Tiger asked.

'Nobody,' Dink replied.

'What?'

'*Nobody Can Beat Us!*' Dink shouted out.

'*Nobody! Right! They Can't Beat Us!*' the players roared.

'What about Carverton?' Tiger asked.

The players roared. Ponce felt like roaring. He roared. It was a mass roaring, carrying far – '*Ho Ho! HO! Carverton! WO!*'

'Can they beat us?'

'*No!*'

'Will they beat us?'

'*HELL NO!*'

'What are we gonna do to them?'

'*CLOBBER THEM! THERE'LL BE NOTHING LEFT!*'

'*Roar, Tigers!*'

The field was filled with the massed blood-curdling roars of the team, and Ponce, and most of the spectators as well, as a matter of fact. It carried far and wide, it lasted a long time. A good bit of Sawyersville now knew, and without a doubt, that its renowned squad was about to start working out.

When the last of the roars had died away, Tiger started talking again. His tone was conversational this time, though vigorous. It could be heard by them all. He walked around as he talked, his gaze falling on them one and all.

'I guess you're all wondering about Jim. Well, you know as well as I do that he'll be back one of these days. Just when, I don't know. They're still playing around with him. Don't blame them. They don't know what to do. Anyhow, the fact is we might not have him around for the Carverton game.' He paused, and Ponce, for one, was certainly surprised. Had something gone wrong? Or was Tiger just preparing them for the worst? He hoped that was all. Tiger went on, 'We've got some changes in a couple of plays, and I'll tell you about them after a while, before scrimmage.' Again he paused. 'Joe Moran – you jump into Jim's slot tonight.' He paused, letting that news sink in. It was news to Ponce too, though Joe was the one he too would have picked. 'How about that?' Tiger was saying now to that lad, 'Think you can handle it?'

'Sure, Coach – ' the lad said, '*You bet.*'

'O.K. – you're the man.'

He looked all around again.

He called out, with a clap of his hands, 'Let's Go!'

And without another roar and whoops, and yells, the circle broke up and the players started taking their long laps around the field.

Calisthenics followed, for about half an hour.

Then kicking, receiving, passing, blocking, tackling practice.

Finally, the climax of it all – Scrimmage, where men were made out of boys.

Ponce loved this most of all, of course. All his theories were put to the test, and Tiger's too. He wondered what would happen tonight, with the new plays. He set the portable blackboard up for the prescrimmage drill and briefing always given to the team by Tiger. He sent Billy King to the locker room for some chalk.

Tiger, after a few last-minute consultations with Ponce, talked to the boys for about ten minutes, outlining the new ideas, sketching them on the blackboard.

Then Scrimmage began.

Tiger was a demon of activity and surveillance. He was everywhere and saw everything, with Ponce's excellent assistance, of course. There was quite a crowd of spectators now. Any Carverton spies? Ponce wondered – not that he gave a damn. What difference would it make? He looked around though, in any event. He didn't think he spotted any strange faces. Once he had mentioned this matter of spies to Tiger – he had only laughed, what a good laugh he had over it. It just didn't worry him. Hell, send them all the plays, he had said, just before the game we'll change them all! How about that? And he had laughed some more. Since then, Ponce hadn't really worried about it.

'Beep! *What the hell are you doing there, Beep!*' Tiger yelled out, in there in a flash, after a particularly furious onslaught unleashed by the offensive squad had been stopped dead in its tracks, amid a crashing, crunching, thumping, battering, yelling melee. Ponce stared, aghast, What a mess! Had Dink survived that mess? What about Pope? Tiger roared, '*You're not supposed to be there!* Christ, Beep, Look What you Did! LOOK! What'd I Just Tell You! WHERE YOU SUPPOSED TO BE? Beep! LISTEN TO ME! Ponce – C'mere, *Ponce* – SHOW HIM AGAIN!' And as Ponce jumped in to do just that, having spotted Beep's bloop himself, as a matter of fact, Tiger turned his attention elsewhere, 'Pope!' he yelled out, '*What the hell kind of a decoy was that? It fell flat!* C'mon, get off your back! You screwed up the works! Look I'll show you once more – Watch This – *And don't screw up anymore!* Wanta get everybody killed? Christ! Pope! Like This –' And Tiger demonstrated expertly, to the lad, who had made it up off his back. And then, pulling Dink out from under a pile of defensive men – 'You Handed Off Too SLOW! Dink! *You're gonna get yourself Murdered!* I told you so! Now look – *listen* – you have only a *Split Second* – Got that? *And no more!* What the hell you think I got Pope *decoying* for? *How's Joe gonna go?* Christ! *Try it once more!*' And on he went, up and down the team, pointing out this and that, not neglecting to praise those who had got it right. He hammered away, and had them do it again. And again. Until finally, breaking out of their huddle with their characteristic roar, everything went perfect, they were streaking for paydirt, and Tiger could be heard yelling loud, '*Go! That's right, Right,* GO! GO JOE GO! ATTAWAY TO GO! THAT'S IT! *Great! Beautiful!* THAT'S BEAUTIFUL, GANG! GO GO! WE'RE ALL GO! *GO!*' They scored.

The whole team, Ponce, the crowd of spectators roared. . . .

48

Jim Green was thinking, *Practice would be just about ending up, just about now, wonder what Tiger had figured out* – when –

'What did you have for breakfast, Jim?' Follo asked.

The boy lifted his head and stared at the man. He had taken

Surcher about fifteen minutes ago. He was fresh. Jim
plenty of go. They were really screwing him up though,
lost a lot of his go. Where was Surcher? And Grady?
he be seeing them again? Now, looking around the room,
saw them sitting in the semidarkness of shadows cast by the
le light on in the room – directly above him, though not in his
eyes. Follo himself was in that semidarkness too, in fact. Though
nearby.

'Bacon and eggs,' answered the lad, almost in the mood to
giggle at the inane question from the man. Where was his
lawyer? What had gone wrong? Were these white pricks bottling
him up? He wondered and worried about that. How long could
it go on? What the hell was Surcher's game? Just out to make a
name?

'Well done?' Follo asked now.

Jim only stared. It was incredible. Could they go on all night?

'Sunny side up,' he answered now, just for the fun.

'What about the bacon?' he was asked.

He was hungry, alright, he suddenly realized. When would
they come through with some food? Christ, they were going to
be in hot water, when this was all over. He thought how he'd like
to meet each of these pricks one day, especially Grady boy, all
alone, in some nice quiet place, an alleyway say. . . . Would be
great – *just great* –

'What bacon?' he asked, surprising himself. He was losing
track.

'You said bacon and eggs, didn't you?'

Follo asked.

Jim stared at the man. . . .

Ponce, nearly home now, after Practice, felt pretty good. In fact,
great. That had been a practice and a half, without a doubt of it.
Even if somehow things got screwed up about Jim Green, he
wasn't all that worried anymore about the game. The plays he
and Tiger had worked out had gone great. The boys were now
right with them. Joe Moran was no Jim Green, that he knew, and
everyone knew, but he was alright. He was only a Sophomore,
after all. Ponce was sure proud of Tiger, the way he handled the
team. Even now. He knew they would go out next week and win.
In spite of everything. If Jim came back before then, great.
Better than great. Though Ponce saw now it wouldn't be a bad
idea at all to let Joe play that game, just to give him a break, in

any case. He was all keyed up, and would be hurt bad, to be pulled out at the last second say. Or even day. Ponce had mentioned this to Tiger, after Practice. And Tiger had said, after thinking a minute, that he might well be right. They had talked about a lot of things. For example, Ponce was worried about Dink's Jump Pass On Three, which somehow Tiger didn't seem to have noticed out there. He had definitely gone to the right too far, and had only just got the pass away, each time. He had been dumped hard. *Too far*. Why had he done that? He had plenty of time, Beep had blocked beautifully, and Al too, just like they were supposed to. Ponce hadn't called Tiger's attention to it at the time because he was on top of a couple of the defensive men, hollering away. And then Dink had called another play right away, one of Ponce's new plays, as a matter of fact, and he had become involved and hadn't recalled until back in the locker room. On that new play, Feef had blasted through a ten-foot hole, at least. It went great. What decoying work!

Ponce had just said so long to Dink and a few other boys, as a matter of fact, having walked home from Practice with them, as he often did. Dink lived just a block away, on Jefferson Lane. That was one quarterback Sawyersville would have a job replacing! Ponce knew, and Tiger above all knew, and they were working on it already. Ken Smith, a Sophomore, was the boy they both had their hopes on. Tiger had only told him tonight he would stick him in next week in the second half, if things went O.K. in that first half, that is. Funny enough, Ponce just recalled, he hadn't asked Tiger if he had contacted Surcher yet. . . . Maybe tonight, he would call him up, and ask. Though he knew there was nothing to worry about. He probably had, or would soon, if he hadn't, anyhow. . . . What a mess. . . . Ponce turned back to Football. He loved the game. He never realized just how much until he got out on the field each day and found himself totally involved in it, like Tiger almost, he mused, grinning to himself, if such a thing were at all possible. Tiger had casually mentioned something tonight after Practice that made him feel pretty great. He had said it might not be a bad idea if he, Ponce, gave some consideration to coming back to Sawyersville one day, after college of course – to teach, to write – *and to give him a hand!* He mentioned this after Ponce had said to him how much he was going to miss the old team one day, when he went his way.

That wouldn't be bad! He hadn't ever really thought about it that way, but it sure wouldn't be bad – at all. Of course, he wouldn't be with Tiger until after four years of college had passed – and a heck of a lot could happen in four years, of course – but in theory, and as a long-range plan, it was O.K. Not bad! He wondered how the team would make out in those four years. They did alright before he ever came on the scene, so why shouldn't they when he went away? Ponce grinned, musing, Who do I think I am? Tiger, he thought, must have given him a big head. . . .

Now Ponce was just a few yards from his house; prowling around along the side of the house he saw Peppy, that crazy cat. Ponce smiled as Peppy looked up suddenly and saw him, and loped in her funny way toward him. Ponce loved that cat. He called her name, and she came the rest of the way, comically slinking along, and turning sideways to him. Ponce picked her up, stroked her, and went around the house toward the back door, talking softly all the while to her.

He thought of Miss Smith.

Wouldn't it be great if she still happened to be around – five years from now!

But Ponce grew sad, thinking, fat chance of that. She'd be married with a houseful of kids – at least. . . .

He reached the back door, he saw his mother in the kitchen, she smiled at him, he smiled at her, and with Peppy dangling from his forearm, purring away, he opened the door. . . .

49

Chief Poldaski was in the corner poolroom, just across the way actually from his usual post in front of the Memorial there at Twelfth Street and Whitmaker Avenue. He was having a hamburger and a cup of coffee for himself at the moment in fact. During the day, when things were normal, he usually dropped in a few times for such a repast. And often in the evenings too. Of course these past few days, during the day, he hadn't had the chance. And so he was especially glad to be there tonight. He had missed the place. He liked it there quite a lot, for the boys were always talking about this and that, and he learned a lot. Besides, he liked their company, they were a great bunch of guys. He

They all laughed. The Chief did too. He took the first shot and scattered the balls. A couple went in. He lined up for a second try as Ben marked up the two.

'How's the huntin' gonna be?' Poldaski asked, taking aim.

'Aw – I dunno. You all set?'

'What you gonna use this year?' Joe Bedenk asked, watching Poldaski's shot clip one more in and then sink itself too.

'Scratch,' Ben said, moving in with his cue.

'Goddamn,' Poldaski said, 'That nig's ruined my aim – '

They laughed. They all had a good laugh.

'Hey – tell how you caught him, John – ' Joe said.

'Did he have his pants down?' Ben said.

They had another laugh. This time Poldaski didn't join in the laugh. However, he finally grinned a little bit.

'He had it out, right out,' he said, with that grin on his face.

'What color is it, John Boy? No shit – Cherry red?'

Another long laugh.

'Red-hot cherry red,' Poldaski said, at last.

'Is that what you grabbed him by, John?' Ray Shuddick said.

That brought a big laugh.

'You fuckin' guys,' Poldaski said, good-humoredly.

'How's the wife?' Ben said.

'Pain in the ass.'

'Hey – know those jig school gals? Know what? No shit, some ain't bad – ' Joe said.

'Aw Christ – you'd lay them, huh?' the Chief said.

'Hell Yes!' Joe said.

Another laugh.

'He'd lay anything,' Roy said.

'*They ain't bad!*'

Joe sank his shot, as they laughed.

The Chief was having a good time, and without a doubt. He always did – up here. He would hang around probably until the place closed – around midnight. And then he would probably hit Selmo's for a few brews and a plateful of that ravioli. *Yeh.* His mouth watered even now, thinking of it. Who the hell in the whole world made ravioli like that? He knew, *no one.* . . . Unless something came up. What could? What now the hell could? He knew nothing would. Another burst of laughter, from the boys at a table nearby, hit his ears. He grinned, feeling good. . . .

50

After getting home from Practice and giving Looby Loo a big kiss and a hug, Tiger had supper with his one and own. It was just great, as usual. She was some cook. Then, after that delicious meal, and some small talk, including of course the whole thing and Jim Green, and another hug and kiss, he never could get enough of her, Tiger went upstairs to give Jane a little help with her homework. Often he did. She had a lot of names and dates to memorize for History, her favorite subject, she had straight A's in it, and she wanted her dad to see if he could help her get them down pat. He liked helping her with her homework. She was a cutie of a kid if ever there was one, it sure was fun being with her. You never could tell what she would come out with next. The things she came out with really made him laugh. He didn't see much of her during the school year, especially during football season, of course, and he was always glad when the weekends rolled around. Her cute face was a lot like Lobby Loo's, though to tell the truth she had her daddy's eyes, and they were nice eyes, too. He was very fond of his little girl, he loved her to the point of almost spoiling her, he knew – which was something he didn't want to do.

'And on what day was the Constitution actually signed?' he asked, looking at his little hon.

She tossed her long blond hair, what a girl, she gave a little pout.

'Wednesday?' she said.

'Just the *date*,' Tiger said.

'Did you and Mom used to date?'

Now why had she said that? What a playful little trick –

'Did you? Hmmmmm? Daddy – Hmmmmm?' she asked.

'Ask Mom.'

'You mean *Mother*, don't you?'

Recently, she had decided it was best to address her mother in that way. She was growing up, she had said. Tiger didn't mind. He understood little girls. He grinned. She was really the cutest thing. She loved her daddy so much.

'That's what I mean,' he said.

'Well why didn't you *say* so?' she asked. 'Know what we did in school today ? Want to know ?' she also asked.

'And what did you do ?' he said, knowing that's what he had to say.

'I'm not going to tell you,' she said.

'Was it bad ?'

'Oh, no – I'd tell you if it was bad!'

'*Were* bad,' Tiger corrected, fondly.

'Is it, Daddy ? I never can get that – '

And there she was, kidding him around again.

'I can't wait to get to high school, Dad.'

He smiled at her. It would be great.

'Will I be in any of your classes, Daddy ?'

'I think you will.'

'Which ones ? Oh which ones, Daddy ? Will you give me all A's ?' She was excited. He saw her warm face, all pink with excitement now. Her PJ's were the cutest things. Pink and frilly, very sweet. She was a feminine thing. A copy of her mother's really, come to think – though she usually wore nighties to bed. Her body was all warm under those PJ's. He knew. He smiled fondly at her.

'Didn't I tell you once ? And you'll have to work for your A's.'

'Oh I forgot – Daddy, tell me again!'

He did just that.

'I hope I pass them!'

'I think you will.'

She gazed at him.

'How was Practice, Daddy ?' she said, warmly.

'Very good.' And it had been.

'I want to be a cheerleader!' she suddenly said, her eyes sparkling at him, 'When I get to high school – oh, Daddy, I want to be!'

He smiled again, 'Well, if you try hard enough, I'm sure you can – ' And she would make the prettiest cheerleader. He knew.

'Sometimes though I think I'd like to try for Majorette – ' she said, frowning a little bit, still gazing at him.

'Well, you have some time to decide,' he said.

'And what happened to Jill Fairbunn, Daddy ?' now she asked.

He sighed. He said, 'She died, Jane.' He always told her the truth.

'She was *murdered*, wasn't she Daddy ?' his little girl asked.

Again he sighed, reflecting that no doubt Looby Loo had already handled these queries, sad as they were, and painful too.

'That's what they say,' he nevertheless said quietly.

'It's horrible, it's awful, isn't it, Daddy?'

'It is,' he said.

'I hope no one murders me!' And she meant that.

'We all hope that.'

'What do you mean?'

'Well, nobody wants to be murdered, little hon.'

'I know they don't.'

He smiled at her, she fell into his arms, wanting a hug. He gave her a hug. Her body felt so good and warm and young. He felt good. She snuggled up on his lap. She had always loved sitting on his lap. She was growing up. She would have a lovely form. He caressed her and gave her a little kiss. She kissed him. He was crazy about her.

'I love you so much,' she said to him, blushing again.

'Now what about those dates?' he said to her, kissing her pretty nose.

She wrinkled up that nose.

'Oh Daddy! *Spoil Sport* – '

He chuckled at her, eased her off his lap, giving her warm, cute bottom a little smack. She had a full life before her.

'Come on – let's go – ' he said to her now, picking up the books again.

She sat on her bed, knees drawn up, her arms resting on them. Her cute face was turned toward him. She waited for the questions to begin. . . .

After the homework session with his Janie, Tiger tucked her in and went downstairs to Looby Loo. He found her, and their cute little cat Sheba, in the kitchen. He played for a few minutes with that playful cat, that little orange cutie, only ten months old, a kitten really, then helped Looby Loo with the dishes. What he did was dry the knives, and forks, and spoons, and similar things, and put them away. He had offered to buy her a dish-washing machine once, but she didn't want one. She was funny that way. He liked drying those things for her. They chatted about this and that. Then he went into the parlor and sat down in one of the comfortable chairs. The small sofa, actually, just big enough for two. Their love seat. Tiger had a nice, spacious parlor, actually very tastefully arranged and furnished – by Looby Loo, of course. He had just switched on the TV when she walked in and sat on the sofa with him. They held hands. She gave him a few little kisses. Tiger gave her a real kiss and knew she was in the

mood. She was nice and warm. How he loved her. She cuddled
up to him, the TV came on. Ads about soup. Then, *Lucy*. It was
one of their favorite shows. That girl was really a card, she made
them laugh and laugh. Sometimes, she made them roar. They
liked Quincey Mayhew too, and Jack Benny to boot. But *Lucy*
flew.

'Is the little angel asleep?' murmured Looby Loo.

'I think so.'

'Did she learn her dates?'

'Yes she did.'

'Are you going out tonight?'

'Don't think so.'

'What's new?'

'Nothing much.'

'What about that boy?'

'Oh, he's not the one.'

'And they're holding him?'

'They made a mistake.'

'There's a lot of prejudice around –'

'I know.'

'So you really think –'

'I think so.'

'How do they make such mistakes?'

'They do.'

'What will they do?'

'Release him – I hope.'

'The poor boy.'

'I told them what I thought.'

'You did?'

'That Captain sent the boy to see me – to see what I thought –'

'Why didn't they let him go?'

'They're up the creek.'

'Well, you did right –'

'I'm pretty sure I did –'

'*How are you?*'

'*Looby Loo* –'

They kissed. A long one.

'Ummmmmmmmm – you –'

'Love you –'

She said, at last, 'Want to watch this – ?'

'Yeh – let's have a few laughs –'

'Oh – Mother wants us to dinner Sunday –'

259

'Sunday? Good.'

'Shall we go after church?'

'Good idea. Yeh.'

'Dad's feeling a lot better.'

'That's good.'

'I'm just not letting you *watch* this!' she said, with a soft laugh. She snuggled up to him even more. She kept quiet now. They watched the show.

'Is Saturday the funeral?' she murmured, once.

'That's what I heard.'

She sighed, they watched the show. Sheba slinked in and made herself at home on her favorite easy chair – the best one. They both smiled at her. . . .

After the TV show, Tiger retired to his den for a while. He had a few little things to do. But soon, in bed, he would be seeing Looby Loo. '*Don't forget*,' she had said. smiling warmly at him, giving him one more sweet kiss. He had grinned and said, '*You kidding?*' And left for his den.

No sooner had he arrived there though than the phone rang. It was Proffer, no less.

'What's new boy?' the wonder said.

'Nothing much.'

'How did Practice go?'

'Oh, great. Those boys are really great. They're something, Harry.'

'What about Jim Green?'

'Are they still holding him?'

'Holy Hell are they – I hear his lawyer can't even see him – all kinds of hell is breaking over *that* – I hear – I guess you didn't hear – '

'I didn't.'

'You still sticking to your theory, boy?'

'Right, I am. He's not the man.'

'They're gonna look awful silly – '

'You know it. They can't help it though.'

'Listen, Mike, what about this funeral Saturday?'

'The whole school should go.'

'All *together?*'

'Why not?'

'We'll have to work it out.'

'It's in the morning, isn't it?'

'Yeh – eleven o'clock.'

'That's what I thought.'

'Well – you don't want to force anybody – '

'No, I guess not – '

'If they get there early, say about eight o'clock, why – maybe everybody could file by – before they close the coffin – that is, everybody who wants to – '

'Right. That's right. That's what I thought.'

'I guess I better announce it in Assembly tomorrow – '

'Yeh, I think you ought to.'

'What about flowers ?'

'Well – I guess the best idea would be for each Home Room to send some. Don't you think ?'

'I guess that's the best way.'

A silence followed.

'Boy, if your theory's right, Mike, we're still in the soup.'

'Uh huh.'

Another silence.

'How's Hilda ?'

'Fine.'

'Jane ?'

'Just fine.'

Silence.

'Well, I'll see you tomorrow, Mike boy. Haven't heard anything from Surcher, have you ?'

'Not a thing.'

'Just wondering if they're going to be around tomorrow – '

'Haven't heard, Harry.'

'O.K. – I'll see you, boy – ' He paused – 'Who'd you put in at End ?'

'Joe Moran – Not bad – '

Proffer chuckled.

'O.K. – See you boy.'

'So long, Harry.'

Hanging up, Tiger sighed. He also shook his head, slowly, from side to side. Then he sat down at his desk. He unzipped his handy slim briefcase and pulled out a few things he had brought home to work on. First of all, the book he had been reading earlier in the day. He wanted to examine it a little further tonight, here in his den, before tucking into bed. Then a folder or two, of this and that, including his Schedule of Activities for the next day, which he wanted to fill in. He mused over that, now, as a matter of fact. Ten-thirty of course Marie Amis, as arranged, so he penciled that in right away. He grinned, looking forward to that. He checked his notepad to see what else was on. He didn't have to write down to *contact Surcher* of course. That he would do first thing, probably right after Assembly. He wondered if Mummer's four million fellow Masons, among other things, would rise to his defense, or contribute to it, at the minimum. A fat lot of good it would do him, in any event, as far as his early retirement from the school was concerned. That he knew, Tiger mused, grinning away. What a character! Where would he peddle his Teaching Machine next, he wondered? Mr Programmed Instruction Queer, Tiger chuckled away there, thinking of him. What about Crispwell? Tiger mused over that one. Maybe he should see if old Ponce had any interesting scoop on that one. What a kid. That great kid though. His new plays had worked beautifully. Tiger viewed the future, blissfully almost. In spite of everything. . . . Peggy Linski at nine-fifteen, after Assembly and that contact with Surcher. She was completing Part II of the Brooder of course. He jotted that in. Was she the most promising of the younger Majorettes or wasn't she? She looked a real sweetie out there on the field, or anywhere, for that matter, in front of the band. He grinned. That's the only way a girl can get to wear a miniskirt in Sawyersville. Tiger was more than fond of her. Those Polish blonds were something that never failed to captivate him. They were a class of their own alright, without a doubt of it. Marjoie was lucky she was graduating actually, or that kid could press her pretty hard for her job alright. Tiger was still grinning, musing over the complex intrigues and processes of high-school kids' social life. Sandy was scheduled for twelve o'clock, he noted, and penciled that in. He stopped a moment, thinking over that one, for it was pushing close to lunch hour, wasn't it, and maybe – but in any case it wouldn't take all that long to give her the Bernkrokker, that was the beauty of that inventory. When had he last tested her, that talented kid? He checked up on that. . . . Then there was luncn and Health Ed. and a little bit of Phys. Ed. and at 3 p.m. or a little after, he made it after, Barbara Brook, whom he hadn't seen for a couple of weeks, at least. He hoped her problems were coming along alright, she actually was pretty bright. *Pretty and bright*. He grinned, warmly. . . . He thought of Jeannie Bonni – but then remembered she wasn't due in until the following day, which in a way was good because it was cutting things a little fine again, though it could be worked in, he knew, if anything could. Who had a sweeter smile than her? *Looby Loo?* Maybe. He felt warm, and content, thinking of Jeannie – and Looby Loo. Soon he would be seeing her. He checked over the whole schedule again, carefully, making sure everything fitted in right. He realized he would have to make allowances for a phone call or two, probably a visitor or two, Proffer most probably, but possibly others too. Jim Green, maybe. He might be around tomorrow. He hoped so. It would be interesting to hear his account of State Police treatment and technique. It would. He sighed, feeling sorry for that lad. But, once again, thinking, it was an experience, it was life, wasn't it. . . . *Look what I've been through.* . . . In a pensive almost melancholy mood, he checked over a few more things and then pushed himself back from his desk and went to his easy chair, with his book. He wouldn't keep Looby Loo waiting too long, but he did want to read just a little bit. He sat down, the book in his lap. He sat there like that for a minute, just thinking about that sweetheart of a wife of his, and his Jane, now asleep no doubt and God knows dreaming of what, and that lazy, sensuous, absolutely selfish little animal Sheba, that treasure cat. . . . He thought about Practice. What a Team, what a pool of material, how could Sawyersville be so lucky, anyhow? Year after year, those kids, *what* material. And Ponce! He grinned fondly. What a fantastic kid. He had finally casually mentioned his ideas and dreams and vision to him. The lad certainly had seemed responsive, his eyes, his whole face had brightened. Four years though. *Five.* That was a long time. He hoped to God he could maintain that responsiveness all that time. A sharp kid like that – no telling who might latch on to him at college and spirit him away, somewhere. God knows those corporations were always combing the campuses for the best. But – there was a good chance, he knew. Ponce was a kid with deep roots, and those roots were right here, in Sawyersville, he knew. He wouldn't desert the old place that easily, he was pretty sure. *Time would tell.* Time, Time, *man's unique Hell.* . . . Four years. What might happen to the team? Tiger found himself growing a little bit apprehensive. Sometimes it happened to him. *Would the pool dry up?* That was the worst question. For a moment Tiger was more than just a little apprehensive. How could it? That was the next question, and Tiger began feeling better. . . . *He knew it couldn't.* . . . He felt a lot better, in fact pretty good. He opened the book now.

The Human Vagina

He tried to recall, had he perused this before?

This very essential and interesting anatomical structure, which can be referred to as the vaginal barrel, has two main functions : (1) Heterosexual psycho-physical contact of the highest and most intimate order and (2) to serve as the main pathway for the Human Male's contribution to the Human Female's total conceptive apparatus . . . He might have, he wasn't sure. He read on, in any event. Content. . . . *The vaginal anatomy and physiology of the Human Female are instructive, in all respects, and provide the most important cluster of clues to an understanding of the very basis of her sexual life, in all its ramifications* . . . Tiger nodded his head, admiringly. . . . Would Looby Loo let him undress her tonight? He hoped so. . . . *For on the one hand while the Human Female's vaginal barrel prepares itself as described earlier for penetration by the fully tumescent penile shaft, so on the other hand the Human Male's penile shaft, fully erect and engorged, demands to penetrate – and readily accepted the invitation on the part of the fully prepared vaginal barrel* . . . to be mounted, unquote, Tiger tagged on, in a frolicky mood, growing warmer thinking of Looby Loo. She often liked him to remove her bra and other things. Those dainty, cute other things. He smiled, warmly. *Those things.* How he loved that gal. On he read. . . . *[See Table 34-D-LX(e)]* . . . He flipped the page. . . . *Anatomically speaking, the very foundation of the Human Female's orgasmic experience is vasocongestion (or engorgement) of the labia minor as well as the vagina* . . . Those wonderful letters she used to write him, they had pulled him through, what else could have? For a moment he glimpsed the nightmare. He saw the letters. They were there. He felt their warmth, sustaining him, there. . . . He had known her since high school days, though he hadn't actually dated her much then. She was going more or less steady then – Freddy Gilpin, wasn't it – He was a banker now. That was it. He worked in a bank in Kitston now. Surcher's stamping ground. Tiger grinned. Now . . . They had really started going together just before the Army, and Korea. That was when. He had finished up at State. . . . He was aware of a surging warmth, thinking of her. Who, outside of Rochelle possibly, could ever take her place? He mused. In life you never knew. He grew sad again, knowing how life was, seeing it for a moment without Looby Loo. . . . For no one ever knew. What was around that corner – you couldn't view. . . . Especially after thirty-five. That was the time. *Time* . . . *Nipple phenomena* . . . Tiger read on. . . . He studied a series of diagrams showing the changes in the size of the Human Female's nipples during the various phases of sexual activity, including mounting. The measurements were precise, down to the hundredth of a centimeter. . . . Tiger browsed on. . . . *The Orgasm of the Human Female* . . . Tiger stopped. . . . *Orgasm cannot be separated from primal socio-psychologic factors* . . . He knew it was thus. . . . *It is the peak, the most ultimate point, the zenith, in short, of the entire drama of sexual activity; it is deeply rooted in the complex biological history of the entire species* . . . Tiger nodded. . . . *It is the* sine qua non *of the very existence of the species, in its present form, bio-psychologic and socio* . . . Tiger pondered it, rereading it. . . . He moved on, finally. . . . *Penetration of the Human Female while she is in a supine position (on her back, i.e.) demonstrates clearly and dramatically the high intensity vector of this phenomenon: Her hands and feet clutch her partner, she cries out, her face contorts in definitive spasms of release and ferment* . . . Tiger nodded. . . . (*See Chart 02-CX-9*) . . . Tiger looked for it. . . . *The Sex Blush is at its most diffuse at this climatic moment* . . . Tiger noted. . . . *The Human Female is capable of re-forming her spent tensions soon after orgasm, and in this connection it is apropos to examine in some detail the phenomenon known as STATUS ORGASMUS* . . . Tiger halted, right on top of it. . . . *This extremely interesting phenomenon can come about as a result of simultaneously surging orgasmic peak levels almost nonmeasurable in their singular entities* per se, *i.e. – or it can simply manifest itself as a definite, continuous, mono-orgasmic wave-surge of the highest dynamic order* . . . 'Hmmm,' Tiger murmured, enlightened, definitely. . . . *STATUS ORGASMUS has been observed to last for as long as 160 seconds in certain instances, though on the whole it is true to say that the normal curve of distribution applied to the phenomenon. [See Table 64-1-D(2) and Diagram]* . . . Tiger checked that. . . . *How does orgasm affect the vaginal barrel? Can the Human Female fantasy to orgasm?* Tiger turned to the Diagram again. He loved that normal curve. He read on again. . . . *At the peak of orgasm, an all-engulfing, wave-like suction-surge overwhelms the vagina* . . . Tiger nodded. . . . *Respiratory rates are very rapid at the peak point – in several cases, rates of 60 per minute were definitely observed and noted* . . . Tiger noted it. . . . He flipped a page and ran into a photograph of a most interesting piece of apparatus devised and constructed by the investigators for the purposes of investigating. It did everything the Human Female vagina could conceivably require of it, under any circumstances. Tiger admired it. There were also detailed diagrams. Tiger browsed over them. What a piece of work. Electronically controlled, instantaneously and delicately responsive, it could match the real McCoy anytime. Anywhere. Its thrust was formidable. Tiger mused, intrigued, definitely. The female subjects must have loved it. Tiger grinned a grin, an image popping up in his mind, many images, as he thought of it ... all of it. ... Now he put the book back on his desk and just sat back in his chair, relaxing, thinking about things. He was thinking a whole range of things, from the mysteries and paradoxes of creation itself right along and down the scale to more mundane details, such as getting a haircut this week, due as he was for one. Hadn't Looby Loo mentioned it to him, in her loving way ? Soon he got up, coming to no definite conclusion on the primal mysteries, in fact baffled as ever, and walked out of his den to the bedroom, thinking only of Looby Loo. ...

She was just slipping out of her dress, and Tiger was glad he had timed it just right. She was standing with her back to him, her hands were reaching behind her shoulders for the zip, or little hook. 'Hello – ' she murmured low, stepping out of the dress. He came up to her and gently slipped his arms about her, his hands cupping her breasts, tenderly fondling the beautiful things. She gave a little murmur, and a soft sigh, her right hand touched his face. She caressed his face, and her face turned toward his, and she kissed him on the lips, as he unhooked her feather-light bra and received the superb gifts that fell into his hands, marvelously. The bra slipped away from her. He looked down at her, loving the view. He loved her flanks flaring out, they were sturdy beauties alright, what a well-formed girl she was. He loved her. *Darling –*' she murmured, as he caressed her breasts, and her belly now, and downward, gliding exquisitely over her, over the silky things, starting them downward, as she exquisitely helped him ease them off her. They stood there, and he continued caressing her, so gently now inside her thighs, circling, back and forth, finding finally the sublime terrain, lingering there. His phallus was prodding and pressing against her marvelous buttocks. He caressed them. He kissed her along the neck and shoulders, and one hand still fondled her fabulous breasts, their sweet pink sentinels fully alert now. "*Take off your things –* ' she murmured to him, reaching for him, kissing him, *as only she could kiss.* ...

At a little before midnight, just as Chief Poldaski was about to hang up his cue and call it a day, the place having thinned out quite a lot in fact, most of the boys heading for Salmo's, Harding's, or similar places of refreshment, for a few brews before retiring for the night, Sam Roto's phone, stuck under the counter, rang, and it was somebody asking for the Chief. Thinking it might be his beloved, who once in a while did give him a call at Sam's place, Poldaski walked reluctantly and even somewhat resentfully to the phone and answered it in not his most dulcet tones. However, it was not Mary. It was Larry Mellish, who ran Sawyersville's most bustling electrician's business (he had wired up the town hall, Sam's place, the school, Selmo's, and many other local establishments, including the Chief's own little abode). He gave a piece of news to the Chief in very worried tones, and demanded that he do something about it. The news was: his daughter, Yvonne, was gone.

Missing.

Poldaski heard the news and nearly fell off the stool he had perched himself on. For a moment he said absolutely nothing, hearing only Larry's voice saying over and over, 'John? Hey, John? John?'

Then he said, 'You home, Larry?'

'Yeh –'

'Stay there. *Don't do nothin'* Understand? *Nothin'.* I'm comin' *right over.*'

And he hung up.

A moment later, as Sam stared, he tore out of the place, jumped into the Borough Police Car, roared off, nearly plowing over a bunch of the boys, and rocket-powered for Larry Mellish's place. . . .

Surcher felt they were getting somewhere. It was 1 a.m. and not only had all attempts by the lawyer (and others) so far failed to dislodge the boy from his grasp, but the boy himself seemed more and more like the culprit to him. He wasn't as yet one hundred percent sure. They had been working on him nonstop, the three of them, taking turns of course, as per Change Up, Phase Four, and he seemed to be wearing down, or approaching the threshold, at any rate. Just now, Grady was questioning him, in his unique way, having taken over from Surcher, who at the moment was grabbing some shuteye in the special Police Slumber Room, well equipped for such vital breaks from prolonged periods of strenuous activity, or duty beyond the call, as it might be called.

'How much more shit you think we're taking from you, Cassius?'

The boy mumbled something. He was obviously tired.

'What? Can't you talk? Can't hear you, Hot Shot!'

'Fuck yourself – ' the boy mumbled.

'You didn't get much fucking out of her, did you, Boy?' Grady threw at him, 'Not a thing, not a bunt, nothing, *right there*, Big Boy?'

'She was a honey – ' mumbled the lad.

'Yeh! *So Long Honey!* That's what you mean – ' Grady fired at him. 'That's what you're trying to tell me – C'mon, come clean – Where'd you write that – in the lavatory? What made you pin it on her? Tell us all about that. Who the hell are you? What was it, a joke, or something: Pretty funny? Give everybody a good laugh? That it? *What's your name?*'

'One of these days – ' Jim mumbled.

'What's your fucken name?'

'You know my name – '

'Is it Muhammad?'

'*White prick – wait – *'

'You don't have a white prick – what a shame! A Goddamn Shame! That poor gal would still be around! Right, Jackson? *White*. Big and *white*. That's what you needed. Right? *Kid?* What a kid! Answer that one! Listen – *when did you pin that note on her?* Was it hard – getting her head down the head? C'mon, Kid! You sure must have worked fast! How'd you prop her up like that? We figure you did it all in *ten minutes flat!* That's fast! A jump pass! *How'd you do it, Kid?* Start from the beginning, that's what, don't skip a thing – '

'When do I sleep?' mumbled the lad.

'Sleep? Christ! All this on your mind and *you wanta sleep!* A little snooze for Frooze! Pull out the bed! The Best bed! Floating Slumbertime mattress for you, Kid? Sweet Christ! Know when you can sleep? *Now listen to me* – Don't drop off that chair because Jesus Christ I'll just kick you to – *Understand?* Listen Boy – *you can sleep when you've told the scoop.* The *Whole Scoop*. Understand? Ready to do that? You'll be here until you do just that! *Better face that!*'

51

Ponce was in his Home Room standing up with the rest of the class Pledging Allegiance to the Flag (and to the Republic for which it stands) the next morning when Jim Green's ordeal ended, though unbeknown to him or to Ponce, or to Tiger, who at the moment was finally putting in a phone call to Surcher with his interesting news. It happened this way: The School Janitor, Bill Honeywell, opening up his broom closet in the basement not far from the boilers, for the purpose of selecting the appropriate brooms and associated equipment to commence his early-morning brush-up, found himself confronted with a totally unexpected and jarring sight – the lifeless form of Yvonne Mellish, Assistant Head Cheerleader – inside. She was propped against the back of that closet and she was leaning over a broom, she almost seemed to be using it, in fact. She was completely naked, save for a pretty pair of briefs, on which was pinned the message – *SWEEP, HONEY* – written in pencil, in large capital letters on a standard sheet of school paper.

52

'Hello, Peggy – ' Tiger said to the blond young lovely as she entered his office, right on time. He felt pretty good in fact. He had just finished talking to Surcher and he felt pretty certain it wouldn't be all that long before his star Right End was back again, none the worse for wear, he hoped. Tiger didn't know it, of course, but Surcher was about to get another phone call which would make that practically certain.

'Hi – ' said that sweetie of a kid, giving him her sweetest smile.

'How are you this morning?' Tiger asked, with a grin.

'O.K.,' she said, so sweetly.

And certainly she looked O.K., Tiger mused, surveying her. Never having really discovered the exact nature of the special something about this girl which so much appealed to him, he nevertheless loved it. The warmest instincts in him, as soon as he laid eyes on her, or, for that matter, thought of her, responded to her.

'Well, what's new?' Tiger inquired, after she had made herself at home.

'I dreamed about you last night,' she said.

'You did, did you?' Tiger said, admiring the maid.

'It was a funny dream – ' she said, moving in her chair, rearranging herself, so to speak. 'You were asking me to come out for the football team.'

That was some dream. Tiger nodded, thinking about it. He had a few himself coming back to him now. He thought about them. He saw Looby Loo.

'And then – when I said *no* – ' Peggy said, 'You said I was probably too young anyhow – '

Fascinating, and how. Tiger mused.

'That sure was a funny dream,' he said at last.

He gazed at the lass.

'Can I sit on your lap?' she asked.

Tiger grinned, she was some kid, a sweetie and a half of a blond Polish kid, what a kid.

'Hold on – not just yet – we have Part II of this Brooder to take – '

'Oh – Brooder-pooder,' she said, pouting at him. And then, 'Do I have to take it?' she said.

'Well that's what you're in here for – ' he said.

'*Tiger* – ' she sounded so bored.

'It won't take long.'

'Promise me?'

'I do.'

'My sister's getting married – ' she said, out of the blue.

'Which one?' He knew three or four of them.

'Eleanor.'

She was a dream.

'Oh yes.' He knew her fairly well.

'She's twenty-two.'

'I remember her.'

'She was a Majorette – Remember that too?'

'Sure I do.'

'Can't I sit on your lap?'

Tiger grinned again. What could he do? They'd never get through the Brooder.

270

He said giving in, looking at her warmly, fondly, 'Better go and lock the door —'

She got up, he admired her form. . . .

53

It was after Peggy had departed that Harry Proffer phoned through with the startling news. It took a little while for him to get it out, for he was in pretty bad form. In fact, he could hardly speak. It was a series of grunts, and squeaks. Finally, having somehow and somewhat calmed him down, Tiger got the drift. In the quietest of tones, he told Proffer he would soon be around. He checked his watch — it was just ten o'clock. He hung up and just sat at his desk for a little while, he just sat, numb almost. Finally, he moved. He shook his head, slowly, from side to side. He sighed. He wrote a brief note — four or five words, at most — *Back soon as poss.* — and placed it on his desk. He got up. He left the office. . . .

Ponce took the news like a man. He was stunned of course, and wondered just what in the hell Sawyersville and this world were coming to, but also he felt mighty glad that now without a doubt Jim Green would be released. And he knew who would be picked up. Only a few minutes ago, and incredibly enough, in fact, he had seen the freak. Ponce had given him two miles of berth, at least, and knew that before too long, everyone would. . . .

The frantic and barely comprehensible call from the school, in effect putting Surcher back to square one, was the first he had heard of Yvonne Mellish. And that had come on top of the call he had received a little earlier from Mr McDrew, with his bit of news, which had set him back to square seven-eighths, at least, just possibly. For Chief John Poldaski had not bothered to contact him about the worried phone call from the father of the late Assistant Head Cheerleader last night. He had taken matters into his own hands. He had decided that. He would handle the matter himself, for he had taken the last bit of guff he would ever take from a goddamn Statie. And he had been doing that, however unsuccessfully, all night in fact. He had interviewed the distraught parents, carefully, skillfully. He had searched far and wide. And in fact, he had been making good progress there, for at the time Bill Honeywell was opening his broom closet, the Chief was just about to begin an examination of that notorious lavatory, having slipped in there very stealthily and cleverly during Assembly, the best time really, as he had concluded, for such improvised activities. . . .

He had found nothing.

54

Despite the development, and the tumult, not to mention near-furor following thereafter, Tiger managed to get back to his office in fairly decent time, after consultations and commiserations and a general review of the situation with Proffer, Surcher, and others. For he had an appointment. And above all, he hated missing appointments, though he might be late, in certain and very rare circumstances. This was one of them.

'Hi – ' he said, to Marie Amis, who sat there, waiting for him. She had found the note. 'What a mess – ' he added.

'Did you see her ?' she asked, without formalities.

'Uh uh,' Tiger told her, sitting down at his desk.

'Will they close the school ?' Marie asked, intelligently.

'Uh uh,' he said, to that bright miss.

'Think they should ?'

'No, I don't.'

'It's getting pretty dangerous though – '

'Well – in a way – ' Tiger said, quietly. 'But – all of life is a dangerous thing – Isn't it ?' And he paused. 'Stop to think about it – Sweet Marie.' And he stopped.

Marie sat quietly a few moments, gazing at Tiger. Certainly, she appeared to be thinking about it. Tiger knew, as he sat there gazing at her, that if anyone, outside of Rochelle possibly, could seriously think about such a matter, it was this maid, this sweetheart of a girl. This dream. She had early shown a considerable talent and coolness under fire, so to speak, in her approach to the production of drama, and other matters, and life in general.

And it wasn't long before Tiger had designated her Student Director, in short, his Assistant insofar as matters in the Dramatic department were concerned. They had enjoyed a long and successful collaboration, and it was only a shame, to put it mildly, that she was graduating this year and heading for State, enrolled in the School of Dramatic Arts, no less, last report. She would do well there, Tiger knew. And one day, without a doubt, the world would hear of her – unless she married, raised kids, which was always a possibility. Which wasn't a bad idea at all in any event, Tiger mused, gazing at her, fondly. That fundamentally, was what any normal woman really wanted anyhow, he knew. Who could deny it ? Tiger knew what fulfilled them. He knew only too well the unassailable truth of that matter. It was beyond discussion, Marie knew it, he knew, within herself.

'I guess it is,' she said, sadly, keeping her gaze on him, 'That leaves the Cheerleaders without any leader at all now,' she also said, quietly.

Tiger nodded, reflecting on that. Certainly it had also crossed his mind, the cheerleading squad was being decimated, without a doubt. Apart from anything else, he was certainly sorry about that. For they were vital. Who could take over ? Was there a natural chain of command ? What about Barbara Brook ? He made a mental note to casually mention that to her. It wasn't up to him of course, for that area didn't fall within his sphere of activities at all, well he knew. But he couldn't help wondering about it. He loved the Cheerleading Squad, and knew how much the team did too. It filled an essential role, however you looked at it.

'You'd make a good cheerleader,' he said to Marie, almost wistfully. He knew she couldn't fit it in.

'Would I ?' she said bemused by it.

'You would,' he said, utterly seriously.

'*Oh Tiger* – ' she said, laughing at him, and warmly.

Now he chuckled at her. He had got the pitch.

'How are you ?' he said.

'I could feel good,' she said, with a soft sigh.

'What do you hear from your brother ?'

'He doesn't like Vietnam.'

'I'll bet he doesn't.'

'He says it's criminal, Tiger, is it ?'

'It's a dirty war, no doubt of it.'

'What do you think of the protesters ?'

'Well – I don't know – Marie – ' He paused, reflecting on it, 'I don't know. Should Americans protest?' He halted.

'Why not, Tiger?'

'Well – we're involved in it – ' He stopped again.

'It's pretty sickening – '

'Yeh, I know, I know.' He paused – 'That I know – Marie.'

For a moment, silence. They were looking at each other.

'Well, anyway, Tiger – ' she spoke quietly. 'There won't be any protesters in Sawyersville – ' She paused – 'Will there?'

Tiger grinned, wryly. He was struggling with it. That statement was true, without a doubt, no matter who felt what about it. What a world. What a rough world it was. And no doubt of it. He thought of Old Cornpone. Dallas was on other planet. Would things have been different? He wondered. Gazing at her. He thought of her brother. Everything. He turned to other things –

'What about the play?' he asked.

'Do we have time to talk about the play?' she said.

She had a point there. What a girl.

'What shall we talk about?' he asked. 'I sure like that blouse,' he said.

'Shall I lock the door?' she said.

'I did.' He grinned at her.

'You think of everything – '

'*You're a dream – *'

'*Let's dream – *'

She reached out for him and touched him. He admired her red hair. *What hair*. She murmured to him and stroked him. *What a girl*. 'What are you thinking of?' she said.

He grinned. 'Being a good girl?' He touched her nose.

She smiled at him, a little flushed. She bent over and toward him and rubbed her nose against his. He saw those green eyes, he never could see enough of them. She smelled fresh, and good. She was in some mood and a half alright, Tiger mused. He was pulling away from darkness. He was alive, again –

'I'm always a good girl,' she said, kissing him, her eyes closed. He took her in his arms, and kissed her too, warmly.

'What I am going to do without you?' she said at last, murmuring softly to him, in his embrace.

'There's a whole year to go,' he murmured to her, gliding his hands over her.

'It goes quick – *so quick* – ' she said.

'That's life – that's how life is – *I'm going to miss you* – ' he said, helping her out of her blouse, delighted at the exquisite sight. She had the whitest flesh. Her slip was the prettiest feminine thing. The feminine principle was the thing. She had on nothing. He fondled her breasts, lovingly, through the sheer slip. She slipped out of her skirt. She clasped him in a passionate embrace, murmuring his name. She pressed against him. That was always her way, Tiger mused, very warmly, caressing her hips. . . . A girl with her own mind, who really knew her own mind, and what a mind. . . . He caressed tenderly. . . .

'A really good one – *Tiger* – *sweet* –' Marie said, rubbing herself against him, loving the strong phallus probing against her, ready for her. . . . '*Oh God I need a good one* – ' she said, in a murmur close to a whisper. . . . '*Tiger Sweet* – ' She was kissing him, merging with him, *who could kiss like that* –

'I'll try my best,' Tiger told her, murmuring low to her, slipping her out of her slip. . . .

55

Surcher was up against it. He had released Jim Green, amid a fusillade of promises from his lawyer Phil Marlowe to 'tear the State Police apart,' which he would no doubt attempt to do, Surcher knew. He had picked up Mr Mummer, as per Mike McDrew's tip (via the kid, Ponce de Leon), and he had released him too, after several hours' questioning, having found absolutely nothing to connect him with things, not to mention that he didn't for one moment believe him capable of such feats, if only on physical grounds, alone, however much of a fag he was, potential or otherwise. (He had finally admitted as much. He would fight, but he would disappear from the school, Surcher knew.) Certainly not. The man, or kid, who had lifted those girls around was no skinny thing. He had muscle on him, without a doubt. On any grounds, Mummer just didn't fit. He would be the last man on his list unless he actually caught him in the act sometime, and then he would have his eyes tested. He was up the creek, he knew. Not only was there obviously a first-class and prima-facie kook loose in the school, having the time of his life dispatching young maids, but he left no clues. What would lead him to him ?

Again, outside of that crazy note, with not a print on it, he had nothing, absolutely. In a way he had hated releasing that kid, Green, for he looked good. But certainly he had no choice. He couldn't possibly have dispatched the latest one by remote control. A search of the girl's home had revealed nothing. This time, not even a note. Pressure was starting to build up around Surcher from all quarters. The Governor himself might soon be sticking his nose in, he knew, being that sort of vote-catcher, he well knew. Not to mention the Attorney-General, who would soon be on his tail. And what about the carloads of media men who would be turning up? He was glad he had plenty of Troopers. He mused over things. The girl had been strangled, that much he knew. She was full of jism, someone had had a good time with her, that also he knew. It was no rape job, certainly. The pathologist absolutely discounted it. There were no signs of struggle, the girl had been dispatched almost effortlessly, it seemed, almost *with her co-operation* – bizarrely enough. It was bizarre, alright. Surcher shook his head over it, thinking of it. Who was the jerk? How many more Sawyersville girls would bite the dust? Would it be best to recommend a closure of the school? This point in particular worried him and caused much conflict within. The parents would probably want the school closed – if they didn't, they might well just keep their kids at home. He couldn't blame them. God knew he couldn't blame them. But – on the other hand – he also knew that was the surest way to prevent the discovery and apprehension of the lunatic, whoever he was. *Who he was.* Surcher slowly brought his fist down on Proffer's walnut desk, four or five times at least, soundlessly. Was it a kid? *Or a teacher?* He had already crossed one off the list. What about the others? What about Proffer? Surcher weighed that a moment, then discounted it. He even grinned a bit. Then, serious again, he knew he would have to examine the possibility that one of the teachers was nuts, and not just like Mummer was. Who could that be? Who was the vicious nut? Surcher twisted around in Proffer's comfortable chair and stared out the window. He saw the expanse of the athletic fields – the football stadium – one of the best in the whole area, he knew – the Practice field – the baseball diamond, what a fine setup Sawyersville had though, he mused, taking everything in, admiring in spite of himself the unbeatable powerhouse they were. Maybe, he mused, he could pick up some tips, before he was through, and pass them on to G.A.R. – courtesy of Mike McDrew. He thought about Jim Green. He felt a little bad. He hoped he hadn't harmed him. Without a doubt, he had put him through a little bit of a rough time. For nothing, as it had turned out. He thought about seeing him, in a couple of days, and maybe apologizing – if Marlowe and his gang hadn't got him thrown out of his job by then, he mused, grinning a little, over that one. . . . What a one. . . .

But who was the nut? How would he find him? Would he just have to wait until he turned himself in? How many healthy young Sawyersville maids would by then have been done in? The grin had completely disappeared. Surcher sat in that chair, staring out at those fields. . . .

Ponce stared down at the floor. He was in the Library, and Mona had just left. She had helped him a lot right off the bat. If it kept up like that, before long, he would actually know what was going on. But now she was gone, and he just stared at the floor. He was actually between the stacks, having wandered there shortly after she had left. He had heard about Mummer being released. Well, he supposed Surcher and his crew knew best. Would the guy still be around though? He wondered about that. He would talk to Tiger about that, he would wait and see. Certainly, quite a few people by now knew the score. And how long could a guy hang around with that on his door? Ponce stared at the floor. It was no good pretending he could hold up his head. The only good thing was that Jim had been released, though he wasn't around yet. Maybe tomorrow he would be. *Tomorrow.* Would *anyone* be? His head carried a ton of dead concrete weight. He knew the score. Would they close down the school? He thought of old Bill Honeywell, and felt sorry for him. He certainly knew how he must be feeling, and above all, what he felt upon opening that broom-closet door. What a deal! For real. What about the team? He hadn't been able to get an answer yet from Tiger about practice tonight. *And the game?* Poor Yvonne. . . . Twice he had been by the Guidance/Counseling office and twice the sign had been up, TESTING. He had almost broken all the rules – and barged in. He was dying to see Tiger and talk about things. He felt bad. True, he had taken the news initially like a man. But that was partly because he thought they had got their man. Now – the full impact of things was making its terrible way through him, utterly muting him. And what was wrong with that? How should he act? Couldn't he feel bad? *That* was a man. Ponce, hanging his head, pondered all that.

'Hello, Ponce,' a warm and familiar voice said to him, between the stacks. He looked up and saw Miss Nectar. Immediately, he felt a little better. He even managed to smile at her, though not quite the usual one specially reserved for her.

'Hello, Miss Nectar,' he said to her.

'Feeling blue?' She had on a dress that was the color of Autumn, Ponce suddenly realized, and it looked absolutely perfect on her. *Beautiful. . . . The leaves of autumn – still – on the trees – beautiful there. . . .* The fragmented sentence ran through his head on its own, having sprung up, suddenly, all on its own. It held him, almost haunted him. Would it depart from him? He listened to it. He saw her. He had always admired her, not as much of course as Miss Betty Smith, that dream of dreams. But – certainly –

'I'm sure blue,' he told her, sighing almost.

'I know how you feel,' now she said.

'What's going on around here?' Ponce asked.

'I wish I knew –' she murmured, 'I wish someone knew,' she also said, tenderly, to the lad.

'Will they close the school?' Ponce asked.

'I don't know. It's awfully bad –'

'I hope they don't though,' Ponce said, feeling the warmth between them, longing for more. He wondered if she felt it too. He looked at her. He was sure she did. What a wonderful, warm woman she was. Like his mother, almost. That's what it was. He gazed at her breasts.

'What are you looking for?' she asked, in a low voice.

'I don't know,' Ponce said, truthfully.

'You poor boy,' tenderly, Miss Nectar said.

'What's this place *coming* to?' Ponce, in a voice full of anguish, asked, between those stacks.

'How can I help you?' Miss Nectar asked, obviously affected, reaching out and touching him on the side of his face with her hand. He felt her hand. The warm, marvelous soft hand. He, mother hand. He caught her fragrance, which was wonderful. He stared at her face. There was warmth, a million years of itr tenderness, and human love in her face. Her brown eyes. Her hair. She had the nicest brown hair. Her lips were lovely. Full, soft, so receptive. He knew. His eyes were hot. Would he cry? There was just the barest hint of a tender smile on her lips, just for him, he knew, understanding him.

'I don't know,' Ponce said, 'I just don't know,' he also said, only hoping she would keep that hand there.

She didn't though. It slipped away slowly, he watched it slide to her side. He remained there, just staring at it. Then, at her. Next to Miss Smith, and his mother, she was the warmest woman on earth. He wished she would take him in her arms. He wanted to nestle against her, on her breast. His heart began to pound.

'There's a big meeting going on soon,' she said, softly, 'I heard.'

'Is there?' he said, still hoping she would.

'Yes. So I've heard,' she said, 'School Board members, County Superintendent – Our Principal – ' she said, 'The State Police – '

'Surcher?'

'Is that his name?'

'That's it.'

She sighed. He saw her eyes. His heart pounded so hard.

'And I guess they'll decide – '

'About closing down?'

'So I've heard.'

Now Ponce really wanted to cry. Between that thought and his powerful desire, it was all he could do from bursting out crying. The tears were there, ready to pour out. What restrained them? He wondered, and marveled, staring again at her breasts.

'M-Miss Nectar – ' he said.

'Yes?' What tenderness.

'*You sure are nice.*'

A moment, silence.

She smiled. When had he seen a warmer smile?

'Ponce – ' she said, very softly, and tenderly, 'That's awfully nice.'

Ponce felt like shaking. Now, inside, alongside his rampaging heart, he was already shaking. Once it started, he knew, he was lost. There was no stopping it. He was getting in quite a state. He was really glad they were between the stacks. He hoped no one else would dive in. The Library wasn't very busy just now – but – you never could tell. It would be embarrassing as hell. He'd really be a laughing stock – they'd have him in a hammerlock – *How he wanted her to take him in her arms!*

'Miss – Nectar – ' he said.

'Yes?'

He couldn't get it out. He knew he never would. He vibrated

wildly. Disaster was just around the corner now. She would know all. Anyone might pop in. The warm and loving creature stood there, looking at him. Would she burst out laughing at him? Ponce dreaded that.

'Ponce – ' she said, her voice caressing him, 'What's on your mind?'

He barely heard it.

'What are you looking at?'

'Your – face – '

She smiled.

'Just – your face – ' he added.

How she smiled.

'*Gosh you're nice* – ' Ponce got out.

'What were you looking for?' she asked.

'Jonathan Wild – '

'That's a wonderful book – '

'Fielding shows an unrivaled mastery of the art of irony,' somehow he got out.

'I agree there – '

'Have you read it?'

She smiled, 'Of course I have.'

'I want to read it again.'

'I'll get you a copy – '

'That's what I was looking for – '

She smiled.

'Do you like football?'

She smiled, but didn't answer.

He said, 'I like it a lot.'

'I know you do.'

'Do you like it here?'

The question was odd. He realized now. No sooner had it come bubbling out than Ponce realized how odd. He didn't know what he was saying anymore, Ponce realized, suddenly. They remained standing there, so close. *What would happen next?* She was a warm flower. *Would the stacks come crashing down?* Ponce wouldn't have been surprised – '

'It's a very nice town – ' he heard her reply.

'Even now?'

She gave a little shrug. He loved that shrug. The shoulder moved, it was a shrug. Her dress moved too, upward slightly, over her breasts, gliding.

'Even now.'

'Do you go to bed late at night?'

She smiled, Ponce felt on fire. How had *that* one come out? He clamped down hard, nothing more would he say. He loved her smile, he wanted to fall, head first, into that smile –

'You aren't the murderer – are you, Ponce?' she asked, murmuring very low. It staggered him.

'O-of – Of Course – N-Not,' he said.

'I know you're not.'

'I couldn't murder a flea.'

'I know, Ponce.'

'How come you asked that?'

'I was only teasing you, Ponce.'

He knew she was. Though what a thing it was. She was teasing him out of his mind, *she was*. How much more could he take? How long could they stand there? Would he finish up his days there? Ponce, wild for her, wondered what to do. He thought of Miss Smith. *Betty Smith*. Within, he sighed her name. That wonderful, *muffed* opportunity. He should have known what to do. Who wouldn't have – outside of him? Now, here, it was clear to him, a second opportunity was rapping hard at the door – miraculously enough. How could it be? *Twice?* in a *row?* Ponce pondered hard, over that one. How could it happen – *to him?* Time passed.

'D-Do you think – you have the book?' he asked, at last.

'*You sweet boy –* '

He saw what was happening and was sure he was in a dream. He would wake up any minute, wet with the dream. *She was putting her arms around his throbbing form.* She was – *pulling him gently to her.* Ponce hit a spin. Wildly, he spun. *She caressed his head, and laid it on her breast.* Ponce shook like a locomotive. He felt her hands caressing his head. She was murmuring, over and over to him '*You sweet boy –* '

Ponce felt the sweet, soft breasts under his head. Was there anything so soft, so sweet in all the world?

He started to sob, suddenly. She kept on murmuring. He sobbed softly, uncontrollably. The tears cascaded from him. She held him like a son, caressing him, murmuring. . . .

They were deep in the stacks.

Marie, in a double-action furor on the Guidance/Counseling floor, let out a scream that could have shattered two or three chandeliers, even four. She thrashed her legs in the air, begging for more, *and more*, as she and Tiger soared *and soared* . . . clearing the summit of Mount Mighty Road. . . .

The Chief was sore, mighty sore. He had come within an ace of discovering the body himself, which he knew in his bones would be around somewhere. If he'd only had ten, fifteen minutes more! He could have moved in, told Surcher and his gang the score. Now, he was only sore. Surcher had curtly relegated him once again to traffic duties, which had now assumed monumental proportions, of course. Staties were all over the place. He had heard there was talk about closing the school. He had seen John Slater and a few others on the School Board show up. Other major domos had showed up. Were they powwowing in there? About what? The Chief wondered. Would they close the damn school? *What for?* What good would that do? He pondered on that, thinking about going in and telling them a thing or two. He could tell them too. They had turned the jig loose. Well – o.k. – *o.k.* – maybe they had nothing on him, *he* wasn't the one – *But what about the other jigaboos?* How many of them? Eleven? Seven? How many were there? Anyhow, how come Surcher and his bright boys weren't working on them? Poldaski, burning now, trying to unsnarl his end of the traffic, exchanging verbal fire from time to time with the friggin' Staties milling around him, here and there, vowed he would find the fiend. *He would show all of them*, for they hadn't a goddamn clue. He knew. This was his lay of the land, and he knew – if anyone did. He would turn the tables on all of them. And then Surcher could suck hotchies – all day long, gong-dong. He had his plans. And how he did. He looked forward to it. He knew he could do it. Surcher was going to find *nobody*. But *nobody*. He knew. Not unless the guy decided to walk himself into handcuffs. . . . *That he knew.*

'Chief – how 'bout moving your goddamn car out of there?' one young Trooper shouted at him. Poldaski hadn't seen him around before. And where the frig had he come from?

He bellowed out at him, *'Don't worry about that car, bud! Look at that goddamn Plymouth there! Move It, Boy!'*

The Statie looked around, the Chief kept on bellowing at him. It was a torrent of abuse.

'*MOTHER FUCKS!*'

He ended up. . . .

56

In the Teachers' Conference Room, around that large and fairly shiny table there, sat Surcher, Proffer, School Board Members, the Area Super, a few others, and Tiger. They were tussling with the knotty problem of closure vs. nonclosure, for the time being, at any rate. From time to time Tiger checked his watch, for it was all a matter of time, and if he showed up too late no explanations would do, he knew. Such were young maids. Well he knew. Whatever the circumstances, it wouldn't do. Sandy especially, that angel in blue. So he hoped this powwow wouldn't go on that much longer. It was all a hell of an affair. Once again he had been forced to cancel practice. Now, here they were seriously discussing whether or not to close the *school*. A major blunder if ever there could be one. Tiger, like Surcher, and Bowlby, the Area Super, was against it. It was some of the School Board bozos and Proffer, apparently, probably sucking up as usual, who wanted to close down. One thing great has been accomplished: Mummer was finished, they had decided on that – unanimously. He wouldn't be allowed in the school after today, though he would be paid until the end of the term. Fair enough. That might just give the jerk time to find work. Good luck to him, Tiger mused. Would he try G.A.R. ? He grinned, picturing that. Right now, Surcher was patiently and calmly explaining why there should be no closure. How else could they corner the nut ? He told them the only way was to keep the school open, regardless of risk, and of course there was a certain risk, no denying it. There was just no other way that he knew of. As for the parents, he thought most of them would understand and cooperate, once they know the facts. Tiger nodded, and spoke along the same lines, leaning, to a certain extent, on his reputation, the respect they had for him, and the awe they held him in. Of course he utilized all the effective techniques of interpersonal communication at his command, internalized over the arduous years of experience in the field. For it was his field, every day. Surcher talked some more also, when he had finished. Finally, and to Tiger's great relief, they swung the right way, starting with John Slater, the best one of the bunch, without a doubt. Tiger knew. Proffer was no problem, once he saw how things were going. Tiger, and Surcher too, he knew, breathed sighs of relief, within. There was more chitchat of course. They decided to invite all the parents to the school for a mass meeting in the auditorium, so they could talk to them and get their fullest cooperation, which was essential, possibly and probably vital, of course. Finally, they broke up. Tiger checked his watch again.

'What about the game, Tiger?' John Slater asked him.

'Yeh –' Tiger said, noting the Board Members beginning to mill about him, 'We'll have to work on that.'

'Hell, cancel the whole thing,' Jack Hitchner said, 'You won't stand a chance – two, three Practices maybe shot to hell –'

Tiger eyed him, knowing what a football expert he thought he was, though of all of them, he knew, he was the dumbest jerk.

'We'll work on it,' he told the dope. That satisfied him, whatever Tiger finally did.

'Why don't they have a double funeral?' Hitchner now said. Tiger took that in. What could he say? He said nothing. He checked his watch. Hitchner had actually connected. They were talking about it. Tiger heard forlornly. Surcher was talking to him.

'Well, you've got your boy back,' he said, giving that little grin.

'Thanks,' Tiger said, meaning it one hundred percent.

Now Surcher talked to him about his plan to interview all the teachers thoroughly. The male teachers, of course, he meant. Tiger listened, concurring, and wishing him the best of luck, and offering him his fullest possible cooperation, as always, of course.

'I don't mind telling you,' Surcher told him, 'I've hit a wall here.'

Tiger grinned, 'You'll get over it –' He paused, 'Or through it.' The man needed encouragement. He patted him on the shoulder.

A few more words with Proffer now, about this and that, and Tiger finally made it out of there.

He checked his watch, with a frown.

Ponce couldn't stand it. No matter how hard he tried. He knew he was on that long slide, and stopped fighting it. And so, after emerging from between those stacks, having done nothing but sob his heart out, on that heaven-sent, he made a beeline for the lavatory – and jacked off. He was a failure, utterly, he knew it. She had offered treasures, well he knew it. Now, finally gaining relief with a series of hot convulsive jolts, a pounding heart, and

284

screaming pins and needles all over, Ponce started pondering morosely, as usual – only more so. He stared at his red-hot and healthy young organ, detumescing slowly. *How long could he go on like this?* How many guys, in one lifetime, were presented such golden opportunities – *twice not once* – like this? And what would they have done? Ponce, in despair, stared at his healthy pal. *Miss Nectar would have adored it!* He had kept it from her. What was the only thing he was capable of doing with it? *Playing with it.* He felt sick. And dizzy. *Keeping it from them.* He nearly fell over. His head would fall into the toilet. That's what should happen, really, he thought, *it was all he was good for*. When would he stop playing with it? He thought he was on his way, he thought he had, these past few days he had fought and controlled himself – And now – *Here He Was.* He hung on in that cubicle. When would he grow up? Be a *man?* That was the trouble. What good was this? Afterwards, he always felt like this. Sick, sick. He was almost seventeen now, it was time to get the hell off this bubble. Did the other guys worth mentioning in the school carry on like this? What the hell would Dink have done with her? What if he knew? Ponce was so low. He would end up in that toilet. *Wham.* Dink's wang would have gone all the way home. He knew it. He pictured it. Deep in those stacks – *What a setup!* He sank lower. No getting away from it. He couldn't go on like this forever, he knew it. It was all up to him, he knew that too. *He* would have to be the one to put the brakes on it, really on it, and start growing up. *How the hell else could a guy grow up?* That was it, that was how it happened alright, he knew. Tiger had told him – not that he had ever discussed his problem with Tiger, he just didn't have the nerve to – but just talking in general, skirting sort of around the area, about growing up in general – developing – he had told him. And Ponce knew that was right, for it wouldn't just *happen.* How could it? He had to *make* it happen. He was sure. Otherwise – and he suddenly shuddered at this, the closest yet to being sick – he could spend *the rest of his life like this!* Ponce stared at his now pendulous organ. He placed his hand around it, letting the last drops of semen slide into his palm, and fingers. *Wasted.* He felt. All down the toilet. He also felt. Loving its feel. And smell. Knowing how much a heaven-sent like Betty Smith or Hetty Nectar would love it, the feel of it. How did it feel, that lovely stuff, that warm-like stuff, inside them? *Sliding in them?* He felt warmly sad, *he was getting excited again*, thinking of that. He was absolutely seized with the most overpowering desire to *know that.* How could he ? He never would. Not that, anyhow. No matter how much progress he made toward being a man, that was something he absolutely and totally would never know, or could. He knew it. He felt more than sad . . . He sat down, on the toilet seat, after getting himself together again, and thought about things. Other things. Everything. He felt worse. He could never remember feeling worse. What would happen now ? Would the kook strike again ? When ? *What about the game ?* Would there even be a game ? *Or a school ?* Was this the end of *Sawyersville High School ?* What would happen to the school ? *And Betty Smith ?* Would he have the guts to go to her place once again ? What about Practice ? Would there be Practice tonight ? *Poor Yvonne.* What a heck of a swell girl, what a girl, that Yvonne ! Her old man. Her parents. Ponce thought about her parents. She was the only child – the apple of their eye – he knew – Larry Mellish had built up that business over the years – all those years – What a raw deal. *Rotten !* What a stinking rotten deal ! *It was !* Ponce thought about going down to see Tiger. But then he remembered, he still would be in that meeting. Well, he would see him after, he had a lot to ask him. Most important, outside of Mummer, even ahead of Mummer, the straight scoop as to whether or not the school was closing. He was almost afraid to ask that one, for he knew the answer *could be* – he prayed it wouldn't be. He prayed silently to a God he didn't even know the scoop about, let alone the truth about, for he had to. Really troubled, he always had to – whatever the truth was. *Did it matter ?* He was beginning to discover what seemed to him to be one of the saddest truths of life – *so many things didn't matter.* He thought of the percentage of his fellow citizens who totally supported the bombing of North Vietnam, *and more*, according to the latest Gallup Poll he had read about in the paper this morning. He thought of that miserable, backward country. All those countries. He thought of the might, the power of his own country. He thought of Cornpone. It was incomprehensible. It was pathetic. He felt so low now he didn't think he could ever get up off that toilet. He would just stay there and they would find him there. *Like Jill.* He leaned forward, his hands over his face, thinking so many things, everything. . . . If he had the nerve tonight he would see Betty Smith. He had to see her, and talk with her. . . . There just wasn't anyone he loved so much – outside of his mother. . . . His profound despair lifted just a little bit, thinking of her . . . and his mother. . . .

'How many hands do you see?' Tiger asked Sandy Seymour. She only pouted and shook her head so that her red hair, today in a cute ponytail, shook too. Tiger loved that ponytail. And the red hair.

'Why were you so late?' she only asked, for the fourth time at least. They would never get through the test.

Tiger sighed, put his hands down.

'I know how you feel – ' he said, 'But try to remember my explanation, *honey* – '

'Well why didn't you phone here or something? You just let me *sit* and *wait* for you – '

'Didn't I leave you a note – Lovely?'

'Tell me about the meeting,' she demanded, in a pet, crossing her legs. Tiger wondered what she had on today, the honey. He remembered seeing her at the community swimming pool last summer in a bathing suit. Come to think of it, that's when she had joined his list. What a girl! It had been so hot that day. He had shown her a dive or two. She had caught on right away. *Some girl.* Next to Rochelle, she was definitely the most talented of the Drama group. She had a class way beyond her years alright, despite the tantrums at times. *Temperamental.* They were worth putting up with. She knew the score.

'I told you already,' Tiger patiently said.

'I hope nobody murders *me*,' she said.

'Amen,' Tiger said.

'*You* wouldn't murder me, would you, Tiger?' she asked.

He grinned at the lass, 'Not today.' Definitely, she was warming up. At last.

'I'm awful mad at you,' she said.

'How many hands do you see?' He held one up this time.

'One,' she said, without a doubt coming around.

'And what if *you* put one hand up?'

She did.

'That makes two,' she said, with a pretty smile.

'Put up the other one,' Tiger said, grinning away.

She had a cute T shirt on today, and with her hands raised her breasts stood out more prominently than ever under it. He observed them, loving them. He didn't think she had one on today.

'Don't you look great,' he said.

'Do I?' she said, invitingly.

'Come over here,' he said, grinning fondly at her, 'With your hands up.'

'Oh – whatrya *gonner* do ?' She was great. She tickled him. She got up.

He observed her as she walked toward him. There might be better forms somewhere, Tiger mused, but he didn't know where. He was prouder than ever of Sawyersville, its young maids, among other things. She walked slowly, the teaser, toward him. He knew she was dying for him. Those marvelous orbs of love. He couldn't wait to get his hands on them. He waited though. She came nearer to him.

'O.K. – let's frisk you,' he said, standing up. He ran his hands up and over her. Expertly.

'Hey –' she said, playing it well. His hands had stopped at her treasures. He was behind her, fondling them through that cutest of T shirts. No bra. He had guessed right. *What a girl*. She leaned her head back until their faces touched. Hers burned.

'*Hey* –' she said again, whispering low. Her hands came down, slowly, and began caressing his neck, his head, he loved it.

'Hey Hey –' she said, very soft and low, as he played with those marvelous gifts. Her warm breath on his face. He stroked the tips. She burned ever more.

'How's everything ?' he murmured to her.

'You'll see – ' said the maid, murmuring to him. She turned her face, her lips met his. 'Oh – ' she said, giving him a luscious kiss, her eyes closed, '*Gosh – oh –* ' she said, turning slow, melting into him. He held her close.

'What's new ?' he said.

'That feels nice – ' she gasped, pressing ever closer to him.

'Does it ?' he asked.

'*Tiger – oh –* ' she barely gasped, quivering a little bit, kissing him wonderfully again, her soft, full tongue gliding marvelously. He loved it. She certainly was true blue, Tiger mused, sliding his tongue over hers, feeling her quivering more. He was near quivering too. Now his tongue slipped through her wet lips, she gave him a little nip. They played gloriously in her wonderfully sweet mouth. She gasped. He unhooked her skirt. He helped her wriggle out of it. What a cute skirt, *what a slip*. That was the prettiest slip. He caressed her hips, gliding around, and inside her thighs. There was silken paradise. He helped her slip off her T shirt. He was dazzled by the sight. He kissed and suckled them, like a famished man.

'*Tiger* –' she moaned, her heart pounding hard. She burned. Tiger lifted her in his arms. He kissed her neck, and breasts, he carried her to the couch. Her head was back, she moaned in his arms. He kissed and glided over her smooth belly now. He laid her on the couch. Gently, he slipped off her silky things, admiring True Paradise, drenched, of course, tropically. *That heavenly way.* How he loved red hair. He stripped and lay down beside her, and she played with his formidable shaft, murmuring, and murmuring to him. Now she moaned again. She moved, gently, stroking, caressing it, from time to time kissing it, gliding her sweet tongue over it, and once letting it slip past her lips, which closed over it, tenderly, as she held it in, exquisitely, a little while. Tiger gently withdrew, finally, she gave a long sigh, he mounted her –

'*OH* –' she cried, as he entered her, '*I love you so,*' now she cried, as he slid deep into her, and began those inimitable divine thrusts into her, again, and again, deep into her. '*TIGER DARLING!*' she cried, beside herself, moving magnificently under him, with him. He held her delightful behind, he rocked with her, his thrusts hit a fantastic rate, he was out of this world again. . . .

57

Surcher had before him Mr Golden, one of the best of Sawyersville's English teachers, and Ponce's home-room teacher, of course. In a way, Surcher felt bad about it, interviewing all the teachers, male that is. As he felt bad about the whole rotten thing, disrupting and disturbing, as he knew it must, the entire educational process of the school, not to mention the kids. He hated anything doing that, for he was a firm believer in Education and all its processes. It was after all the very backbone of our democracy, well he knew, only too well what kids turned out without it. But he had to. That too he knew. Without a doubt it was one of the most frustrating, and certainly distasteful cases he had ever been obliged to turn his attention to, on that account alone, if no other. Unprofessional, and almost unethical, as he knew it was, he couldn't help wishing in a way that the colored kid Jim Green had been the one. At least, now it would have been over and done with. As things were, here he was, back where he'd started from.

'How old are you, Mr Golden?' Surcher asked.

'Thirty-eight,' the teacher answered. He was a mild, almost shy man, slightly balding, of medium build. He just had the beginnings of a paunch, Surcher noted. He felt in his bones this couldn't possibly be the man. In fact, Surcher felt somewhat sorry for him, imagining life around the school at times getting tough for him, some of those wiseacre kids. He wouldn't keep him long.

'I'm sorry to take you out of your classes, Mr Golden. I hope you'll understand why I have to ask you a few questions. They won't be many, believe me.'

Mr Golden nodded, and waited to hear more.

'Are you married, Mr Golden?' Surcher asked.

The teacher hesitated before answering, obviously uncomfortable.

'No, I'm not,' he replied.

'Bachelor?'

'That's right.'

Surcher nodded, and grinned that little grin, 'One of the lucky ones,' he said, to put him at his ease.

Mr Golden also grinned.

'Not for much longer though,' he said.

'Taking the plunge?'

'Afraid so.'

'Swell, congratulations.'

'You're from Kitston, aren't you?' Mr Golden ventured.

'That's right.'

'That's what I heard –' Mr Golden paused, about to say more, 'My bride-to-be teaches there.'

'Is that right? Where?'

'G.A.R.'

'What do you know! My kids go there.'

'Well, well. What a small world. Ask them if they know Miss Burke – English Department.'

'Miss Burke? Oh yeh – I've heard of her –'

'That's the one.'

'What do you know!'

'I lived with my mother a long time,' Mr Golden said, 'She died two years ago,' he also said.

'I see.'

Mr Golden grinned, or tried to, 'I guess I was a mamma's boy.'

'Uh huh,' Surcher said.

'I wish I could help – with the trouble – ' now Mr Golden said, dropping his tone low, 'It's an awful mess.'

'Know of anyone who might conceivably be our man?' Surcher asked.

Mr Golden stirred in his chair. He certainly was uncomfortable there. Surcher guessed he could name at least twenty-five wise guys right off the bat – though he wouldn't, he knew. A lucky thing.

'I don't, I really don't – ' the teacher answered at last.

'Not one?' Surcher thought he would ask.

Mr Golden shook his head, 'I really wish I could help. I wish I could.'

Surcher nodded. He had nothing else to ask the man. He was absolutely sure of this one. However, out of pure devotion to professional technique, he had to ask –

'Mr Golden – where were you last night?'

The teacher blushed, bright red, and replied, 'With Miss Burke.'

Surcher jotted that down.

'Well, that's all, Mr Golden,' he said, 'Now if anything comes up, anything at all that comes into your mind, that you think might be useful to us, or important in any way, just let me know – o.k. You never can tell.'

The teacher nodded and said, 'Oh, I certainly will.'

And he left.

Surcher, checking his list, noted that Mr Crispwell, Commercial Studies department, was next. He gave a sigh, checked hs watch, and the phone rang. It was Follo. The State Attorney-General's Office was on the other line and wanted to talk to him. He thought it might be the Attorney-General himself. Surcher more than sighed. *Oh, oh,* he said, to himself. This was it. From now on, he could look forward to quite a lot of this. He would have a fight on his hands, to keep control of things. If he wanted to, that is. And he did.

'Put him on,' Surcher said, bracing himself, and staring hard at the list. . . .

58

What Tiger did after the eventual departure of Sandy Seymour, that classy sweetheart of a honey maid, what he did, after that, and some lunch, and a phone call from Looby Loo, that true blue, was revise his list. He inserted a few stars, and half-stars, and even quarter-stars, here and there, appropriately, in his judgment, which was fair. In short, he brought it up to date. Finally, and sadly, and very reluctantly, he drew a line through the name of that late and sincerely lamented gem among gems, Yvonne Mellish, that victim of a most tragic fate. And that just about brought everything up to date. He stared at the list. His mood was funereal. There was no doubt. Two of the most divine and sublime – gone forever, and ever, and forever and ever – from his list. *From life.* He couldn't come to terms with this, no matter how hard he tried. All he could do was stare at the list, forlornly. *How many more?* Would there be more? Just exactly what was Sawyersville coming to? What was the score? He had been born and brought up here, lived all his life here, he thought he had known the score. At this rate, he knew, as any rapid calculation would prove, his list would be decimated within the year. *This year.* He felt blue. Even though the superb lusciousness of Sandy's kisses, among other things, still lingered vividly and warmly in him, he was blue definitely. It wouldn't do. What a mess. *Definitely.* Who in his right mind could deny that? No one. He knew. Tiger, staring hard at that list, *that shrinking list*, could think of no one, utterly. He sighed. He knew if he sat there long enough, he would have cried. It didn't matter, why shouldn't he cry? He had plenty to cry about. Again he sighed, and also checked his watch, thinking of that appointment at three o'clock. He looked forward to it. It had been some little while. When had he seen her last? He would check. She was a mighty fine girl. Of course, Barbara had a unique advantage in life, in a way, it couldn't be denied. Her father, the Reverend Timothy Brook, was the head man at Tiger's own church, no less. He mused about her, for as things were there was definitely a vacancy for the position of Captain of the Cheerleaders, not to mention Assistant Captain, of course, and although Barbara was only a Junior, in Ponce's class, as a matter of fact, it seemed possible she might qualify for the job, *one* of the jobs, that is to say. She was on the squad. In addition to her church connections and interests. For Tiger was well aware of her interests. How long had she been on the squad? What was her seniority rating? They would take that into account, among other factors. No doubt. Tiger mused. She often spoke to him about Religion and the Religious life, for it couldn't be denied. she was a quasi-fanatical not surprisingly, all in all. *The Right Way to Paradise*. Again and again, she hit that theme. In fact, that was how she always began her sessions. And Tiger couldn't agree more. There was only one paradise, he was aware, and one way to get there, he was only too well aware. They hit it off. They hit it off well together. Tiger was feeling better. Three o'clock couldn't come soon enough for him. He thought about Surcher. What would he be getting up to now? Who could tell? He was aware that the scope of the investigation could at this point well involve the entrance on the scene of other levels of Law Enforcement. In short, Surcher, like Poldaski before him, could be out in the cold. Would he take it? Fight it? It was a test. His mettle. How would it turn out? Tiger wondered. He awaited the answer. Would they call mystics in? A seer or two? What about LSD? Wait and see. A possibility. Certainly it wasn't a matter for the CIA. They had other things on their hands. But the FBI – ? Possibly. Possibly one of their unique experts on such matters would be asked to render advice and assistance, however, unofficially. He wished him the best of luck, not at all envying his task. What a task. Tiger pondered, entering deeper waters. Though America, his only, and beloved, country, was, of course, the best place in the world to live in, he didn't know a person in the world who didn't know it, it had to be said it had this problem, of crime, that is. Definitely. Most particularly distressing to Tiger in particular, and personally, was its high incidence among youngsters, juveniles, that is. In short, Juvenile Delinquency. He knew it was a problem which cut across and into every stratum of American life, from the President on down, theoretically, if not literally, of course. Certainly, its inroads were wide. And grave. It could of course only be solved, he well knew, or at least ameliorated, to take a more realistic view, through the intense and concentrated cooperative efforts of all concerned, all segments and levels of society, that is. *All Adults*, in short. Especially and certainly responsible adults in responsible positions and most especially of all – *parents*. For there was the key. The core. Patriotism had its role to play. Certainly, a sojourn in Vietnam, if nothing else, could do wonders for a wayward kid. Religion had its place. He was back to Barbara again. Though sometimes Tiger had to ponder the question, awkward as it was, she would be the first to admit, why was it that the country which had the highest percentage of churchgoers, of *bonafide* members, no less, in the entire civilized world, had also the highest crime rate ? It baffled him. What was the connection ? Could there be ? And how could there be ? Tiger was in the deepest waters. Perhaps *life* was the answer. Repressed, tight-lipped societies, for example European, and, for a more specific example, Britain, would appear on the face of it, to take statistics as evidence, at any rate, to have a much lower crime rate, or incidence of the scourge, on all levels. Was this so ? Truly so ? If so, why so ? What did it add up to ? What conclusions could it lead to ? Notoriously, despite from time to time the show and surface of things, the British these days were practically an agnostic culture. Certainly, a thoroughly *nonchurchgoing* culture. Put it that way. That was the way. In short, religion was a joke there. He knew it. Who didn't know it ? Didn't Barbara know it ? Tiger pondered, shaking his head slowly, from side to side, holding the list, aware he was gazing at it. *Bad*. It was bad, bad. The older you got, especially after that thirty-five mark, that was the mark, the more the awareness of all the badness, and paradoxes, and baffling conditions, situations, and problems of this life, this world, this one and only human life, and world, pounded at you, from all quarters, giving you no quarter, hurting you, and finally – smothering you. Was that it ? All of it ? What about bewilderment ? Resignation ? Was that the end ? Whose end ? Tiger floundered. . . . He would have to talk to the parents at that proposed mass meeting, he knew. He wasn't looking forward to it. But he would have to. Only he knew how to. He would have Proffer say a few words of course by way of introduction. Of course. Then he would speak. He would do his best. And Surcher. That would be a good idea, Tiger thought, having Surcher speak also. By all means, the school should be kept open. There should be no bowing, no knuckling under to intimidation, or adversity. Had Americans ever ? *Never*. And they would never. Tiger was in a superpatriotic mood just now, he suddenly realized. He grinned to himself. It happened, sometimes. Uncle could always count on him, in a pinch, anytime, when the chips were down. Wasn't he in the Reserves ? Was he still ? Tiger mused, from time to time he got letters from them, full of gobbledygook, he never read them, it was a lifetime affair, wasn't it, however inactive you were. There was quite the little active Reserve Unit in Sawyersville, he knew. They looked pretty great out there too, in Fourth of July parades, Decoration Day. Great. What about Vietnam? Would they get the chance? Some of them were a little old. Old. Chic Angelli was a grandfather, wasn't he? Sure he was. Grandfather Chic, he was. The business of the game would have to be carefully looked into. He knew. Tonight of course there couldn't be any Practice. He didn't think it would hurt them much. He looked forward to seeing Jim Green. To hear the scoop. Just how were those Staties? What was the scoop? He would have a long powwow with him, soon. There would be practice tomorrow, of course, if all went well. And he hoped it would. Tiger, now, feeling somewhat sad again, finally put the list back in its folder. Reverently, he put that back in the drawer. He got on the phone to see what could be worked out about the prospective game. Something could be worked out, he knew, once he started working on it. . . .

59

Ponce, seeing the coast was clear, entered the Guidance/Counseling Office. And there was Tiger.

'Ponce!' he called out, obviously glad to see the lad.

'Hello, Tiger,' the lad said, in a minor tone.

'I don't know what this place is coming to,' he then said, having made himself at home.

Tiger nodded, understandingly, though he himself at the moment wasn't feeling too low. He had just finished making a few phone calls.

'I know how you feel, Ponce, believe me,' he said, 'But listen, I have a little bit of cheerful news, anyhow –' he then said.

'You do?' the boy said, glumly.

'The game's set.'

'It is?'

'That's right.'

'No practice tonight though – ?'

'That's so.'

Ponce couldn't help it, he grinned, 'Think we can do it?' he said.

'Sure we can.'

Ponce actually found himself feeling better.

'So the school won't close?' he asked, with hope.

'Not if I can help it.'

'Is that the word?'

'So far so good.'

'That's *real* good – Tiger.'

'Let me tell you.'

'Will the kids come to school though? Think their folks will let them?' Ponce asked, upon reflection.

'Well – we hope so. We're working on it,' said Tiger.

Ponce nodded. There too he was hopeful.

'Tiger – ' he said, 'What about Mummer?'

Tiger surveyed the lad. 'Well – as you probably know – Surcher let him go.' He paused, watching Ponce nodding at him. 'I guess he just had nothing at all to hold him on, Ponce. That's all.' He paused again, keeping his eyes on the boy. 'He won't be around any longer though.' He stopped, watching Ponce's face light up.

'He won't?'

'No sir.'

A pause.

'*Hot dog!*'

The lad said, grinning away.

Then, inexplicably enough, he again was blue. Tiger noted this.

'I just don't feel like going to any classes,' said the lad.

Tiger nodded. Then said, 'Force yourself.' He paused. 'I know that's a hard thing to do, but it's the best thing, Ponce, believe me.' He paused, his eyes on the lad. 'I'm forcing myself all day around here, Ponce, let me tell you.'

Ponce understood.

'I sure feel sorry for her parents,' he said.

'So do I,' Tiger said.

Ponce shook his head slowly, and looked down.

'No kidding, Tiger, sometimes I think it's a bad dream – ' he said.

'I know how you feel.'

'Here we are, clipping along just great – '

'That's it, how it is. That's how it is,' Tiger said, gently –

'That's life, Ponce.' He paused. 'It's a hell of a thing.' He was speaking very low. Ponce barely heard him now – 'How it's always been – ' He stopped, trailing off.

The lad nodded his head.

'Anyhow, we got back Jim Green – '

'Right, Ponce. That *is* something. There's always something. I hope to see him tomorrow – I hope he shows up.'

'I bet he will – '

'If I know that boy, he will,' Tiger said.

Ponce sat down there now and just gazed at Tiger. What a guy and a half he was. If he could grow up and turn out just one-half as good as that – he'd be doing all right. *Alright.* Could he though? What about next time? *It was up to him,* Ponce reminded himself. He knew it well. Tiger was right. *Force yourself.* He wondered if there was any way he could force himself to talk over his problem with him. Ponce, at the mere thought of it, blushed furiously inside at it. He just couldn't do it. *Not now* – anyhow. He would work on it. Was it fair, anyhow, to burden Tiger with it? Didn't he dump enough stuff on him?

He said, 'Miss Nectar sure is nice, isn't she, Tiger?' Out of the blue, quietly.

Tiger gazed at the lad.

'She is, you're right,' came the reply.

'I was talking with her in the Library before – ' Ponce blurted out, 'I was feeling mighty low. She sure helped me out – ' He stopped.

Tiger nodded, his gaze on the lad.

'One of the best I've seen,' he told the boy. 'Librarians are funny, sometimes.' He stopped.

Ponce grinned, 'Remember the last one we had?'

'Do I!'

It was a fact, she had been a pill and a half, if ever he saw one. She had retired. Miss Nectar, fresh from the Library School at Rutgers, had come along.

'I saw your mom and your little brother this morning,' Tiger now said, grinning.

'You did?'

'On my way here. She was taking him to school, I guess.'

Ponce nodded, and grinned, 'She was.'

'Sure is a cute little kid,' Tiger said, 'Where'd he get that red hair?'

'That's what we'd like to know.'

They both grinned. Now Tiger chuckled.

'Well, we'll see him up here one day,' he said.

'We sure will,' Ponce told him.

'That's the beauty of this job, Ponce, believe me,' Tiger now said, 'New ones always coming up, fresh ones, young ones, full of life of course – they keep you going, even when you want to lie down and die. And no kidding, Ponce, sometimes, when you get up around my age – ' He grinned, 'What a thing to say to you – ' He paused, still grinning, 'I guess I'm getting old.'

Ponce had to grin. He just couldn't imagine Tiger old. Though in his heart, he knew that's just how it was, everyone grew old – it seemed he'd always known, too. *Yvonne and Jill wouldn't though*. Suddenly, Ponce had that thought.

He stared at the floor. . . .

60

Tiger took care of that Health Ed. class after Ponce left. It was a Freshman class. In it, he made good use of a lot of the material (and technique of presentation) from the book he had of late been perusing and thoroughly enjoying. Of course, he had attuned it to their level, here and there. At this point in the term they were on the subject of Sex, of course. He had been a little apprehensive at first about utilizing the book, because there was just the chance that some of the kids might break out with some so-called typical adolescent giggles, and such. But, they hadn't materialized – so far, at any rate. It had gone well, as a matter of fact, they had given him their rapt attention. He would certainly press on with it. In fact, he thought, it wouldn't be a bad idea if they all had a copy of it. Maybe not right away, but in about a month – He would check with Hetty Nectar about it. He was just musing over that and checking his watch, about halfway down the hall from his office, when he was suddenly aware of Jeannie Bonni, beside him. She had materialized out of nowhere. He grinned at her, and said Hi. She certainly looked cute today.

'Tonight, Tiger ?' the girl said, in a voice unmistakably full of go.

'All right,' Tiger murmured, after a moment or so. He was aware of her urgent tone.

'Eight o'clock?' she murmured, still in that tone.

'Fine,' he told her, admiring her verve.

And she moved on, after a delightful smile. He walked on. He had barely been thrown off his stride. He couldn't help smiling. She certainly had verve. She was a girl with verve. And with no practice tonight, as well she knew, or had guessed, the time was just right. . . . He smiled more. . . .

He reached his office, and walked in.

'Hello,' Barbara said.

The brown-haired maid with the cutest fringe turned around on the couch as she greeted him. She looked well. Very well. And this surprised Tiger just a little bit, considering how close her relationship was to her ex-sister cheerleader, so to speak, and Assistant Captain, no less. She had on the sweetest yellow outfit – a dress. Tiger stood there a moment, admiring her. Who had a cuter fringe? A long time ago, it seemed, Looby Loo had a fringe – definitely. He thought of that. He kept on looking at that fringe. It went just right with her slightly turned up nose. He loved that nose. She always made herself right at home. *Now the Holy Hour*, Tiger thought.

'What's new?' he said, crossing to his desk. He had taken care of the door.

'Haven't you heard?' Barbara asked.

What did she mean by that?

'Everything O.K.?' he asked. He had given her a good supply last time, so, assuming she had been a good girl –

'Oh – I'm O.K.,' said the girl.

Tiger sat down in his chair and surveyed the girl. He knew what she meant.

'That was a blow, a blow,' he said, quietly.

'She was such a nice kid,' Barbara moaned.

'I know – ' Tiger said, 'I know – ' His voice was very low.

'So was Jill – ' the girl said, with another moan.

'I know – ' Tiger murmured. The dress fitted her like a glove, he observed.

'It doesn't even do any good praying to find the murderer, does it, Tiger, because *that* won't bring them back, will it?' She paused, shaking her head from side to side, 'No, no – ' She moaned low, 'It won't.'

There was an indisputability about that that jarred Tiger. It hadn't crossed his mind just that way, ever. Nevertheless, he knew he should be ferreted out. Whatever. It was essential. He told her.

'If they don't find him,' he said, gently, 'Who knows what will happen next?'

Barbara wasn't impressed.

'*But it won't bring them back –* '

Tiger could think of no comeback to that. What could he say to that? She was dug in, impregnably. Now she was gazing at him, from that couch. He let her. Her eyes were moist, and in contact with his, and soon he felt a hot pressure building up in him. He knew how she felt. Exactly. Empathy couldn't be more complete. He admired her fringe. Her eyes were almost exactly the color of her hair. She had lovely hair. Tiger felt his own eyes going moist. Would he break down, at last? he wondered. Would that help her? Without a doubt, she had a powerful effect on him. Would they both go over the brink, and break down together? He gazed at her.

'*Whosoever cometh unto the Lord –* ' she began.

'That's right, that's right,' Tiger said.

The girl cried. She sobbed and sobbed.

Tiger held on, knowing he ought to. There was something more he could do. He got up, he went to the maid. He put his arms around her, and let her cry on his chest.

'There,' he murmured, softly to her.

'Tiger – ' she sobbed, 'Oh Tiger – ' she sobbed and cried, '*I love you so much –* '

'I know you do,' he murmured to her, sitting back with her on the couch. She nestled in his arms.

'*The Lord giveth and the Lord taketh –* ' she said.

Tiger, murmuring softly, nodded his head. In his arms her sobs gradually faded away. Now, once in a while, she gave a tiny one. She sighed. He helped her dry her eyes. She raised her hand and gave his face a caress.

'You're so good to me,' she said.

'I want to be,' he said, returning the caress. She raised her face to his. He saw her fringe. He was looking into her eyes. Tiger loved her warm brown eyes. And the fringe. He passed his hand over her eyes. And the fringe. She gave his hand a kiss.

'I'd better not talk about them anymore,' she said, 'What can I do?' She paused, 'What can anyone do?'

'Not much,' Tiger replied.

She kissed him on the lips. Tiger fondled her, through that nice dress. He fondled her breasts, soft and free.

'Ummmm – ' she said, '*I don't have it on,*' she said, which he already knew. She gave him a marvelous kiss, her arms behind his neck. He was warm.

'I know – I know – ' he murmured to her, 'You're a good girl – ' he murmured low. He found their tips. He lingered there.

She came up for air. She was very warm, she sighed, her face next to his. Tiger's hand caressed her thighs, and glided slowly toward Paradise. She closed her eyes. She sighed.

'Don't you have a nice dress – ' he murmured low.

'I'll take it off – '

'I'll help you get it off – '

'Like it – do you – '

'Really swell – '

'Ummmm – well – '

'How's everything?'

'Just nice – '

Tiger gave a soft chuckle. He draped the sweet dress carefully over a chair. He admired her slip. He took her in his arms, and they kissed again. She was more than warm. His hands drifted downward again, caressing all the way. Her heart pounded hard against him. She gave little moans.

She came up for air. Now his hand was traveling upward, he loved gliding over her stomach and bumping into those fabulous breasts. They were treasures, just for him. He fondled them, and brushed their tips. He kissed the tips.

'Tiger – ' she gasped, soaring toward bliss, 'I have to tell you this – *Tiger –* ' she said, '*Let me –* '

'Tell me – ' he said, his lips on those tips.

'I dreamed – ' she said, trying hard, 'Tiger I had this dream last night – *darling Tiger* I – ' she tried and tried – '*I dreamed you were Jesus Christ –* ' She stopped, as Tiger thought, *escalation*, that's all. He waited for more. He held, he continued to caress her throbbing form.

'Is that right?' he said, at last. Hoping for more.

'Yes – *Oh yes –* ' she replied, her hands straying wonderfully over him. Her lips brushed his ear, she whispered, 'Is that blasphemy?' A little gasp. '*My love!*'

'I don't think so – ' Tiger said, though he wasn't all that sure. Could a dream be blasphemous? He thought that one over, in the heat of the moment, and wondered more. He could check with her father one day. That was the way. Next time. Sunday, maybe. But maybe before, for often he ran into the Reverend here or there, in Sawyersville. On Sunday certainly during the course of conversation, possibly after the sermon, he could put the question to him for his consideration. It was most interesting and worthy of expert consideration. The finer nuances of Theology certainly weren't in his sphere, Tiger was well aware. The Reverend was the man, definitely. They were standing up now, which was something he knew she loved to do, he was behind her, caressing those magnificent orbs. She bent her face back to his, and sighed, and kissed him. She leaned against him, and his organ.

'Aren't they gorgeous – ' Tiger murmured, fondling her. He couldn't find praise enough for their marvelously soft fullness. She sighed, and gave sweet little cries, whenever he brushed the tips. She kissed him about the ear, and caressed his head.

'What was I doing?' Tiger inquired, drifting back to her dream. He was interested. Definitely.

'Well – *Darling* – ' she said, 'My sweet darling – ' she said, and what a state she was in, 'This – I think – Tiger – *Honey* – ' She fought for her breath, 'Do I – *have* to – tell you?'

She didn't, of course, but it would be more than interesting to hear. It intrigued him, no end. He stroked gently between her exquisite thighs. He found treasure island.

'*Tiger* – ' she cried, as her state fused with his more and more, 'You were – *on the Mount* – you – I was there – ' She paused, gasping divinely, '*You weren't giving a sermon* – ' She paused again, she had to, '*Is that blasphemous?*'

'I don't know,' Tiger had to reply.

'*Oh* – ' she cried, as her silky slipped off.

'What was I doing?' Tiger murmured again, tenderly fondling her. His hand was drenched.

'*This* – ' she cried, '*Just this* – ' She managed to cry – '*Oh – I – Love – You – Tiger* my Darling my Honey *my Only I Love You* – ' Once more she cried, barely, '*Is It Blasphemy?*'

Tiger gave no answer this time, she fell back on the couch with him, she caught sight of his formidable shaft, she took hold of it, she held it.

'Oh JESUS!' she cried out, raising her knees, utterly gone now, writhing, dying for him, '*GIVE IT TO ME!*'

He obliged. . . .

61

What about Honeywell? Surcher wondered, in the middle of interviewing Mr Crispwell, Commercial Studies teacher. He had of course interviewed the Janitor after the discovery of the body but had no grounds for any suspicion whatever toward the man. The same was now true of this Mr Crispwell, whom he didn't like very much, to tell the truth. He was a Bircher. He had proclaimed that fact, right off the bat. But that had little to do with the matter. That was the matter. Honeywell. It was odd his thoughts should turn to him once again. Perhaps it was that phone call from the Attorney-General's Office. For that phone call had certainly made very clear to him, as if he didn't already know, that swift and prompt action, and the leaving of no stone unturned, were expected in the matter. Assistance, in the form of a small platoon of Special Investigators from the Attorney-General's own office, would be on its way within twenty-four hours, unless he came up with an answer, or something pretty close to the answer. The FBI was also mentioned. And the Governor. In short, Surcher had an ultimatum. Looked at from any angle, it was, *put up or shut up – Buddy.* Well he knew. That was it. And not that he minded all that much, for he was of course a man not easily ruffled, whatever the circumstances. He was also well aware of the special problems and sensitivities of politicians, who would come and go, Attorney-Generals or whatever. Especially ambitious Attorney-Generals, he mused, not unhopefully, formulating his next question for Crispwell.

'How old are your children, Mr Crispwell?'

The man answered, precisely, tightly.

Well what about Honeywell? Surcher reflected, jotting down the answers. Was he possibly a Don Juan of the Furnaces? Or Broom Closet? He mused. Not to mention the Lavatory. He seemed like an ordinary enough fellow. In his working clothes, he was no Brando. He was in what appeared to be a genuine state of shock, or close to it, when he had interviewed him. He was married, with a couple of kids of his own. Middle forties. No record. Well thought of. Should he have another talk with him? Surcher wondered. Certainly, it fitted in with the Attorney-General's directive. Or would he just waste his time again? *Jim Green.*

Surcher almost sighed, thinking of him. There was the honey. He almost shook his head too, forlornly. His hunch still was that the nut was some kid, not a member of the faculty. Though the latter couldn't be excluded totally. He and his assistants would know more about that by the end of the day. Naturally. He thought of Poldaski. His Troopers had reported he was a hard man to work with. He had to grin, picturing that.

'Well, now, Mr Crispwell – just one more question, and then you can go. Just a routine question, please understand. Would you account for your movements between the time you left the school yesterday afternoon – and this morning?'

The teacher sat back, somewhat taken aback.

'You understand it's strictly routine, Mr Crispwell,' Surcher told him again, in his friendliest way.

'Yes – I understand – ' Mr Crispwell said, finally, adding, for the record, 'I know what you're up against.' And he began answering.

Did he? Surcher wondered, as he began writing.

He doubted it.

He would check out Honeywell – just once again. . . .

62

Ponce, taking the bit in his teeth, was on his way to Miss Betty Smith's place that evening. More than ever, he was aware of being caught up in a matter of unprecedented historical importance, so far as he was aware, in the story of Sawyersville, and possibly the whole state, at this rate. And though on the whole it appalled him, it also undeniably excited him. He was well aware. When had Sawyersville known such excitement? The football team was exciting, but in a different way. Nothing like *this* way. Where would it end? What would the end be? That added to the excitement, of course. Ponce was caught in a paradox, he was aware of the most bewildering spectrum of emotions about the whole affair. He began to reflect, for one thing, on the fascination that catastrophes of all kinds, natural or manmade, most particularly manmade (such as wars, e.g., the current Vietnam war) have for humans. What a strong pull. It made all life touch and go. It was hard to deny, Ponce now felt, on that track, that there did seem to be some connection between his going again to see that dream and the matter. The situation. The disaster. He seemed to sense that it had in some odd way boosted his courage, in fact given him a verve, so to speak, and nerve hitherto non-existent, or certainly totally dormant, *inaccessible*, in him. It had affected him. Stimulated him. Infected him. This, he was well aware. And it only meant more confusion. For he was basically and had always been a prudent, careful boy, as he and the whole world knew. Certainly, the whole of Sawyersville knew. In some way, the situation seemed to free him, it seemed to open up a whole new vista of long-buried, only dreamed-of, occasionally thought of, but definitely and powerfully longed for – *raw freedom*, as such. Certainly, such. Ponce knew it, though he was ashamed to admit it. His heart pounded, in a new, fierce kind of way. He felt he had in his grasp some unparalleled and spectacular experience whose essence was Treasure, *pure Treasure*, no less, and *fabulous*. It would be equal at least to the hoard of eternity, with the universe thrown in, for free. That's how it was. He felt great. He felt bad. He felt appalled. And he swayed, back and forth, a mad pendulum, on the one hand genuinely in need of rapport, contact, a meeting of minds with Miss Smith – on the other – *where was the measure?* He was in a state. *That Treasure.* His head whirled as never before.

He rang the doorbell a few times before she answered it. Of course, she wasn't expecting him. Ponce had taken her at her word. That was it. She opened the door finally and his heart pounded like artillery. For a moment she was startled, or very faintly appeared to be. Then, she broke into the warmest smile imaginable, welcoming him. Ponce grinned even more warmly back at her. He was relieved. For a fraction of a second there he had thought she was going to slam the door in his face. Did she think *he* was the lunatic?

'Ponce, well, how nice to see you!' she said, 'Come in. Come on in. What a nice surprise. I'm telling you – ' the divine creature said to the lad, as he stared at her, and then found himself floating in. He was under a massed bombardment, floating in. She had on a dressing gown, and it was the prettiest thing. *And what else?* The question flew up in him, embarrassing him. Also, it inflamed him. And raced around in him.

'How are you?' she said, 'Here, let me take your jacket – ' And she helped him off with it. It was a lightweight, lined, all-weather jacket. The latest thing.

'Ah – not too bad, Miss – *Smith*,' Ponce said, hardly stuttering. He couldn't help noticing. His eyes were glued on her.

'Listen, now you call me *Betty*,' she said, and Ponce hit a spin.

'*Betty* – ' he said, in a dream. Would his feet ever touch the floor again?

She stood there, smiling warmly at him. A troop of cavalry were thundering inside Ponce, across the parched plains. Was that a bugle call? Rusty Joe loved them. Ponce grinned at that. And – Miss Smith. *Betty* –

'That's better, isn't it?' she said, Ponce wondering what she meant. 'Isn't that a nice sweater!' she said, touching it lightly with her hand. The sweater was soft wool, cashmere, in fact, a special present his last birthday. He had rarely worn it.

'Thanks – ' he said, grinning again. His face was burning.

'Sit down, Ponce. Want to?'

He followed her. The small sofa.

'I was just thinking about you, Ponce, isn't it incredible?' She sat down. 'Sometimes I think there really is something to this extra-sensory-perception business, that business, you know what I mean – ' Ponce sat down, a foot from her. She smiled, and reached for a cigarette. 'That's one of the reasons I think I may have looked a little startled when you turned up – I was – you know?'

'You were?' Ponce only said.

'I certainly was. I was,' she said, lighting up, taking a puff, Ponce's eyes fixed on that puff. He went in with it.

'What – were you thinking?' Ponce said, like that.

'Oh – ' she said, withdrawing the cigarette, he loved the bit of red where her lips had been, holding it just to one side, near the left side of her face, her arm just resting against her breast, 'I was feeling a little blue, to tell the truth – ' she now said, lowering her tone, 'You know, after – today – ' She paused – 'In a way – ' Another pause – 'I was thinking how you must be feeling, and taking it – as a matter of fact – ' She stopped. Ponce lowered his head.

'Is that why you came?' she asked, tenderly.

'I – ' he said, staring at her lap, 'I guess so – ' he said, at last.

She sighed. She puffed. Ponce saw the smoke drifting by him. And above him. It smelled good.

'I guess so – ' again he said, continuing to stare at that lap. It moved.

'Partly – ' he said.

'I'm almost scared to go back to that school,' she said.

'You are?' Ponce said, slowly raising his head. She was just taking another drag. Ponce wished he *could* go in with it.

'Ponce, let's face it, there's a nut loose there.' She blew out smoke, slowly.

'Yeh – I know it – ' he said.

'Aren't you scared?'

'Well – ' he said, groping for it, 'I'm not a girl.'

She smiled.

'That's true,' she paused, 'That certainly is true, isn't it.'

Ponce nodded his head.

He said, 'But I'm scared, don't get me wrong – ' He paused – 'Just – well – not in the same way – '

'Yes.'

A pause.

'Aw – they'll find him – ' he said.

'But *when*?'

'Yeh – ' Ponce said, 'That's it.'

'Isn't it!'

'Gee – I'm sorry you're scared – I really am – '

'I'm going back though,' she said.

'Aw, that's good. Real good. Wonder how many kids will though? That's the thing. It'll be something to see – won't it?'

She nodded her head.

'I'll bet a good number of the girls stay home – '

'Yeh, I'll bet – ' Ponce said, 'But – wait and see – '

'It's a *terrible* thing – '

'It's like a – dream – '

'Nightmare, you mean – '

'That's what I mean.'

She pulled on her cigarette again. Her eyes were on him.

'But – ' she sighed, smoke going for a ride, 'That's life – ' She paused – 'I'm afraid.'

'I guess it is.'

They were quiet. Ponce wished suddenly they wouldn't talk any more about it. What good would it do? And – it spoiled everything. And that was a funny thing, because he thought that was supposed to be one of the things he really wanted to talk about. In fact, wasn't it the *main* reason he needed her so badly to talk to – tonight? Ponce pondered, thinking hard all around that one. More smoke enveloped him. He loved it.

'How's your theme coming along?' now she asked, gently.
Ponce was glad she did. She moved her arm. The dressing gown
moved too, however slightly. Ponce caught a fleeting glimpse of
the tops of her breasts. With a casual movement of her hand, she
adjusted the dressing gown. The treasures were lost from view,
save for their glorious, soft fullness outlined under the gown.
Ponce's head swam.

'I – was up in the Library today – doing research – ' he said.

'That's good. Find much?'

'Well – you know – '

She nodded understandingly.

'Poor kid,' she said, very tenderly.

'Miss Nectar's – very helpful – ' he said, suddenly.

'Oh, Hetty's awfully nice,' Betty said.

'She is,' Ponce said, feeling strange, hearing her first name used
so familiarly.

'Did you discuss the theme with her?' Betty asked.

'Well – I mentioned it – ' Ponce said.

Betty nodded.

'I just – mentioned it – ' Ponce again said, hoping to get away
fast from that debacle. He nearly blushed.

'I think your approach is so good, Ponce. I hope you develop
it. I can hardly wait to see the final item. Know that?'

'Hope I can do it!' he said.

'Oh you will, you will,' his English Literature teacher reassured him, giving another warm smile.

'What do you think of *Crochet Castle*?' Ponce suddenly asked,
surprising both of them.

Betty's lovely arm was moving. She was seeking an ashtray.
Finding one, she put the cigarette out in it. She looked at Ponce.

'One of the finest of satirical novels,' she said.

Ponce nodded, and said, 'The dialogue abounds with eccentric
and sardonic wit – '

'It does,' Betty said, 'I think it's definitely Peacock's masterpiece.

'Oh, *yeh*, it is – '

'I think it is.'

'What about *Jonathan Wild*?' now Ponce asked.

The dream moved, and Ponce's eyes followed every nuance of
the move. Was she getting another cigarette? No, Ponce observed.

'Well – ' she said, 'In having a thief and a gallows-bird as a hero, Fielding shows an unrivaled mastery of the art of irony – '

Ponce nodded, for he couldn't agree more, of course.

'But probably, Ponce – you know – probably the greatest piece of satirical writing of all time – now that we're on it – with a unique approach and a more than unique appeal for young and old alike, on quite different levels, is *Gulliver's Travels* – don't you think ?' she said.

'It sure is up there,' Ponce replied.

'I think it's on *top of there*,' Betty said, 'Definitely.'

Ponce remained silent, for he couldn't commit himself on that. He wasn't exactly positive. She ought to know though, he thought, if anyone did. Maybe one day he'd see.

'I like Donne's *Poems of Love* a lot,' Ponce ventured, blushing just a little, having said it, however quietly.

Betty Smith's warm eyes stayed on him, as she said. 'I love them. I really do – ' She paused – 'Ranging from a lyrical ecstasy to – arid despair, those poems, both sacred and profane, are a supreme reflection of the eternal conflict between the flesh and the spirit, Ponce, you sweet boy – '

'They are – ' Ponce could only say.

She smiled, 'But don't let all this take you away from Milton – will you ?'

'Oh, it won't – it won't – ' he said.

Sitting back relaxed and cuddled up in her dressing gown, she looked terrific. Warm, wonderful, and terrific. Ponce waited for more.

'Literature's so wonderful, isn't it, Ponce ?' she said, soft and low, turning her head upward a moment, toward the ceiling, as the lad gazed at her lovely white throat. 'I don't know what life would be like without it – ' She faced him again, those warm eyes on him, 'I don't. I can't imagine it. Ponce, can you ?' she asked.

'No,' he said.

She laughed softly, and Ponce loved it. 'You know what I'd like ?' she said, 'I'll tell you my dream – I'd like to have one copy of all the world's masterpieces – I mean, really nice copies – all about me, up and down the walls – well, most of the walls!' she said – 'Oh, I'd like that, Ponce – ' She paused – '*Surrounded by them.*'

The boy nodded, vowing he would do all he could to help her fulfill that dream.

'How are you, Ponce ?' she asked, tenderly, reaching out toward the lad, taking his hand, 'How's your family ?' she said.

'Oh – they're all right – ' Ponce said, the whole world hovering about that beautiful warm hand, on his.

'Your brother's awfully cute, isn't he?' she smiled, 'Where did he get that red hair?'

'I – don't know – *Betty* – '

'You have nice hair.'

Her other hand moved to the side of his head, and he felt it pass through his hair.

'Don't you?' she asked, her hands still there. She was drawing him closer to her. Ponce trembled.

'What's the matter?' she murmured low, '*Hmmmm?*'

'*Wow* – ' he managed, though how he didn't know.

'You're the sweetest boy – ' Her hand now caressed his face, she was looking right into his face, 'Aren't you, now?' And leaning forward just a bit more, she gave him a gentle and tender kiss on the lips.

'*Gosh* – ' he said, '*Holy Cow* – ' he also said, trembling more, and wondering when he would wake up.

'Ponce, I've got an idea – ' she said, continuing to caress his face.

'You have?' he said, staggered at what it might be.

'Yes, I have,' she said, withdrawing her hand. 'Would you dance with me?' she said.

Ponce answered, shakily, '*Sure* – Miss Smith – '

'*Betty* – ' she smiled, gently reminding him.

'*Betty* – ' he said.

'You're shaking an awful lot, Ponce – you'll have to calm down – ' she murmured to him, 'Come on, let's calm you down – ' she added, sweet and low.

Ponce was suddenly aware only of being nestled in the most divine of arms, on that sofa. She was stroking him and murmuring little sweet things to him. Ponce tried hard to calm down. Her fragrance, a rose, made him float. He lay against her breast. 'There – ' she murmured, 'There – ' she kept murmuring, '*You sweet boy* – '

'I – dream about you – a lot – ' he said, at last.

'You do?'

'To – tell you the truth – Betty – ' he suddenly said, 'I – *I'm in love with you* – ' he heard himself say.

'You're such a sweet boy – ' she said, hugging him, her face against him, 'That's an awfully sweet thing to say – ' She spoke just near to his ear, her voice soft and low – 'Want to dance, Ponce?'

'I'll – try – ' he said, hoping he could stand up, mortified by what she would see – if he did make it up.

'*Come on* – ' she said, gently helping him. . . .

63

Looby Loo's luscious kisses still lingered on Tiger's lips when he left the house to have a look around that night. It wouldn't take him long to get to where Jeannie should be waiting for him, that little doll, the honey bun, *The little sweetheart*, Tiger mused, thinking of her. *What a verve.* And ingenuity. How many Sawyersville maids could have persuaded their parents to let them out of their sight – that night? Very few, Tiger knew. *Few, few*, he mused. *If any.* Cruising along through Sawyersville's streets, passing the Town Hall, the Fire Station, the Roll of Honor, the pool room, Chief Poldaski's favorite station, catching a glimpse of his car parked outside there, putting in a little over-time tonight, no doubt, the poor guy certainly with a job and a half on his hands, those crazy reporters and other media men milling about, making his life hell, plus the general curiosity-seekers, and so on, Tiger found himself thinking somehow of an ad he had seen in some British weekly some time ago. *The New Statesman?* It could have been. He had been looking through this weekly doing some off-hour looking around in the Library, as he sometimes would, Hetty had shown it to him, he recalled, for she had some friends working over there for a couple of years and they sometimes sent her such journals, weeklies, and such. This advertisement read, and it had stuck in his head, photo-graphically, almost – 'First Director for NACRO – this new national organisation [and that's how it was spelled, all right] concerned with community involvement in the prevention of crime and the after care of offenders, seeks to appoint its first Director. Salary up to £4,000 per annum, pensionable.] That was about $12,000, not bad, over there.] The post will be London-based but will involve travelling. It is desirable that the candidate should have academic qualifications and experience in social administration. Application should be made to the National Association for the Care and Resettlement of Offenders – ' He had forgotten the address. Like the snatch of nursery rhyme that from time to time ran through his head, he didn't quite know just why this should have stuck in him, or why he should be thinking of it, as a matter of fact, at this time, or any time, in fact. He chuckled, turning a corner and drifting out of Sawyersville's seat-of-government area – was he planning on applying for the job? He wondered, still chuckling away there. Certainly, it had its appeal, no doubt – though he couldn't even begin to see those people considering an American – No, he mused, he really wouldn't dream of pulling out of Sawyersville, for *any place*, no matter the job, let alone England, that corny old place, that place, filled with snobs, fobs, fags, and Royalty – and Harold Wilson, don't forget, Old Cornpone's best buddy, not to mention girls who wore skirts up to their ears – He chuckled again, thinking of that, and how a few of the Sawyersville kids had tried imitating that – it had fallen flat. Then he thought, still chuckling a little bit, was it connected up somehow with that exchange teacher from England who was due to arrive at Sawyersville next term? For a year. She was a young Englishwoman, and from her photograph quite a fair maid. Tiger, as Assistant Principal, knew all about her of course, having in fact dictated the letters finalizing the matter, though Harry Proffer had signed them, the tube. It could be, Tiger mused, looking forward to seeing her. He had never encountered an Englishwoman. He might learn a lot more than he already knew or anyhow thought he knew about the place, maybe even find out just what the trouble with the place was, nearly flat on its face as it always was, or so they claimed. Suddenly, he felt sorry for the place. *Maybe it was just too old.* Maybe nations, like people, reached a certain age and then irreversibly started sliding downhill. It could be. *It's going to happen to me*, Tiger mused, sadly, *already I'm on the wrong side of the hill*, he reflected, somberly. And when would it happen to the USA? he wondered. Or would this place never see it, having blown itself and everything around itself to kingdom come before that time rolled around? He wondered, pondering sadly on the matter. He cruised past the swimming pool, the Community Recreation Area. That area. What would be left of Vietnam, he wondered? What was Old Cornpone after? Did he know? Anyhow? Tiger chuckled, however sadly, thinking of that current occupant of the White House. *That crafty boor.* Perfect. He mused, was it true a country gets the leaders it deserves? Generally speaking, that statement could be said to be true. He knew it. Did that make him unpatriotic? He wasn't. He knew. *Didn't I prove it?* he mused. Who wanted to be a leader, anyway? *Anywhere.* What types were attracted to it? What kind of personality and character structure was essential? Tiger grew sadder, pondering all this. . . . He thought of the Englishwoman. She could turn out to be interesting, and how, and no doubt of it. Would she come equipped with miniskirt? Tiger grinned. What would the School Board say? The P.-T.A.? He loved the P.-T.A. They loved him. When exactly was she scheduled to arrive, anyway? He made a mental note to check the date. Things should be part of History by then, he mused, hopefully. And what about Nursey Mortlake? he thought, taking a corner, getting nearer to his destination. Was that as walled off a situation as it looked? Could it be? Well – wait and see. It could be. It wouldn't be the first – or the last, definitely. There was hope. She had a powerful pull. That was always grounds for hope. Well he knew. *Always.* He mused about her. She was worth it. Was she fighting, and hiding it? That could be, also. Well he knew. And it wouldn't be the first either, that's how those married sweethearts were, always. He tended to steer clear of them. But – *this one* – he sighed, thinking of her. Caution, patience – wait for the moment – *judge it.* That was all-important. The *most* important. For failure in judging it – he shuddered, almost. What a trial it was. A supreme one. It could unhinge one. *Was* it worth it? What a pull though. He couldn't stop feeling it. What would Rochelle say? Or Betty? Those two had brains in the highest reaches. Should he talk it over with them? He wished he could. It would be something, talking it over with Rochelle. He could see it. That incomparable sweetheart, that darling, that possible life-partner – he felt he could talk over anything with her – practically. There was a limit. He was aware even there of a limit. Was there though? Should he give it a whirl – subtly, tactfully, *obliquely?* Would she see it? That was it, in a flash she would probably see it. No, he mused, a frontal approach, with her, or nothing. Tiger's thoughts drifted on, he lost that one. He was thinking now of all the poverty in the world, still. The unfairness. *The ass-kissing.* He knew the enormous feat of strength, of *character strength* it took to go through life without ass-kissing, say twenty or thirty times a day at least, for a start. Tiger knew it. That was another facet of the beauty of his Sawyersville setup – there was nobody's ass he kissed. Not that he would, he knew, no matter where he would be. Had he ever? Even in the Army – *in Korea* – He was proud of that. Not many could say that. Tiger mused, on other things. He grinned. It would take a hell of a lot more than the Offenders' Directorship to pull him away from here. . . . He thought of Janie's last birthday party, that cutie, and all those little games they played, the same as a matter of fact he used to play at parties when he was a kid. Post Office, he grinned, that was some little sexy game. He used to love it. They all loved it. He knew Janie did. Parties. As a kid. That all seemed like a million years ago, out of another world, somewhere. Again, Tiger felt blue. He was on his way, on his way, nothing could stop the undirectional slide down that way. Oblivion. *Nothingness*. He thought of the game. It was set for next week. He hoped he was right and that everything would go alright. Tomorrow, unless unforeseen developments prevented it, there would be practice. Tiger was in somewhat of a quandary about this, and made a mental note to talk it over with Ponce tomorrow morning, first thing. The quandary was this: Should he put Jim Green back in and scrap the new plays they had unfurled? How would Joe Moran take this? Wouldn't it be best to utilize him – for a quarter say – at the minimum? Tiger thought about it. He would have to talk very seriously with Ponce about it. No doubt of it. That poor kid certainly was low, he was the most sensitive kid he'd ever met, which was one of the reasons he liked him so much, on top of the talent he had, of course. It hurt him though to see him suffer so much. He was young, he didn't yet understand fully, did he, the hammer-blow cruelty of life, from all quarters, and any, any-time, the most unexpected of times. Tiger sighed. The boy was like a son to him. Also, he would talk to Jim tomorrow. Though no doubt things would be pretty tight tomorrow. *What a mess.* Anne Williams might have to be cut by half an hour, and she would love that. He pictured that. And Sally Swink. What would *she* think? He didn't look forward to it. Could he make it less? He would do his best. Now Tiger's mind crowded with a whole host of things. How many of those parents would really keep their kids away from school? He wondered. He turned into Chestnut Avenue. He thought of the Kennedys. There she was. He thought of Vietnam. He pulled up. Grinning, he opened the door.

'Hello Tiger honey – ' she said, immediately cuddling up to him, as he drove off, smoothly.

'How's everything?' he asked, warmly, aware only of her

sweet form, near him. He glanced at the dark-haired maid.

'I almost didn't make it,' she said. She looked great.

'I can imagine,' he said.

'There's school tomorrow, isn't there, Tiger?'

'There is.'

'That's what I told them.'

'Didn't they think there was?'

'They said there couldn't be –'

'We'll fool them.'

Tiger suddenly thought of the back yard of his house when he was a kid. The pear tree in it. The grass. The way he used to cut the grass. His father was dead now. So was his mother. He only had a few cousins around somewhere – and a brother. He was a couple of years older, he was in California, he taught at the University there, Berkeley. Looby Loo wanted to take a trip out there this summer. They were working on it. *The back yard.* He saw himself, that kid, running around the back yard. He was there, in it. He was climbing the pear tree. He saw his father working in the garden, which took up about half the yard. He was always working on it, they had vegetables all summer from it. He even grew watermelons, though it wasn't hot enough to bring them to maturity, of course. How far was he up that pear tree? His father turned, and saw him. He grinned at him. Tiger grinned. He was a little scared, up that tree. His father would help him down. Often, he dreamed of him. He had always been close to him. His death, while he was in Korea, had been a cruncher for him. And when he got back – his mother. That was another one. *He saw his father, tying up the tomato plants. His brother was running out of the house – he was going out to the field – to play baseball –* 'Bob –' *he called out to him.* 'Hey Bob –' *He wanted to play with him –*

'Where are we going, Tiger honey?' the little darling asked softly. She smelled sweet. So sweet. What a sweet –

'Oh –' Tiger reflected, 'Let's see –'

That delighted her. 'A *surprise?* Oh Gee!'

Tiger chuckled, 'Let's just see.' He hadn't thought of it. But now an inspiration hit him. The fields – behind the high school! *Great.* Nice and quiet, private, he had never thought of it. *Really great.* The beauty was, it took no time at all to get there. That was the beauty of it. Why had he never thought of it? He would have headed automatically for the hills, and Rochelle's favorite nook, with its spectacular view. Of course it was rare that he saw a maid after school hours, very rare, outside of Rochelle, that is. That was it. Probably. She insisted on it –

'Where did you tell them you were going?' Tiger asked her, suddenly. It had come to him.

She gave that sweet little laugh she had, and said, 'Majorette Meeting.'

'With Marjorie?'

'That's right.'

She was dreamy.

Tiger grinned, what a kid. He was thinking of her now in her majorette outfit. He had first taken notice of her out there. Who cut a cuter figure than she did, in that outfit? That was when, alright. Maybe Marjorie did, it could be – but in a different way. They all had their ways – she had this sweet, cute appealing way. It was hard to say. She was a fine majorette. A twirler.

'I hope we have a nice meeting,' she said, the little devil.

Tiger chuckled, he couldn't help it.

'How's your dad?' he inquired now, for he hadn't seen her father, Dr Bonni, for a couple of months at least. He was Tiger's dentist, in fact his whole family's, and without a doubt the best one in Sawyersville. He was sure of it.

'O.K.,' said the maid.

'Mother?'

'She's O.K.'

Tiger nodded. Looby Loo was friendly with her, in fact they belonged to a few clubs together. Once in a while she came over to the house. She was from Jersey. Not far from Atlantic City. Was she a bathing beauty? Tiger wondered. Even now she had a form. Though not like Looby's. He grew warm, thinking of Looby Loo. And Jeannie. And Jeannie's mother. He pulled into the road that led to the back of the high school. Tiger drove slowly. He grinned. It certainly was dark back there.

'I know where we're going!' Jeannie suddenly said, lifting her head from his shoulder.

'Uh huh,' he said.

'That's a *terrific* idea,' she said as they rolled onto the fields and Tiger cruised around for an ideal spot. Probably down by the baseball diamond, he thought, driving carefully, avoiding the various benches and paraphernalia, here and there.

'Glad you like it,' he said.

'I guess you won't see me tomorrow now, will you?' It was true, she was scheduled. 'I just had this urge to see you tonight –

Tiger. Were you surprised ? In the hall, that is ? I just had to – '
He chuckled.

'That's alright, believe me. You little sweetie.'

'What about tomorrow ?' she asked again.

Probably, he would reschedule her.

'Aw – don't worry about tomorrow now,' he said, 'O.K. ?'

'O.K.,' she said, though Tiger knew rescheduling wouldn't go
down well. In fact, she hadn't finished the Brooder, Tiger mused.

He pulled up, just beside the baseball diamond. It was pitch
dark. Would there be a moon later on ? Tiger mused.

'Are you crazy about me ?' she said, in the darkness, putting
her arms behind his neck, as soon as they had stopped.

He felt the warm young form against him, eager and throbbing
for him. He gave her a little kiss and touched her face, passing his
hand over it. She kissed the hand.

'Don't you know it ?' he asked, caressing her warm, smooth
face. She closed her eyes. He brushed his fingers over her lashes.
They felt so nice. He was more than crazy about her.

'*Yes* – ' she sighed, turning her face upward, kissing him. . . .

64

'Ponce, you're a very nice dancer,' said Betty Smith.

'I am ?' Ponce asked, surprised himself at how well he was
doing. There was a smooth, slow number on. Vibes. It was
dreamy, nice. Full of warm life. They were close, in spite of
things, in fact she had her cheek next to his, which of course was
a burning fire, or more. He tried hard to keep the lower half of
himself out of contact with her, for he was in some state, but she
didn't seem to mind that, in fact she seemed definitely to like it,
and even want it, and so Ponce had to stop trying, finally. He let
himself merge with her.

'You *are*,' she said, as they flowed, about the floor, 'You certainly are,' she said, as Ponce began trembling again. 'Do you
like dancing with me ?' she asked, tenderly.

'M – M – *Betty* – I think it's great – ' the lad said.

'What's wrong ?' she murmured, aware of the trembling.

'W-*Wow* – ' he said, barely murmuring.

'Now now – ' she told him, 'There now – ' she murmured, in his ear.

'Am I hurting you?'

'Of course you're not – ' she spoke so softly, her warm breath caressed his ear, she smelled so sweet, '*Certainly not*,' she murmured, 'Certainly *not* you're not – ' she told him. His heart pounded, his body bounded. Without a doubt she liked it. She pressed even closer and held him tighter. Softness. Warm, divine softness. He still worried about hurting her. He didn't want to do that. He didn't know if he was here, or there, or in a dream somewhere, but he certainly worried about that. Could it hurt *him*? That was something else to worry about. Ponce was a bundle of worries now. The whole thing was something he always had trouble with anytime he danced, which was one of the reasons he didn't do too much dancing. He wore a jock strap whenever he did go dancing, and that helped a lot, though it was uncomfortable, to put it mildly. At last year's Sophomore Hop he had danced quite a few with Anne Williams, who was just a Freshman at the time, and it had really saved his life. Where had that kid learned to dance like that? *Why hadn't he worn one tonight?* He wondered, trembling, aware of Betty's soft murmuring –

'That's a very lovely thing – how could it hurt me?' And her hand caressed his neck. He had never felt a hand like that before, not even his mother's. What was she doing tonight? he wondered. He thought and thought about her.

'*D-Do you have a mother?*' he asked, in one breath.

She laughed so softly he was barely aware of it. Her lips were brushing his ear.

'*D-Do you?*' he asked again.

'*Ponce –* ' she said, 'Dear Ponce – ' she also said, softly, in his ear, once again giving that little laugh, 'Yes, I have a mother,' she said, both her arms around his neck now, as a matter of fact. Ponce found himself with his arms around her. He was a pounding, trembling, burning form, pressed against her. 'A *very nice* mother,' she said, warmly, pulling away gently from his ear and looking into his face, 'Almost as nice as yours – ' she said.

'G-Gee – ' Ponce said.

'Tell me about your mother,' she said.

Ponce looked into her face. Where had he ever seen such eyes? Such hair? *Was he there?*

'I-I – *love* her – ' he said.

318

'Does she kiss you goodnight?'

'Y-Yes –'

'*Like this?*'

Soft, full, warm lips pressed against his, luscious dream lips on his, Ponce had never known or heard of anything like this, where was the dream taking him? Would he be the same again?

'Ummmm –' she said, breaking away for a moment, warm, moist, '*Like that?*'

What kept him from exploding? She was the softest, most exquisite dream. He held tight to it –

'*G-Gosh* –' he could only say, '*Holy Gosh* –' he said.

She kissed him again. He was shaking fairly violently, certainly uncontrollably. Her hand caressed his head. He was about to fall over. The kiss was a warm tongue of fire now, exploring him –

'B-B-B-Betty – *Betty* –' he said, barely, he was fighting for breath –

'What's the matter?' she murmured, continuing to caress him. He noticed another number was playing now. It was a soft jazz tune, slow and low. When had it dropped on? How many more had? They were in the middle of the room, holding tight and close, not dancing, just sort of swaying. How long had they been there? She was kissing him.

'I sure – like to dance –' he said, 'With you –' he also said.

'What else can we do?' he heard her.

Roses. Only roses. How warm her face was. She was looking at him now. Her hand passed along the side of his head and face now, tenderly.

'Ponce – listen now – you sweet kid –' she told him – '*I want you to control yourself.*' Her voice was soft and warm, divinely for him. He only wondered – How could he control himself? He was only just barely still around now – How had he done it? He tried thinking about football plays, and variations thereon, and next week's game. He tried hard. He thought of his mother.

'*Try* –' she said, 'Please try –' she only said, 'Because we can do something *awfully nice* –' she said, 'Know it?' she murmured los, 'Close your eyes –'

When had he vibrated more? He closed his eyes, as ordered. He thought of his father. Of Peppy. Of Rusty Joe. Of Jill. Of Yvonne. Of Hetty. *Hetty*. Exquisitely gentle fingers were unbuttoning his shirt – *Tiger* –

'Ponce,' she said, her voice a dream. What would she do next?
He only stood there, letting her. He would die there, what did it
matter? He saw a well, a deep, dark well. He was waiting,
vibrating – He thought of *The Reader's Digest* –

'Open your eyes,' she ordered, in that caressing voice, a million
years later. Somehow, Ponce did that.

She was naked, utterly, before him, breathtakingly beautiful –
Her form – *Her divine form* – Her dressing gown on the floor –
He was wild at the sight of her. *There was red hair*. Music was
playing. *Tristan and Isolde*. Could it be? *Red hair*. It was all he
remembered. He fell over. . . .

65

Tiger was unaware of it, but his nocturnal penetration of the
playing fields of Sawyersville High School had not gone unno-
ticed. The observer was none other than Chief John Poldaski,
whose car Tiger thought he had seen outside the pool room, just
a short while ago. And in fact, he had. For the Chief was a cunning one, had left it parked there deliberately, as a ruse, while he
drove up to the High School in Sam Roto's car, on a special
mission, all his own: surveillance and investigation, based on a
hunch. Which was – There might be something worth seeing
around that high school, at night, if you stuck around long
anough. And he hoped to. For he was determined to do one thing
if it was the last thing he ever did do in this world – *Give those
Staties the crunch*. The whole bunch. They weren't around the
school tonight, of course. Nobody was. It was dark, deserted, he
was the only one who was. With his hunch. He had parked Sam's
snazzy car in a cleverly concealed position overlooking the school
and the athletic grounds, the whole works, and the road leading
to those grounds. He had been sitting there, calmly, patiently,
occasionally uttering a curse at those Staties, or at his wife Mary,
for an hour and a half, at least, ever since nightfall. He had been
thinking a lot of things. All kinds of things. He was even back at
the Second World War, in which he had served as a Military
Policeman. He had pulled plenty of long stretches of lonely
night-guard duty, of which this reminded him. A long time ago.

He had checked his revolver. His rifle. His club. His duster. His flashlight. His notepad and pencils. His pen. Everything was right. Then – he saw the headlights. And he just about kissed Jesus Christ. He watched those headlights circle around, and down, slowly, he watched them playing on the stadium wall, the football practice field, the baseball diamond – he watched them go out, just beside the diamond. And then – pitch darkness. He sat there awhile so excited he couldn't move. He could see Surcher's face, and those other hot guys, Follo, Grady, all the rest of those wise guys. He wouldn't tell them a goddamn thing. He had it all planned: He would capture the jig, hold him at the Station, call in the reporters, the photographers – and then the D.A. That was it. And the Staties would read about it, and hear about it – most of all, *his name*. He could see the headlines. No question about it: spectacular fame. And all those hot Staties hanging around – sucking hotchies. Yeh man. Down the lane. *Way down* that lane. He only wondered, still sitting there, which of those jigs would it be? There was no doubt at all in his mind, *one of them* it would be. All these things, these images, these predictions, raced through his mind in a furor, as he tried to calm down, as he congratulated himself more and more. It was brilliant. Ten minutes passed at least before he could move. Finally, he got out of the car, quietly, drew his revolver, held it in one hand, hauled out his flashlight, held it in the other hand, slung the rifle over his shoulder, checked everything, and started to move, soundlessly, classical commando style, toward the area. For it was only an area, so dark was it. He couldn't see the car and he wouldn't until he was practically on top of it. That was great. He was an expert at that. And had always been. He could prowl around in the dark like a cat. That was one of the reasons he had so often been detailed that night-guard duty, long ago, he knew. His technique was perfect. Over the years he had utilized it. He moved steadily, silently. He made progress. At last, he was upon it. He moved in on it. Every muscle in his body got set – to pounce on it –

66

Ponce was floating in the warmest darkness he had ever known. He was a million miles from anywhere. Everywhere. And nowhere. He wanted to get out of it, for it bothered him. At least if he could just touch down somewhere – this was the most dangerous thing in the world, in the whole of the universe, he knew – floating around nowhere, in that darkness, far out there – no matter how comfortable he was, and no denying it there wasn't anything uncomfortable at all about it. He just knew it would end, and disastrously, somewhere. Where? On the moon? A crash landing on the moon? Would he be the first? Was that allowed? He wasn't even an astronaut, or a believer at all in the Program, in fact, it was all a colossal waste of money, the whole space malarkey, that was his view. Malarkey. It had always been. Well what was he doing in it? On it? Upon it? He heard music. No doubt about it: *Tristan and Isolde*. It grew, it flowed all about him. It was magnificent, and powerful. He was riding on it. . . . Now, a voice spoke to him. Out of the darkness, somehow the voice came to him. Part of the music, it sounded right next to his ear. He couldn't identify it. But it was asking questions, at first he couldn't at all comprehend the nature of the questions, but gradually he realized they were part of a test – in English Literature – '*And what's an Elegy?*' it asked, pausing, obviously waiting for his answer. Could he answer? What was the answer? A voice, his, yet completely dissociated from himself, answered, '*A lyric poem that is a lament for the dead.*' It was his voice, no doubt of it. '*And what is a Requiem?*' The next question came. He answered, '*A sad song or chant which is in reality a prayer for the repose of the dead.*' The examination was over. He knew. No one told him, definitely knew. Now, the music, only. . . . Suddenly, he was no longer floating. Without even knowing it, he had landed. He was amazed to have been so gently landed. There would after all be no lunar crash landing! Ponce, on his back laying on something hard and flat, found the courage and strength, not to mention curiosity, to open his eyes. He found a strange sight. He was on a hill in a brilliant, warm climate. At first it blinded him. Then, gradually it came to him. To the right and left of him: tall upright columns. Doric? He seemed to be in the Parthenon. Flat on his back, staring up at a cloudless blue sky, between two Doric columns, magnificent things, in the Parthenon. This was all he could see. Those columns were massive, and endless. From where he lay, Ponce could not see an end to them. They seemed to penetrate the sky. Ponce tried to move, he wanted to see just where they ended. He could not move, however. He could see, he could hear, and feel, but there was nothing at all he could do about moving. Instead, in a moment, the columns were moving. Ponce was alarmed. They were moving toward him, closing in on him, and would surely crush him, within a matter of minutes, like two gigantic pincers. Now Ponce fought desperately to move. He couldn't. More: He couldn't move his head to the right or left anymore. It was fixed, he could only stare straight ahead. In anguish, he awaited his end. He tried to close his eyes but found that he couldn't even do that. What fiend, what forces had dreamed up this end? He saw the columns, before him, suddenly. They had not crushed him! They had merged into each other so that now they were one enormously massive column, a colossal one – stretching upward – and upward – ad infinitum – *and it seemed to be growing out of him!* Ponce couldn't see, but he was absolutely sure it was part of him! Ponce felt so hot, the sun was burning him. *Was this his end? Would he lie here, forever, tortured by that burning sun, that column part of him, probing the universe?* He heard a voice –

'Ponce – *Ponce* – '

He saw Miss Smith – *Betty* – he had come to, finally. She was beside him, leaning over him, gazing down on him. It wasn't a statue. She was so soft, and warm. So warm. He was flat on his back on the floor. *He was naked* – utterly – *as was the divine form.* . . .

67

Which jig would it be? the Chief wondered, just before pouncing. Would his black prick already be in her? How far in her? He pounced – he yanked open the car door – his light flashed on – he leveled his gun –

'*Tiger!*' he hollered out, when he finally realized what he saw, totally astounded at the sight.

In the glare of the Chief's powerful flashlight, Tiger turned, shielding his eyes with one hand, trying to see what it was, out there, all that noise. The maid was still in his other arm, though now she was clinging to him in a state of fright and near-shock. . . . They were still clothed, having spent the relatively short time since their arrival talking and kissing and playfully petting, only. There was silence now. In the glaring light, Tiger finally understood what it was, going on. He almost smiled.

'John – ' he said, in the friendliest way, 'How are ya?'

The Chief stared. He could only say, after a moment or two – 'Tiger.'

In a much more subdued tone, however, than his initial greeting. Which in a sense it was. He was surveying things, thinking hard, figuring out things. Or trying to. *Who was that girl?* Half hidden as she was, he couldn't tell. He stood there, collecting his thoughts. He couldn't talk.

'What's new, boy?' Tiger said, utterly calm.

'I – geez – Why – ' The Chief was trying hard. His light came down. Tiger, surveying him, saw that he bristled with arms.

'Working a little overtime?' Tiger said – 'How's the wife? Hey – let's turn off that light – look, there's a light – ' He pointed at the dim light in the car, which had come on when the Chief pulled open the door.

Poldaski switched off his light. Tiger saw the revolver in his hand, leveled at them. He grinned.

'Hey, what's that in your hand?'

Still in a daze, the Chief looked down at his hand. Tiger watched him for a half a minute at least, staring at that hand. He felt the maid trembling, though possibly just a little less, against him. He gave her a squeeze.

'Put it away, John,' he said, quietly.

Slowly, the Chief did so. He stood there. Tiger surveyed the rest of his armory. Certainly it was formidable, he mused, almost bemused. Though now he grew sad. He looked a long time at the Chief, who just continued standing there.

'Coming to the game, John?' Tiger asked, finally. Definitely, the maid's trembling was less. She remained buried against him.

'Yeh – Tiger – ' the Chief replied, mumbling really. He stared at them.

'Who's out there with you, John?' Tiger now asked, casually.

'Nobody,' At once, the Chief replied.

A moment's pause.

'We'll beat them,' Tiger said, 'Might be a little rough, though. And tough.'

'Yeh – ' the Chief mumbled.

'I'm using Joe Moran for this one, at End. We worked out some new plays – '

'Yeh ?' Poldaski asked, interested.

'Yeh, we had to. Other ones were built around Jim Green – '

The Chief stiffened at that name, but he was definitely glad to to hear about Joe Moran. He lived just a couple of doors from him, as a matter of fact. Sometimes he shot a few games with his old man, up at Sam's. He wasn't bad. Last year they had gone hunting together, couple of times. In the mountains –

'Who you startin' at half ?' Poldaski slowly asked.

'Left ?'

'Right.'

'Pope, I think.'

'He's good.'

'You're not kidding there, John, that's gonna be one to replace, huh ?' He chuckled, 'You want the job ?'

The Chief chuckled too, somewhat. Years ago he had been a pretty fair back, of course, under old Hink Henderson, right here at Sawyersville. He might have got a scholarship, only his grades weren't too good, and then, anyhow – along came the war.

'Old Fifi at full ?' he now asked.

'Sure,' Tiger said, 'Who else ?'

'There's a boy – '

'See him go last week ?'

'Jesus, he don't need holes – '

'You said it.'

'Just get down to the ten – hand off to him – '

'That's what we always do.'

'What about Jerry ?'

'I'll start him.'

'He alright now ?'

'Oh, yeh. Wasn't broken.'

A pause.

'Tough about those Practices though – huh, Tiger ?'

'What can ya do ?'

'Yeh – how it goes.'

'We'll take them though.'

'Think so ?'

'I think so.'

'Geez, I hope so.'

'Keep your eye on Moran.'

'No kiddin' – you really got some good new ones?'

'Beauts.'

'From the T?'

'Mostly.'

'Deployed wide?'

'Wait – I'll come out and tell ya – I'll show ya – '

Tiger eased his way out of the car, gently sliding away from Jeannie, leaving her sitting there, fairly calmed down.

'Who's she?' the Chief murmured to Tiger, outside the car.

'Jeannie Bonni,' Tiger replied, 'Know her?'

'Oh, yeh – ' said the Chief, 'Yeh. Nice kid,' he said.

'Real nice kid,' Tiger told him.

'I go to her old man,' said John.

'Yeh? So do I.'

'Good man.'

'I like him.'

'Real nice kid – '

'I like her.'

'Did I scare her?'

'Aw – not too much.'

'She alright now?'

'Oh yeh.'

'Some dentist. No kiddin' – ' the Chief said.

'I know it,' Tiger said, 'Here – John – got a pad and pencil? I'll show you – ' he added.

The Chief, after a search, obliged.

'Let's go over there,' Tiger said, indicating the benches near the diamond. He stuck his head in the car and murmured a few words to the maid. Then he walked with the Chief to the benches. They sat down.

'Shine your light on it,' Tiger said. Poldaski did so.

Tiger expertly sketched two opposing teams on the pad. He began drawing lines this way, that way, just about all ways. It put the Chief in a spin. Tiger chuckled.

'This is the age of razzle-dazzle, red-hot football,' he told John, who chuckled also. 'Little different from your days, huh, John?' he added.

'You're not kiddin'.'

'Listen, that old single wing was pretty good though, let me tell you – '

'It just about went out when you hit State, right, Tiger?'

'That's right, John.'

'This "*I*" is what gets me though – Jesus!'

'Yeh, well, I'll show you some with that too. In a while. But take a look at this, John. See here, that's Dink there of course, at quarterback – ' Poldaski nodded. 'Well, this is T-Fifty-four Left Decoy Pass Right Five On Two – ' He paused. 'With me?' Poldaski nodded. 'Check. Well that's how it was anyhow with Jim, see here he is cutting out and in and swinging hard right after deploying left, notice the decoy there too. See it?' Poldaski nodded, slowly. 'Check. Well, here's old Dink faking off to Pope, and Jerry, and getting set now to drop back – here he is – and left – that's it – there it is – that's the beauty of it there, see?' The Chief nodded. 'Check. Right. So – what happens?' He paused. Poldaski waited. 'Well, with Joe Moran we switched the fake on Pope and flicked him left, while Beep there on the line does the good work, opening up that decoy hole – see it there? Right there. That's great. That was Ponce's idea, I don't mind telling you, John. That kid is great, and no kidding about that at all. O.K. So there goes Pope and all hell breaks loose. What happens now? He's plastered at the secondary – carrying nothing, of course – while Dink juggles around, spinning right, and hands off, though he doesn't, and there goes Jerry into the line – drawing the rest of them off – he's carrying *nothing*. Of course. And that's the *second* beauty of it, John. See what I mean. No kidding, it foxed hell out of our defensive boys at Scrimmage the other night. It all happens so fast of course you don't even know it. But watch out for it. O.K. So what happened? *He hands it back*, see what I mean? Just like that, it takes half a second. And all the time Joe Moran's drifting left. *Left*, I said – '

'*Wow* – ' Poldaski said.

'Yeh – now – there he goes – see him there – he's going – who sees him going? Bill Linski there, the other End, he's deployed too – *and* decoying too. What does he do? Look – watch – just look – ' Poldaski gave a low whistle, as Tiger's hand raced here and there on the paper – 'And so? Before they know what's hit them, Joe's out there, alone, open – Dink's right – see him there, well protected, though, Hell, by now he doesn't need it, getting set there – right – he flings it – What a catch, man! What a pass! Chalk up another one!'

'*Goddamn*,' Poldaski said, astounded, admiring it all, though in truth, baffled totally.

'That's one,' Tiger said, grinning.

Poldaski nodded, studying the pad, '*Wow Wow* – ' he said.

'Now take the Jump Pass – remember that? We scored our first TD last week on that – '

'Oh yeh – ' the Chief said.

'Well, get this now. And we can do this because Dink can jump and pass a mile, you know that – '

'What a kid!'

'Is he! Notre Dame's getting him, you know – '

'Yeh, I heard – '

'You'll hear about that kid – '

'Geez, he's in all the papers now, Coach – ' the Chief said.

'So here we go, Jump Pass T-Twenty-one Jump and Run Decoy Right On Three – ' Tiger's hand flew this way and that, over the paper. The Chief tried hard to follow. Tiger talked rapidly, engrossed in it, totally. He explained all the dazzling intricacies, pausing to check with the Chief once in a while – 'And what about that?' at last he said.

'That's some Jump Pass!' John said, more baffled than ever. He stared at that paper.

'Sure,' Tiger said, 'And only Dink can do it – but notice Joe Moran? Notice?' Poldaski nodded, 'He'll go for yardage – big yardage – maybe all the way – after picking that up. Hell, he's not slow! He could *go*.'

'I'd like to see that – '

'You will. Don't worry – '

'He just lives a couple houses down the road – '

'That kid's got it, I'm telling you.'

'I'll bring his old man. Know him?'

'Sure I know him. O.K. Look now, John – Here's the "*I*" – ' He paused, starting on a new sheet and sketching rapidly, flashing all over that paper. The lines went everywhere, crisscrossing here, there. Poldaski stared hard. At them.

'Christ!' he said. 'Holy Christ!' he also said. 'How do those kids do it?'

Tiger chuckled, 'They do it.'

'I'd never do it. *No kiddin'*, Tiger – '

Tiger nodded, still chuckling. Then he spent ten minutes at least outlining that one.

'And there he goes!' at last he said, triumphantly.

'Boy!' the Chief said, only.

'See that?' Tiger said, enthusiastically.

'Oh Man!'

Tiger chuckled.

'Wait till the game,' he said quietly.

'You'll clobber them!'

'Now this one – '

And Tiger sketched that one, and two other ones, and then it was over. A little more chitchat, about this and that, and they got up from the bench and started walking, still talking. Tiger gave the Chief back his notepad – and pencil. The Chief said he would be at next Practice, come hell or high water, tomorrow night – wasn't it? – to see the action. He wanted to see those plays in action. That's all. They walked past Tiger's car. Tiger thought about the maid inside. They walked on, still talking, until they got quite a way from the car.

'Where's your car, John?' Tiger asked him.

'Aw, just up there – ' the Chief said, pointing toward the general direction of the school. In the moonlight, which had just emerged and probably wouldn't last too long, Tiger mused, he just saw the vehicle. Was it John's? he wondered. Could just be. Couldn't it? They were about halfway up there, no doubt of it, Tiger mused, glancing at the night sky, noting all those clouds, the moon getting set to dive once more into them. He was growing sad again, thinking about John Poldaski, one of the best Police Chiefs the town had ever known, without a doubt of it, in many ways, he knew it. He wondered, growing even sadder, thinking about his wife now who wasn't at all bad-looking, what was her name, *Mary*, a good wife for him, he knew, even though she had that temper, he grinned a little bit, through his sadness, he had heard about it, even heard it, once, somewhere, here or there. Somewhere. He hoped Jeannie was alright. He had told her he wouldn't be too long, and he was pretty sure she'd still be there. She should be. She was that kind of girl. But he couldn't stop thinking about John Poldaski. It was so painful he wished he could stop thinking about it. But the forces that govern all destinies, he mused, in the depths of himself, sometimes worked out this way, converging at just a certain, unbearable unfortunate point, as only too well he knew, so well he knew. That's how it went. It was a process alright, and nothing could stop it, no matter how much you knew about it. And who knew more? Tiger knew it didn't count, not in the crunch, the confrontation, with that convergence of tragic forces, whenever that might be, and who knew that, no one, that was true, until face to face with them, facing them, or running head first into them. He knew. It was tough. And John had seen plenty of action too. The Legion didn't have a better man on its rolls. They'd turn out in force.

'What's with that little gal ?' the Chief suddenly asked, in a low tone, indicating a genuine concern, and that he wouldn't turn down a turn.

Tiger almost shook his head at that, from side to side, as sometimes was his way, slowly, so much was he affected by it. It was a fact. He couldn't remember ever feeling so sad, not just now, anyhow, though in time, he knew, reflecting over everything, things, he knew he probably would. It went that way. Remorselessly. He was in the depths.

But he said, quietly, 'She's got a few little problems, John.'

'Yeh ?' the Chief said, curiously.

'Yeh,' Tiger only said, gravely.

He didn't know what else he could have said. For the process now was irreversible. It put words into his mouth, no doubt of it. There was absolutely nothing he could do about it. For the years had come. And gone. They were gone. He thought of John's wife again. Insurance. The concept of insurance fascinated him, revolving as it did around the darkest corners of the processes, irreversible as they were, and had always been. Complexes. For it could be said, certainly, well he knew, that it all consisted of innumerable factors, processes, interacting, interweaving, clustering to form these complexes. Life was such a complex. The process a combination of complexes. Death another. The other side of it. He knew. And where they touched – He sighed, almost. Life was an organized affair. There was nothing random about it. That was probably, in fact without a doubt, the saddest part of all. He knew. The interaction of human beings – He thought of Looby Loo. From the first time, so long ago, that he had really noticed her, he had been drawn to her. He loved her. He had always loved her, and so far as he knew always would. She loved him. He knew their lives touched at just the right point and intermingled – perfectly. That's what it all meant, what it was all about, man and wife. John. Mary. John loved Mary. She loved him. He knew. It must be. Despite her hot temper, which after all was just one of those innumerable factors. It too found its part in the process. The complex. For the other side was darkness. Emptiness. Nothingness. That was it alright. This was the only reality we would ever know. We hung on to it. Clung to it. Fought tooth and nail for it. What else could we do? Tiger pondered, touching depths of sadness he had rarely known, in fact had he known – aware at the same time that with the passing of time he would touch still further, deeper, and more frequently, and descend in fact, who knew, the depths were immensely profound there – He thought of Jeannie. He sighed, within himself. That wonderful girl. He saw her at the football games, in her majorette outfit. He saw her in Health Ed. class, without doubt the healthiest in the class. In his office. She had done pretty well on the Stummper, much better than he had anticipated. He thought of her parents. Without a doubt the moon would disappear soon, diving head first into those clouds. Lost for a while. It was a matter of normal distribution, who disputed that was in peril, for the entire spectrum of human activities, attributes, acts, what have you, fell in that pattern. In fact, anything, so far as he knew, did just that. And where the lines converged – where they dared not diverge – Where did John Poldaski at just this moment lie on the curve? Tiger wondered. Did he know it? How many knew it? He himself, he knew, didn't know it. What was it – all fantasy? What did it mean – in terms of fantasy? He thought of teaching machines. There was the matter of teaching machines. He was aware of himself on the Practice Field. He saw his eternally triumphant football teams. He saw John Poldaski. Was he at all aware of where he stood? Had he ever heard of the curve? Tiger groped in the depths, as he stopped, and said to the Chief.

'I'll see you, John.'

It was true, strictly. Tiger thought this, as John answered –

'O.K., Tiger.'

He watched him turn, after a moment or so, and start to walk off, no doubt heading for his car.

'John – ' Tiger called out, softly.

The moment, no doubt of it. *Now.* And Tiger knew it. Fused with it. Poldaski turned, curious, hopeful, who would know it, and a karate blow, deadly, true, already slicing the night air with the speed of sound at least, struck him like a bolt – though he never knew it. He fell in a massive heap, at Tiger's feet. It killed him instantaneously.

Tiger looked down on him, mournfully. There was nothing now but to mourn him. He thought of his widow. He shook his head from side to side, so slowly, he murmured two or three times, just audibly. The moon had ducked into the clouds again. He left him.

68

Ponce found he was paralyzed. Stretched out, like Christ almost, though the arms were a little wrong of course, and he was flat on his back on the floor of course, one thought now ran through his mind, terrifyingly: *Was it permanent?* Betty was doing all she could for him. She stroked him, murmured to him, so softly. She kissed his lips, his face, his wide-open eyes, staring starkly. She caressed him, all over. She leaned over him, and lay beside him, pressing herself to him. She reached down for him, she fondled him, she leaned over and kissed him there.

'Ponce – can you hear me?' the divine voice came to him.

He couldn't answer. He wanted to, but just couldn't. What would she do with him? Who would find him? Would she phone up an ambulance now? What about his mother? He wanted to cry. Who had undressed him? *Had Betty actually undressed him?* What would become of him? What would Tiger do?

'What am I going to do with you?' she murmured. Now she was leaning over him with her magnificent treasures. They were right over him. He longed to touch them. He saw her face. There was concern for him.

'I just can't understand it,' she said, 'You *seem* O.K.'

What did she mean by that? He wanted to ask. How hard he tried to ask. She was caressing his face, he was aware of the warmth of her, next to him. Her breasts brushed him, he felt the tips. They brushed his chest.

'What shall I do with you?' she asked again, her face just above his. What a lovely face. Her red hair touched his face. 'Can you see me?' she asked. How he wanted to tell her. Would he ever again tell her? She moved her legs, he felt her thighs moving against him, and gliding onto him. One of her gliding thighs touched a column. Definitely a column. He was aware suddenly it was *his* column, colossal, pointing straight upward. How he wanted to look, for he wondered: Did it go through the roof?

How else could it probe the sky? The ceiling. What about the ceiling? He tried moving his eyes. He tried to see. Why was he having these crazy thoughts? He thought, suddenly.

'You're *huge*, Ponce. *Lovely* – ' divinely, Betty murmured – 'As lovely as I've *ever* heard of – ' she said – 'Know that?'

He wished he could answer. He thought of Ivanhoe.

'Shall I just go for a ride on you?' He heard the voice. Ponce didn't know. It was up to her what to do. She should know. Besides – what could he do? If she did what she said, he couldn't answer for it. Certainly. He loved her, he worried about her, but what could he do about it? She could hurt herself. He wished there was some way to warn her that she could harm herself. Didn't she know it? Couldn't she see? Why didn't she? How he wished he could see!

'Shall I?' he heard her, sweet and low, murmuring to him. She was moving. He felt her form, warm, wonderful, hovering over him. Warm, gentle hands fondled him. 'Ummm – ' Her sweet voice. '*U*mmmm – ' He fought for his voice. '*U*mmm – *U*mmmm – ' If he had a voice – '*O*hhh – ' He was in agony. '*O*h – *O*hhh – ' Where was his voice? '*Ponce! Oh!* . . .' He felt her upon him. . . . Her soft treasures were on him. . . . Her face over his. . . . Her lips pressed to his. . . . *The column was sliding, sinking.* . . . *He wanted to scream . . . a profound, warm depth beckoned it . . . and enveloped him.* . . .

69

'Gosh! Hi!' the maid said, breathlessly, as he slipped back into the car, and beside her.

'Hi,' he said, cuddling her. She was warm in his arms, that sweet young form.

'Is he gone?'

'Yes.'

It was definite.

'Brrr – he scared me!'

'Do I scare you?'

She laughed, in her way, so sweetly. She kissed him.

'Never, Tiger.'

'That was some surprise,' he said to her, kissing her. He caressed her form. He certainly was hungry for her.

She murmured, 'Let's lock the doors.'

'I did.'

He told her. . . .

Was there anyone in the world with a sweeter form? Gently, presently, he slipped the clothes off that form. She sat on his lap, playfully. She certainly could play, well he knew. He admired, kissed, caressed those young breasts. She played, marvelously. She murmured to him. She wanted to straddle him. He let her. She kissed him a thousand times about the face. He held her at last so close to him, in a tight embrace. She wouldn't get off his lap. She cried out with delight as he penetrated her, the first time, on his lap, he ever had. She clung to him, giving little cries, wonderfully kissing him. . . . Gently, at last, Tiger eased her over, and off him, very gently, barely interrupting a kiss, until she lay on her back, under him, on that ample seat, for he loved her that way. She sighed, she murmured, she raised her knees. She was really enjoying herself, as Tiger was. Of course. And he thought about her. For certainly there was quite a lot to be thought about, in connection with her. He thought and thought, connected, exquisitely, to her. Without a doubt she was a treasure of a maid to be connected to. And how she moved. A little sweetheart. True. She gasped his name. The thrusting, eager, warm young form, under him, putting its life into him, renewing him, pulling him back from the brink. For there was the brink, and over into it he had to gaze, well he knew. He thought of John. He would have to go back to him. Get that notepad and pencil off him. He thought of that. He hadn't thought of that. He gazed and gazed. There was the brink. There, his life had become fixed, at that point, what else could be done? There was nothing else to be done. It had all begun – How had it begun? What a process. There were these processes. Did he have to? Was it true? He knew he had to. Nothing else would do. She was whispering to him, whispering the sweetest things to him. Once the process had begun – Soon they would reach the highest peaks of ecstasy, and she would scream. There was absolutely nothing to be done – He remembered the first time she had given that scream – It had a life all its own – It wasn't all that long ago – And took hold of his own – It had undoubtedly been the most thrilling moment of her young life for her, he knew, wonderfully supple maid, for she had been a virgin, one of the few – What could he do? *Do?* When it was time to. He hadn't hurt her, he had been exquisitely gentle with her – He remembered it. *What could he do ?* Fate played it this way, and had beckoned her, touching her, guiding her to him in that hall, today. It had. Or she wouldn't be here, now, he knew. The process was extraordinary beyond any and all comprehension, and he knew he never could hope to begin to achieve a penetration of it. The threshold itself was as far beyond his reach as the origin of the universe. He was a part of it. That he knew. Only a part of it. Well he knew. He remembered his mother, once his only universe. Now there was Looby Loo. He knew what there was to do. In a sense, in a very real sense, she was his mother now. And always would be. And what was he ? Escalation was this way. She loved him deeply, without reservations, that was clearly the thing. Perhaps it was all that mattered, finally. The only thing. When he held her, when he penetrated her, she was the universe to him. The process was more than a dream. In a dream his mother was calling him, when he turned, it was Looby Loo. Where was Jane ? Out of her had come Jane. That sweetheart Jane. Janie. Jane. His little Jane. He thought of Jeannie's mother. That was the thing. The hardest thing. He tried veering away from it, but it wouldn't do. There was absolutely nothing he could do. The forces, the processes, the complexes, and fate moved and converged this way. In this way. What else could he do ? It had begun. If there was anything else at all he could do – gladly, he would do. This, he knew. He knew –

'*I love you so much so much so much Tiger – OH – '*

The young thing was mounting the highest reaches, he knew, Heaven was not far, he was supremely aware. Her voice was a column of fire, next to him. She rocked, she rolled, her knees were high in the air. This was life, the undying source of it, as far as we were concerned, no doubt of it. The wet edges of life pulled and pulled him, ever in. He was pulled in. *The depths.* Where had he been ? Divinely, she caressed him. He caressed her. Held her. He caressed her hair. She had the nicest dark hair. Where was there a sweeter young girl ? Could there be ? His hands caressed her face, her mouth was part of his, she smelled so sweet, love sweet. They were drenched. The USA was sweet, sweet, what a treat, despite everything, *crime, corruption,* so many things, *teaching machines,* all those things, *Old Cornpone,* everything, *Vietnam,* everything, when they came, in the night, the moonlight, *there was the moonlight, we opened up, we cut them down,* my

God they fell down, and down, *down*, thousands down, well placed, machine guns, what guns, *they were guns* – He knew. True. Wasn't it true? What other place would do? What place *was* true blue? No place. He knew. *For the complexes – all the processes* – There was a cherry tree his father used to graft branches to. Branches. What was the world full of? He knew it. He felt sorry for those Vietnamese, but what branch of civilization did they want to be part of? That was the issue, he knew, and everything else was a sad, tragic, dirty, bloody ancillary of it. What about India? The misery, the poverty, the disaster of those vast hopeless masses was staggering, beyond all comprehension. Who could comprehend it? Help them? Who had helped us? *That* was the key issue. Well he knew it. *He knew it.* We had done it. They must do it. This sweet place would do what it could, naturally, however at times clumsily. *We were human.* Only. *Korea.* War was clumsy. *As in Korea.* We did what we could there. He had played his part there. Now the boys were again over there, another part of course over there, doing what they could, there. Here, slowly, white supremacy and tyranny were coming to an end. Here. One day, even those rotten Southern African nations, as he and Ponce had discussed only the other day wasn't it, would wise up to themselves. They had to. *There was one life, only.* This was it. Wasn't it? *Wasn't it?* How many times had he fallen off that tree? His father never fell off, that he knew, and what about Bob? Tiger caught a glimpse of that stranger, his brother, that bookworm, if ever there was one. He thought about Jeannie. He thrust deeper and deeper into Paradise, and he knew they could go on all night. *Not tonight.* She was burning hot, the rocking young thing, crying out and crying out to him, she tasted so sweet, he could live the rest of his life inside the young thing, to hell with the brink – *What brink? Where was the brink?* Tiger wanted to laugh, to shout, to roar – *He could roar –*

'*Tiger!*'

She screamed.

'*OH GOD TIGER!*'

She screamed and screamed. . . .

70

How Ponce got home that night, he'd never know. *How he got home!* He just didn't know. He knew only that morning had come, and he was in bed, and Peppy there too, lying luxuriously, blissfully, supremely comfortable, as often she did, on a select corner of the bed. He gazed down at her. Crafty cat, she had one eye slightly open, loving him, but warily surveying him, as he stirred. He grinned at her. He felt nothing but love and admiration for her. *What a cat.* What creatures they were. Dogs couldn't even begin to compare with them. How had she got here? He moved. It was strange, for a minute there he thought he wouldn't be able to move. Why should that be? He remembered a dream. Miss Smith – *Betty – was here.* She was talking to him. Murmuring low, all sorts of things. How had she got here? It almost seemed – in the dream – she had brought him here! He grew warm with that dream – or fragment of dream. *Was it a dream?* Ponce stared at Peppy. Soon, Rusty Joe would be cruising about. All hell would be loose. Peppy would have to hide – and that's something she was absolutely expert at, as she was at so many things. Clawing and spitting, for instance, if someone screwed around with her too much, or in the wrong way. Or a stranger! She dived like a streak behind the nearest sofa, or ran behind the stove in the kitchen, at first sight of a stranger. Ponce grinned. He loved that animal. Maybe she did have nine lives, but she sure wasn't going to take any chances – just in case. Ponce felt good. He couldn't figure out how come he felt so good. He lay there, just feeling good. It almost was – it felt – it was like – *something extraordinary* had happened to him. When had he last felt like this? Christmas – as a kid? He grinned. He really felt good. Or maybe when he had been to a nice dance at the school – or even at a juke joint? Dancing slow and easy with a real nice girl? It always made him feel all dreamy, and good. Right into the next day. But what dance had he been to? He remembered the first time he ever danced with a nice girl – *Rochelle, wasn't it* – at the high school. He had danced quite a few with her, and he had dreamed about her. He was a Freshman then. He had gone through a phase there of a terrific crush on her, almost right through the whole of his Freshman year. She had even liked him a little – it seemed – then – she had drifted away. She had lost interest. She had – grown up. Girls quickly grew up. She wasn't interested in kids like him – He grinned. Ponce, lying there, gazing at Peppy the Great, and out the window, where it looked like a really beautiful Autumn day, felt great. Warm, dreamy. He could lie here a long time, and would, if there wasn't school today, which of course there was, or if Rusty Joe let him, that crazy poke. He remembered he used to feel something like this when he was younger, when his mother used to tuck him in and read stories to him, or talk to him, or hug him. Ponce smiled. He loved her so much. He mused. What was up? The dream. Was it the dream? More of it drifted back – *Betty Smith was talking to him – talking so softly to him –* was she tucking him in? What a beautiful day it was. Ponce could only see clear blue. Rusty Joe burst into the room –

'Hey! You going to school today?'

Ponce turned from the window and surveyed him. Peppy had already scurried under the bed. Rusty Joe was diving after her, but wouldn't have a chance of reaching her. Ponce grinned. He'd be lucky to even see her!

'How come she always runs away from me?' the boy asked, on his hands and knees, trying hard to see.

'Don't ask me,' Ponce said.

'You gonna get up?'

'Sure I am.'

'Mom's been calling you.'

'She has?'

'Is there school today?'

That one stopped Ponce, and he began remembering things. That was a good point. Tiger, he remembered, said there would be. What was Rusty Joe asking that for? Ponce guessed he must have heard a lot. And guessed the rest.

'Sure there is,' he replied to the lad.

'Well I'm glad!' the lad shot back.

Ponce grinned and moved out of the bed.

'Hey! You have different tops and bottoms on!' the lad said.

Ponce examined himself, and sure enough it was true, strangely enough. He wondered how that had come about. Now Rusty Joe would have something to broadcast to Mom about. Standing there, before the mirror now, Ponce had to grin. Though it puzzled him no end. He almost looked like a clown – salmon-colored tops and green bottoms. He shook his head. The boy

338

started to laugh.

'You sure look funny, Ponce!' He shouted out.

'Aw shut up,' Ponce replied, suddenly feeling *very* strange.

He got dressed in no time flat, while Rusty Joe watched – and poked around too. under the bed. No luck.

'I'm playing football today!' the lad said.

Ponce heard Peppy spit, the kid must have come close.

'Hey, leave her alone,' he said, as if that cat couldn't take care of herself.

He went downstairs, Rusty Joe trailing after him, close.

'Think I'll ever make Tiger's team ?' the boy asked.

'I don't know.'

'Uncle Brucie says cats are for the birds!'

'Aw – ' Ponce started to reply, then toned it down, 'He didn't mean it – ' he said, though he wished the lunatic were here so he could punch him right in the nose.

Ponce's father had already gone to work, of course, and so Ponce sat in the kitchen with his mother and little Joe. His mother was cooking him bacon and eggs, his favorite breakfast dish. Joe sat there, monkeying around.

'I didn't even hear you come in last night, honey – ' his mother said.

'You didn't ?' Ponce said, feeling stranger and stranger.

Now Joe started, 'He had different tops and bottoms on! *He did !*'

'What!' his mother asked, smiling at that.

The lad played it for all it was worth. and wound up making a penetrating jingle out of it, which he repeated over and over.

'Well, Ponce – ' his mother finally said, 'Whatever's got into you ?'

'I dunno – ' he replied, sheepish.

'You must have put them on in the dark – when you got home,' his mother told him, reassuringly.

'I must have,' Ponce said, staring at the bacon and eggs on his plate. He felt hungry.

'What's the matter ?' his mother asked, leaning over him, an arm around his shoulder. Rusty Joe had finally left the room, in search of better things to do, before going to school. 'I know – I know – ' she now said, softly, 'It's just *awful* – ' she said, putting her face next to his, and hugging him. It felt good.

Ponce said nothing. He only nodded, and started working on the bacon and eggs. He certainly was hungry. *Very.*

'Want more toast ?' his mother asked him. . . .

71

The lifeless forms of Chief of Police John Poldaski and Drum
Majorette Jeannie Bonni were discovered on the playing fields of
Sawyersville High School by Art Murray, night watchman at
Feldman's Furniture Factory, on his way home from work that
morning, at just about the time Ponce was lying in bed all dreamy
and warm, all over. Art lived near the high school and always took
a shortcut across the athletic grounds except when it snowed
hard. He was pretty shook up by his find. But so was Surcher,
who uttered, when he got the news, '*Holy Christ !*' and that's all,
for quite a while. He uttered those words in a tone most unusual
for him. For now, he knew, things were not only much worse –
but all hell would break loose, certainly. The place would be
swarming with 'assistance,' courtesy of the Attorney-General.
The Governor himself, especially in this election year, might even
show up and start personally directing operations. *Against what ?*
Surcher wondered, starkly aware of what he was up against. This
was turning into a real circus, without a doubt, and fifty gover-
nors couldn't help, ex-Attorney-Generals, D.A.'s, whatever they
had been, on the way. He shook his head, slowly. Not only had he
two more victims on his hands, but the entire Sawyersville Police
Force had been wiped out. And whatever the limitations of local
police forces, they certainly were essential, they had their role,
without the slightest doubt. Surcher's head kept shaking. Undoubtedly, the same madman had struck again – Two notes had
been found. On the late Chief, the caption read, *GONE ON*. On
the young girl, pinned there: *OH MY HONEY*. And that was
that. A double-header. The Chief's mode of death had not yet
established, though Surcher had observed a certain slight bruise
on the neck and had his own theory on that. The pathologist
would have the answer in a couple of hours. The girl had obviously been strangled and – 'sexually molested' – though that was
the wrong term, he knew, if ever there was one, for there was no
sign of any struggle, absolutely. She had just – gone on. The
same pattern. The same blank wall. No clues at all. And John
Poldaski. A walking arsenal. What a cruncher ! What had he been
doing here, the poor sucker ? Surcher wondered. Just what had
happened ? Honeywell was out of it. He had eliminated him,

definitely. Not that he had ever seriously considered him. Surcher reconstructed the affair. As far as he could tell, the late Chief must have been on the prowl and stumbled head first into the arms of the quarry. Had he surprised him while in the act with the girl? If so, how in the world had he succumbed this way? He was a dope, but a hunk of a man, to put it mildly. What had happened? He could have held his own with a small squad of full-sized Troopers, he was sure. And he was armed – to the teeth, no less. Just what had happened? What was he supposed to do – comb the school for a karate expert? A *super* expert! That was his theory. He could have moaned. What kind of a fiend were they up against? Was he, after all, not connected at all with the school? Could that be? Surcher shook his head again, worried, wondering, and feeling sorry for that poor hunky. A dope, alright, but he had run into it. If only he had lived to talk about it! Or – Surcher wondered – *Or hadn't the poor dope realized he had it?* Was *that* it? It could be. It just could. He knew. He mused. It could explain a lot of things. It could. If it would! Surcher was stuck with it. He had to work with it. At least until the army of 'assistants' arrived. He knew it.

He was at the school, which was now besieged by a small army of media men, local citizenry, and curious onlookers. He was in serious conference with his assistants and the two key men of the school, Harry Proffer and Mike McDrew.

Proffer was saying, 'My God, *what are we gonna do?*'

That was a fair question, Surcher knew. 'Try to find the bird,' he answered.

'What are you gonna do to protect these kids?' Proffer asked. Surcher said, 'Station Troopers all over the place – that's one thing – ' He paused, 'And tell those parents to keep them in at night, for another thing.' He paused, 'Until we find the answer, that is.'

Proffer nodded, but had grave doubts about the second thing. He knew his Sawyersville kids.

'Poor old John!' Proffer said now.

They all agreed.

'He sure gave his life, didn't he?' Proffer added.

They all nodded.

'He did, alright,' Surcher told him. 'And – he had found the answer,' he added.

'I hope his insurance and everything was alright,' Tiger said, quietly.

'My God, if it isn't, the *town* ought to provide it,' Proffer said.
'Well, he no doubt had police insurance, most local forces
have – ' Surcher told them. 'It's not bad. Not too bad at all,' he
said, quietly.

Tiger nodded his head. As did Proffer.

There was silence.

'Mike – ' Surcher said, finally, 'Are there any karate experts in
the school – that you know of ?'

Tiger looked his way. Thoughtfully.

'Not that I know of.'

'Was John killed that way ?' Proffer spoke up.

Surcher nodded. 'I think so.'

Silence.

'You're not one, are you, Mike ?' Surcher inquired, mildly.

Tiger grinned, 'Wish I was,' he told him.

'Don't get me wrong – ' Surcher put in.

'Aw, don't worry – ' Tiger grinned.

'I just thought you might have some Phys. Ed. class in it – '

'My God no,' Tiger told him.

Again, silence.

Surcher mused. He had a lot of looking to do. And looking out
too – when that 'assistance' arrived. He knew. He had a lot of
looking to do in Jeannie Bonni's house today – this morning – for
example. There was something he would find one of these days
which would lead him straight to the lunatic. He knew it. But
there was also something else he knew, which wasn't too good:
he might not. *Nothing*. He (and/or the 'assistants') might just
have to wait like chumps until the thing had run its course, grim
as that could be. For he knew these things did run their course,
chilling thought though it was. It was even possible that one day
the nut would just hand himself in. It had happened.

He spoke now to his assistants.

'I want you to ask every girl in the school one question: '*Has
anyone ever made a pass at you, a sexual pass, with sexual inten-
tions ?*' He paused, letting that sink in. Tiger mused, hearing it,
it was some question. 'I mean *anybody*. This is very important.
It could be a teacher, a classmate, some guy out on the street –
I mean anywhere. Take all the names down.' He paused again.
'There should be a good batch of them.' He stopped, surveying
them, and Proffer, and Tiger. This was one approach to the
matter he had so far not put enough emphasis on. First he had
wasted too much time with that colored boy and then that

Janitor. Though he had done right, he knew. For anybody –
within limits – could be the culprit. Sitting there, musing, he
tried to build up a picture in his mind of the kind of man he
would be, when and if they finally cornered him. Obviously,
someone with something. A way with the girls. And Police
Chiefs. Something. An expert killer. More and more, as he sat
there, he saw his man as an adult, a formidable one. Though he
couldn't discount a school kid. Anyone. So far, no one impressed
him. He sighed, within himself, almost glad in a way that
'assistance' was coming. Though of course he would prefer to see
the affair right through to the end, possibly the bitter end, with
his own team. He gazed at Proffer, and Mike McDrew. No,
neither of those two. On that karate thing, which he had sneaked
in, McDrew hadn't even batted an eye, he knew. Surcher was up
the creek.

'I'll bet you quite a few of the girls won't be around today,'
Proffer told him.

Tiger wondered about that, casting a passing glance at his
watch, in the process.

'We'll see them at their homes, that's all then,' Surcher told
him. He turned to Tiger, 'Things all set up for that meeting with
the parents?'

'All set,' replied Tiger, 'Tomorrow morning, here in the auditorium.'

'Good,' said Surcher, still looking at him. 'I hope we can get
their cooperation – ' For a brief moment, his eyes locked with
Tiger's.

'So do I,' said Tiger.

'We'll certainly try our best,' said Proffer.

Surcher's eyes left Tiger, and he sat quietly a few moments,
looking down at the table, tapping his finger against it, half a
dozen times at least.

'Two cheerleaders – a majorette – ' he murmured.

'A police chief – ' Tiger put in.

'*God almighty* – ' Proffer winced. . . .

72

On the sidewalk in front of his house, just a few minutes after stepping out of the door, Ponce remembered – *everything*. It roared through him like a flood, staggering him. He had to lean against one of those big shade trees to keep from falling over. He was poleaxed. His heart was pounding. He was sweating. He hoped to God his mother wasn't near one of those big front picture windows. If she saw him, she would come running out after him. Rusty Joe had already buzzed off to school on his bike, with his pals, so that was o.k. Ponce just leaned there against that tree for a few minutes, absolutely about to keel over. There was no doubt about it – *It Had Happened*. He closed his eyes, he almost swooned, only the tree kept him from toppling over, as the details fell into place, in him. He saw that dream, the world's most beautiful thing, Miss Betty Smith. He was with her, they were doing things. He had never known or even heard of such thrilling, incredible, miraculous moments as when they were doing those things. *What things*. Ponce hung on. *When she was doing things*. For Ponce remembered: He hadn't done a thing. *Nothing*. He had just lain there, totally unable to move, a hot, massive column between his legs, pointing straight upward, *for her*. How she loved it. How she had loved it. *It*. He remembered it. He had never in his wildest dreams touched close to such mystery and ecstasy. He remembered the wild climax of it. *Fantastic moments there*. Hours. *Eternity there*. Her cries, her divine cries as that climax swept and surged all through them, her body had surged, and jolted, like a – *volcano !* Or was he the volcano ? That was it ! Certainly ! Ponce remembered, leaning against that tree, propped up there, his heart battering at him. The hot fluid, the love fluid, bursting out of him, shooting into her, filling her. She was crying out – Ponce remembered it. She had clutched him, surging against him. She had kissed him and kissed him. . . . *Was it still in her ?* How she had cried out ! Calling his name. . . . Ponce opened his eyes, coming around somewhat, calming down, little by little, somehow. . . . *And afterward* – he remembered now – she had lain there, upon him, murmuring and talking, she had talked such a long time to him, kissing him, caressing him, tenderly. He saw her face. Her sweet mouth. Her eyes. Her warm, sweet

breath. Just above his face. . . . Ponce closed his eyes again. . . .
Then, she lay by his side, and helped him, murmuring softly all
the while to him, stroking him. Helping him – to move. *To
regain his power of movement.* . . . What a long while! Ponce
opened his eyes again. He moved off the tree, and after a few
wobbly moments, started walking away, up the street. . . . He
didn't know how long it had taken, only finally he found he could
move his head at least. Sitting up, she had supported his head in
her lap. *That divine lap.* Above him, *her breasts. She let him
suckle her breasts.* . . . Ponce walked like a man in a trance, up that
street, remembering that. . . . And then – *when* – he didn't know
when – she had helped him get dressed. He could still only move
his arms and head by then. *She made him something warm to
drink.* She caressed him and talked to him more. . . . Finally, *she
had driven him home.* He remembered it, late, late at night – or
was it dawn? He could just barely walk, with her support, he
remembered his arms about her neck, and shoulders, and her
arm about his waist, as they made their way slowly. . . . In the car,
as she drove, his head rested on her shoulder. . . . She kept murmuring, talking softly, all the way home. . . . *It wasn't a dream.*
He knew it. . . . At his house, she had opened the door. . . . Upstairs. . . . Up those stairs, with her. . . . She helped him to undress. . . . The only light was the moon. . . . He remembered the
moon. . . . It ducked in and out. . . . *Where were the PJ's?* There
was trouble finding PJ's. . . . He got into them, with her help. . . .
He sat on the edge of the bed. . . . She held his face in her hand.
. . . *She had tucked him in.* . . . What sleep. What bliss. *What
sweet bliss.* . . .

'Hey! Ponce!' The voice crashed against Ponce like a barrel of
ice water. It jolted him out of his reverie. Looking around,
shaking all over, he saw Dink, calling to him. He was catching up
to him.

'Hey – What's up?' Dink said, finally pulling up to him, 'I
been hollering and hollering to you!'

Ponce had walked right by his house, he suddenly realized this.

'How come you didn't call me?' Dink asked, surveying his
friend.

Ponce was acutely embarrassed. What a hell of a thing! How
could he explain things? What could he tell Dink? *About this?*
He couldn't. He wouldn't. *It was something he wouldn't.*

'Holy Poke! I'm sorry, Dink! Gee! Know what was going on?

345

I was thinking of plays. New plays. Honest, Dink! I'm sure
sorry – '

Dink grinned, still surveying his friend. He was a funny guy,
but some guy, he knew it. Who didn't know it? And all that
trouble at the school didn't help. Well he knew it. He knew how
he felt. He let it go.

'I hope they're good ones!' he said, walking off with his friend,
toward the school. . . .

73

For what is momentum? Tiger mused, opening the door to his
office. The very stuff of life, upon which its renewal is based.
Could life possibly exist, without it? How could that be? And
Surcher and his karate expert. From the beginning it had been so.
It had been the history of this staggeringly successful Republic,
for example – wasn't that so? There certainly was a batch of
funerals coming up. Jeannie would have quite a funeral. He
knew. Her father was a devout Catholic, well he knew. The
Majorette squad had definitely suffered a blow. *He* had suffered a
grievous blow – He saw Anne Williams.

'What's your favorite band, Tiger?' that brown-haired Sophomore asked him.

Tiger grinned. And closed the door. She was standing near the
desk. She must have got here just a minute or so ago. He admired
her form. She wore a sweater and skirt, white socks, her hair was
held back by a band, she had long hair, just long enough, Tiger
mused, he didn't like it too long, like some girls wore. Down to
the waist, almost. He grew warm. He admired her curves. Nature
had blessed this girl with the most perfect curves. He thought of
curves, Nature's most perfect form. He just stood there, looking
at her, which was something she always loved.

'You're beautiful,' he said, spontaneously.

She smiled at him. She moved away from the desk. She
touched this and that. Now she stood near his chair, behind the
desk. *What a fifteen-year-old.*

'Am I?' she said, just standing there.

She was a little tease, it was her little game, but that added quite a lot to her appeal – bar none.

'You know it.'

Tiger felt more than warm. If he had all day, he could spend it admiring that form. *This* is momentum, from *here* it sprang. He reflected on that. Was it in the Bible? Ask Barbara next –

'Aren't you going to *tell* me?' she asked.

What was she referring to? He remembered.

He grinned again, acknowledging momentum's surge, 'Ralph Marterie – used to be – ' He moved, toward her, 'Don't know anymore. They still have bands anymore? I don't know. . . .' He paused, two feet from her – '*How are you, hon?*'

'I'm alright,' she said, and he could see she was.

'How's everything?'

'Do you like Tim Clean?'

'Who's he?'

She giggled at him.

'Oh, never mind,' she told him. And then, 'Do you like *me?*'

'What do you think?'

'*Take me on a trip.*'

He grinned. Soon, they'd be traveling marvelously. Partly, that was what she meant. She had a style all her own, and where had she learned it from? These things came naturally though, that he knew. It was a function of the individual personality, each one just that much different, if no more, and that's what made life fun. And momentum.

'Where shall we go?' he asked that, standing there, just looking at her. So warm, so young. Young warm form. Tiger knew she was warm, her heart was pounding away under that form. He loved to fondle that form. Her eyes were a very light brown. She was still teasing, still on that game, but definitely trembling a little bit. She wanted that trip –

'*Gosh oh* I want to go!' she said, and, 'Promise you won't murder me though.'

He grinned. She was some kid. Reaching out now with one hand, he touched her face. It was warm. 'Why should I do that?' he murmured, good-humoredly.

'*I know you won't* – ' she murmured too, her voice very low. Her eyes were on his. She moved her face against his hand and gave it a little kiss. Her breath was in the palm of his hand, warm, sweet. He loved it there.

'I'm scared,' she said, falling against him, '*Know that?*'

Why shouldn't she be? It was something anyone could under-

stand. He took her in his arms, and kissed her. She gave a marvelous kiss, soft and luscious. He felt her soft form, against his. Her
arms were about the back of his neck, caressing it. Now they
locked in a tight embrace.

'Still scared?' he said, after a while. Now he fondled her form.
Good girl, she hadn't wrapped that form. That marvelous form.
He would reach under the sweater soon, but for now, for a little
while, he fondled them through it, they felt wonderful to him.
He felt the tips, through it. What a soft sweater. What a form.

'*Uh Uh –*' she said, in a husky voice, giving a little gasp when
their mouths parted finally from that long kiss. She went limp,
she was sighing now, and trembling more, as he fondled those
tips.

'*Uh Uh –*' she repeated, obviously being carried away. She
sought his lips once again.

He picked her up, he carried her across the room.

She loved that. She didn't like the floor.

'*Where did you used to hear Ralph Marterie?*' she murmured,
somehow, fondling him. They were on the couch.

He told her, helping her out of her things.

'Someday –' she said – '*Take me there –*' She sighed – 'Will
you? *Darling –*' She clutched him.

He nodded his head. . . .

74

Miss Craymire spoke to Harry Proffer, urgently, in the outer
office, as soon as she got him alone – His own office had of course
been once again commandeered by the State Police.

'Mr Proffer –' she said.

'Yes?' he asked.

'I don't think I can *work here* anymore,' she said.

Proffer looked at her. Obviously she was quite distressed. On
top of everything, *the whole damn thing*. The phone hadn't stopped ringing all morning. Policemen, people, all kinds of people,
big and little people, barging in and out, everybody checking
things out, and only that strong cordon of State Troopers out
there keeping things from turning into a rout. He certainly

thanked God for them. Above all, Surcher, on the lookout for a karate expert. He admired that man. He kept his head. He kept on looking at her. He sympathized with her, knew how she felt. In fact, he felt the same. He couldn't walk out now – *but* – when this whole thing was over – He sighed, seeing that TV store. She could work for him. He was strongly attached to her, they had worked together for years, ever since he had been appointed. If she went, he went, and he didn't want to, *how could he*, just yet? More and more, he saw that TV store.

'Now Jane, listen to me – ' he said to her.

'I just can't *take* any more,' she cried, suddenly, 'I'm a *bundle of nerves*,' she said, sobbing at him, '*That's all.*'

'I know – I know how you feel – ' he said, putting an arm about her, the first time in all these years he had laid a hand on her, 'How do you think I feel? I feel the same way – *Believe me* – ' he said to her.

'I don't know what to do!' she sobbed, against him.

'Now, Jane – There now – I know how it is – Jane – ' He wondered what he could say, what should he say, or do, he really felt for her, 'Maybe – maybe you could do with a rest – ' he said, groping desperately, 'Why not take a few weeks' vacation, huh? Jane?' The idea gripped him, he wouldn't mind a month off himself, right now, 'By the time you got back – they'd have cleared up – the mess – ' He paused, praying hard, 'They're *bound to!*' he said.

'I don't know – *I just don't know* – ' she moaned.

Proffer could have groaned. If she left, on top of everything, it would be the final blow. He cursed the murderer. A bright idea hit him, out of the blue.

'Listen, Jane – ' It really had him, 'Why not do me a favor – *and* yourself a favor – heck, *everybody* a favor – and have a talk with Tiger – *Mr McDrew* – ' he said, 'You know how great he is at talking to people – *helping* them – ' He paused, 'You know that.' He was quite excited by it – 'Look at all the kids he's helped! My God, *you* know – '

Her sobs diminished somewhat. Proffer dared to hope. He continued standing there, his arm about her. Gradually, hoping more, he was aware of her sobs running low.

'Maybe – ' she said, as Proffer hoped and hoped, 'Maybe – I will – ' she said, remaining there under his protective arm, quiet – and snug –

'I wish you would,' he said now, in his gentlest tone, 'I'll bet it would be an awful lot of good – ' He paused, very slowly with-drawing his arm, 'A lot of good – Jane – ' he said to her.

She stood there. near him. looking miserable, once again. She was about to sob, a lonely figure in need, indeed.

Then – she nodded her head, slowly, as Proffer nearly gave a deep sigh. He stood there, watching her, not daring to move. He was offering up a dozen prayers, in all the languages he knew –

'Yes,' she said, 'Yes, you're right,' she said, her face turned to his. 'I think I will –'

Proffer could have kissed her, then and there.

75

The new developments hurt Ponce very much, of course. He was particularly staggered by the demise of the Chief. He had known him since he was a little boy, he was in his mind a monument, not a human being, as permanent a feature of the Sawyersville scene as the Roll of Honor – or the Town Hall. He had just never associated the Chief with the concept of mortality at all. Ponce was shook up, deep down. *And Jeannie Bonni.* That was it. And all that crazy mob around the school. He thanked God for those State Troopers, they were great. He had always admired them, in any case. Without them, he would still be outside the school. They sure knew how to handle those jerks. Without a doubt. What a crowd. *And those goddamn reporters and stuff.* Ponce hated to curse. In fact, he couldn't remember the last time he had. It was something that would hurt his mother very much. But – in thinking of *them* – it was the only way he could. It was the right word. The *only* word he could honestly employ – He was fussy about words, as any budding writer would be.

Inside the school, he had found things not too bad, to his sur-prise – and relief. It was almost as if the – thing – were getting to be *routine.* He rebuked himself for having that thought. It was an evil thought. Classes were going ahead, all the kids seemed to be more or less around, he had been glad to see Jim Green, looking none the worse for wear. A whole gang had gathered about him, firing questions at him before classes started. He was a hero more than ever. Ponce would wait till later, to have a talk with him.

Now Ponce wondered: *What would they do?* For it was pretty bad, he knew, no matter how near-normal things seemed to be. Things couldn't go on – like this. The kids didn't seem scared – in fact, they seemed to be getting kicks out of it, Ponce had to note, in spite of himself. He even got caught up in it. He felt it. Look at them there, with Jim! A burst of raucous laughter hit him. It must have been a good one. Turning away, by himself again, he felt as he knew he should feel – *pretty low*.

What helped him from sinking down to the lowest depths he'd ever known was the spectacular memory of *last night*. What helped even more was actually seeing his dream, in Eng. Lit. class, of course, which he had second period that morning. He sat there in that class, utterly unable to follow a thing. A dreamy-warm mist enveloped him. And it smelled good. He looked up once or twice and there, in front of the class, wearing the prettiest pale green dress, was his dream. He flushed. He burned. He yearned. He had to look away from her. He would have exploded right there, like a low-yield nuclear device at least, if he had kept his eyes up there. As it was, trying to stare at his books was hard enough. His body shook. His heart pounded like mad. He was in love, hopelessly. *And would always be.* With that dream. He was aware of her fragrance – even in the classroom filled with plenty of sweet-smelling maids. There was only one fragrance like that. *It was enveloping him.* He thought – of everything. *She had done it for him.* Ponce wanted to marry her, right away. And here he fell low once again. For it would be a long time, he knew, before he was in any position to marry her. At least – *at the very least* – until he finished high school. She wasn't all that much older than him – there were guys right here in Sawyersville, he knew, married to ladies that much older – *and more.* Wasn't Kishner's wife *ten years* older than him? Or was it *fifteen?* It might have been. That's what he'd heard. His mother had even said it, once. If she didn't know – who did? She was good friends with Ruth. . . . Two years at least, Ponce pondered, despondently. And what – he suddenly thought – *what if he had given her a baby last night?* Ponce nearly panicked. It hadn't come into his mind at all before this, and certainly – it should have. He knew. It was something that *followed logically* – as a result of. Why hadn't he thought of it? The amount spilled in her! Ponce was sweating. She didn't seem worried about it. He took a peek at her. In fact, she didn't seem worried about anything. The few glances he had cast upon her told him clearly she was as perfect, as beautiful, as absolutely divine and marvelous as he had ever known or seen her. She conducted the class, he heard her voice, the same as ever, no less. It absolutely amazed Ponce, and increased his admiration for her, if that was at all conceivable, at least twofold. Certainly, one-half a fold. He worshiped her. Could it come true? *Was there any chance at all of his wildest dream coming true?*

'Ponce – ' Her voice.

Was that her voice, calling on him? What should he say? He was in a hell of a way. He hadn't any idea at all what the class was about today. He would have to answer, and look up. *Their eyes would meet.* How could he manage that?

'Yes, ma'm?' he said.

Their eyes met. He was a pounding, quivering thing. He was zooming to the heart of heaven, he was almost there, *those divine eyes were on him –*

'Would you say Milton was *the* outstanding figure of his time?' she asked, and he heard the voice.

Ponce had heard. Now he pondered the words. They had a meaning, he knew. And there was an answer somewhere. Somehow, that warm, steady, divine gaze of hers was definitely and lovingly guiding him there. In spite of the calamatous clamoring and hammering within, he was *getting there*. He kept his eyes on hers.

'I would say – ' he heard himself say. . . .

76

Tiger looked up. He hadn't even noticed her come in. He was working on some papers on his desk – tests, football plays, interviews, a sketch of the stage, this and that – when she walked in. He had just about given up hope of her walking in. He checked the time.

'Hi – ' Sally Swink said.

'Hey, you're late,' he said.

The honey blond, whose hair was exactly the color of his own Jane's, and worn in just about the same style as a matter of fact, smiled at him, though she looked wan.

'I'm sorry, Tiger,' she said, crossing toward the desk. She

stood before it. She certainly looked depressed. And there wasn't all that much time. Tiger thought, *another time?* It just might be best. Rarely did it have to be, but he understood, completely. And if it had to – it had to. That's all. That was all. He looked at her. What a sweetheart of a girl, that's all. He was warm. He observed her. She had on a pale blue sweater, and what a sweater. She looked the picture of the sweetheart she was. In that sweater. He was unhappy though, seeing how low she was. Another time. That's all.

'What's the matter?' gently, he asked her.

'Oh gosh, I've been having a rough time – '

'Everything alright?'

She looked up at him, and seemed to blush a little. There was just the hint of pink on her. It made her look even prettier. She was so pretty, pale green eyes. He loved those eyes.

'Oh, *that's* alright,' she murmured, 'I'm pretty sure.'

Tiger was glad to hear that. Pretty sure meant sure.

'Running low?' he asked, tenderly.

'Oh – I could use a few more,' she said, in the softest way.

Tiger nodded, and reached into a drawer. He handed her the small bottle. Their fingers touched as he did so. She smiled, still standing there, and her eyes seemed to come a little bit alive, he observed. So did his. Sally was one of the most sensitive of maids. It was one of the things that made her such a treasure, he knew. He treasured her, and handled her supertenderly, and gently. There was poetry in her. She stood there, from time to time her eyes meeting his.

'What's the matter?' he asked again.

'Oh – ' she said, '*All this trouble* – ' She halted.

Tiger nodded, understanding completely, and in total empathy.

'Want to sit down?' he murmured.

The girl nodded, and moved to the chair beside the desk. She sat down, and Tiger observed her. *Who could sit down like that?* She had an exquisite class. Even the simplest movement told you that.

'I know,' he said, 'It's bad.' He meant that.

She was looking into his eyes. He was admiring her hair, her face. The way she held her hands. This girl could be a ballerina. What grace. What a naturally classy girl. As a woman, one day, she would be *elegant*. He knew. That was the only word. Well he knew. Her eyes were tenderly sad. Her father worked at the electronics plant. He was an engineer.

'They're questioning *everybody* –' she said, unhappily. 'All over again.'

Tiger knew. But he said, 'Oh?' Nonetheless.

'That's why I'm late.' She gave a wistful smile. She reached out, suddenly, with her hand. She reached for his hand. 'I'm sorry I'm late – *darling* –' she said, her hand meeting his. She gave it a squeeze. Tiger admired her beautiful hand.

'That's o.k.,' he whispered almost, 'I'm glad you came.' He checked his watch. Though who would have known. It was too late. He took that blow.

'You know what they asked me?' she said, distressed. Tiger waited to hear, understanding her state.

'What?' he asked, gently. Though, of course, he knew.

She spoke in the lowest of voices. But at the same time, Tiger couldn't help but observe, was that the trace of a *smile* there? It could have been. Well he knew.

'*Had anyone ever made any sexual passes at me* –' She paused, as Tiger sat there, fascinated by her face. 'That's what they wanted to know.'

Tiger nodded, perfectly composed.

'What did you tell them?' he posed.

'*No.*'

He grinned, in his way, tender and warm.

'*No?*'

She gripped his hand, '*I love you so much.*'

He knew. He told her, '*You're in a class of your own.*'

Her hand was so warm.

'Am I too late?' now she asked.

Tiger knew she was. But she was approaching some form. It was a problem and a half to grapple with, though he didn't shrink from it. And never would.

'How are you?' he asked, murmuring low.

'*Great,*' she said, and he knew that was so. Her heart was pounding hard. Well he knew. *Yes, some form.* He mused, grappling hard. She would never forgive him, if time won out. He knew.

'Get on the floor,' he told her.

It would be fast, but sometimes that could be fun. Certainly, he would do his best. And she would appreciate that. If possible, he would try working her in again – later today. Maybe after Civics class. He thought about that. For half an hour at least. She squeezed his hand. He murmured to her. Tiger mused, warmly, watching her do as he asked.

What a lass. . . .

77

Surcher knew he was at the crossroads. Certainly, *a* crossroads The trouble was, well he knew, each of the roads led nowhere. For example, *where was the karate expert ?* So far, he hadn't unearthed one. Nobody had even heard of one. He just got blank stares. Calm, steady investigator though he was, experienced and seasoned man of the force, he was nevertheless uncomfortable. He was idling low. He knew that before this thing ended, there was more than a good chance that he would need at least a minor overhaul. He was frosted. Certainly, he was buffaloed. He had all his men working full steam, all his resources were beamed. A squad was combing the school, interviewing every single girl available, including teachers. Those who weren't in school – and surprisingly that didn't even amount to a handful – would be checked out at home. In fact, it had already been done. And he and several assistants had gone through Jeannie Bonni's house meticulously, leaving no stone unturned, despite all the difficulties. For that home was a pathetic scene of supreme catastrophe. Her mother was in a state of near-hysteria. Neighbors, relatives, thronged around her. Her father was in a state of collapse, on the sofa. A doctor was with him. Despite his mandate, Surcher had barely been able to go through with it. In the end, he might just as well skipped it – He found *nothing.* Definitely frustrated and unhappy, but even more determined than ever, and unrelenting, he slipped away from the place, with his assistants, and returned to the school. There, after breaking through the considerable crowd gathered there, with the assistance of his club-waving Troopers, he found his men hard at work, checking all the girls. Otherwise, he noted, everything else was pretty much in order. Classes were being conducted, though he wondered just what could be going on in them, and everybody seemed to be reasonably calm enough – under the circumstances – in a way, he was glad to note. The one place where calm didn't reign was in Proffer's outer office, of course, where the phones rang and rang and people came and went, mostly students, policemen, plus a number of local dignitaries and functionaries, including men of the cloth, of course. Proffer himself, sweating, his tie loosened, shirt collar unbuttoned, jacket draped over a chair in fact, seemed to be talking to everybody at once. Surcher felt sorry for him. It was a mess. What had happened to his secretary, Miss Craymire, he wondered? She seemed to have disappeared. He wasn't surprised at that – last time he saw her she was in some shape. *Something like you'll probably be, old buddy, before this is over,* Surcher mused, to amuse himself.

'Captain – ' It was Grady, calling out to him, above the voices.

'Yeh?' Surcher turned to him.

'Attorney-General's been on the line again. Wants you to call him back right away.'

Surcher nodded. He had expected this.

'Any message?'

'I think they're sending an army down.'

Grady was a fairly young man, not long assigned to the Investigating Branch. He was excited, even though he was trying to hide it. To him, this was war, and platoons brought victory. No doubt of it. Surcher, gazing at him, before going toward a phone, knew that in time he would learn.

'No helicopters, I hope,' he said to him, picking up a phone. Grady grinned. He had a sense of humor. He admired his chief.

78

Tiger wasn't feeling too bad. It was lunchtime, or nearly so. He had taught a Civics class, among other things, talked to Looby Loo, that true blue, on the phone, quite a little while, that honeybunch, his only one, and he had just come back from quite the harrowing little session in the Conference Room with Proffer, the Area Superintendent, Burgess Totsi, practically the whole School Board, Reverend Brook, that peach of a theologian, officials of the P.-T.A., assorted and varied sundry others – and Surcher. Tiger stopped. *Surcher.* He shook his head, slowly. The barrage that guy had to face was murderous, they just couldn't believe he was doing his best, or in fact if he even knew what he was doing – that had come out, from at least two of them. Tiger admired him. He had handled it beautifully. He was a man to watch, alright, no doubt about it. Tiger admired him, unqualifiedly. If ever a man was up against it, and knew how to handle himself, there, he was it. Without a doubt of it. But what had really uplifted Tiger, so to speak, was the decision taken then and there to (1) keep the school open, and (2) go on with the game. It was something they had all more or less agreed on, after a while, thanks in no small part to Surcher's efforts, not to mention his own effective advocacy of both matters. The only problem now might be the parents. At the meeting tomorrow, Tiger would put all he had into it. He was impressed however with the massive turnout today and so he had hopes they wouldn't be too much of a problem – if any. After all, despite everything, the parents of Sawyersville were interested in the education of their children, not the cessation of it, and were, on the whole, *rational*. Well they knew how meaningless it was, statistically, to worry unduly about the possible dispatch of one of their loved ones by the fiend, whoever he might be. Besides, State Troopers would be everywhere, and certainly no young maid was going to be allowed out at night – until the situation was settled. And it would be settled. So Tiger, all in all, didn't feel too bad – though he was in mourning. Nothing could help that. It had gone on all morning. It was a process as inevitable as the sun rising. Or setting. The moon waxing. Waning. That was life. Name it. It was the case. Place it. There, without a sound, soundlessly, converged all the forces. Without a doubt, a part of him hovered low. There was Alice Patmore.

'Hi – '

In that frock, that bosom friend of poor Jill's looked fetching. It was a pretty pastel shade, close-fitting, and could almost pass as a mini. With her blond hair – worn in the latest and cutest style, what a style – it was perfect. Tiger grinned at her warmly. *Right on time*, the honey.

'What's new, Pretty?'

He knew she liked that, almost as much as he liked saying it. In fact. She sat down.

'Are they going to close the school?' came the query, right off the bat, as he admired her lipstick. He wanted to ask her what shade that was. And he would.

'No,' he said.

She sighed, 'That's good.'

Who could sigh like that?

'I like your lipstick,' he said.

'Do you?' She was as coy as they came. No doubt of it. He loved it.

'What shade is it?' he asked. 'What do they call it?'

She smiled. She had perfect teeth.

'*Coral Wonder.*'

'No wonder.'

'A *cool* number.'

Tiger grinned, and she was smiling. Her position on the curve was – *Tuckwell*. The last name of the teacher due from England next term popped into his head, suddenly. Without warning. He toyed with it. She would have one of those nice British accents. He loved that accent – on the fair sex. The *young* fair sex. At any rate. It had something. He always thought of English maids as friendly, fresh, in love with life – and that sweet accent. His favorite accent of all of course was American. Except southern. He thought of him. *Old Cornpone*. He smiled.

'How's everything?' he asked Alice.

'Oh – alright – ' she answered.

Tiger nodded.

'Tiger – ' She halted. He gazed at her hazel eyes. Intriguing color. In it, were all colors. He loved them. He waited. 'Those little pills – ' She paused. He waited. *Here we go again*. 'They can't hurt me – can they?' she murmured.

'No,' he told her, 'Not if you take them as directed – ' he reassured her, quietly. She sighed, reassured once more. *Until next time*. She had this quirk. Tiger sat there, gazing at her. She certainly thrived on reassurance. It would be o.k. now. He knew. He loved those eyes.

'Aren't they wonderful,' she murmured.

'I think so,' he told her.

'Just like you're wonderful,' she murmured. He loved blond hair. He thought of Jill's blond hair. He had loved it. It was slightly different from Alice's. There was nothing like blond hair. Or red. Or brunet. That was true of hair. There was this subtle and intriguing shade of difference between heads of hair. The hair on their heads. No two blond-haired maids for instance had *identical* hair, he mused, anywhere in the world. He knew. What color was Miss Tuckwell's?

'Where were we?' he asked her.

'Oh – ' she said, and she spoke softly, 'On the couch.'

He grinned. There was a memory. But it wasn't what he asked her.

'I mean the project.'

She was looking at him, and pouting.

'Was it the one with all the drawings?'

He said, 'We did that one.'

'I finished it?'

'Sure, you finished it.'

'Can't we sit on the couch?'

This was the other side of her coyness, and no ignoring it. He gazed at her form, outlined invitingly under her frock. It was true of all coyness, as he had gleaned, through experience.

'Then – ' she said, very softly, '*You could tell me how I made out* – ' She stopped.

He gazed at her. He would do that. There was nothing like comfort. Above all, she was for comfort. He got up, opened the filing cabinet, and pulled out her folder. He grinned at her. He gave a little nod at her. Her form was warm.

'Come on,' he said, warmly.

He walked toward the couch.

Smiling, she followed him. . . .

79

Surcher said into the phone, after a pause, 'What am I supposed to do – give everybody the third degree?'

He said it very calmly, after reflecting on it, in response to the Attorney-General's last sally, a brilliant one: '*It's somebody in that school. I know it. It has to be.*'

'No – no – nothing like that – ' said the voice in his ear, almost astounding him. The guy had taken it *seriously*? Surcher mourned the lost sarcasm. Wasted. And studied too. To boot. Well, it could be. He was the Attorney-General. Who now went on, 'But Christ, listen – how big of a place *is* it? Listen, you can pin him down, my God I'm *sure* of it – He must stick out a mile! *No kidding.* Once my men get there – ' A pause. 'I know I can count on your total cooperation – ' Another pause. 'Got that?' Surcher had. 'Listen, this is dynamite. *We've got to find him.*' There was another pause, while Surcher said nothing. *Why?* He felt like asking him. Just for the hell of it. What would his answer be? How many votes, he wondered, would it mean to him? He almost asked him. He could have chuckled – under different circumstances. 'Here's another thing – ' Pause. Surcher waited for it. 'Captain? Are you with me?' He confirmed this. 'Good. Listen – there's going to be a writer coming along with my men. *Ben Shingle* – you've probably heard of him – *he's one of the big ones*. He just flew in and the Governor passed him on to me. He wants to write a book on this, the whole case, from start to finish, eventually. That will be quite the book you can imagine, Captain.' He paused again. Surcher could have groaned. He pictured it. 'Well, now get this, *take good care of this man, Captain* – as far as I'm concerned he's on the same footing as any of you directly working on the case – I mean, as far as access, *within reason of course*, to information is concerned. You've got to use your judgment there, naturally, on certain things, I know, I know just at the present moment you won't be able to tell him *everything* – but within these limits, you see what I mean, tell him what he wants to know, let him circulate – ' He paused. 'Got that?' Surcher grabbed it. 'Later on,' the man went on, 'when it's all over, you can fill in the gaps for him.' He stopped.

'Do we get a cut of the royalties?' Surcher asked, full of fun.

There was a long pause, and then, another surprise: a burst of hearty laughter. There was a sense of humor, Surcher noted, forlorn.

'Who knows! Wait and see!' he next heard, finally. And then, again serious vein, 'O.K. Is everything all clear? Do you have any questions?'

'Not that I can think of – at the moment,' Surcher told him, dryly.

'Alright then. Don't be surprised to see me around there – tomorrow – next day – when is that Carverton game? – Though by then, *I hope*, everything will be O.K.'

There was menace in that hope, Surcher couldn't help note.

'We'll try our best.'

'Right,' said the man. '*Find him.*'

And that was that.

Surcher put down the phone, thinking, *what a good idea.* He turned around, as Follo crossed the room to talk to him. Maybe, now he thought, Ben Shingle would have an even better one. Despite everything, he had to grin. . . .

<h1 style="text-align:center">80</h1>

When Tiger returned to the office, after a quick Health Ed. class with the Freshmen, he found none other than Miss Craymire sitting there. She looked unhappy to an extreme degree. He had been expecting her. Proffer had contacted him and made arrangements for him to see her. Checking his schedule, he had agreed to do that. It would just fit in. Tiger also found a tiny note on his desk, reading simply, '*When?* – *H.L.*' He had grinned. *Hilda Linder*. Yes, it certainly was time for that maid. He was glad she reminded him, though he hadn't forgotten her. He would set her up, he mused, tomorrow. First thing. That was it. He thought about her. She was a fair-haired maid. As soon as Miss Craymire left, he would set her up alright. What time was it?

'Well, Jane, how are you?' Tiger asked the secretary, in his open, friendly way.

She wasn't exactly the most beautiful creature in God's creation, but there were points in her favor. True, she was on the wrong side of that curve, of course, as he himself was, well he knew, of course, but – her eyes, for instance. They were a beautiful, clear green. Beautiful eyes. Her figure wasn't all that bad either, though she kept it hidden. Her hair wouldn't be bad at all – if she did more with it. Her teeth – well, they were a little big, true. But not offensive. Her face, *in toto*, wasn't *unpretty*. Certainly, there was warmth in it. And it could be pretty. She was an old maid, Tiger mused, but didn't have to be. He didn't think she was born that way. He felt for her. It was the first time he had ever had a chance to really talk to her. Maybe, he thought, he just might help her. Maybe, he also thought, the whole sad chain of recent events would have at least one fruitful offshoot. He hoped. It could be. In any bombed site, flowers grew. Tiger stopped. It could trigger off a whole day's review. But he thought, *for this too is part of the process. Complexes. Normal curvature* –

'I'm really feeling awful, Mr McDrew,' she confessed, 'In

fact, I *can't stand* it.' She would sob. He knew. In a minute.

He nodded, gazing at her in that friendly way. He thought that under the circumstances, at least to start off with, it would be best to utilize a strictly nondirective approach. He would try it.

'You really don't feel too good,' he told her.

'I feel *awful*.'

'Everything seems pretty bad.'

'*Awful*.'

Tiger thought of soccer. He had always taken a dim view of that game, so called. It made him unhappy to see what a tremendous drive was now going on in the athletic-commercial complex to establish it as a major sport in the USA – of all places. They might even succeed. The scoundrels. He saw signs of that. It would be a sad day, and no kidding. He hated the game. What would come next? Cricket? Jane Craymire remained silent.

'It's really got you down,' Tiger said, 'Under the floorboards.'

'*Oh God* it has. *It has*. Yes,' she told him.

Soon, she would sob. Tiger decided to shift his approach. As always, he sensed it, intuitively. 'What's upset you most about it?' he put to her gently.

She blurted it out, surprising him, '*The sex. The sex in it*. Oh God! Disgusting!' And she burst into tears, a flood of them.

Tiger sat quietly and calmly across from her, watching her sob her heart out, as he knew she would. It was a release triggered by the depths, and no doubt of it, he mused. Not to be tampered with. He watched her.

After a while, she said, 'I can't *possibly* work here any longer.'

He nodded. Certainly, he agreed with her. But there was more. No process ever had more. And he was out to help her. He recognized the limitations of the help he could offer her, but his obligation was clear. A frontal assault was called for. He would do what he could, if no more than that. Proffer might even thank him. He was fully aware how much the man leaned on her. For one. He must be about ready, he mused, for that TV store.

'Do you feel you might be the next one?' Tiger asked, as soon as her sobs had abated, somewhat.

She looked up at him. She certainly looked miserable.

'It's possible!' she said, 'I've thought of it!'

'I think the thought dominates you,' he offered her.

'Well it *is* possible – Mr McDrew – *isn't it*?'

Tiger searched for an answer to that.

'*Isn't it*?' she demanded.

362

Where was the answer to that? And her need was total.

'Well,' he said, finally, finding words as he went along, as he did, often, his gift being what it was, 'You and I, we both know what kind of a world it is – ' He paused, letting them take him along, 'Anything's possible – isn't it? Jane?'

He waited. It was a process of serial approximation. And this was the challenge, the heart and life, the excitement in it. Well he knew.

'*But I don't want to die that way!*' she cried out.

He couldn't blame her. He was in total sympathy with her. He gazed at her. Those green eyes were just beautiful. He knew. He thought of Rochelle.

'How do you want to die?' he asked, gently.

'Why – ' She was choked for words.

'How many of us choose how we die?' now he asked her.

'What do you mean?'

'What do you think I mean?'

'What – ' she gasped – 'What did I come *in here* for?'

'I wonder.'

She sank back in her chair as if she were dissolving into it. Tiger watched her. Her eyes never strayed from his, they were terror-fixed. He felt for her.

'Sex has always been associated with death in your mind, hasn't it?' he said, softly. 'To have sex is to die, in your mind. Am I right?'

She sat there. She seemed paralyzed. He wondered if she would scream.

'Am I right?' He pressed on with it.

'*Yes.*' she said barely above a gasp. It was like the last word she would speak. She sat there, soundless.

'Have you *ever* had sex?' he asked her.

'*No.*' she answered –

'Do you masturbate?'

'What?'

'Play with it – ?'

'I – '

A pause. She was about to cry.

'*Yes I do.*'

Her head sank toward her chest. She hadn't passed out. She began to sob quietly.

'How do you play with it?' now he asked.

'I – ' she said, barely, through her sobs.

'At night ? On your bed ? All alone ? In the dark ?'

'I – play with it – '

'How ?'

'I – rub my hand – over it – ' he barely heard.

'All of it ?'

'It feels so good – '

'Do you talk to it ?'

'I rub a long time. I get very hot. I sweat. Mr McDrew – *I'm all wet* – ' The words emerged slowly, little drawled bunches of them, barely audible.

'Are your legs up ?'

'They're up – '

'Open ?'

'They're – open – '

'Way up ?'

'I'm on my back. My knees are – up – '

'Way up ?'

'Up – '

'Is your hand wet ?'

'So wet – '

'What else do you do ?'

'I – do – '

'Do you put anything into it ?'

'I – '

'How deep into it ?'

'I – '

'What do you think of ?'

'All – sorts of – things – I – '

'Do you like it ?'

'Oh – I – '

'How often do you like it ?'

'I – '

'What do you think of ?'

'Sometimes – '

'How high up ?'

'So – oh – High up – '

'Do you play with them ?'

'I – caress them – '

'The tips ?'

'I – stroke the tips – '

'How are you ?'

'Way – oh – way up – '

'Who are you thinking of?'

'I – '

'Harry?'

'What?'

'Harry Proffer?'

'I – '

'Do you think of him?'

'I – think of him – '

'What do you do then?'

'I play – I play – '

'And then?'

'After a long time – '

'Yes?'

'*I come* – '

'Yes – '

'It's beautiful. *For a moment*. A moment – ' She paused. She was murmuring inaudibly. Then, '*I get so wet* – ' Another pause. A long one – '*I curl up* – I have – *spasms* – ' She paused. 'Then I'm sick.'

'That's death.'

'*Sick, sick* – '

'You're dead.'

She remained with her head down.

'You're in love with Harry Proffer,' he told her, quietly.

Strange, but true. He knew. How well he knew. He sighed to himself, in wonder, at the byways, the under-the-surface ways, as always, the multiple intersections and skyways, all ways, of human life, that most astonishing of processes. What a process.

'*That's right*,' she murmured, barely there.

'Do you think he's the murderer?'

'*No*,' she told him.

He watched her moving. Her head, very slowly, was moving. Soon, she would be looking at him.

'*In your mind* though – he *is*.' he told her. 'Because you *want him*. You know what I mean. And since all these – sad events – these tragedies – ' He paused, surveying her, '*These murders* – ' He paused again, 'You can't bear being in the same room with him – *for you know what you would like him to do to you* – and you know what *that* would mean – *in your mind*, that is – ' He paused once more, he continued speaking very quietly. '*That's* why you want to leave here – ' he told her, 'That's what you're really terrified of – ' He paused again, 'Don't you think so?'

She said nothing. She only stared at him. Those beautiful green eyes were staring steadily at him.

'Sex, Death,' he said. '*Sex means death to you.*'

This much he told her. He knew well there was much more. But he had plans for her. There would be plenty of time to get down to it. Deep down. All of it. He knew it.

'What kind of a figure do you have?' he asked her.

Those eyes stayed on him.

'Stand up,' he said to her. She did so. 'Take off your jacket.' She did so. She had on a blouse. And under that, he knew, a tight bra. It nearly flattened her. 'Take off your blouse,' he told her. She hesitated. 'Take it off,' he murmured. Slowly, she did so. She stood there. 'Now the bra,' he told her. Very slowly, she slipped out of it. She held it. She stood there, nothing on from the waist up, still gazing at him. He gazed at them. He had been right. Not bad at all. They were white. Fine uplift, free of their straps. Tips. He liked the tips. Very fine uplift. They screamed for kisses, caresses. Her hands only fondled them. He knew it.

'Do you look at them?'

'What?' Her voice was far away.

'Before your mirror – when you're undressed – do you stand there – looking at them?'

'Yes – ' she told him.

'You can't suckle them – '

'No – .

'You'd 'like to – '

'*Yes* – '

'They're very nice.'

He murmured to her.

He thought about her. There was plenty to think about there. He continued gazing at her, quite a while. *And she was permanent.*

'Turn around,' he told her. 'Slowly.' She did so. There was the side view. Beautiful. 'Slowly.' She completed her turn. She faced him – ready for anything.

'Get dressed.'

Slowly, after a long moment, she did so. She said nothing.

He told her, 'I want you to come to see me here once a week.' He paused. 'At this time.'

She was just slipping back into her blouse.

'Can you do that?' he murmured.

Slowly, her eyes on his, she nodded.

His eyes stayed on her. . . .

81

Ponce floated down the hallway, after the class. She had called to him, just as he was about to go out the door, and he had turned, and gone up to the desk. *To her.* The others had by then all left the room. He stood before her, rubber-kneed and trembling, too afraid to look at her, waiting to hear her. He was ready to stand there all day long – if necessary.

'Ponce – ' he heard. Her dulcet tones.

Somehow, and slowly, he looked up. He almost saw her face. There was her – chest –

'How are you, Ponce?' she said, and he thought he would melt.

'O.K. – ' he said, fighting hard, his eyes still on her breast.

'Look at me, Ponce,' he heard. And he lifted his head. Her face. He fell, head first, into those divine eyes –

Now she said, as he swam, 'Keep up the good work,' she paused, he gave a nod, it was his head, nodding, her voice was so warm, so low – soft and low – '*I want you to keep up the good work.*' She paused once more. 'Promise that?' She stopped. He nodded his head again. He wanted to rest it on her breast – 'That's all,' she said. 'You can go now,' she also said.

And he said, only dimly aware of the words being said, 'Can I come to see you again?'

She had smiled. That warm smile. He lived for that smile – '*Of course.*'

He had heard. . . .

Ponce, floating along down that teeming hallway, heard only those words. . . .

82

Lieutenant Follo was interviewing Rochelle. He was struck by the maturity of the girl. Her records said she was a Junior and age seventeen. Yet, if someone had asked him, and he was no fool, he would have said she was at least in her early twenties. It was her *way*. She had some way. Follo knew she was no kid. She had seen life, and how. That was sure. He was getting nowhere with her.

'Now – Rochelle – ' He had some trouble calling her that. It would have been better, would have *sounded better*, if he said, *Miss Hudson*. That he felt. But – he had started out this way, as of course with all the others. Come to think of it – some of the others – he mused – *kids these days !* They grew up so fast. He thought of his own, ten years old and already wearing a bra – of some sort. *Pre-bra*. That sort. Sure, he knew, nowadays they all did that. He had heard – the latest rage. He knew that. He was nuts about her in any event, no matter how many bras she wore – 'I'd like to give you another chance to think about that question – ' he said – 'Because I'll tell you, if you can help me, it would be helping yourself, in the long run, and all the girls in this town, you know it – '

The girl nodded, and sat there. All Follo could do was stare. She was a beauty. That dark hair –

'I know it.' at last she said.

'Well – what about it ?' he said, patiently.

'Lieutenant – ' she said, looking him straight in the face, 'What kind of a girl do you think I am ?'

He didn't know. *What a voice*. She had this low, soft voice. It shook him. No doubt about it. Just what were kids coming to ?

'Well, I think you're a nice girl – ' he said, '*A very nice girl*, in fact – don't get the whole thing wrong – Rochelle – ' He stopped.

'And that's exactly what I think I am too,' she came back.

'I know that – '

'Well, what kind of a question is that to ask of a nice girl ? Hmmm ? Lieutenant ? Tell me.'

Follo sat there. This kid was beginning to make him feel like ten cents. And it made no sense.

'That's not – ' he started to say.

'What kind of girls get that kind of thing said to them ?' She trampled him – 'No man, no boy, would make that kind of an approach to a nice girl. Don't you know that, Lieutenant ? *They wouldn't dare*. When they want to proposition, they're very careful to select just the *right type* of girl. Not my type. I'm not that type. Do you follow me ?'

Somewhat stunned, Follo just sat there, and even became aware, gradually, however dimly, at first, of the pun she had

368

played on him. He began hating his name. Also, Rochelle. Could she be next? He began wishing, he was aware. . . .

'O.K. That's all. Thanks,' he said in a low monotone. To the girl.

She left. . . .

83

What monolithic consensus drove a notion say along paths that could be described as heinous? *Flagitious.* And all with pious, righteous phrases? This was the crux of it. No doubt of it. Was it a nonevent? The worst crimes perpetrated by mankind, on vast national, international scales were wrapped in pious, righteous phrases. It had always been. So had it always been. We were no exception. The best, yes, but no exception. But why the consensus? Tiger mused over this, and could only return to the concept, the basic concept of all the complexes, and processes; normal curvature. *That* was no nonevent. It seemed an unchangeable, tragic factor, that inescapable and irrefutable concept. In the whole complex of processes. There was the bulging center, the bulk. And the edges. And only along those edges – Tiger pondered, sadly – that tapering right side edge, that edge, was there any real hope of redemption, mitigation, release from consensus. The light of day. Blue sky. Daylight. It was tragic. Nature had cast the tragedy. What could men do, bound as they were – by their nature – to act out the tragedy? *Reparation. Amelioration. Restoration.* They were all. Ever. Or what tentative steps could be taken in those directions. For once on that downward slope – that slope – the wrong side of the slope – Tiger floundered, shrouded in shadows. He petted Sonny Swingle. She liked to pet for a long long time. She was a playful thing. Whom he would have called *Pussy* all of the time, not just some of the time, as he did now from time to time, if she let him. She preferred *Sonny.* Except for those few times – He didn't belabor the issue. He would have to see about setting up something for the evenings, after football season, for certainly it was clear that more than an hour was required here. Where had she learned it? It all came naturally. He knew it –

'Going to purr for me?'

'Sure . . . ' she said, and did so, with that word, and who could purr like that? Not even Sheba. . . . He loved her purrr. . . . He kissed her cute nose. What a nose. Her eyes. Her brown hair. He let her frolic with him in the chair. *Who could frolic like that? There –*

'How's everything?' he inquired of her. He heard a tune. It was his tune. *It came, it went, it was the cutest tune.* Long ago, he remembered, his mother sang him that tune. Looby Loo and Jane. *The tune –*

She was lying in his arms, her eyes closed, letting him fondle her bundle. 'Pussy – ' he said. And she sighed, and kissed him again. His hands caressed those sweet breasts. They were delightful, and soft, nice-sized, the tips were aflame. *Great.* 'Pussy – ' again, he said. She caressed his face. She kissed him again. They played. . . .

'I took it off for you,' she said, her sweet mouth next to his.

'Good girl,' he murmured low.

'Were you mad at me last time?' she asked.

He grinned. How could he get mad at her? She had arrived last time with it on. He hadn't complained. He hadn't minded at all. Together, they had slipped it off. Off. The treasures fell in his hands. He thought of Mrs Mortlake –

'Are you kidding?' he said, kissing her. Her kiss was luscious on his. Their tongues met. And strayed. They played. . . . 'How could I be?' he said, fondling them. . . . They kissed, and kissed. She could set a record. He knew. *He loved this maid* – 'Sweet Pussy – ' he said, in her ear. . . . She sighed a deep sigh, she clung to him, pounding hard, hot, and quivering. . . .

'Ummmm – ' she said, 'Ohhhh – ' she now said, fighting for air.

'How are you?' he murmured, nuzzling her ear.

'*I love that* – ' she barely said.

'Where did you get that bra?' he mentioned, referring to last time. It was the cutest thing.

'*Like it?*' she managed, playfully gliding her finger along the bridge of his nose, she stopped at his mouth, and he gave the sweet member a little nip, she loved that, he knew, as he did. *Nip, nip.* She gave a little cry. 'I saw it in *Glamour* – ' she said. 'I fell in love with it – isn't it sweet? *Sweet* – ' A little gasp – '*It's called the Curveallure* – it has *curve-caressing allure* – allure – *oh sweet* –' She was limp in his arms. He was slipping off the rest of her things. '*Are my curves alluring?*' she said, her eyes closing. . . .

'They are.'

He picked her up. . . .

Looby Loo he knew, once in a great while, bought that magazine. He leafed through it. There were lots of cute things in it. There were. He hadn't realized it interested Sonny's age group. He learned a lot. Every day. . . .

They were on the floor.

'*Glamour?*' he asked, sweet and low. She was dying for him. He knew. But she gave that sweet little laugh. There was a laugh – Her knees rose. She gave little moans. She was trembling. Eyes closed. There they were. Rising. He observed her. 'It was on the table *in the dentist's waiting room* – ' she said, though how, he never knew. '*Oh Tiger – Please – *' now she said.

'Dr Bonni?' he asked, admiring the view.

'That's right.' It was a moan. '*Is he your dentist – too?*'

He loved her.

He was on top of her.

He kissed her, and played with her. They played, more. She trembled beneath him, she was on fire, and wet, more and more. She moved, and moaned. She fondled him. *More*. . . .

'How do you like the play?' he murmured, after a while. She wasn't a bad little thespian. She would have a part. She looked great – up there – He was fondling her breasts.

'*I – like it,*' she gasped, her pounding heart –

'Do you like your part?' He was on fire.

'*I love it – *' she said – somehow –

He was kissing the precious orbs, the soft treasures all for him, he was lingering at the tips, sucking them, gliding his tongue over them –

'*Tiger – Please – *'

She could have screamed.

'On the couch?'

'*Anywhere – *'

He thought of Rochelle.

Slowly, he got to his feet. He helped her rise. They embraced, tightly, in a long kiss. He loved that kiss. She moaned. She trembled more and more. His shaft pressed against her form. She swayed, she moved, her body was a hot undulating form. He caressed her back. Her hips. Those marvelous hips. His hands glided now over her thighs. She was purring, he knew. It was a purr like the world never knew. He touched Paradise. She gasped and sighed. She thrust herself against him even more.

He thought of Hetty Nectar.

He asked, 'How's your folks?'

She moaned, she would go up in smoke –

He turned her around, slowly, she gave little cries, his phallus touched her, her shoulders and hand rested against him. A blissful kiss. Her lips met his phallus. He fondled those curveallure breasts – Now his loving hands gently glided between her thighs, and caressed Paradise. . . .

She said, her whisper red hot, *'Let's play all day –* ' And, strangely enough, *'Poor Jeannie –* '

It was her way.

He thought of Mona.

He said, 'I wish I could – '

He carried her to the couch.

On her back, her knees high, she was a beautiful sight. He gazed on her. He stroked, and caressed her. He loved gazing on her. They played and played, she was a trembling form, on fire, they played in her way. He loved it. Could they burst into flames? He wondered. She cried out, just gasping the words, finally, hoarsely, *'Do you love my pussy?'*

He thrust home.

'What a pussy.'

She moved and moaned, wildly, exquisitely. *Here was glory.* He stroked massively, marvelously. . . . He stroked the depths, gloriously. . . . His pace broke all records, known. . . .

'Oh Tiger! OH!' she screamed – 'OH – 'OH-OHHHHH!' They were drenched, from head to toe, they rocked, they rolled – *It was all glory.*

'TIGERRRRRRRRRR!'

She screamed beautifully. They rolled off the couch. They hit the floor with a thump, they never felt it, they rolled, and rolled, *they rolled timelessly.* . . .

84

A week had passed. The funerals of the deceased had taken place
There had been no new developments, outside of the strange case
of Mary Holden, which, however strange, did not appear to be
connected with the case, in Surcher's opinion. Nevertheless, he
reflected once again on the bizarre details. She had been found
dead in her bed by her mother three days ago. She was completely naked. Her legs were apart and her hand was between her
thighs, over her genital. She was curled up, as if in a spasm. In
her vaginal barrel, inserted as far as it could go, was found a
device that remarkably resembled an erect penis. It was made of
a substance which turned out to be plastic. Just what the object
was had not as yet been determined. Certainly, it remarkably
resembled a phallus. There were no signs of foul play. Pathologist's report: Heart Failure. He had said to Surcher, privately,
'Died Loving it.' And, wryly, 'Her epitaph.' Surcher hadn't
replied, he knew his Pathologist. A record had been on her
phonograph, it had been playing over and over, loudly, this had
in fact been the reason her mother had gone up to her room – the
record was by the fellow Tim Clean, and his group, The
Cleaners – *What The World Needs Now Is Love, Sweet Love.*'
And, ready to drop on, though it had never made it, due to some
technical hitchup, *You're Gonna Know What It Means To Be
Lonely.*' Same group. That was all. Nothing else was found.
Yesterday, she had been buried. . . . Today was the big game
with Carverton. Surcher had a seat on the fifty-yard line, in the
magnificent Sawyersville Stadium. Next to him sat Ben Shingle,
who had turned out to be a lot better than he had anticipated, not
a bad guy at all, in fact. He was quiet. Modest. He got in nobody's
way, and yet had a sharp eye. He was on the ball. Surcher had
respect for him. When he asked questions, he didn't mind at all
answering them. He had stayed at the motel the first two nights
after arriving, but now was staying with Mike McDrew, who
had become pretty good friends with him. They hit it off alright,
they spent quite a bit of time together. Surcher had taken time off
to come to the game, for he was in need of a break, despite all the
'assistance.' And – he wanted to see this phenomenal Sawyersville team in action. He couldn't deny that. He wondered how

they would fare. It should be some game. Carverton, so far this
year, was unbeaten. In fact, Sawyersville had been the *last* team
to beat them – last year, he remembered. The stadium was packed
full, in spite of everything. Secretly, he was rooting for Carverton,
though he felt slightly guilty about it. He had become almost a
part of Sawyersville. That he knew. So far as the case was concerned, there had been absolutely no developments – despite the
intensive work by himself, his men, and the Attorney-General's
platoon of Assistants, including an FBI man attached in a purely
advisory capacity. In fact this man had so far given no advice,
confining himself in the one talk Surcher had had with him to
delivering a long, quiet, very sober panegyric on the distinctly
remarkable, supremely unassailable, and untarnishably super-
American qualities of The Director. Surcher took it in stride,
like a man. The Attorney-General had turned up today. He was
sitting a few rows above Surcher – surrounded by local dignitaries, and Assistants. Surcher hoped he enjoyed the game. He
was tired. He only was grateful there had been no further
departure of maids, outside of Mary Holden, of course, which
didn't count in his book. Maybe, he hoped, watching the teams
line up now for the kickoff amid thunderous cheers and rolling
roars, the madman had run his course. Maybe, he further hoped,
he would turn himself in, having regained lucidity and having
become aware of the horrors he had committed. Surcher mused.
It was a theory he had discussed at length with Shingle, who saw
some merit in it. Much as he wanted to find the fellow himself,
Surcher wouldn't have minded, for it would have solved the
problem. That was the only important point, well he knew.
There were plenty of State Troopers in and around the stadium,
and in the high school. No chances were being taken. The parents
were cooperating excellently, and he owed it to them to give their
kids the fullest possible protection, possibly in spite of themselves, and no matter what the overtime came to. He watched the
ball sail through the air as the Sawyersville boys kicked off. A
beauty of a kick. What a kick. Who was that kid? The crowd
roared. Surcher relaxed. He liked a good game. He needed this
break. And he was going to enjoy it.

'That sure does look like quite the little team,' Shingle com-
mented as the Carverton ball carrier was clobbered by a swarm
of Sawyersville players.

Surcher turned to him, and he couldn't help grin, in spite of
his secret wish.

'Keep watching.'
He told him. . . .

Tiger was leaping on and off the bench, striding back and forth, yelling here and there, pulling players out, sending others in, shouting for Ponce, holding conference after conference with him, the cheerleaders were working hard, the stands were roaring, and Ponce was worried. He hovered over Tiger's clipboard. Sponges, towels, water bottles, equipment, were all about him. He studied everything going on, with computer speed. Profoundly. He tried hard not to show it, but he was worried, and he knew damn well Tiger was worried. Things weren't going too well. The first quarter had gone by – and no score. True, *they* hadn't scored, but the fact was they had once come mighty close to scoring. Only Beep's tremendous work had saved the day. As for Sawyersville – they had been completely stoppered. They hadn't even moved out of their own forty-yard line. It was awful. Everything had flopped, even the special-pass plays, and variations thereon. That Carverton defense was rock solid, it had even broken through and dumped Dink three or four times, while he still had the ball. Tiger had pulled Joe Moran out. Jim was in there. Now, it was halfway through the second quarter. And things were still awful. *Look at now.* He jumped off the bench like a shot, with everybody, Tiger was hollering and hollering, there was the Carverton fullback down to the twenty – the ten – and dropped, but hard, finally, just beyond there. *On the five.* When had a team last hit that five ? *Time out.* Ponce and Billy King raced out there with their stuff, Tiger sent in four or five fresh men, hollering all the while. The whole team stood around them, down in the dumps, no doubt about it. Ponce felt awful. He talked to them, but it wasn't time. Al Bartholomew limped about. Fifi looked in a daze. He had the wind knocked out on that play. He had made that tackle. Time out was over. Ponce and Billy left the field. And on the next play, Carverton scored. *And converted.* Their side of the stadium went mad, off their rockers, Ponce had never seen cheerleaders vault so high. He felt bad. Bad bad. Tiger, all of them, looked glum. They sat on the benches, stunned. There was no further scoring that half. . . .

In the locker room, at halftime, while out on the field the Sawyersville band and the Majorettes put on their show, Tiger gave the team hell. Ponce hoped to God it would ring a bell. Ben Shingle had slipped into the locker room, Ponce observed. He was tucked in a corner, out of everyone's way, but, Ponce knew, taking everything in. Ponce almost grinned. He had been pretty thrilled to hear about him, not to mention actually meeting him, for who was a more famous and celebrated writer than he? He was a real nice guy too, that was the best part of it. And no doubt about it. Ponce had talked to him quite a lot, since his arrival. Especially since he had moved into Tiger's house. He had encouraged him a lot. He had even said he would try to help him. And that was great. Now he did give a grin, the best he could under the circumstances, and nodded to him, for he had caught his eye. Tiger didn't seem to see him. He was before the team, pacing back and forth, not saying a thing – yet. He called to Ponce. He had a little talk with him. Then – he pitched in –

'Just what were you guys playing out there? *Hopscotch?* What do I have – a *Hopscotch* team? *Where the hell is my team? Are you here?* Where are you guys now? *Out in space?* WELL GET BACK DOWN HERE! You know who you are? WHAT you are? We're playing *Football!* Know what that is? Remember? You played it last week – and the week before – and all of last year – *Just Like A Sawyersville Team!* You know what that is? *You Guys Are That Team!* Know that? Well I'm *reminding* you of that – Alright? Because you sure as hell didn't look like you knew it out there – AT ALL! *Not At All!* GET ON THE BALL! Get hold of it, and hang on to it! YOU KNOW WHO YOU ARE! YOU HAVE TWO QUARTERS TO PROVE IT! What kind of blocking was that, you guys on the line? Beep – I'm surprised at you! Was That You? What about you, Al? And you, and you – Joe – Cal – HOLY COW! You oughta be able to push those jerks back a mile – A MILE: RIGHT OUT OF THE STADIUM! All I'm asking is that you open some *holes.* What's Pope supposed to do? Run through a *Wall?* What about Feef? JESUS, LOOK AT HIM! You just about KILLED him. And Dink! How many passes has he got off? Huh? WHAT'S UP? WHAT THE HELL'S UP? *Is this My Club?* What's the Score? Don't you want me as coach anymore? HELL, I DON'T CARE! I'll quit right now if that's what you want! IS THAT THE SCORE? And your Defense! WOW! They push you around like toys! You're outfoxed every time! EVERY PLAY! The holes are big enough to get a tank through. A Tank! What's up? What's bothering you? Don't blame it on the Practices we missed! DON'T TRY THAT! *You oughta beat that gang with NO PRACTICES AT ALL!* Know That? Well, *I* sure know that!

376

Let me tell you! WHO DOESN'T KNOW THAT? What's Up? What's got you down? ARE YOU TIGERS OR ZOMBIES? You LOOK like ZOMBIES! What is it? *The troubles got you down?* All those sad events got you collared and down, way down, right right down? Is that it? Listen: *Those girls would want you to win* – All of them – to play ball like a *Sawyersville* team – Know that? Look at all Jill did for you! And Yvonne! *Jeannie!* Think of Jeannie! Remember that girl? WELL WHAT ARE YOU DOING FOR THEM! *All of them!* I'll tell you: SITTING FLAT! *Flat!* ON THE MAT! If they could see you now – you look like a bunch of zombie jerks. JERKS! You want this to be a JERK TOWN? *That* what you want? Like Carverton? There's a jerk town if ever there was one? WHAT A TOWN! You know it! AND THEY'RE KNOCKING HELL OUT OF YOU! How many will they rack up? *What about us?* If you get out there and *played ball – rough – tough – Real Football* – If you charged like the Tigers you are – AND NOT ZOMBIES – if you blocked – ran – *opened those holes* – IF YOU PROTECTED DINK!' He paused, just an instant, hitting the highest crescendo yet – 'WHAT A SCORE! WHAT ONE HELL OF A SCORE! A REAL TIGERS SCORE! You wouldn't even HEAR of Carverton anymore! They'd quit the League! Like they ought to! WHAT ARE YOU GONNA DO? *It's Up To You!* I can't come out there and *play* for you! *Ponce* here can't do it for you! IT'S UP TO YOU! ALL OF YOU! Look how you screwed up his plays! Those are GREAT plays! *Think of those girls!* AT LEAST PLAY FOR THEM!' He paused, he thumped his hand on a table – '*ROAR!*' The whole team roared, Ponce roared, he had been electrified by the talk, he roared and roared, he had never heard such a talk, he even thought he saw Mr Shingle roar, '*ROAR!*' They roared and roared, the room shook with their roars, Ponce was sure of the score, Tiger hit the table again, and again – 'ROAR! ROAR!' The walls would fall down with the roars – 'TIGERS – ROAR! NO PUSSYFOOTING AROUND ANYMORE!' Ponce was drowned in the roars. . . .

In the second half, they scored thirty-five points, Carverton – none.

Surcher and Ben Shingle watched a spectacular display of awesome and dazzling Sawyersville might. Everything clicked just right. Their stands roared, the band blared, the cheerleaders turned a thousand cartwheels. At the end, Surcher and Shingle, standing up in a sea of roaring, saw Ponce and Tiger carried off the field – high on the team's shoulders – the band blared – Majorettes' batons flew high in the air – it was a wild scene of pure jubilation – one vast, wild roaring –

Ben Shingle, turning to Surcher, made himself heard somehow –

'Jesus.'

Surcher grinned.

Broadly. . . .

85

Ponce, smiling and happy, on top of the world, after the game, was in Tiger's office. The joy and jubilation, the noise and happy horseplay of the locker room still rang in his ears. He had gone to the office at Tiger's request – to put some football folders and other items away in the files for him, for Tiger's wife was waiting for him outside in the car and he didn't have time for it. 'Do that thing for me, Ponce, thanks – ' he had told him. Ponce of course had been only too happy to do so. This had been quite the day. He had really thought, in that first half, Sawyersville had finally reached the end of the line. He was absolutely amazed, and of course mighty proud of, the way things had gone in the second half. Nothing went wrong! Practically every play ate up yardage! Dink and Jim had clicked beautifully! Jerry had snaked sixty-five yards for one, Pope fifty-five yards for another, Feef twenty-five, after breaking through like a bulldozer, Dink and Jim got the other two. Beauties! What beauties! Perfect! Each one had thrilled the stands, which had gone wild. Twice in the third quarter and once in the fourth Ponce had improvised new moves, and Tiger had approved, and sent them in right away – and they had clicked. It was on the first one that Jerry had got away. They had danced for joy – Tiger, Ponce, the whole bench! What a run! What a day! Some day. And Carverton had been stopped cold, stone cold. Ponce really had loved the day. And now here he was, putting things away, in Tiger's office, for that terrific guy, *the top high-school coach in the country*, *without a doubt*, among other things, *so many things*, Ponce knew, *whose assistant one day he*

378

would be, just wait and see. Ponce, smiling away, thinking so many things, stood before the filing cabinet and started filing away. There didn't seem to be much room there – it was full of test results, all sorts of Guidance/Counseling stuff. He thought of Betty. He hadn't yet been able to see her again, he wondered if she had seen the game. Tonight, he would see her for sure. He had the theme done. He had promised himself he wouldn't go back to see her until he had it done. He knew she would want it that way. He grew warm, thinking of her, and his possible future with her. For there was no doubt, *it was possible*, and he would try hard. When should he propose ? Did guys still propose ? Or did it just happen ? Should he ask Tiger ? What a day. What a game. Ponce was still spinning. What about it ? Just happened ? Like everything else ? He wondered about that, and also worried a little bit – but not unduly. It was a technicality. *Mary Holden.* What had happened to Mary ? He had heard the craziest stories – it was all crazy. A technicality. He knew Betty would help him out on that. He wondered what his mother would say. He would tell her – one day. He tried picturing that day. Surcher. The troubles. Mary Holden. That sure had been a funny one. He would corner Surcher – or Mr Shingle – and get the straight story. Though by now, Tiger probably had it. When he had asked him, a day or so ago, he hadn't known – exactly. One thing for sure – it wasn't connected with the others. He would find out alright. Everything. He had felt bad, as he had of course *about the others.* He even felt bad still about that poor dope the late Chief John Poldaski. Who would take over ? He had heard talk about Joe Linski, Peggy's old man. Maybe so. In the Army, he had been an MP. That he knew. Right now, there was no one. The town had no Police Force. Dozens of Staties though. He thought of the funerals. He felt sad. Jeannie's had been some funeral and a half. That's how they were, those Catholics. He thought of Ben Shingle, and what a fine guy he was. Out of all this, because of it, he, *Ponce*, had been given the chance to meet and get to know a writer like that, *of that caliber*, no less. They were friends, no doubt of it, what a great guy he was. He felt bad about it though, having happened this way. He felt bad, it was like – cheating, almost. But – Ponce knew that's how life was, or certainly *sometimes* was. The breaks – deserved – undeserved – out of the blue – Things happened that way. If he were given the choice, of course he'd want those girls all back alive – and never get within sight of Ben Shingle, or anyone like that. Any day. He knew that. And even the Chief too. To boot. But the choice hadn't been his. He mused. It had happened this way. He knew that. He felt bad that Surcher and all the others who had turned up, including the Attorney-General himself, who had turned up today, he had watched the game, had so far hit a stone wall, and had turned up nothing. It was still, without a doubt, one hell of a mess, despite the great victory today. But things had been quiet, at any rate, outside of the Mary Holden thing, which could have happened anytime, anywhere, to anyone, so far as he knew, from what he knew, and had nothing at all to do with the thing. Only this morning, he had heard Surcher confide to Tiger, while they were having a talk about things, and Ponce happened to be around, Mr Shingle as well, he had heard him confide that maybe it was possible it was the end of the trail. It was just possible, he had said, it was classical, he had also said, Ben agreeing with him. He remembered Tiger nodding his head at that. Looking very pensive at that. In any event, *what a day*. And he was glad no colored boy had been tagged with the thing. He was glad all the dirty pressure from certain elements had been resisted and finally whittled down – to nothing. He admired Surcher. Now, he knew, only the hard-core Birchites were still out for their blood. And everybody knew what they counted for, so they were no worry. This wasn't Mississippi, or any of those crapulent Southern states. Or California, for that matter, that nuthouse of a Reagan State. The phone rang. Ponce picked it up.

'Hello ?'

'Who's this ?' the voice said. A female voice, low, warm.

'Ponce.'

A pause. She was still there.

'*Ponce de Leon,*' he said, to make matters absolutely clear.

The phone clicked. There was the dial tone.

'*Hello?*' Ponce said, just once more. She had hung up. He hung up. Wondering who it was. It almost sounded like, he thought now, in his astute way, his mind working with it – *Rochelle*. He mused, thinking about her. He wasn't sure though. What a girl. It might not have been, or – could just have been. Wrong number ? He mused a bit more. Then dropped it, of no consequence. Whoever it was, if she really wanted Tiger, she would phone back. He could find no room for some of the stuff in the file cabinet at all. He turned and thought about trying the desk. Tiger hadn't mentioned it, but it could go in the desk. If he filed anything there. He didn't know. He tried a few drawers. In the top drawer he saw some folders. One was lying on its back, on top. Possibly put there by Tiger in a hurry, to be filed properly later, when he had time. He picked it up and started turning it over the right way so he could tuck it in the drawer properly. It bumped the drawer and fell out of his hands, spilling its contents onto the floor. He said, 'Damn – ' in a mild way, feeling embarrassed about his clumsiness, and maybe having messed up that folder on Tiger. To boot. He started to pick the stuff up. They were football plays, he noted, grinning about that, fondly. They were rough sketches of plays, he and Tiger had worked on from time to time. Here was the old Reverse-Shuffle-Fake From The 'I' On Three. That was a one. He liked that one. Pope had clipped off forty-five the first time Dink had called it today – in the second half, that is. He looked through the sheets, each one a different play. He put each one back in the folder, carefully, after a glance at it. Then there was other stuff. Referees' names, Coaches' phone numbers, colleges, universities – their head coaches – all that stuff – clubs – that kind of stuff. Ponce hastened to put it back in the folder, feeling embarrassed again, as if prying. He felt like a prying kid. Though Tiger wouldn't have minded though, he was that way. Of course. He sure had a nice wife and kid. Tiger did. She was real good-looking, his wife was. He thought of Betty again. He came across the last sheet and was just about to tuck that in. He stopped, for some reason. Incurably curious as ever, his eyes were perusing the sheet. It was just a list of names, girls' names. His eyes ran up and down the list. He saw the names. He began feeling funny, suddenly. Just a little funny, suddenly. There were marks beside each name, stars they looked like. That's what they were. His eyes saw the names. Four of the names had lines drawn through them. A line, through each of the four. They were crossed out. That's what they were. He could just make them out though. He felt funnier now. Just a cold kind of feeling coming up in his stomach, and at the top of his spine. That was it. *Jill Fairbunn,* he made out *– Yvonne Mellish – Jeannie Bonni* – He could make out – *Mary Holden* – He also made out. He halted there. All he could do was stare. He felt funnier and funnier. The cold was spreading. *What the hell was this list?* What were those blue stars beside *Rochelle's* name? *What was Betty's name doing – on this list?* Look at those stars there – three and a half – red ones – *And what did they mean?* There was Mrs Mortlake's name – the School Nurse – number 21 on the list – a question mark after her name – *What did that* *mean ?* Ponce felt icy-tingling waves spreading all over him, and through him, he felt mighty cold. What was this list ? Was it *Tiger's* list ? What was it doing here ? What did it mean ? He saw Mona Drake's name on the list. Barbara Brook's. *She just lived down the road.* Her father – Marjorie Evanmore. *Hetty Nectar.* Ponce stared. He digested every name on that list. Each one hit him like a hammer blow. He was more than cold. *What was the score ?* What the hell did it mean ? Suddenly, with a staggering surge that nearly knocked him off his feet, Ponce realized what he had in his hand. He fell back, he slumped into Tiger's chair. He put his head between his knees, to fight hard to keep from keeling over. He didn't want to keel over. His heart pounded, he felt sick, and ice cold. He had never known such a sick feeling as this. He fought and fought, hanging on, going under, surfacing, going under, again surfacing – a dozen times or more. At last, he raised his head, slowly, and sat back in the chair. He was a man near death. He sat there, numb, like a ghost. Or the sole survivor of a shipwreck, after long days on the open sea. Or worse. He had the list. He stared at it, starkly, dumbfounded. His world whirled. He knew one thing: *Nothing again would ever be the same.* For he knew, with an excruciatingly painful burst of awareness he suddenly knew: *Tiger must be insane.* He stared at that list. His eyes wandered over each name. Who was Looby Loo ? He hoped for a moment now that it *wasn't* Tiger's list. That *someone had put it there* – or – that *Tiger had confiscated it, from some nut of a kid.* He hoped. And hoped. But – he knew he was wrong. Somehow, he knew it was Tiger's alright. He had seen that writing a hundred times. That printing. That way. His eyes stopped and riveted themselves on Betty's name. *In the name of God, if there was a God, what was she doing on this list ?* Just what were those stars ? Those marks ? *Could it really be what he thought ?* How could it ? For up to now, Ponce had only grasped part of the matter, the horror had only been associated with the names *crossed off.* Now – *more.* He saw more. With a fresh wave of agony he began to realize fully just *how much more.* His acute intelligence and imagination suddenly flared and filled in the full details. It was before his eyes. And he was rocked – to the depths of his soul. He wanted to cry out, a cry that would echo through all history, and eternity, and reach the very ends of the universe: *What Kind Of A World Was I Born Into ?* He thought of his echoing cry down the hallway that morning. He thought of Betty. His eye was still locked on that precious name, on that list. He couldn't believe it. *He had to*. He thought of Tiger, whose image lay shattered about him in a million bits and pieces, forever more. He slumped back in that chair even more. *What to do?* He was overwhelmed. *Just what was he supposed to do?* He wasn't about to take off on another run, of that, he was determined. He held the list, acutely aware through all the agony that he had come to a terrible crossroads in his young life. *His life*. It wasn't fair. *It just wasn't fair*. That too he wanted to cry out. What should he do? What was there to do – *with his discovery?* Surcher? Take it to Surcher? Put it back? Forget about it? Let somebody else find it – one day? What would the score be? Or – tear up the list? Or – just remain sitting there, until someone came in? *Would Tiger come in?* What would happen, if he came in? *Would he join the list?* He hadn't seen the Chief's name on the list – Would he just disappear? *With the list?* Was that it? Ponce moaned. He was aware of the moan. He wanted to talk to Tiger. He almost wished he would come in. *Maybe if he could only talk with him*. . . . Ponce was stuck at that crossroads. He just sat there. He only saw all the alternatives, crystal clear. . . . *Surcher* – that was the sane, *the only rational thing to do*. . . . *He knew*. He thought about that. He thought about all those girls – on the list. On active status, on the list. He thought of the game. The team. That great team. *It would go to hell*. He knew well. He could have cried. He was in agony. Who could help him? *It would just all go to hell, the team, the school, everything. All to Hell*. He knew well. Well he knew. The shock alone would wreck everything. *And those girls. Betty*. He wanted to die. Was it the end of the line? Was that how things were – in this life? He was plunged into the most profound crisis of his entire life. He was in anguish – and suddenly also angry. *Why him?* Why, at such a tender point of his life, should *he* have to face such a crisis, terrible in the extreme? It was enough to poleax the most seasoned of human beings, adult stage. Why should *he* have to stand at those crossroads, agonizing beyond belief? He hated it. His tender age. Why was *he* selected for it? He wanted to run like lightning from it. *Ben Shingle*. He thought of him. . . . Everything was going along so smoothly. He really hated it. *That stupid piece of paper*. . . . He thought of his mother. His father. Rusty Joe, Peppy. *Surcher*. His thoughts stayed with Peppy, that cute little animal, innocent little creature if ever there was one, or could be, *anywhere*, on this earth, anytime. . . . *He knew he had to face it*. There was absolutely no getting away from it. *The sane thing. To do*. His eyes were wet. His face was getting wet. The list was blurred. How he loved that little animal. He wished she were here now, so he could hold her, and stroke her. *Betty*. The tears flowed. He sat there, staring at that blurred list. *Tiger*. He wept. . . . The moment, the event, for all of them, was momentous, he knew, and ineradicable, well he knew. . . . A million years from now, he was sure, he would still see himself, here, staring trance-like at that list . . . *no matter what he finally decided to do* . . . or who might walk in that door. . . .